Ella's

Escape

Ella's

Escape

Jen Jo Kelly

To all my friends and family who pulled together.

To give ideas, descriptions, editing, cover design.

To help me tell my tale…….

Rebecca B

Molly Z

Alexander F

Alison F

Francisco M

Samantha V

Julie B

Melissa P

Holly M

Noemi H

Chapter 1

Why does this keep happening to me? I thought he was the one. He told me I was the one. Please someone come and save me. It's raining outside. I am pacing back and forth in my room, looking out the window.

"Please come and save me!" I scream.

My boyfriend Zach just left me, and has turned his phone off. My heart is pounding and I'm beginning to freak out.

What's going on? How could this possibly happen? What did I do wrong? Why did I have to find out from someone else that we are no longer together? Is he not even man enough to tell me to my face? I have so many unanswered questions.

I am angry. I am hurt. *Please, please help me. Please help me to stay calm.* I feel out of control, this is not fair.

Zach and I have been going out for over four years. We have had our ups and downs in the last year, but I never thought this would happen. *What have I done wrong?* He said he loved me and wanted to marry me. I just don't understand. *What did I do?* I just don't understand. *What? What? What?*

"Aaaaaahhhhhhhhhhhhhhh!"

I can't handle this. Zach just started working with my brother's wife at her Legal Firm. As far as sister in laws go, she's great. Victoria is a partner, and got him in as a favor to me. Sebastian, my older brother had just called and informed me that Zach is going around work telling people that he and I broke up. *What? What is going on?* Victoria called Sebastian immediately once she collected all the details she heard at work, and of course, the news had finally gotten back to me.

This is how I find out he doesn't want to be with me anymore? I begin to try and make sense of what has just happened. *This is why he has been so distant lately?* How immature. I've invested four years with him. I just can't believe it.

"Please come and tell me you're sorry. Tell me you're an ass!" I scream out the window.

This can't be happening. This isn't happening. I begin to repeatedly rub my face in frustration. I collapse to the floor and begin to slowly rock back and forth with my arms around my knees. *Please come back to me Zach, please...*

I continue a pattern of pacing, rubbing, rocking, pacing, rubbing, rocking, and all the while willing him to answer his phone. My eyes repeatedly check the front window, like he's going to show up. I'm here all alone, which I'm not used to. *Please Zach, please Zach, please come back, please come back.* I've never been this sad before. I just don't understand.

I seem incapable of deciding what to do next. Should I go find him? Should I go to his house and demand to talk? Why is his phone off? He must know that I found out today. I'm lost, spiraling down. I dial his number over and over. *He has to turn the phone on eventually doesn't he?* I sit down and put my head between my knees, trying to catch my breath and control the sobs. I'm pulling at my face, pulling at my hair, when suddenly I hear my name.

"Gaby. Gaby. Gabriella, are you home?"

Zach! He's come over to set everything straight.

"Gaby, answer me."

Oh shit. My roommate is home. Fuck I don't want him to see my like this, again. I try my best to wipe my face and stand up. I really don't want to talk about this. I walk into the living room.

"Hi Lucca."

Fuck. Fuck. Fuck. I want Zach, not Lucca.

"Gaby, what's going on? I have been trying to call your phone. Sebastian called to make sure I was coming home tonight. He wanted me to check on you. He said you hung up on him."

He reaches to hug me. He's talking so fast.

"Oh Lucca. I just can't handle this anymore. Zach is telling people at work that we broke up and it got back to me, which was obviously his goal. And now his phone is off."

I'm breathless. I can barely get myself to whisper the words.

"I mean we've been having issues, but this is too sudden. What should I do?"

I take the brief silence as a chance to admit something to myself. I think deep down I knew this was coming, but I didn't want to face it. I never expected it to happen this way. I'm beginning to cry again, and resume rubbing my face.

Zach has put me through some shit, but this is the worst. Lucca pulls me down to sit next to him on the couch. I put my elbows on my knees and my head down in my hands. He hugs me, and strokes my hair. That's his usual routine when I get like this. He knows how to bring me back down to normal. He's the best friend I could ask for.

"Gaby, it will be all right. Zach is an ass. Don't waste anymore tears on him please."

Lucca's voice is calm and slow.

"What did I do? Why doesn't he want me anymore? He said he would take care of me forever," I sob into Lucca's shoulder.

"Stop this. I've called the girls and they are coming over. We are taking you out. NOW. The fights, crying, out-of-control shit is done. Let Zach go. This was his choice, and what is best for you. You don't deserve this!"

Lucca is getting angry. I don't usually see him angry. He hates Zach.

"There is no way I can go out. Look at me," I point to my face. "I'm a complete mess. My face is probably puffy with mascara all over. And I'm really not in the right frame of mind to get ready. I am not going anywhere. Zach is avoiding me and I can't take it."

I'm yelling. I'm babbling. I can't gain control.

"Well they will be here in twenty minutes, and you know how Simone is. She will get your ass up and ready."

He laughs, still stroking my hair. For some reason, that helps.

"Please give me a minute. I need to call him one more time. Please."

I must hear his voice. I miss him so much.

"You have one minute," Lucca holds up one finger and walks away.

I look out my window one more time in hopes that Zach's car will be there. It's not. This is really happening. We are breaking up. I still don't get it!

I take my phone out of my pocket and push the picture of us together at a happy time. His phone is ringing. Holy fucking shit. It's ringing, not direct to voice mail. *Oh my God, Oh my God.*

My heart is thumping and I can barely breathe. I don't know what to say. *Please answer. Please answer.*

"Hello."

Zach answers in his deep voice and I am literally shaking.

"Zach, what's going on? Victoria said you're telling people we broke up at work. I don't..."

He interrupts me before I can say anymore.

"Gaby, this just isn't working anymore. I know this isn't the way to do this, but I can't look at you and tell you I don't want this. I..."

Now it's my turn to interrupt him.

"You really are done with me? What about all you promised me? All of our hopes and dreams for the future, our plans? You said you would always be there for me. You said you would take care of me and watch over me. You said you loved me. What happened?"

I'm screaming into the phone.

"Gaby, please."

"Please come over. Please, please. Please let me look at you. Please make me understand. Please tell me what I've done wrong. I'll do anything. I promise. Anything. Please."

"Gaby, I..."

"Zach. I need you. I can't do this. Please don't do this to me." I can't stop crying. I'm begging, holding my hands up like I'm praying.

"Zach, please. Where are you?"

"I'm driving around."

Was he going to drive by and save me like I hoped?

"Will you please come over? Please, please, please. I need to see you," I plead.

"I don't think that's a good idea Gaby."

He sounds angry now.

"Please Zach. You owe me this. Please." Why do I sound so desperate? I hear him let out a big sigh before he answers.

"Fine. Be outside."

Okay, he is coming over. *Will this be the last time we see each other?* No, surely we will remain friends. We can get past this. I will seduce him and he will stay with me tonight. My mind is all over the place. If he leaves I don't want to be friends.

"Aaaaaaaaaahhhhhhhhhhhhhh!"

I have to make myself somewhat presentable in the couple minutes I have to get myself downstairs. I want to be down there waiting when he pulls in so he doesn't change his mind and drive off. Fuck. I can do this. Be calm. I stand to let my breathing slow, but it won't.

I run to the bathroom, right past Lucca who has the most confused look on his face. I look like shit. Fuck it. I'm just going outside. Maybe he will feel sad for me or bad that he's putting me through this. Maybe he will change his mind. I have to get out there. I run past Lucca again and out the front door. Simone is approaching and it's still raining. Just great.

"Don't ask," I say to her.

I sense that she and Lucca are watching me out the window.

Zach pulls into the driveway. He gets out and stands with his arms crossed. *Why on earth does he look pissed?* I haven't done anything. I'm the pissed off one here mister.

"Hey," I say as quietly and calmly as I can.

I wrap my arms around him but he pushes me back.

"Hey."

His voice is completely void of any emotion.

"Why did you want me to come over here Gaby? I told you on the phone this isn't a good idea. I don't want to do this anymore. And now I'm fucking getting wet. Please let's just take some time."

"Time? Time for what Zach?"

Now I'm getting angrier, sadder. I don't know what to feel.

"Zach. Please tell me what I've done. I just need to know. Please tell me so I can fix it."

"You haven't done anything. I just don't want this anymore."

He is shaking his head.

"But why? This doesn't make any sense. You promised..." I pause for a moment. "Wait. Have you met someone else?"

"Of...of course not Gaby."

I don't believe him. *Why is he hesitating?*

"Are you su...?"

He cuts me off.

"I shouldn't have come here. I need to go."

Go? What? Wait. We haven't resolved anything. He gets back in his car, slams the door and starts it.

"Wait, Zach...Wait!"

I'm screaming, pleading, crying, sobbing, and losing control again.

"Zach, please, please don't go."

He screeches off and I'm running after him. I stop when he speeds up. It feels like slow motion, like I'm watching this all happen in a movie. The screen slows, it's blinking on and off, and everything slows down. It's all a blur of running, screaming, yelling. *NO!* I'm watching myself run and he doesn't even turn around.

"Zaaaaacccccccchhhhhhhhhh, noooooooooooooooooooo!"

My body is numb. I sink to my knees in the middle of the street. *What just happened?* I'm getting soaking wet and all I want is for him to come back. As I lay my head in the street, I hear a door slam. I'm startled and momentarily distracted from my hysterics. Lucca and Simone are running out into the street after me. Together they pick me up and we stagger back into the house.

I hang my head. I feel broken. I sit on my favorite chair in the living room. They are both sitting on the coffee table in front of me, stroking each of my hands.

"Gaby, please calm down. Please, please."

Simone is trying to calm me down, but it's not working. She's not very good at this.

"I can't. If I understood... If I knew what I could do to fix things. Why is he doing this to me? If I...," I pause as anger floods into my voice, "this would be different. And did Lucca tell you how I found out?"

I'm yelling at them.

"Yes, and this is no surprise. I've always known that Zach is immature. What a baby."

Simone speaks with a knowing tone in her voice that says "Well duh, of course this is how he broke up with you."

"Simone, I know, I know. I know how you feel about him. Lucca please help me out here," I squeak.

Lucca comes to hug me.

Simone jumps up.

"That's it."

She points to Lucca.

"Lucca isn't defending you this time. Sam and Kelly will be here in ten minutes and the five of us are going out."

She puts up a finger to stop me before I can argue.

"No. No excuses. You are coming out with us, Gaby. You will not sit here alone and wallow. Zach's an asshole, he left, his loss. He doesn't deserve you. You have always been too good for him."

I look at her, and then glance at Lucca who just shrugs his shoulders. I squint my eyes at Simone, but give up and retreat to the bathroom.

Once I've shut the bathroom door, I give myself a reassuring hug. I look in the mirror as if to ask myself what went wrong. *What did I do? Why doesn't Zach want me anymore? Why can't I find someone to take care of me? Why did I trust that he would?*

All I want is for someone to mean what they say, damn it. Someone to love me, live for me, take care of me, protect me, be strong for me, spoil me, sweep me off my feet, take my breath away.

I glance down for a brief moment and return my gaze to the mirror.

Who's inside there? Who am I? What can I be doing better?

My mind is all over the place. How can I possibly go out with my mind racing like this?

I take one final look and say, "Same old me again today."

I go to my room and grudgingly pick out something to wear. I don't want to go, but I know if I don't get moving, Simone will be in here and put me in the car, ready or not. After the day I've had, I simply can't allow myself go anywhere looking like this. I may feel like Zach's punching bag, but I refuse to look like it.

Simone, Lucca, Sam, and Kelly are all sitting on the couch downstairs drinking wine and waiting for me. They all look up in unison as I descend the stairs and I hear a collective gasp.

"That's what you're wearing out?"

Kelly points at me and makes a face.

"What's wrong with what I'm wearing Kelly?"

I give her my evil glare and an eyeball roll.

"Well it's just so...plain," she sputters.

I should be hurt by Kelly's words, but the fact is, I'm not. I know in my heart that I won't be trying to impress anybody. I always look plain anyway.

I sigh loudly. I just want to get this over with. Pass some time so I can be alone. Sleep. Escape from this pain.

"Oh girl, you look fine. Let's go."

Sam saves me from Kelly's accusations and we all pile in Lucca's new Nissan Pathfinder.

He is driving of course, which of course then that puts Simone in the other front seat. I am in the middle of the back seat, sandwiched between Sam and Kelly. These two could be clones. They look like petite little blond twins. They aren't twins, but they are both slender with long blond hair. And they style it the same on purpose.

I glance up at the front passenger seat. Simone is what I call my perfect friend. She is tall, thin, long dark hair, outgoing, and is what I would consider to be the total package. She can pick up guys just by thinking about it. Single guys seem to flock to her and she ends up having to practically fend them off with a stick. Sometimes it's plain ridiculous to watch. We could be walking down the street, and guys actually pull over in their cars to talk to her.

Me? I'm just the friend. They ask her out and say, "Oh, your friend can come too".

Oh can I? Gee thanks.

All of a sudden, I am overwhelmed with memories from earlier this evening, and I am once again in a state of devastation. I sink back into my seat as I listen to everyone go back and forth about their days.

I allow my mind to drift back to a few weeks ago when Zach and I were in bed. He was so sweet, and loving, and slow, and sexy. He always tried so hard in bed. He had the same routine almost every time-- candles, music, wine. The routine was sweet, but also predictable. He probably thought that I enjoyed it. He was so careful and he made love to me like he thought I might break. He was so...

"Hey!" Simone yells at me. "Snap out of it."

Her comments quickly bring me back to reality.

"What?"

"Stop thinking about that asshole," Simone commands. "We are going out to get your mind off of him. We are going to cruise the strip on our way to Ghallagers. Now what do you want to listen to?"

Simone is a force to be reckoned with, and she always says exactly what's on her mind. I love that about her.

As we make our way down the strip, I realize how blessed I am to have such close friends that all live within five miles of Huntington Beach. Ghallagers is our favorite group hangout. Well, it's not really Lucca's favorite, but when Simone picks a favorite spot, she doesn't really tend to care what Lucca thinks.

We continued to follow the strip as it curves along the beaches of the Pacific Ocean. It's the place to go to blast tunes and just cruise. It's actually pretty fun and relaxing on days when it's not too crowded. For a moment I wish I was alone cruising in my own car. I could listen to my kind of music and clear my head.

"Simone, please just play something. It doesn't matter to me."

I throw my hands up in the air.

Oh fuck. Simone is giving me a skeptical look, probably questioning her decision to bring me out tonight. She hates when I'm in this mood, but I don't care. She turns around and ignores me, turns on a random mix and starts to dance. There she goes, doing her own thing and drawing all the attention. She really is in her glory tonight.

Why can't I be that happy, that free, that outgoing?

All the windows are down and everyone is singing and dancing along but me. They each make a few attempts get me to dance, but I shake my head.

Zach pleaaaasssssseeeeeeee! I scream in my head. *Please come back to me!*

I open my eyes and we are stopped at a stoplight. There is a car with four guys next to us. I roll my eyes. Just fucking great.

"Hey boys," Simone yells to them.

I sink further into my seat.

"Hey!" the boys in the car yell back. "Want to pull over?"

No we don't want to pull over.

"We are going to Ghallagers. Follow us there... if you dare," Simone taunts them as she throws her head back with a laugh.

"Oh my God, Simone. I thought this was about us going out," I spit out in anger. "You know, making me feel better. Remember? Or did you forget?"

An uncomfortable silence fills the car.

"I'm really not in the 'meeting guys' mood," I mutter under my breath.

Why doesn't she see what I mean? She always puts herself first. *Can't someone put me first? For once?*

"Oh Gaby, loosen up. It's not like they will really follow us. I'm just having a little fun," Simone retorts.

Sure enough, when we pull into the bar the car of four boys parks right next to us. *Fuck, really?* Simone practically pulls them out of their car. She waves all of us in and finds a table for nine.

I shoot a look of annoyance her way, which she immediately ignores, and she leads the group to our seats. I'm following way behind, not wanting to be part of this.

"So where are you boys from?" Simone asks in her sexiest voice.

"We all live here in Huntington Beach," one of the guys says.

Why is he looking at me? I didn't ask the stupid question, and really don't care to hear the answer.

"So do we," she smiles, showing her perfectly white teeth. "What are you up to tonight?"

"We were just cruising on our way here. A boy's night out after a long week. What are your names?"

This guy is still staring at me.

Can he tell I've been crying? No. Probably not. He's probably wondering why I'm with all these pretty girls. I'm sure I must look out of place.

"I'm Simone, and this is Lucca, Samantha, Kelly, and Gabriella," Simone says as she points to each person as they're introduced.

Leave it to Simone to use our full names. *Bitch.* And of course she introduces all of us. Wouldn't want the attention being diverted to any other members of the group.

"Hi, I'm Aidan. This is Nicholas, my brother, and those two are Matt and Mateo," Aidan says as he points to each of the guys.

Matt and Mateo. Interesting combination. They look nice enough. I smile at each of them.

"What do you girls like to drink?"

Aidan is taking control of his group just like Simone controls ours. *I guess each group needs one*. I giggle to myself. They would go perfectly together. I look over to Mateo, and notice Lucca is watching him. I think Lucca wants to make a move on him. Not sure that Mateo is gay though. He is very tan with dark hair and dark eyes, exactly what Lucca likes.

Aidan calls a waitress over and orders two bottles of wine. Simone and Aidan rule the table with their conversation topics. They ask what we each do for fun, weekend plans, regular small talk. I watch Simone in awe. She is so comfortable in her own skin and body.

I wish I could be like that.

I want to feel beautiful. It amazes me how she doesn't seem to have a care in the world. She keeps tossing her hair back. I usually twirl mine. It's a nervous thing.

As I sit at the table, I realize for the first time that all five of us are currently single. That hasn't happened in quite a long time.

Single.

I close my eyes. *Oh my, is this real?*

Zach, I miss you. Zach, come back to me. Hug me, hold me, rescue me. Show up here and take me from this crowd and tell me it's all a big mistake. You want me. You miss me.

"So, Gabriella is it?" Aidan moves next to me.

Wait, where did everyone go? It's just him and I at the table.

"Gaby," I nod and give him my uncomfortable smile.

"Well, hi Gaby. I'm Aidan. It seems all of our friends have left us to go dance."

Why is he still here with me then?

I thought he was hooking up with Simone. I look over Aidan's shoulder and see Simone dancing with Matt, Sam with Mateo, Kelly with Nicholas, and Lucca with...

Who the hell is Lucca with?

Must be some guy at the bar. Figures. Lucca is and always will be quite the player. He always knows who he can hit on and who he can't. Don't ask me to dance, don't ask me to dance.

Why is Aidan, the sexiest one of the group hitting on me? I am never hit on. *Am I just who was left so he is stuck with me?* Of course that's why. I'm not the sexiest one in my group.

This is confusing. Zach left me today, and I'm not interested in small talk. This is too much. I have a new guy talking to me. But why?

"Yes, I see them all dancing with each other. Nice how that worked out. And here you are stuck with me," I say quietly.

"Stuck with you? Are you kidding me? Do you know how beautiful you are?"

Okay, that's not what I was expecting to hear. I forgot how nice it is to have someone else say it. *Do I dare believe him?*

"Oh thank you."

I can barely talk. I am not outgoing like Simone. I don't start conversations.

"Gaby, your eyes," Aidan says, "are they brown or hazel? They are breathtaking."

My eyes? I do love my eyes. They switch between brown and hazel depending on what I'm wearing.

I find myself becoming distracted by Aidan's voice. He talks so slow and smooth, so seductively. Then I remember he's waiting for my answer.

"My license says they're brown," I say matter-of-factly and put my head down.

"That's funny. Brown it is then," he laughs.

"What do you do Aidan?"

I can't think of anything else to say.

He is the traditional tall, dark, and handsome. Brown hair, brown eyes, and olive skin. He's so muscular and he's the type that just oozes sex appeal. His hair is just long enough that it starts a curl. It looks so soft. I wish I could run my fingers through it. And his deep voice…that's his best quality. It's rough, manly, scratchy. I imagine hearing dirty things from that voice.

He gazes at me and I look deeper in his eyes. He looks confident, but deep down like he's hurting. He's putting on a front.

Why can't I do that? Why am I imagining these things?

"I own a local consulting company and do motivational speaking on the side," Aidan offers.

Wow, that sounds boring. Zach I miss you.

"And what do you do, Gaby?"

"I work at a software company. I help implement our software at new companies."

I'm not really in the mood to talk about work.

"How old are you Aidan?"

I must know.

I try to change the subject because my job is private. I am truly stunned that his attention is on me.

"I'm thirty," he responds casually, "and I'd like to take you out to dinner some night this week."

Whoa. He is bold.

I'm taken aback. My annoying self-critical voice still says he should be with Simone. I'm not used to this attention.

I'm not ready to date someone new am I? I can't do this. I want to call Zach.

"Um, I don't think so." I look down.

"Ok." He rubs his hair forward with his hand, and then rubs it down his face.

Oh, that's kind of cute. Wait -- did I just hurt his feelings?

"It's just that I…" I stammer, "I just broke up with someone. Like just, as in today broke up with someone."

Ok now I'm rambling. I sound stupid.

"I understand."

He pauses.

"I mean, it's just dinner."

He sounds a little annoyed, or maybe sad? I'm not sure which.

I glance back to the dance floor and see all the couples still moving to the music.

Aren't they tired yet? Maybe I should get out there and burn some calories and get out of this one on one with Aidan? He sure is hot. *Maybe dinner wouldn't be so bad?* I am single now. *I am single.* The truth of those words begins to finally sink in. I take a minute to compose myself.

"I'm going to make a quick call."

I call Zach's phone from the restroom. It's off. Again. I want him to come over tonight and sleep with me one last time. Hold him, feel his warm naked skin against mine. He obviously doesn't want the same thing.

I take a deep breath and stand up straight. That's it. I'm going back out to Aidan. Maybe he will order some more wine and my liquid courage will start flowing.

My mood begins to lighten as I walk back toward our table. Aidan is still sitting alone. I stop and take a minute to admire him. He looks deep in thought and that hurting feeling comes back to me. I watch him for a few minutes. He stands as I approach, and I sit next to him.

"Could we get some more wine please? I could really use some after the long day I've had," I explain. "Thank God it's Friday, right?"

He seems to lose that hurt in his eyes as he smiles at me. He looks around for the waitress and orders another bottle. I slam what's left of my glass. The wine comes and I pour myself a full glass and guzzle it down in a matter of seconds.

"You know what? I would love to go to dinner with you," I blurt out.

Aidan's face lights up.

"How about tomorrow night?"

Before I can answer, the group is back at our table. They all are smiling and chatting. They brought more wine back with them. *Good.*

Our friends take turns telling us about the crazy couple that took over the dance floor and kept knocking everyone over.

Everyone laughs, followed by an abrupt silence. They're all looking at Aidan, who is looking at me.

"What's going on over here?"

Simone directs her question to me.

"Gaby has agreed to go out for dinner tomorrow night with me," Aidan says proudly.

I sink in my seat. I didn't say yes to tomorrow night yet.

Tomorrow, as in the day after today. I thought he meant next week or something. The girls are going to think I'm crazy for doing this so soon. I'm so confused. I need time to think. I want to go out with Aidan. *But how could I want that when I'm still thinking about Zach?* I don't know what to do.

"Of course she will go," Lucca says as he winks at me.

I'm going to kill him when we get home.

"Yes, I'll go," I say through a tight smile.

"I will pick you up at six," Aidan says confidently.

"Sounds great."

Everyone resumes their conversations and appear to be enjoying themselves. The girls and Lucca all do a "thumb ups" motion in my direction, giving Aidan their stamp of approval.

Lucca leans over and whispers, "He's hot."

Don't I know it?

Lucca is so funny, and he makes me smile. Like me, he has a thing for the brown haired men. Lucca is skinny and very muscular. His hair and clothes are always perfect, no matter whether he's going to get gas or attending the opera.

Sitting, chatting, and drinking wine make the hours fly by. I look around the table. Matt is still talking to Simone. *He's not sick of her yet?* I note that he is on the tall side with red hair. I had no idea Simone was into red hair on a man. He's also very quiet. *I guess opposites attract?* That's the only conclusion I can come up with.

Aidan is still sitting by me. He only talks to me unless someone asks him something directly. It's a little uncomfortable at first, but after a while I realize that I'm actually having a nice time. I haven't thought about Zach in almost two hours. *Holy shit!*

I find myself beginning to miss Zach all over again. *Stop. Stop!* I command myself to stop thinking about Zach.

I refocus on our table. Matt, Mateo, and Nicholas all seem to be so close. I wonder if Nicholas is older or younger than Aidan. They kind of look alike I guess. Nicholas is also tall, dark, and handsome. *But not as handsome as Aidan,* my inner cheerleader giggles. Lucky me.

Aidan stands up and holds his hand out.

"Shall we dance?"

Chapter 2

Kelly gives me a little nudge and I jump up. I don't want to dance, but everyone is looking at me. I take Aidan's hand and he pulls me out to the dance floor. There is a slow song playing, which is good. I am not a dancer and really don't like people watching me.

"Are you having fun tonight?" he asks.

"Yes I am. You have certainly taken my mind off some things," I blush.

His hands are on each side of my waist and mine are resting on his shoulders. This feels nice, comfortable, not weird at all. Another man is touching me, and I'm enjoying it. He clasps his hands a little tighter around my back and I lean in and rest my head on his shoulder.

There's a slight hint of weird energy between us.

We slow dance to two songs without saying anything. After the second song, I lean back and he leans in, like he might kiss me. I stiffen. I am horrified. This is way too soon for me. I shake my head.

Sensing my hesitation Aidan drops his hands from my waist and grabs my hand.

"Let's sit down for a while?"

I nod and he pulls me back to the table.

"Lucca."

I try and get Lucca's attention.

"Lucca."

Fuck is he ignoring me?

"Lucca!"

He finally turns around and makes eye contact with me. I mouth to him that I'm ready to go. He nods.

"Ok ladies, it's late. We should head out."

Lucca gathers all of us, orders the rest of the girls to finish their drinks, and after a few moments we head to the car.

"Hey Gaby, may I walk you to your car?" Aidan asks as he runs next to me.

"That would be fine," I hesitate.

He asks for my number, and hastily programs it into his cell phone. Before we go our separate ways, we've made plans to see each other tomorrow evening at six.

I feel nervous. Everyone is loaded in the Pathfinder, waiting for me. I hope they're not watching me too. Aidan reaches for my hand. I lift it and he kisses the top.

He kisses me on my cheek and whispers "goodnight" in my ear. I can hear him inhale my scent and feel as he exhales slowly. It sends a zing right to my groin. *Fuck.* All of a sudden thunder crackles overhead. Aidan's eyes widen.

He carefully steps back.

"I have to go."

And within seconds he's in the car and out of sight.

The drive back home is a lot quieter than the cruise to Ghallagers. Everyone seems to be tired after the night's events.

Friday's usually aren't my favorite nights to go out. Zach and I normally stay in on Fridays and prefer to go out on Saturdays. *Stop thinking about him,* I order myself.

There is soft music playing, and no one is talking. Once again, my mind drifts to Zach. I imagine him kissing me, touching me, looking into my eyes. Aidan kissed my cheek. *Where did that come from?* My thoughts drift back to Zach. *Should I try to call him again before I go to sleep? Should I have Lucca drop me off at his place?* No, of course not. That would be stupid.

A series of memories, realizations and affirmations wash over me. *Aidan's eyes are so deep. I could get lost in them. Zach screeching away in his car and not looking back at me. He hasn't called to check on me. He doesn't love me anymore, he told me. Aidan wants to take me out. I go back and forth between these two men. I can NOT jump into a relationship with Aidan. Rebounds never work do they? No they do NOT.*

Kelly leans over and says to me quietly and lowers her voice to a whisper.

"So, Aidan huh? What do you think about him? He is so cute."

"I know. I keep thinking about him. Maybe Aidan is what I need to get me through this?" We are both whispering now.

"I think he is. I don't want to see you suffer over that asshole Zach anymore. He's been different for a while now. We all see it."

I can feel myself start to get defensive and then it hits me. Kelly is being honest with me. It's odd to hear her say bad things about Zach, and I had no idea that everyone had hated him all along.

"Kelly, I just don't know. I suppose he would be a nice distraction."

I replay my goodbye with Aidan in my head. He kissed me close to my ear. My body begins to tingle just thinking about his warm breath on my skin and the zing it gave me.

I realize I'm smiling when Kelly gives me a reassuring wink as we pull into the driveway.

"Girls, do you want to crash here? There is plenty of room," Lucca offers.

Leave it to Lucca to play Mr. Hospitality. He loves having people stay over at the wonderful house he inherited from his grandmother. The more the merrier for him. Lucca and I have been best friends since high school, so when he offered for me to move in with him, I simply couldn't refuse.

"I'll stay," Kelly says while stifling a yawn. "I'm exhausted and I always have my bag in the car, ya know, just in case."

She skips away to retrieve her overnight bag.

"I'll stay too," Sam says, "but I need to borrow a t-shirt to sleep in from someone."

"Well it won't be a proper slumber party without me."

I guess that means Simone is staying too.

We change, get comfortable, and start a movie on the big screen. We have more wine, and some popcorn to soak it up. After about a half hour, I look over, and everyone is sleeping except for Lucca.

"I'm going to bed Lucca."

I give him a small hug.

"Sweet dreams honey. Get some sleep."

He pats my shoulder.

"Thanks, I'll try. Thanks for everything earlier."

I smile and turn to head up the stairs.

I perform my nightly beauty rituals once I'm in the bathroom, brushing my teeth, and throwing my hair up before climbing into bed. I fall to my pillow and let the tears come. Zach always sleeps here on Friday nights. This is so crazy. I'm in my bed alone. I miss him. I hug my pillow close. I reach out with one hand but Zach is not there. I finally fall asleep on a wet pillow.

I wake a couple times during the night tossing and turning. I wake again and notice that it is becoming light out. I am feeling really good. Oh my goodness. *I am touching myself.* Then I recall the few times in the night when I woke and realize I was touching myself then too. I imagine him lying next to me. I want him in my bed. *Wait. What? I've been dreaming about him?* All I know is I've woken up touching myself, yet still wishing *he* was touching me. Fulfilling that desire he had sparked with that kiss in the parking lot, the zing. AIDAN.

I sit up in disbelief. *I've been dreaming of Aidan?* Something about him is sticking with me. He is so dark and mysterious. *And those dimples, fuck!* I remember him kissing my hand and my cheek and I heard him take in my scent. His exhale made me feel...made me feel *good*. Then the loud thunder and he was gone. *How weird was that?*

I hope I hear from Aidan today. *What if he doesn't call?* I cut off my endless list of "what ifs", and throw off my covers. Waking up happy is a refreshing feeling, especially after the drama of yesterday.

I slip on my slippers and go to the living room.

I must have a smile on my face, because Lucca, Sam, Kelly, and Simone all smile and greet me in unison.

"Good morning sunshine!"

What the hell? I panic for a moment, thinking they know about my dream and then I let out a breath. They certainly couldn't predict what I've been dreaming about. I think of how Simone would have a heyday if she became privy to this information. Perhaps I will confide in Lucca after the girls are gone.

"What time is it?" I ask, trying to stifle my smile.

"It's eleven o'clock. You never sleep this late."

Sam looks concerned.

"I guess I needed it."

I shrug my shoulders.

Only I know that I was dreaming of the dark knight, but I can't tell her that.

"What's the plan today?" Kelly asks.

She doesn't like going home. She likes when we are all a group.

"Well Gaby has a date tonight."

Simone lifts her eyebrows and looks to me.

"That's only if he texts me. Maybe he changed his mind?"

I shrug again. *Oh I hope not. Maybe he is sleeping late too*? I move to the kitchen to avoid questions.

"Who got phone numbers from the guys last night? I'm sure I'm not the only one."

"Gaby, you had us leave when you snapped your fingers, so, uh, no we didn't," Lucca informs me.

"Oh, sorrrrryyyyy," I say and roll my eyes. "You could have said something."

After a moment of uneasy silence, Lucca waves us all into the kitchen to start cooking breakfast. Er, well lunch. Okay, maybe by now it's brunch.

Lucca starts up the blender and the vibration reminds me of my phone. *My phone*. Wait, where is it?! *Has Zach called?* I hope so. Or at least, I hope I have a text from Aidan about tonight. *Fuck, I'm wishing for two men?*

Flustered, I make a quick exit from the kitchen and sprint up to my room.

I hear the vibration of my phone as I enter my room. It's a text. I flop on the bed and see it's an unknown number. *Well, it's not Zach then*. Aidan, I hope? I look at the time and see the message is from three minutes ago. It says:

Gaby, see you at 6!

Eek, I am so excited! I have that butterfly feeling in my stomach that I almost don't recognize. It's been so long since I last felt this light. The feeling of dating someone new is indescribable. *Dating?* No, I'm not dating him. He said it's just dinner. *Maybe it's not a date?* No, it's definitely a DATE.

I quickly tap a few buttons to send a text back.

Yes, sounds good!

I save his number in my phone and it vibrates again immediately.

Looking forward to it. What's ur address?

We text back and forth enough times for me to give him the address and quick directions. I am very excited, but also feel nervous. I quickly text Sebastian and let him know I'm doing okay and will see him soon. I almost forgot about the plans we've been making to visit our parents in a few weeks.

What should I wear? Is it weird to go out with someone alone when I barely know them? Unable to make any first-date wardrobe decisions on my own, I go back out to the kitchen and find all of my friends are eating without me. *Nice.*

"Lucca, will you be home tonight at six? I'd like you to be here when Aidan arrives to pick me up."

"Yes, I should be."

Oh good!

"Good. I'm kind of nervous about going out with someone new."

"Gaby," he winks at me, "let's talk about this later."

Oh I get it. He wants to talk when the girls leave.

We finish our brunch and discuss plans for the afternoon. We decide to get ready and go to the mall to pick a new outfit for my date. Yes, it's a date. I have to keep telling myself that. Aidan is picking me up tonight, for a date. It is such a surreal feeling. Just yesterday morning I was with Zach, my love for four years, and tonight I have a fucking date with a new man. *Can I really get over Zach so quickly?* I think about Aidan. His smoldering eyes. His dimples with his boyish grin. His touch. I just want to kiss those dimples and his neck, and move my way down his body. I shake my head to refocus. I need to get ready for shopping.

In the bathroom mirror, I repeat my daily mantra.

"Same old me again today."

Yep, there I am. My brown/hazel eyes, my long brown hair, blah, blah, blah.

"Ready?"

Simone pushes the door open. *Gee, she can't knock?*

"Yes, I'm ready Simone."

I hope she can hear the annoyance in my voice.

"Good, let's get out of here."

"Right behind you."

Once again we find ourselves riding in the Pathfinder. It's the only car the five of us can fit in comfortably and Lucca likes to drive. He thinks he's the leader of the group then, when we all know that Simone would never let that happen. And it's really *my* group of friends anyway. Lucca just likes to tag along.

We go to four stores until I finally find something that I like. Sam keeps having me try on these ridiculously short dresses, but I don't dress like that. Kelly is more conservative, so her choices aren't really jumping out at me either. Then there's Lucca's style. His taste in clothes is always my first choice. I'm lucky that we live together, because he's often ready to lend a hand and help me choose outfits for work, dates, and weekend plans. He knows how different brands fit my body, which is very helpful. I'm not the best decision maker, but if he says something makes me look fat, or skinny, I believe him.

Lucca runs into the dressing area while I'm taking my last mini skirt off, that I nonchalantly toss in the 'HELL NO' pile.

"Gaby, you must try this on."

He sounds so excited and a little short of breath.

"Lucca, what the hell are you doing in here? I am in the women's dressing room! Emphasis on the word WOMEN'S," I snap.

"Yes, Gaby. Just slip this on."

"Ok, ok. God!"

I take the black dress as he slides it over the top of the door. I hold it up. It doesn't look half bad. It's all black, which I love. It's not too short. It doesn't look too tight. Well maybe it's a bit snug – but in all the right places. I giggle to myself. I do want to look sexy for Aidan. But I will not sleep with him. *I will not sleep with him.*

What do people do on first dates nowadays anyway? Do women sleep with men on the first date? Do men expect it? *Fuck.*

Zach, my comfort zone. I am so out of touch with the dating scene. *What if I want to sleep with Aidan though?* But I won't. Nothing ever good comes out of one night stands. No one ever falls in love after that, do they? But the way Aidan made me feel when he kissed my cheek… wow. He sent shivers through me. Zach never did that. Zach just got so boring in the bedroom. I realize that after a long time of settling for boring that I really missed the butterflies. I shake my head and focus on the task at hand.

Lucca is waiting to see this black dress on me. I slip it on and it fits perfectly. It is tight where it needs to be, not too short, where I'll feel stupid when I sit. I feel comfortable and a tad bit sensual and sexy. It's nice to feel this way. *What has Zach done to me and my confidence?*

"Gaby, are you coming?" Lucca yells.

At least he didn't come back in here again.

I step out of my dressing room and Sam, Kelly, Simone, and Lucca all look at me stunned. Simone actually starts clapping.

"That's it!" She says. "You look fantastic."

I feel myself smile.

"YES!" Kelly and Sam say at the same time.

"Let's pick some shoes."

Lucca nods his approval, which is exactly what I need right now.

I pay for the dress and heels that Lucca picked and we drive back to the house, where they all wish me luck and tell me to text them as soon as I get home.

I'm kind of relieved to have some alone time with Lucca. *What would I do without him?* He follows me into my room.

"Hey, what's this nervous business you were talking about?"

"Lucca, I need you to pep talk me like you always do. I haven't been on a date with someone new in forever. You know how I am with small talk. I'm just..."

"You will do great, Gaby. Aidan obviously likes you. He was like a magnet to you as soon as we all got out of our cars last night. I was watching him with you from the bar."

"You were? I thought you were hitting on that super skinny guy."

I laugh because the skinny guy was not cute.

"Ha, well I was hoping for Mateo, but that didn't work out. He is so damn hot."

"I knew it!" I say.

I could tell he was looking at him with that look in his eye.

"The girls each grabbed a guy, so I went up to the bar. I felt a look from Aidan that he wanted to talk to you alone."

He did? I didn't notice.

"Lucca, when he kissed me on my hand, then my cheek, I practically melted in the parking lot. It felt incredible."

Well, *more* than incredible.

"I think this is good for you. Get your mind off of Zach. Just go with it and see what happens. You deserve someone that will treat you right and take care of you."

He's stroking my hand.

"That's what I was wishing for," I whisper.

I don't tell him about pleading out the window yesterday when I was here alone.

"I even had a dream about Aidan last night."

I wink.

Lucca's eyes widen and then he smiles.

"Come on. Get yourself ready. It's already five-thirty and we have a lot of work to do," he smirks.

He watches while I do my hair and makeup again. He instructs me to leave my hair down because it gives me an innocent look. He touches up my face and I'm off to get dressed.

It's now ten minutes to six. *Shit.* It's almost time. Aidan will be here soon. I'm almost ready. I'm almost ready. Deep breaths. *This will be fun.*

I decide not to tell Lucca everything about my dream last night. He would have laughed or encouraged me to do something I am not ready for. Maybe I'll confide in him tomorrow if tonight goes well.

The doorbell rings.

Here goes nothing. I open the door and Aidan looks gorgeous. He flashes a smile, and there are those prominent dimples I've been longing to kiss. He's wearing black jeans, a black jacket, and a crisp white button up shirt. How is someone so good looking interested in little old me?

"Hi. You look beautiful," he holds up a bouquet of flowers.

"Why thank you. Please come in."

I shut the door and follow him up the stairs. He looks so nice in those jeans.

"Gabriella. I hope you're hungry."

Gabriella?

"We have reservations at six-fifteen. We need to get going."

He gives Lucca a nod, and Lucca nods back.

"Hi Lucca."

I put the flowers in a vase on the table before we head toward the door.

Lucca mouths "good luck" as we leave.

I smile and shut the door. Aidan holds out his elbow and leads me out to his car.

Turns out Aidan drives a sleek, dark grey BMW. I have no idea what kind it is, but I know it's a BMW. I'm not very good with cars, but even I can't help but be impressed. *Where did he say he works again?* I try to hide my smile. Good looking guy, hot car, sounds like a good mix to me. Zach just drives a Toyota. *Stop thinking about Zach. Stop thinking about Zach.* Aidan opens my door and I slide in. *What a gentleman.*

"Where are we going for dinner?" I ask quietly.

"We're going to Capone's for Italian food." He smiles.

Those dimples again, fuck me!

"That sounds good."

Italian food. Good, I need something with carbs to settle my stomach.

"How was your day?"

He looks to me.

"It was nice. Just hung out with the girls and Lucca. What about you?"

I'm twirling my hair.

"I was counting down the minutes until our date tonight. I've been thinking about you since I saw you all quiet and shy in the back seat."

Wow he is so bold and direct. I am so embarrassed. I've been thinking about him too. Well more than thinking... but I can't say that.

"Oh."

I find myself not knowing what else to say.

He reaches over and gives my knee a little squeeze. I start to melt. *Don't stop, don't stop.*

My phone rings. Zach is calling. *What am I going to do?* I don't want to answer. Well, I do want to answer, but not when I'm with Aidan.

It rings again. I push the Ignore button and slip my phone back in my purse. Aidan's hand is still on my knee. I just stare at it, wishing he would slide it up my leg slowly. Oh, so slowly.

"We're here."

He startles me from my thoughts. That was a quick drive. I didn't know this restaurant was here, so close to my house.

"Wonderful."

All of a sudden I go weak in the knees. Aidan gets out of the driver's side and holds his finger up, signaling for me to wait. He walks around the car and opens my door.

"After you."

He gestures and puts out his elbow for me to grab on to. *Does he know my knees are weak?*

"Thank you, sir."

I see him smile.

We walk up a few stairs into this beautiful, elegant restaurant. There is a fire blazing in the entry way, and all of the décor is accented by dark mahogany. I can smell the oils and the spices mix with the fire. It's a heavenly combination. *Why have I never heard of this place?*

Aidan shakes the host's hand.

"Good evening Mr. Scott. Welcome back sir."

Mr. Scott? I didn't even know his last name. I like it. The host leads us to an intimate table for two.

"This is lovely. Thank you."

"Just like you Gabriella."

He pulls out my chair. I really do need to sit down.

"You've been here before I see?" I ask, twirling my hair again.

"Yes, a few times," he smirks.

He orders two glasses of white wine before turning his attention back to me.

"Is there anything you don't like or are allergic to?"

"No. At least not that I know of."

Why? He wants to order for us? Interesting. A take charge kind of guy. I could get used to this for sure. Zach was always so wishy-washy. *Zach, fuck. Why did he call?*

Aidan extends both arms on the table and holds his palms up. *Does he want me to put my hands in his?* This is awkward. Holding hands signifies a level of comfort in a relationship. I'm surprised to realize that I feel so comfortable with Aidan so soon. I place my hands in his and he grabs them firmly.

He looks directly in my eyes and says, "Gabriella, you are very beautiful. I can see the brown shining in your eyes tonight. I guess your license is right."

He's teasing me.

"Yes, I guess it is," I smile back shyly.

His touch is welcome.

"Like I said in the car, I can't stop thinking about you."

I wonder if this is a line he uses on all girls.

"There's something about seeing you in between all of your friends, so shy, not giving a fuck, that intrigues me."

Intrigued? I guess I would say I find him intriguing too.

"Intrigued?" I ask.

"Yes, intrigued. You're not all out there like your friends are. I want to get to know you better."

Ok now I'm getting that feeling in my stomach again.

"You put me in a trance when you speak. And you smell intoxicating." He smiles and then his brow furrows as though he's trying to figure out how to phrase his next thought.

"Gabriella, who called you on the way here?"

Oh shit.

"No one important."

I really don't want to discuss Zach tonight.

"Are you sure? You put your phone away rather quickly."

"Yes, I'm sure."

I'm relieved as the waiter chooses that moment to arrive and pour our glasses of wine. Aidan lifts his glass in a toast.

"To beautiful Gabriella. Thank you for coming out with me this evening."

I smile and we clink glasses.

"I love your dress, and your hair looks lovely."

Ok, enough with the compliments already.

His constant smile, those damn dimples and the steady flow of honest flattery is causing my body to react – and I mean in a *good* way. His eyes lock on mine and his thumb brushes over my fingertips, making me wetter and wetter. *Wow.* I take a deep breath and break eye contact for a moment to regain control over my body's reaction.

Aidan takes the brief pause to call the waiter over, and he orders us a bruschetta appetizer, a greens salad, baked rigatoni for dinner, and some fancy-sounding dessert I've never heard of. *Wow.* He just ordered a four course meal, as easily as if he'd ordered a Coke. I experience a moment of hesitation, as I try and determine if my stomach will even be able to handle that much food.

Aidan puts his hands out on the table again and I place my hands in his.

"I'd love to take you for a walk on the beach after dinner. It is so nice outside, and the waves here are amazing."

"Ok."

A nice stroll on the beach. I can do that. He strokes my hands with his thumbs and looks into my eyes.

I think he wants to ask me about the phone call again, but instead he says, "Tell me about yourself, your family, I want to know everything."

I take a deep breath.

"I have one brother. His name is Sebastian. He is older than me, and very protective," I warn. "He is married to Victoria. They don't have any kids, but they are trying. My parents live in Northern California. I see them about once a month. Either they come down or I go up for a weekend. It's only three hours away. We are planning a visit in a few weeks. "

"Sebastian. You have so many protective men over you."

Protective? I wish that were true.

"What? Who?"

"Lucca seems very protective over you as well."

He puts his finger to his mouth like he's thinking.

"Lucca is a good friend. He likes your friend Mateo."

"Mateo? That's hilarious. Mateo is not a man's man. Now that you say it, I can see that Lucca is." He switches to his next question. "Sebastian. How much older is he?"

"He is four years older."

"I don't think you ever told me how old you were."

"I'm twenty six."

"So Sebastian is my age? Interesting."

The salad arrives before the bruschetta. We are sipping wine and eating our salads and my phone rings again. *Why didn't I turn the ringer off?* It's Zach. Again. *What the hell?* I push Ignore one more time and put it back into my purse. I can see Aidan narrow his eyes at me. He knows something is wrong. I do my best to try to pretend that didn't just happen.

"What do you like to do, Gabriella? Do you have any hobbies?"

"Not really."

I really don't.

"Do you like to go to movies?"

"Yes."

"What kind of movies?"

"Action, romance, anything really."

I'm starting to act weird. I'm distracted by the phone calls.

"Have you seen any recently?"

I have to think for a moment. Toward the end of our relationship, Zach never took me out.

"No, the last movie I went to was full of teenagers laughing and giggling. It completely ruined the experience."

"What are your goals? Your dreams?"

Crap. I can't concentrate.

"Um. I'd like to travel. I'd love to get a beach house that's suspended over the water."

Okay that's good. I'm opening up a little bit.

"Interesting."

He's looking at me like he didn't completely understand my answer.

"What about your family?" I ask.

I don't want to be the center of all the questions.

"It's just Nicholas and I. We grew up in a small town in Italy, without much money. We all moved to the states when we were twelve. Our parents died when we were young."

Oh how sad.

"How old is Nicholas?"

"He is also thirty."

"You are twins?"

"Yes. We are close now that we are older. We used to hate each other, but we had to bond together once our parents passed away."

"How old were you when they died?" I ask, as the appetizer arrives.

"We were fifteen, and we were homeless for a while."

He closes his eyes, as if the memory is replaying in his mind.

"Nicholas and I have been close ever since. Our parents taught us so much and how to be proper gentlemen."

His eyes open.

"Enough about that. What kind of music do you like?"

"Um, I like rock music. Some good heavy guitar and drums always get me in a good mood."

I smile hoping he will smile back.

"I like something a little lighter, alternative I guess you would call it. The heavy guitar and drums give me a headache. I can't listen to that."

He shakes his head.

Throughout the rest of the dinner, I grow quiet. I think about Zach and what he wants. *Why is he calling me? I miss him, don't I? I want him back, right?* I am having a lot of fun with Aidan. I excuse myself to the restroom in order to break up the silence.

Aidan stands as I walk away from the table.

Once I'm in the restroom out of sight, I check my phone. I have a voice mail from Zach. I hit the button to replay his message:

"Gaby, what are you doing? Where are you? Sam told me you were out on a date tonight. And now you're not answering. I'm sorry about yesterday. Gaby, please call me back. Tonight. I have something to tell you."

I feel the anger start to bubble to the surface. *Are you kidding me? How does it feel for me not to answer Zach? And why does he sound all frantic?* He broke up with me. He shouldn't care where I am or what I'm doing... And what was he doing talking to Sam? Sam always tried to make him jealous over the years, but it never worked. But me on a date – now *that's* something for him to get pissed about. *Why the fuck does he care where I am?* I'm so mad at how left me in the street yesterday. He never did give a fuck about anyone besides himself. *I hope Sam didn't tell him where I was.* Oh, of course she didn't. She couldn't have. I didn't even know where I was going. I resolve to shut off my phone and let him suffer. It feels good to turn the tables.

I hastily shove my phone in my purse, realizing Aidan is probably wondering what's taking me so long. I take a deep breath and go back to the table. I see the dessert has arrived. Aidan's chair is now on my side of the table.

"Sorry for the delay."

"Dessert just got here and I ordered another glass of wine."

He smiles but looks angry. We are sitting so close that our legs touch. I am feeling a pull to him. I want him to run his hand on my legs like before. I'm aching.

He lifts his wine and says quietly, "Gabriella, I'm going to kiss you."

Fuck. My ache gets deeper. He takes a sip of wine, and reaches up to my face. He strokes the back of his fingers down my cheek. He moves closer and leans in to kiss me near my ear. I hear him do the inhale again and my knees feel instantly weak. He sits back, looks in my eyes, then down at my lips, and kisses them softly. He stops. I close my eyes and relish in this new and welcome feeling I'm having all over my body. He leans in again, and kisses me. *Oh Aidan.* He sets his hand on my thigh and my heart starts beating harder. I curse myself silently for not wearing a shorter dress, so I could feel his hand on my skin. I feel him part his lips, so I part mine. He licks my lips gently and sits back. *Wait, don't stop. Don't stop.* He has literally taken my breath away.

"Thank you, Gabriella. Let's have our dessert."

I am panting inside. I want more of his touch. We are in a restaurant, but I don't care. *These feelings.* I'm not used to them. Aidan begins eating his dessert. It's some sort of chocolate cake. I'm watching him, and he offers me a bite of his. I can barely move. I don't want to lift my fork. His lips are so inviting. He runs his tongue over his lips, almost seductively, between bites and sips of wine.

"Eat your dessert, so we can go for our walk."

He points to my cake and winks.

I eat my dessert quickly. *This cake is so good.* I wish I could slow down and savor the flavors, but I want to get out of here. My heart is racing. While I finish my wine, Aidan pays the bill and stands. We don't speak. He watches me as I finish my dessert. I want to kiss him again.

"Let's go."

He puts his hand out and I take it.

He leads us to the back of the restaurant. The beach was right here, this close. I thought we would have to drive a bit for our walk. I am holding his elbow again and as we get closer to the water I can see the moon light glisten over the ocean. The waves crashing create a romantic soundtrack for our walk. This date has been perfect so far.

"May I carry your shoes for you?"

His voice is so silky and seductive.

I take my shoes off and hand them to him. It feels nice without heels and to have the sand surround my feet. I look up at Aidan. He must be at least six feet tall. I am only five feet six inches.

I lean down to fix my dress, and as I come up, he grabs my chin and kisses me, this kiss rougher and more intense than the first. I feel it everywhere-- my stomach, my throat, my knees, my groin. He lets go of my chin and wraps his arms around me. He pulls me close and I can feel him growing hard against me. I put my arms around the back of his neck. Our lips hover together. *Please kiss me. Please kiss me again.*

My heart beats faster and faster. His hands go into my hair and we are still pushing our bodies together. He is consuming me with his hands, his breath, his body. There is that zing of energy again. *I want him so bad.*

I told myself I would not sleep with him tonight. He steps back, reaches for my hand and pulls. We start to walk again. My legs are trembling and the waves are crashing over our feet.

Aidan relaxes me. He is so calm and slow. I am really enjoying the evening. I'd like to go out with him again, but only if he asks. The waves are coming up to our knees now. He suddenly stops and turns.

He looks deep into my eyes.

"I want to make love to you Gabriella."

My heart skips a beat.

"Something is pulling me to you. I can't describe it. I don't know what it is. But I don't want to fight it."

I want that too.

"Aidan, I..."

He pulls me to him and kisses me softly. We are still holding hands.

"Aidan, I'd like to know more about you. This is so sudden. I told you about what happened yesterday, but I feel the same pull towards you too."

"You feel the pull?"

Is that all he heard from what I just said? He looks so hopeful.

"Yes, I do. Please let's just..."

He puts his finger up and I stop talking. He hugs me, breathing into my ear and it sends a shiver through my body.

"I will wait until you are ready to make love, Gabriella."

He keeps one arm around me, while the hand from his other starts to touch my breast. He circles it so softly and kisses my neck. When he touches me, I lose myself. I lose all train of thought, my willpower. I am in his trance too. His hands move down the front of my thighs.

He touches my skin just below my dress line. *Go higher, go higher please.* As if he could read my mind, his hand does go higher, up towards my wet panties. He grazes me softly on the outside of them. I lean forward welcoming and encouraging his touch, but he doesn't change his rhythm. He skims his finger up and down, while kissing my neck, my ears, my lips. I want him *now.*

"Aidan," I whisper.

"Tell me, Gabriella," he whispers too.

"Please touch me. Touch my skin."

I can barely speak.

The waves are getting higher. He moves his fingers to one side of my panties and slowly slides them over. His middle finger opens my lips and spreads my wetness. It slides so easily. He doesn't go inside, just the slow strokes up and down, up and down. My heart is beating so loud that I can't hear the waves anymore. I can't feel anything else. I might not be able to stand much longer. I'm shaking. This slowness, this teasing is torture. He stops and pulls back.

"Gabriella," he kisses me, "Gabriella, let's keep walking."

Keep walking? I'm not sure if I can.

He pulls lightly and we walk hand in hand down the beach. I think we are the only ones here. I hope no one saw us. This section of the beach appears to be very secluded, so we must be alone. We walk for a few minutes when he stops and turns to me again. I'm hoping we are going to pick up where we left off.

"Tell me whose calls you are ignoring."

Oh Fuck. I don't want to talk about this now.

"It was Zach who called."

"Who is Zach?"

"Zach is the person that broke up with me yesterday. He left a voice mail. He knows I am on a date right now, so I turned my phone off."

"Good girl."

Good girl? Who is this guy? He is so hot and controlling. That turns me on.

I continue explaining.

"He left me yesterday in hysterics, and I am very angry with him. He didn't even tell me we broke up. I had to hear it from Victoria."

I start babbling.

"What? Wow. Sounds like quite a guy," Aidan says sarcastically shaking his head. "I would never..."

He stops himself.

"I don't want to talk about him. I'm having a really nice time with you."

I squeeze his hand.

"Me too."

His demeanor changes.

"Let's head back towards the car."

Head back? I don't want to go home.

He's silent as he strokes my hand with his thumb. We don't talk. He looks so deep in thought. *What is bothering him?* It better not be Zach and his antics. I've gotten him out of my thoughts, for now at least. Aidan shouldn't be bothered with him.

Just this one date with Aidan makes me want to see what more dates are like with him. I feel very comfortable even though it's been such a short time. I don't want to think about Zach anymore. *What did he ever do for me anyway?* He just made me feel like shit about myself and started doing his own thing. I've never felt the pull with Zach that I do towards Aidan. The pull with Aidan is so strong.

On the drive back, Aidan takes me by surprise.

"I would like you to stay with me tonight. I know it's probably too soon for you. But I wanted you to know what I was thinking."

Oh, I was thinking the same thing too. What I would do to feel his naked body against mine, his warmth, him inside me.

"I'll take you home."

No! As we turn on my block, I push so I sit up straight. *That can't be Zach's car.*

"What's wrong?"

"Aidan, please keep driving. Maybe staying at your place is a good idea."

"Why? I mean I would love that. But what's wrong?" He's getting louder.

"Zach is waiting here for me. That's his car."

I point to the red Toyota directly in front of my door.

"Persistent isn't he?"

Aidan has a mean look in his eye. He parks across from Zach, and we both get out. This isn't happening. These two should not be meeting.

"Aidan, please get back in the car. Let's just go," I beg.

Zach watches us get out together, and he immediately jumps out of his car.

"Who the fuck is this guy?"

He points at Aidan.

"This is..."

Aidan interrupts me.

"I'm Aidan. Who are you?"

He knows who it is.

"I'm Zach, Gaby's boyfriend."

Boyfriend?

"Zach, please go home. Please just leave," I plead.

"Yeah, right. Gaby, I've been trying to call you and apologize. I've made a huge mistake."

"Zach, please just go home." He comes towards me and puts his arms out like he's going to hug me. I put my arms straight out and push him away. His eyes widen. He bypasses my arms and hugs me so tight.

He whispers in my ear almost begging, "Gaby, I'm so sorry. Please forgive me. Please take me back. Please."

I don't know what to do or think. Zach begging for me. He's my comfort, my love of four years. There's sexy Aidan, just watching us. He looks like he is going to pounce. I give him an "I'm sorry" look and he walks towards us. He pulls Zach's shoulder back and takes him off me. Zach turns around and swings in Aidan's direction, punching him across the jaw.

"Zach stop!" I scream. "Please go home. We can talk about this tomorrow."

Aidan and Zach launch into a full out brawl, hitting back and forth, yelling at each other. Zach threatens to sleep in his car. I can't watch this. No one is letting up. Zach's face is bleeding. Oh my God. Aidan is such a tough guy. He didn't even know me two days ago, and now he's fighting for me. *Don't fall, don't fall.* I run into the house hoping Lucca is home.

"Lucca. Lucca." I'm screaming up the stairs.

"Holy shit Gaby. What?"

He jumps up.

"Please come outside. Zach and Aidan are fighting in the street. Hurry!"

"This is ridiculous."

Lucca storms outside.

"Zach. Stop. Stop now. This is my house. I've thrown you out before. You need to go home. NOW!" Lucca screams.

Zach stops. For some reason, he is a little scared of Lucca. I'm not exactly sure why. They must have had an altercation that neither of them told me about. Lucca gives him the stare down. I feel relieved.

"I will be back tomorrow Gaby. Count on it!" He yells in my face and I watch him drive away.

I am shaking, crying, stunned beyond belief. Zach came back for me. *But is it too late? Is he what I want anymore?* I fall to the street, putting my head down. I watch Zach screech off again. And just like twenty four hours ago, he left me here in the street, sobbing. My world is spinning.

"Hey," Aidan says as he scoops me up.

Aidan is here for me. He is saving me, protecting me, taking care of me. *Just what I've always wanted.*

"Please stay with me tonight," I whisper and close my eyes.

Chapter 3

Aidan carries me into the house. I am spent. I've had so much going on in my head the last couple days, I just can't think anymore. I try to focus. Aidan saved me. He picked me up off of the street, while Zach just took off again. Aidan cares about me. He has agreed to stay with me tonight. *My dark knight.* He makes me feel safe.

I don't even look around for Lucca. I'm sure he made it back in the house just fine.

I have my arms around Aidan's neck and am nuzzling him. He shuts my bedroom door behind him with his foot and lowers me to the bed. I'm lying down but he hasn't let go. He leans back and looks in my eyes.

He kisses me softly.

"Are you ok?"

I nod.

"Thank you."

"For what?"

"For staying with me."

He closes his eyes for a moment.

"Gabriella, I am here for you. Tell me what you need."

Have I found the perfect man? He says exactly what I need him to say.

"I need you. I need your touch."

He hugs me tight. This is what I need.

"May I help you out of your dress?"

He undoes his hold on me and I stand at the edge of my bed. He stands behind me and starts to unzip my dress. He kisses my shoulders as the zipper moves down slowly. He pushes the straps down my arms and my dress falls to the floor. I turn around and hug him. He reaches behind my back and unhooks my bra. He kisses my cheek, then my ear, and he takes a step back, allowing my bra to slip off my arms and fall in the pile with my dress. His hands slide down my shoulders and he tickles my arms. We are looking into each other's eyes.

Is he looking for my approval to continue?

He moves his hands to my stomach and puts his fingers under the top of my panties. I don't move or blink. I don't tell him no. He starts to pull them down. Still looking in his eyes, I step out of them as they add to the pile. I want this. I need this. The butterflies are flying. I can do this. I deserve this. I am naked in front of a new man. I feel his pull. I see the care in his eyes.

Is this love at first sight? Is this what you hear about in the movies? You see a guy from across the room and the rest is history?

"What do you sleep in?" he whispers.

"Nothing tonight," I say quietly, "I believe you should do the same."

His eyes widen. I feel him grow harder against me, and I nearly collapse. He takes his jacket off and lifts his shirt over his head. I am seeing his bare chest for the first time, and my heart skips a beat. It is so dark and toned. It's so smooth and mesmerizing. He unbuttons his jeans and is still looking in my eyes for my approval. I don't flinch. This is what I want. His jeans and boxers come off at the same time. He is... *Oh shit.* His erection is very impressive. It looks perfect, just like the rest of him. I can't wait to have it, so deep inside me.

He picks up the pile of clothes and puts them in the corner. *Holy shit he has lower back dimples.* Fuck, I love that. And they match his cheek dimples. His body radiates strength. *Come here. Come here.* I can barely contain myself. I'm trying to stand as still as I can. He turns and walks towards me. He picks me up the same way he carried me into my bedroom, over the threshold kind of carrying.

This is so hot!

He lowers me to the bed, this time coming all the way with me, and lies right behind me, spooning my body. I feel his erection at my back. I want to turn around, but he's holding me tight again. One of his arms is under my neck and his other hand is now on my waist.

Kissing my neck he whispers, "This is nice."

Feeling his hot breath on me is making me shake. The butterflies are flying faster. I have the feeling deep down, a weak in the knees feeling that he gives me with ease.

"What you said earlier, about needing me, needing my touch," he pauses, "I need yours too. Let me take care of you, Gabriella."

I squeeze my eyes.

He has taken my words. He is doing what I've wanted someone to do. He wants to take care of me. He is asking me. I am not begging him. He wants this as much as I need it. He can't see my face, but this makes me so happy. *Who is this man? Sweeping me off my feet in such a short time?*

I turn my head back to kiss him. He is so gentle. His tongue enters my mouth and his hand moves up to my breast. I instinctively push back on him. I want to turn around more than anything. He switches between each breast, squeezing each nipple, kissing me tenderly. I have one hand at his face as he touches me. This is slow torture. His hand moves down past my stomach and to my wetness and I part my legs slightly.

"I feel how much you need me," he says as his fingers linger in the moisture he's created.

I smile as he strokes up and down spreading the stickiness, but doesn't go inside. He uses his arm and moves me to my back. Now I can look into his dark eyes and touch him back. I trace my fingers between each muscle on his chest.

"You are so beautiful. Don't cry anymore. Tell me what you want Gabriella."

I love that he uses my full name. It is such a turn on how he says it, so tender. He is asking me what I want. He's asking my permission to go further.

"I want you Aidan."

"But what do you want me to do, Gabriella?"

He kisses my cheek.

"I want you inside me. I want to feel you. Please make love to me."

"Oh baby."

He closes his eyes and opens them again.

"Are you sure you're ready?"

I lick my lips and nod. He takes my nipple into his mouth. I gasp and stiffen at his touch and he sucks harder. He is teasing me. He touches my upper thighs, my stomach, everywhere but where I want him to touch.

He positions himself between my legs. *Oh finally.* He lies on one of my thighs, and pushes the other down so I'm open wide. He caresses my stomach, my hips, my thighs, and then down to my knees. He is watching me. I feel as though I am going to explode if he keeps this up. I think he can feel my legs trembling because he smiles and leans in and kisses me hard. I run my hands through his soft hair. He feels so good. I can't see what his hands are doing, but I feel my lips part and he slowly sinks a finger inside me. I groan, and he kisses harder. He's moving his finger in and out too slowly and is groaning back as I try to move. I want to close my legs around him. I can't handle this. I can't do this. Closing my legs doesn't help. I need him inside me. *Now.* I push myself forward and get a small graze of his tip near my opening. I cry out and he sits back.

"Easy, baby. Not yet."

Not yet?

I am practically begging for him. I push up again trying to get a little pressure. He slides down, still holding my one side. *Is he going to? Oh shit.* He is. He kisses my stomach, pushes my other leg down to the bed, and uses his fingers to hold my lips open. He teases and stops to suck my throbbing clitoris ever so gently. As he sucks, he slides a finger inside me, then two fingers. They move and push on my front wall, and when he hits that sweet, sweet spot, I cry out. He doesn't stop. He pushes harder, and puts more pressure on my clitoris with his palm at the same time. I'm going to come. I don't want to come yet, but I can't stop it. I haven't felt him inside me. He said. He said he would. Oh! I stiffen as I let go. My body is trembling.

I pull at his hair. I want his face back up by mine. He sits up to look at me. He keeps his fingers moving in and out as I slowly come down from the high of my orgasm.

I haven't had an orgasm like that. *Ever.* I didn't think I could. What is Aidan doing to me?

His fingers withdraw and he comes up to my face and holds me as my body calms. I feel safe, secure, content. I still feel his erection. I pull his lips to mine and kiss him. He leans up on his elbows hovering over me. We both look down and I see him. *So hard. So ready.* He rubs himself in my succulence. My heart is racing. I feel myself open further to draw him in and I push up so the tip enters a little bit again. He looks back up at me.

"Ready?"

Oh Aidan, I'm more than ready. I kiss him and push up. At the same time he pushes down and enters me. I groan loud, almost screaming. A feeling of peace takes over my entire body. My nails instinctively dig into his back. He makes me feel like no one else ever has. We are giving into the pull we have between each other and it feels amazing. He goes deeper and deeper as I adjust and stretch to his girth. My body is striving to accommodate him. The passion in his kisses is overwhelming. I begin to move to his rhythm.

He stops.

"Gabriella, you are amazing. You feel amazing. Your body is driving me crazy. I need to stop and just take you in because if I pull out now, I might come. I want to feel you as long as possible."

I feel the same way.

"Aidan, I don't want this to end either. You have taken all my cares away, all my thoughts."

He closes his eyes and moves again. He takes my hands so we are holding them at the side of my head with our fingers laced together. He bites my neck and I gasp. I wrap my legs around his back with my hard breasts pressed against his chest. In and out, in and out, slow, fast, slow. He keeps a firm pace as he holds my hands and kisses me.

"I want you to come again for me."

Oh shit.

I've never come like that and he wants me to do it again. *Just let yourself go, enjoy this. Concentrate on the fullness inside and feel every inch.* He picks up the rhythm and holds it steady once he's hit that sweet spot again. *Keep going, please.* I moan. *Fuck, here I go again.* I come around him. This is incredible. My body responds to his so quickly. I hug him tightly as he empties inside of me.

"Oh," he says in my ear, "oh baby."

He collapses next to me and doesn't let go as he says, "I'm going to hold you all night."

I fall asleep feeling safe and secure. It's such a confident feeling. Does Aidan need me as much as I need him?

When I wake in the morning, he is still holding me. He is behind me, arms around me, and holding my hand. *Am I dreaming?* I have this hot man draped around me. He asked me if he could take care of me. This is too good to be true. Wait. *What have I done?* I told myself over and over not to sleep with him. *Will he leave the second he wakes up?* I'm sure he will not want to deal with crazy Zach. Simone does this kind of thing all the time. She never told me about any of them staying over all night or holding her hand the whole time. *This is more than that isn't it?*

I don't want to move. *What if he leaves and it's all over?* I take a deep breath and feel tightening on my fingers. I turn and see Aidan is awake.

"Good morning," he says with a smile.

"Good morning."

Please don't leave.

"Did you sleep well, Gabriella?"

"Yes. Thank you again for staying with me."

"You look very beautiful in the morning." He kisses my cheek and hugs me close.

"Thank you."

I swallow.

"I love that you hold my hand."

I look down and slowly turn to face him. I hope he can't see the desperation in my eyes.

He smiles big and says, "You look surprised to see that I'm still here. I told you I would stay with you. I asked to take care of you."

Wow. Can he read my mind or what?

"I really enjoyed last night. I hope I didn't cross the line."

I look down again, embarrassed. Look at his beautiful body. So close to mine. Naked.

"No, you didn't. I enjoyed it too."

He pulls me into a tight hug. He's not leaving.

"What are your plans today? I have something in mind if you're up for it."

He wants to spend more time with me. *This is surreal. Don't get hurt. Don't fall too fast. Not this time.* Before Zach, I did the one night stand thing with Simone. Her and I approached it differently though. She wanted the one night. I wanted to fall in love. It never happened. I've always dreamed of love at first sight. Could this be it? I knew I didn't have that with Zach. He wasn't my soul mate, but I still loved him.

"What did you have in mind?"

"It's a goodie."

"A goodie?"

Oh, something romantic I hope.

"A surprise. I call it a goodie."

He smiles and rubs his hair down.

"Sounds like a perfect Sunday. Wait, I am supposed to meet the girls." *It is Sunday, right?*

"The girls?"

"Yes, I'm sure it will be fine if I cancel."

I want to cancel. I want to spend my Sunday with this perfect man lying next to me.

"Come here."

His eyes look hooded, smoldering.

"You smell so sweet."

He pulls me into a tight embrace. I feel his erection at my stomach. *Well good morning to you.* His hands move up and down my body, tickling my sensitive skin.

"What time were you supposed to meet?"

He is almost panting.

"At. Ten. This. Morning." I kiss him between each word. "Why?"

"Because it's nine-thirty now."

I sit up.

"Fuck, really? I need to call them."

"You go meet them and I will see you after. I have a few things to do at home."

I give him a quick kiss and find my robe. I stumble around to find my phone. I really don't want to turn it on. I don't want any calls or texts or reminders at all of Zach, especially today.

"I'll be right back."

I open the door and go to the living room.

"Gaby, you naughty girl," Lucca says from the couch.

He's drinking his morning coffee and reading the Sunday paper, as is his usual Sunday morning routine. He's just in his robe too.

"I see he's still here. How was last night?"

"Lucca. You're the naughty one," I smile. "Can I use your phone to call Kelly?"

"Only if you tell me why."

He smirks.

"I don't want to turn mine on, and I need to tell her I am running behind for brunch."

I meet the girls every Sunday at ten for brunch. We've been doing it for years. He throws me his phone.

"Thank you. You have her number in here, right?"

"Yes, it's under K."

He rolls his eyes. I give him a fake smile and find her name and push it. It's ringing.

"Lucca, is Gaby ok?" Kelly asks.

"It's me, and yes, I'm ok."

"Gaby. I've been worried sick about you. You didn't text us when you got home last night."

"I know. I should have called yesterday. I'm sorry. I'll fill you in when I get there. I just called to tell you I will be twenty minutes late for brunch."

I hear her sigh and then say, "OK. I'm glad you are fine. Remember we are going to Simone's parents afterwards for their anniversary party."

"Damn, that's right."

I really don't want to go, but I promised, and Simone would never let me live it down if I didn't.

"OK, I'll see you soon."

I hang up and throw the phone back at Lucca.

I hear Lucca call out after me as I skip back to my room.

"Nice to see you smile, Gaby."

I shut my bedroom door. Aidan is still in my bed. What a beautiful sight he is. He smiles up at me. He has both hands behind his head on my pillow.

"So? What did she say?" Aidan asks.

"I told her I'll be late. But I forgot I have to go to an anniversary party today."

"Oh."

He looks disappointed. I lie next to him and circle my fingers around his naval. He keeps his hands behind his head.

"Why are you so smiley?" I ask as he rubs his nose to mine.

"You make me smile. That's all."

I rub my groin against his. He thrusts up once and I moan.

"Let's get ready," he says.

What? He's such a tease. I'd love to lie in bed with him all day. I rub a little harder.

"Can't we stay just a little longer?"

I'm whining. And he's enjoying it.

He smiles and shakes his head no. He wants me to wait for him, long for him. Is this payback for having plans today?

Chapter 4

The hot water flows over me. I replay the night in my head. Aidan slept over. He held me when I needed to be held. *This is craziness!* He hit Zach. He asked me to spend the day with him.

This hot shower feels like I'm washing off all of the old negative memories and vibes and starting over with new ones. New ones with Aidan. New and exciting memories. Today is going to be a great day.

What have I done? Sleeping with someone so soon, I scold myself. I feel tingles as I remember Aidan's kisses, him taking my dress off, his face when I told him what I wanted to wear to bed, his hard body, his back dimples, holding his hands while making love. He made me come twice and I woke up with him around me holding my hand. I smile and let the hot water run down my body.

I am dressed in my favorite jeans and blue button up blouse. I'll wear my boots with a small heel so I'm closer to Aidan's mouth. Oh that mouth, so soft and strong. I brush my hair out and dry it straight. I finish my makeup. There I am.

"Same old me again today."

I wink at myself and open the bathroom door. I can hear voices from the living room. Aidan is up and dressed and having coffee with Lucca. This is a great sight. Zach would never have done this. He and Lucca weren't close. I could get used to seeing my new hot guy getting along with my best friend. *It still seems too good to be true.* Aidan hops up when he sees me.

"Ready to go? Lucca has made you a coffee for the road and I will drop you at brunch."

He holds the cup out to me.

"Thank you Lucca."

I smile at him. He smirks. He knows what I did last night.

"See you tonight."

"Bye Lucca. Have a good day," Aidan says to him.

I wonder what they have been talking about. I thought I heard them mention something about the weather.

"You too."

Lucca waves at us.

Aidan opens my door. I just love this car. Before I get in, I stare at the street, recalling the events from last night. I shake my head to change my thoughts and I sit down.

"So, what was the surpri-- I mean goodie today?"

I hope he tells me.

"I'm not telling."

He grins.

"You're no fun."

The suspense is killing me, but I do love a good surprise.

"Don't say that. You have no idea how fun I can be."

He's so mysterious.

He types the address of the restaurant into his GPS, and away we go. I watch his hands maneuver the steering wheel. I imagine them wrapped around me and teasing me like he did on the beach. I find myself staring at his strong jaw and soft lips. I want them all over me. I sit back and close my eyes. His tongue is slowly parting my lips. His hands are caressing my breasts. His erection is pushing into me. He is breathing hard in my ear, so hard he can't wait one more second to be inside me.

"Hey, sleepy head. Didn't get enough sleep last night?"

He snaps me out of my daydream.

"I guess not."

Staying up with him was worth it. We both giggle.

"Gabriella, thank you for a lovely evening. When can I see you again?"

He smiles seductively.

I kiss him gently on the lips. He wants to see me again. I can't wait to see him again too, but I'm busy all week with work. I turn my phone on to check my calendar, but turn it off immediately. I don't want to see any calls or texts. I think I am free Thursday night. If I'm not, I'll get out of whatever I'm doing.

"Gabriella, may I see you sometime this week?" he asks firmly.

"I would like that. I am free on Thursday after work."

I will be free Thursday after work.

"Thursday it is."

He kisses me softly and his hand grazes my leg. There's that zing again.

I walk up the steps to Sweet Elle. We always have brunch here. It's the sweetest little place. There's a small store front that sells local art and clothing and all the food is homemade. I peek out the window. Aidan waited for me to get all the way in the door before pulling away. That makes me smile. I spot the girls waiting for me at our usual table.

"Gaby, you're late," Simone scolds.

"I called Kelly. It's only a half hour. You could have eaten."

Gee, what's the big deal?

"Don't go changing your plans on us for some new guy."

Oh yeah, because none of them has ever done that. I roll my eyes.

"Simone, calm down," Sam says. "Gaby, tell us about your date last night. Kelly says he slept over?"

I tell them about the restaurant and the walk on the beach. I don't tell them every detail about the walk, just that it was romantic and secluded. They can draw their own conclusions. I explain how Zach was waiting for me when we got back and Aidan picked me up off the street and carried me in the house. They watch me so intently. I can tell they are impressed with Aidan.

"He's different. He asked to take care of me and hold me," I explain when Simone looks confused. "He said he feels some sort of pull towards me."

Now she's rolling her eyes.

She doesn't believe in love, especially love at first sight. Actually, I don't think she's ever been in love, now that I think about it. With guys constantly ogling you, I guess you may choose that attention over settling down.

"Simone, let's give him a chance. He has got to be better than Zach."

Thank you, Sam.

"Sorry I didn't text you guys last night. I was so overwhelmed. I just wanted to go to sleep."

"So you went right to sleep?"

Oh shut up Kelly! I try to kick her under the table.

"I'll never tell."

I can barely keep a straight face.

"Well I think he's hot, Gaby. He's a keeper. You should be happy and have some fun."

Sam steps up again. *Well done.*

"Thanks Sam."

I remember what Zach said on the voice mail.

"Hey, why did you tell Zach I was on a date?"

"Sorry Gaby. I wasn't thinking."

And she does look sorry.

"Please don't tell Zach anything. He chose to leave. Ok?"

I look her directly in the eyes and she nods.

We do our usual routine where we go around the table and say our highs and lows. We talk about the week coming up and if will see each other or not. We probably won't because of my busy schedule at work. We are all very close and try to hang out at least once a week. I tell them about my date on Thursday night with Aidan.

"You're seeing him again on Thursday?"

Simone looks confused again.

"Yes, Simone, I am."

"So you are done with Zach completely?"

I see a look in her eyes that seems as though she wants me to say yes.

"I don't know what I am Simone. I have a lot of thinking to do. But I did agree to see Aidan on Thursday and I'm looking forward to it."

I need to get through today before I even think about Zach again. I'm sure I have tons of messages. He said he was coming back today. *Shit, I forgot about that.* I should have gone with Aidan.

"Um, Gaby. Isn't that Aidan?"

What? He's here?

I look around, and see him by the door. We make eye contact and smile at each other. I start twirling my hair at the same time he's smoothing his down. I look away.

"Yes, that's him."

He looks so hot. He has changed and had a shower.

"Wow, he sure has it bad for you. Did you know he was coming here?" Sam asks.

"No. He dropped me off and I said I'll see him Thursday."

I'm shocked.

What is he doing here? I make eye contact again. He smiles, does a little wave, and walks out the door.

Should I run after him?

I start to get up, but the waitress interrupts me.

"Madam, the gentleman has paid for the table."

What?

"Oh, thank you," I say as the waitress smiles.

"Anything else I can get for you?" she asks.

We all shake our heads and she walks away.

"I can't believe he paid for all of us."

Simone is shocked.

See how a gentleman acts Simone. Not the losers that you see once and it's over.

I think she may be jealous.

"Wow, Gaby. He really does have it bad."

Kelly smiles. I'm blushing.

"Whatever, let's go. Gaby, you can come with me."

And just like that Simone summons all of us. I can see her jealousy is taking over. And I love it.

Sam and Kelly follow behind Simone's Jeep to the anniversary party. I have to turn my phone on to text Aidan and thank him. While I wait for it to power on, I listen to Simone go on and on about how her parents have been married for thirty years and this surprise party wouldn't have happened without her. *Well of course not Simone, you do it all.* I try to give her some encouragement. I don't want her crabby. My phone is ready. I have three voice mails and twelve texts. I quickly check who they are from and each and every one is from Zach. I don't open them. I quickly text Aidan.

TY for brunch

I receive a response immediately.

U R Welcome

I quickly text back.

I'm excited for Thurs

Without missing a beat, Aidan replies.

Me 2

I don't text back. I don't know what else to say. I'm not going to tell him how hot he looked. His hair was still wet and he had fresh clothes on. And he drove all the way back for me. To pay for my friends and I. This is still all so surreal. I make a bad decision and open the texts from Zach.

Gaby, plz take me back

Please call me

Please text me back

I'm coming over

Don't ignore me

It's over for real now

Don't call me ever again

I love you

I'm sorry

Please call me

I'm coming over. Be home

I'm at your house. Where r u?

As I read, my feelings go from an extreme high to an all-time low, the same way his texts did. He wants me one minute and hates me the next. Then he wants me again. I feel the same towards him. I can't decide. I'm being pulled in so many directions just from him, and in another direction with Aidan, and even another with my friends. I don't know what to do.

Now he's at my house, waiting for me? Will he still be there when I finally get home? Oh I hope so. No I don't. Yes I do. I want to see him. I can't do this anymore, and my emotions start to spiral out of control. I'm shifting back and forth in my seat. I'm rubbing my hands in my hair, down my face, squeezing my cheeks tight. I can't hold the tears back any longer and I break.

"Holy Shit, Gaby. What the hell?"

Simone is yelling. That's all I need right now.

"Please call Lucca and have him meet us at your parents," I plead.

"Why?"

She doesn't understand. She doesn't know about me spiraling out of control and how to bring me back down from my attacks.

"I need him Simone. Just do it."

I'm sobbing, scolding, begging.

"Fine," she snaps back.

She calls Lucca and gives him the address to her parents. He must be asking a lot of questions. She keeps saying, "I don't know" and sounds more annoyed each time.

"Gaby, I don't know what's going on with you, or why you won't tell me, but don't ruin this day," she says with a glare. "Lucca will be here in a minute. I'll see you inside."

She slams the door and struts into the house. Sam and Kelly run over and yank my door open.

"What happened?"

Kelly is holding my hand. She doesn't understand either. I try to stay calm in front of her and Sam.

"I just need to talk to Lucca. I'm all over the place. I should have never turned on my phone."

"Why not?" Sam asks.

"There were so many..." I pause, "many messages from Zach. I don't know what to do."

Lucca arrives and pushes Sam and Kelly back. He shuts my door and pulls them away to talk with him. I can't hear what he's saying, but I can see him doing all the talking. He looks firm and is holding up a stern finger. They nod, take a quick peek at me and go inside.

He opens my door and kneels on the curb next to me. We don't speak. He gives me a long tight hug. He leans back and I hand him my phone. He shakes his head as he scrolls through the texts. He knows exactly what I'm going through. He knows me so well.

"Was Zach at the house when you left?" I ask trying to stay calm.

"I wasn't at home when Simone called."

"Oh. Thank you so much for coming."

What would I ever do without Lucca? He hugs me and strokes my hair, just like he always does when I need him. He looks in my purse and pulls out what little makeup I have. He starts to fix up my face and talks me through this mess. I explain my feeling of being pulled in so many directions and I don't know which one to follow. He nods in understanding.

"Just go in there and put your pretty smile on for an hour or two. You can do this. If you don't, Simone will kill you."

He smiles and that makes me laugh.

"We will talk later when you get home. Do you need a ride?"

He is so helpful.

"Yes. I'll call you when I'm ready."

"Oh, no you won't. Don't you dare turn that phone back on. I will pick you up in exactly two hours from now."

He puts his hand out. I take it and stand up. He walks me to the door and kisses my cheek.

"Thank you, Lucca. For dropping everything. For me," I whisper.

"Get in there. I'll be back in two hours." He gives my hand a final squeeze and I go in.

I put on my fake smile for two hours of agony. I don't want to be here. I eat and mingle with the few people that I know. All the girls ask how I'm doing. I keep my smile going and tell them I am fine. Simone's parents look so happy. Even after thirty years together, they hold hands and smile and wink at each other. That is true love. *Has none of this rubbed off on Simone?* That thought makes me giggle.

There are about one hundred people here. Simone pulled this off in two weeks' time. That's pretty impressive. Simone is running around making sure everyone has a drink in their hand at all times. I see Sam and Kelly outside talking with a couple of guys. They look way too old for them. I walk towards the kitchen and check the time. Lucca should be here in a few minutes. I don't see any of the girls, so I decide to sneak out the front door. They probably won't even notice I'm gone.

When I get outside, Lucca is just pulling up. I skip to the Pathfinder and tell him to step on it. I don't want anyone to see me leaving.

"Thank you for coming back. I had to get out of there. My cheeks hurt from this fucking fake smile."

We both laugh out loud. He always puts me in a good mood.

"I'm taking you for happy hour. I don't think we should go home yet."

"I don't want to go home either."

I don't want to go and sit there. I need to get my mind off things. Just go to sleep and get back to work tomorrow. Back to normal.

"Let's cruise for a while. Then we'll go to The Red Chair."

Lucca loves The Red Chair. He always tells me about the hot men he sees there.

We cruise, windows down, blasting the new Foo Fighters CD. We sing every song, word for word in unison. We couldn't speak if we wanted to. The music is too loud. This is so much fun. This music makes me relax, takes my cares away, as I'm cruising with my best friend. We are oblivious to everyone and everything around us. This is exactly what I needed. We pull into The Red Chair just as our favorite song finishes.

"Whew, that was fun." My voice is scratchy from the screaming. I love it!

"We should do that more often."

Lucca gets out of the car.

As we enter, he scans the place. I assume he's looking for hotties or for someone he knows maybe? He pulls me to a little booth in the back corner by the kitchen. From back here, we can see everyone. I wonder if he was going to meet someone here, or if it's just him and me time. I'm in a better mood now, so it really doesn't matter. He orders us two pineapple martinis and an appetizer sampler. We talk about work and my client coming in, the concerts coming up that we want to see, and the dull anniversary party. He keeps the drinks coming. Every time I have a sip or two left, I see him give the waitress a nod, and by the time I'm done, I have a full one waiting for me.

He does see a couple guys he knows and they come and join us. He introduces me to them, and we are in a full fashion discussion. This is awesome. We talk our favorite shoes and handbags. They tell me about their jobs, which are all fashion-related. The night flies by. I dance with each of them. We are up. We are down. We are doing shots. We are dancing in a line. I'm sure all eyes are on us and our stupid antics. *This is so much fun.*

"Whoa, we better sit down for a while."

Lucca pulls me back to the booth.

"What? Why?"

I'm slurring my words.

"Come on, let's get home. You look beat and we have work in the morning."

Lucca says goodnight to his friends and practically carries me out to the car. He wakes me when we get home. I don't remember the drive back. I'm exhausted. He pulls me out of my seat, puts his arms around me and drags me in the house. While he's unlocking the door, I turn to make sure Zach's car isn't waiting outside. It's not. Lucca helps me change and tucks me in bed.

"Sweet dreams, Gaby," he whispers and shuts my door.

Chapter 5

My alarm wakes me at six the next morning. It's Monday. Back to reality. Back to my boring life. Back to work and to the same old routine. I slowly get out of bed and gather my clothes for the day. *I don't want to get up.* I have such a headache this morning.

I check the living room, and Lucca is already gone for the day. I find some ibuprofen and slam four of them. The hot shower feels nice on my head. It's throbbing. I try to rub it under the water to take some of the pressure off, but it doesn't help. I let the water stream over my face. I mentally go through a checklist of what I have to do at work today and what I have to get done this week. I step out and get dressed. I need some new clothes. I look like shit. Makeup won't help me today. You can tell I'm hung over. My eyes are puffy and red.

"Same old me again today."

My drive is a quick ten minutes. I need to work with my door shut today and keep to myself. I see an email from Zach once I boot up my computer. Can't he just leave me alone? I don't want to read it.

I go through all of the other emails from the weekend. We have a big conference coming up next week, so there is a lot to do to get ready. This is perfect timing to keep me focused on work. There is so much to do and arrange for the clients flying in. As I search for the schedule of events, there is a knock at my door.

"Come in."

Who is it so early?

"Good morning Ms. Woods. A delivery has arrived for you."

"Thank you, Lexi. Please leave it on my desk."

Lexi is my assistant.

"Yes ma'am."

She leaves it and shuts my door.

I turn and am almost knocked off my chair. *How did that even fit on my desk*? It's a huge box all wrapped in red tissue paper. I am nervous to open it. *What could it be? Who could it be from*? I stand and notice a small envelope on top that says "Gabriella", and I immediately know who sent them. I pull out the card.

> Happy Monday, Gabriella.
> Four dozen roses for the
> four long days I have to wait
> until I can see you again.
> xo Aidan xo

My knees are weak and I fall to my chair. *Aidan is for real. He sent me flowers.* I sit back and hug myself stomping my feet on the ground like an excited little kid. *Should I call and thank him? Should I send him a quick text?* I don't want to seem too eager and push him away. A ping from my computer interrupts my glee. It's a new email from Zach. *What does he want? Should I read it now?* I take one big breath and sit up to read it. It says:

> Gaby. I have made a huge mistake. I am sorry.

Please don't throw away our four years together over one night of my stupidity.

I've been so stupid. I want to do all those things we said we'd do. I want to take care

of you. I want to comfort you. I want to be there for you. I promise I will do better.

I want to fulfill all of my promises. Please give me the chance. Please take me back.

I love you more than anything Gaby. Marry me!

I am stunned. He asked me to marry him. *Yes!* No, wait. *Do I still want that?* He does comfort me when I'm spiraling. I don't know if Aidan will be able to handle me when I'm like that. I've been waiting for Zach to ask me to marry him and he wouldn't budge. He is trying so hard. *Oh Zach, I miss you too.* I re-read the email several times. Zach wants me back. It's all sinking in. I close my eyes tightly. Breathe in and out. Calm down.

I slowly open my eyes and see the huge bouquet of flowers on the corner of my desk from Aidan. I look at his card and I melt. I need to call Lucca. My emotions are all over the place. Lucca doesn't answer so I leave him a voice mail. He always answers when I call. *What's going on today?* Everything is out of whack.

I type back to Zach.

Zach, thank you for all you've said. I will think about this.

Within seconds, I have a reply.

Gaby. I love you. Meet me for dinner at seven o'clock on Friday night at our place.

I reply.

OK

There is no reply after that. He must be satisfied with my answer. Lucca finally calls back and I explain the situation, about my emotions, me being pulled, not knowing the path again. Bottom line is that I have to make a decision and go with it. Make the decision and don't look back. I have to choose, Zach or Aidan.

The rest of the day goes by so fast. The conference will take up most of my days and evenings in preparation this week. This is our biggest conference of the year, and I have a huge part in it.

Monday comes and goes. Tuesday, the same routine, I get to work and shortly after I settle in and have my coffee, Lexi knocks on the door. Another delivery. Same packaging. The card says:

> Happy Tuesday, Gabriella.
> Three dozen roses for the
> three long days I have to wait
> until I can see you again.
> xo Aidan xo

Same thing Wednesday. The knock on the door. Lexi arrives at the exact same time. The card says:

> Happy Wednesday, Gabriella.
> Two dozen roses for the
> two long days I have to wait
> until I can see you again.
> xo Aidan xo

Thursday has arrived. Tonight's the night and I'm nervous. I'm so overwhelmed by all the flowers. Aidan is trying so hard. I haven't heard from Zach since the Monday email exchange. I can't decide what to do. Lucca tells me to see how the dinner with Aidan tonight goes and he and I will talk when I get home. Aidan is picking me up at work today so I have to wear my date clothes. I put on my favorite navy dress and pumps.

"Same old me again today."

Lucca is still here.

"Lucca what's wrong?"

He's never here this late.

"I'm not feeling well today. I'm going to stay home."

"Why aren't you in bed then?" I scold. "Do you want me to come home after work and take care of you?"

He always takes care of me. I should return the favor. I do need one night to myself to think about everything before tomorrow night. Zach will expect an answer at dinner.

"Don't be silly, Gaby. Go on your date and we will talk when you get home."

"Fine. But I will call you mid-day."

There is already a delivery on my desk when I get to work. I can't even see my computer. It's hidden underneath all of the flowers from the week. This time the wrapping is different. It's all white silk with a red ribbon. I open the card:

> Happy Thursday, Gabriella.
> One dozen roses for the
> one that I'm falling for.
> See you tonight.
> xo Aidan xo

Holy shit. He's falling for me? This is too much. *Am I falling for him too?* We've only had one night together. But what an incredible night it was. He saved me.

The afternoon is full of meetings. I don't realize it's already five-thirty until I hear my phone vibrate with a text from Aidan. He is waiting outside for me. I hurry to finish and shut down my computer for the night.

In the elevator I push the "G" button. I walk backwards until my back touches the wall and I close my eyes the entire ride down. No one gets on the elevator. I'm riding alone. I am so nervous. I need the wall to hold me up. My knees are weak and my stomach has those damn butterflies flying around again.

The elevator pings and the doors open. I push through the revolving doors and see his BMW waiting for me. He is at the passenger door leaning against the car with his arms crossed. He looks incredible, and he's waiting for me. *Unbelievable.* He has on a dark navy suit, which looks so good against his tanned skin. He's rubbing his hair. I realize I'm twirling mine. *Is he nervous too?* Stop over thinking this. We make eye contact and a huge grin takes over his face. He steps back and opens the passenger door.

"Hi," I smile.

"Hi yourself."

He shuts the door and walks around the back of the car.

"You look stunning, Gabriella. I am so happy to see you."

"I am happy to see you again too Aidan," I say softly.

I feel shy all of a sudden.

"How has your week been?"

My week?

"It's been very busy. Thank you for the flowers. They smell heavenly in my office. I think Lexi wants to meet my secret admirer."

"Lexi?"

"She's my assistant. She brought them to me every day."

"You have an assistant? Very impressive, Gabriella."

He's thinking about something. *What's going through his head?*

"Yes, she's worked for me for about six months."

Enough work talk already.

"I do hope you're hungry."

Ok good, not a work question.

"Yes, I am. Where are we going tonight?"

"We are going to try that new fondue place down on the beach."

"Perfect, I'm starving."

I didn't eat today. Shit, I forgot to call Lucca over lunch. I send him a quick text.

On my way to dinner, sorry, r u feeling better?

He replies almost immediately after I push send.

Yes, have fun

"Is everything all right? You seem distracted."

Can he tell I'm nervous? I can't tell him how overwhelmed I've been this week or about the email from Zach, well, proposal actually.

"Yes, sorry. I had to text Lucca quick."

"I really like Lucca. He looks after you. He helps you right?"

Yes he does, but what does Aidan mean?

"Yes, he's my best friend."

I don't go any further. Yes he helps me. I'm sure Aidan would run if he knew all of my issues that Lucca is privy to.

He drives his beautiful car right down on the beach and parks at Simply Fondue. It looks very classy from the outside. He opens my door and puts his hand out. I wonder what we will talk about over dinner. *Should I tell him about the email from Zach? Should I tell him he asked me to marry him?*

I can't. Aidan looks so confident and is so complimentary. He said he's falling for me. I have to choose by tomorrow evening, and I don't know if I can do it. I take a few deep breaths as we step through the door. Aidan has arranged for another private table. It's just the two of us at a small table that has a drape around us for privacy. He orders the same wine we had last week, our meal, and dessert again all at the same time. I sense he just wants the waitress to go away so we can be alone.

As soon as she is gone and the drape closes, he puts his arms out on the table with his palms up. I smile shyly and put my hands in his. He looks deep into my eyes. For a moment I think I see that hurt, but I shake it off.

"Gabriella, you are so beautiful. I have been thinking about you all week. Again, I've been counting the moments to see you."

"I..." I start to speak, but he puts his finger up.

"Let me finish, Gabriella. I need to get this out."

He takes a deep breath and starts again.

"I cannot get you out of my head. I've tried even for a few minutes, and I just can't do it. I think about you constantly. You have a trance over me. I can barely work. I feel a pull to you. As soon as I see you, I feel like a magnet is pulling me towards your body. I look at you, and I hold my breath. This probably is too soon and too sudden. I know what happened to you last Friday. I know this must be hard for you. I know this is confusing. But I also know that I'm falling for you. I hope you feel the same."

He stops speaking. He squeezes my hands and I have to remind myself to blink. I don't know what to say. I can't tell him about my dinner plans tomorrow night. I can't tell him I have the biggest decision of my life to make tonight. I can't tell him that a man I've only known a week up against a man I've been with for over four years doesn't really stack up. *Or does he?* He's right. I am confused. I need to get out of here. I can't do this tonight.

"Aidan, I...." I pause. "I'm so sorry. I can't do this right now."

I put my head down. "Please take me home."

I hear him take a quick breath in. This isn't what he expected me to say. He's angry. He lets go of my hands, stands up, throws his napkin to the table, opens the drape, and storms away. I immediately follow him. He is walking so fast, about six or seven steps ahead of me. As we pass through the crowded bar, he stops and turns around. I stop in my tracks. He looks into my eyes and stares. *Fuck. What is he thinking?* He walks directly towards me not taking his eyes off of mine. My heart is pounding out of my chest. *What is he going to do?* It's slow motion. He looks so serious and determined. He bends down and kisses me deeply literally lifting me off the ground. He kisses me long and hard, right in the middle of the bar. I can't catch my breath. He leans back, not letting go.

He whispers to me as he looks into my eyes.

"I want you to be mine. I have never wanted anything this bad. You make me feel alive. I know you feel it."

He is breathless too. "Think about this Gabriella."

He sets me down. "Meet me here tomorrow night at seven o'clock so we can have our date. If you show up, I'll know you've chosen to be mine."

He lets go and walks away. I am stunned, speechless, dumbfounded. I feel like jelly and might melt to the floor. My body is shaking. I look around and there is an older couple looking at me. I wonder if they could hear what he said. They smile as I start to walk outside. Aidan is waiting for me by the passenger door. He opens it as I walk towards him. I can't look at him.

As he starts the car, he reaches for my hand and I let him hold it. I'm still shaking. We don't speak at all. He parks in front of my house. He gives my hand a final squeeze and lets go.

I look at him and say, "I'm sorry Aidan."

He shakes his head and whispers, "Goodnight Gabriella."

He kisses my cheek. I can hear him inhale my scent as though it may be the last time and wants to remember it forever. I feel that zing again. *Fuck!*

Lucca is home resting. His head spins to the door.

"What are you doing home so early?"

He looks concerned.

I start to cry and fall to the floor by the door. He races over and picks me up. He pulls me to the couch and hugs me stroking my hair.

"Gaby, tell me what happened. Why are you home?"

I haven't told him yet about my email from Zach and the proposal, or all the flowers and cards from Aidan. I haven't had a chance to tell him anything.

"Lucca, I have so much to tell you."

I control my sobs and start from the beginning. I tell him how Aidan paid for brunch last Sunday, the daily flowers, what the cards said each day, and that the Thursday card made me so happy. I read the email from Zach. He shakes his head when I read the last line about marriage. I say what happened at dinner tonight and that Aidan made me melt in the bar when he kissed me. I could barely walk. I feel the pull too.

"Lucca, I'm scared. Zach knows me and how to handle me, like you do. I'm scared Aidan won't be able to."

"Aidan is falling for you. He told you. He asked to take care of you. You said he saved you. He asked you to be his. This sounds like love, Gaby."

Well I see whose side he's on.

"But will he leave me? Will I be too much to handle? Will he love me then?"

Lucca looks frustrated.

"True love always wins. Remember what your dad told you about Zach? He told you Zach was like a cancer, and you need to get rid of it before it gets worse."

My dad hates Zach. Zach has always been so selfish and put himself first.

"Oh, Lucca. I just can't take that chance. I can't let someone else inside."

He hugs me tight and we rock back and forth as I calm.

"Are you ready to be tucked in?"

I nod and he stands and leads me to bed.

"Get some sleep, Gaby. Remember, true love always wins. I love you."

He tucks me in.

"Lucca, wait."

I pull him to sit next to me.

"Did I tell you that they both asked me to dinner tomorrow night at seven? They are both expecting me at the same time tomorrow. I can't be two places at once."

I'm getting worked up again.

"Wherever I show up. Whoever I show up for is who I choose."

"Catch your breath, Gaby. Think about what I said."

He closes the door.

I am alone with my thoughts and a decision I need to make on my own. I love Zach. He knows me. He handles me. He has been my comfort zone forever. He tries his best, even though I need more. I love him. I need him back.

Aidan asked me to be his. He wants to take care of me. I'm so scared. He makes me feel beautiful. I was never insecure until I met Zach, but I can't take this risk right now in my life. I have my work to focus on. I can't let someone new in. Maybe I should get rid of Zach and focus on myself. Maybe I choose no one. Maybe I won't go to either dinner tomorrow night. I do feel the pull towards Aidan. I love that feeling he gives me. I want to feel it again. He surprises me and makes me smile.

AAaaaahhhhhhhhhhhhhhhhh! I'm screaming inside. Too many 'maybes'. I don't want any more decisions to make. I can't risk this. Zach asked me to marry him. *Can I marry him?* Yes, I could. I could be comfortable with him. *Comfort or risk new love?* I'm torn. I can't keep my eyes open another second. I fall asleep again on a tear-soaked pillow.

I wake with a jolt. My morning alarm is not welcome at all. I want to get through the day and fast forward to tonight. I cry in the hot shower hoping I'm making the right decision. Both men waiting for me at the same time. *Should I let the other one know I'm not coming?*

They will wonder where I am. I clear my thoughts and get ready. It would be nice to see Zach. I haven't seen him since last weekend. I'm surprised he hasn't emailed me again. He must be giving me the space I need. He's learning and doing what I ask. His stupidity last Friday made him realize what he's lost. I miss him too. Hair, makeup, clothes, my usual routine before work.

"Same old me again today."

When I get to the office and open my door, I see the flowers from Aidan. There aren't any new ones waiting. *Good.* No emails waiting. *Good.*

Lexi brings me a much-needed extra-large coffee. She is in and out of my office all morning. We are making notes and schedule changes for Monday. She makes suggestions for the clients coming in. Next week is going to be absolutely crazy. She steps out and I finally have a minute on my own to breathe.

I lean back in my chair and take some deep breaths. *I can do this.* When she returns, I can't see her face. I just see her skinny chicken legs sticking out beneath a huge bouquet of flowers. She sets them on the side table. There is no room left on my desk. *Who are they from?*

There isn't a card on top. I open the wrapping. This is the most beautiful bouquet yet this week, but they're not roses. They are the biggest pink and white dendros that I've ever seen. These are my favorite flower and are so hard to find. I'm so excited, I clap my hands. Lexi gives me a quick smile and leaves. They must be from Zach. *Who else would know they are my favorite?* I search for a card. I can barely see it, but there is a small silver balloon on a spike in the middle of the bouquet. It looks like a mirror with nothing is on it. I turn it around, and written in black marker, it says MARRY ME. I feel a lump in my throat. They are from Zach. *Yes, Zach. Yes, Zach. Yes!*

I work as late as I can. I have to make a quick stop at home to change my shoes before going to dinner. I'm blasting my music and singing along in the car. I can't think anymore. I've made my decision and I need to keep my head clear for now. Lucca is in the kitchen. I run past him to change and he's still there when I return.

"So?" he asks with his hands out.

"So what?"

What does he want?

"Where are you going for dinner tonight?"

I should have known that's what he was going to say.

"I'll tell you after."

I squint my eyes. I don't want to tell him. I don't want any questions or second guessing. I've made up my mind.

"Pleeeeeaaassseeeee."

He gives me the puppy eyes.

"No."

"I know where you're going anyway."

No he doesn't.

"I'll text you later, Lucca."

"Fine. You're so stubborn."

He shakes a finger at me.

I start the car and pull to the corner. Turning right will lead to Zach. Turning left will lead to Aidan. I close my eyes, take a deep breath, swallow, and make my turn. I convince myself this is the best decision. This decision is final. There's no turning back after I go in the restaurant. *This is it.*

My music is still playing, but my mind is racing. I turn it down because it's not helping. I park and turn off the engine. It is exactly seven o'clock. Slowly my heart starts pounding harder and harder and my breath quickens. I'm sweating. I'm swearing. I can't hear or think with this pounding in my head. I grab the door handle to get out, but my hand slips off. They are wet with sweat. I hold the handle as tight as I can. I sit back in my seat trying to catch my breath, but I can't. I shake my head back and forth and fist my hair. *I can't do this.* My lump in my throat is back. I pick up my phone to call, but I throw it down. I grab my head and let out a big long scream.

"Aaaaaahhhhhhhhhhhhhhhhhhhhhhhh!"

I sit back and run my fingers through my hair. I grab the handle again, holding it for minutes while my breath comes back to normal. *I can do this.* Finally I get the door open and step out. I walk with as much grace as I can muster to the door of the fancy restaurant. I see him sitting at the table, and his back is to me. My lump grows bigger as I realize that time has stopped. My soul is screaming. *This is the man for you. This is him. I can do this.* I slowly walk towards the table. He looks up and meets my eyes.

I smile and say, "Yes!"

Chapter 6

Aidan jumps out of his seat so fast that his chair falls back to the ground. He grabs me behind my waist, pulls me towards him and lifts me off the ground. Our kiss is so profound. I don't want him to set me down.

He leans back.

"You're really here?"

"Yes, I'm really here."

"You are mine."

He twirls me around. I hug him so tightly. Seeing his happiness engulfs me. I feel that pull towards him.

"I belong with you tonight," I whisper in his ear.

"Hell yes you do!"

He sets me down and gestures for me to sit.

"I'm so..."

He is breathing fast.

"I was so worried you wouldn't come. This has been a day from hell. After last night..."

I stop him.

"I know. You make me feel alive too. You are something I've been afraid to find," I pause to gather my thoughts, "I'm scared. I feel the pull you talked about. I can't break it."

His smile grows. He grabs my hand and pulls me to his lap. Both of his hands are in my hair as he pulls me to his lips. He feels so good. My hands are clasped behind his neck. We kiss long and deep. I'm turned on like never before. I really just want him to take me home to his bed. I want him to rub his hands all over me, between my legs, but they stay in my hair. He sets me back.

"Gabriella, I can't keep my eyes off of you. This is unbelievable."

Just when I didn't think his smile could get any bigger, it does.

"What I'd really like is to get you home. I want you in my bed."

I blush. That's what I want too. He is reading my mind.

"Me too."

His eyes widen.

"Let's go."

He lifts me from my seat and we head for the door.

"Leave your car. We will come back for it."

He's pulling me to his car, almost running.

"OK!"

He opens my door and runs to his side. He locks the doors and lunges at me. We are breathless, panting, we can't kiss fast enough. His tongue is all over the place in my mouth. My body shivers at his touch. He stops.

"You are so beautiful. I could kiss you forever."

His middle finger runs slowly up and down my thigh. I lean back, so my behind goes forward on the seat. I want him to know he's welcome to touch me anywhere he wants. I smile. I don't want to talk.

"Everything you do is beautiful, Gabriella."

He traces the line of my skirt against my skin. He lingers his way up my leg while kissing me slowly. He stops at my panties and rubs between my opening and my clitoris. He's teasing me again. I think he wants me to ask him to touch me. *Does he like that I ask him*? I said yes I would be his, so he can do whatever pleases him. His light touches make my knees shake each time he passes my clitoris.

"Touch me."

I lean forward again.

"Not here, Gabriella."

He shakes his head.

"Please touch me. I need you to touch my skin."

I do need it. It's a need only he can fulfill. The way I feel when we give in to the pull is overpowering. I can't explain it. He increases pressure a little, but still doesn't touch my skin. He leans back, all the way to his seat so we aren't in contact anymore. I immediately lean towards him. A magnet is pulling me towards his body, just like he told me. I move my tongue all around the outside of his ear as he starts the car.

I lower my voice to a whisper.

"Just so you know, deep down I knew my decision the second you kissed me in the bar last night," I continue swirling my tongue, "that was really hot."

I see a smile on his face. I rub my hands over his chest, over his shoulders, and down his arms feeling every single muscle along the way. He is so gorgeous, and I'm his now. I guess that makes him mine. I move my tongue to his neck and he squirms.

"I can't drive like this. You're making me crazy."

"Good," I say between each kiss.

"If you don't stop, I will have to pull over."

I lean back and think about my next move.

"You wouldn't touch me. My skin I mean. I can touch you like this, can't I?"

I cup his erection with my hand and it feels remarkable. I want to unzip his pants and take him in my mouth. I push on him and rub my palm up and down slowly. I shudder as I imagine his length.

I notice the houses are getting larger and larger, and closer to the ocean. *Does he have a beach house? No way.* These houses are huge. He slows near the corner and pulls up to massive entry gates. He rolls down his window and puts his thumb on some weird little box, and the gates open. *OH. MY. GOD.*

I stop touching him. He turns to me and smiles out of the side of his mouth. This place is indescribable. There's a long trail with luscious trees of all different types, even fruit trees. I can see different fruits growing on each of them. There are flower and vegetable gardens and herbs on both sides. There's a beautiful brick road leading up to the house that makes a circle to lead back out to the gates. It's a stunning, peaceful two story beach house. It's now dusk, and the outside lights surrounding the house illuminate the porch that wraps around it. It's simply glowing. There must be fifty light sconces out here. White stone paves the way to the three car garage. The house appears of light wood and gives it a feel of a cabin. There is another small garden to the side of the garage. The plants are thriving, tall as can be and green as the grass. There is a breath taking pond in the foreground. It's surrounded by boulders of all sizes, small trees, white flowers, and wood chips. The pond is a place of peace and serenity. *He must come out here to think.* The trees surrounding the house are things of wonders, standing taller than the house and blossoming with leaves and branches. I am in awe. He parks right in front and gets out to open my door.

"This is your house?"

My jaw is scraping the brick road.

"Yes."

He giggles a little bit. I pick up my jaw.

"Come in."

He pulls at my hand, but I can barely move.

As we approach the door, it opens. A man, probably in his fifties greets us. He looks very formal wearing a dark grey suit and tie.

"Good evening sir, ma'am."

"Good evening, Alan. This is Gabriella."

"Good evening."

I smile and twirl my hair.

"Have Marie prepare us some dinner. We will dine on the South Lawn in one hour."

Aidan, so direct. *Am I dreaming? Who is Marie?*

"Yes, sir."

In an instant, Alan is gone. We are still outside.

"Close your eyes," Aidan smiles wickedly.

"Um, why?"

What is he thinking?

"Just do it."

So demanding.

I close my eyes and suddenly I'm in his arms. He's carrying me like he did when he brought me to my bed. The over the threshold kind of carrying.

"Don't open your eyes."

He stays firm.

"I won't."

I rest my head on his shoulders and look down to resist my urge to open my eyes. I want to look around this place. *Why doesn't he want me to?* He carries me up what seems like millions of stairs. He fiddles with the doorknob with his hand that's under my legs. The door opens and I feel him kick it closed with his foot. *Why is his foot closing the door so sexy?* He lowers me to the bed.

"You can open your eyes now."

I try to look around, but he is immediately kissing me. His lips are the only thing touching me.

"You have made me so happy. And yes, you do belong with me tonight. And always." *Always?*

He steps back and stands at the end of the bed. He takes his jacket off, and then his shirt. He is watching me and I'm looking in his eyes the whole time. He unbuttons his pants, lowers them to the ground, and steps out of them. His hard body is calling my name. I put my hands out hoping he will come lay next to me, but he shakes his head. He walks to the side of the bed and slips off his boxer briefs that hug him in all the right places. I could look at him all day. I need that feeling again of his body taking over mine. I want to look around his bedroom, but I can't tear my eyes away. Now, fully naked, he sits down next to me.

"There are so many things I want to do to you Gabriella."

He takes my shoes off and I hear them hit the floor.

"I want you. In my bed. Every night."

Every night?

He taps the side of my hip and I lift off the bed. He pulls down my skirt and panties and drops them to the floor. His finger starts at my ankle and eases up one of my legs, so lightly, too lightly, over my naval, and down the other leg. He trails back up and stops between my legs. I part them slightly. His finger glides in my heat. He is touching my skin, finally. He doesn't go inside. He must know this is pure torture for me. At the same time he leans down to kiss me, the tip of his finger goes in. I moan and he kisses harder, and he pushes his finger as deep as it can go. I moan again. This feels so good. He spreads the moisture and immediately goes back in again. I lift my hips while he pushes in. He unbuttons my blouse, one button at a time, kissing my breasts between each one. He pulls me into a sitting position and slides it down my arms. He pushes my hair behind my shoulders exposing my neck. He flicks his tongue over my neck and ears and unhooks my bra. Chills run down my spine. All my clothes are on the floor. I am fully naked.

"Let's have some wine."

His voice is so seductive. It's making me wetter.

"Yes."

I look around and see a champagne bucket on a stand next to the bed. I hadn't seen that before. There is a bottle of white wine in ice, and two glasses on the table next to it. *Who put that there?*

He stands and walks to the table. I'm watching his body move around the bed, erection pointing at the ceiling. He moves with such confidence, so comfortable in his own skin. I am lying back on my elbows with my knees bent. *Is this really happening?* He watches me as he pours two glasses. I lick my lips. I need him inside me. He sits and hands me my glass.

"You feel like home, Gabriella."

I take a deep breath. He is so sweet and I feel the same way. It does feel like coming home with him, like everything is falling into place. He clinks my glass. We each take a long sip and he sets both glasses back on the table. He spreads my legs and trails kisses from my knees towards my opening. Gently sucking my clitoris, he puts one finger in, and then eases in a second. I lie back on the pillow and cry out. He backs off the sucking, but keeps both fingers inside. His other hand reaches for his wine. He takes another long sip and with a still cold tongue, he sucks again. The cold makes me moan louder than before as tremors run through me.

"Do you like that baby?"

"Yes."

I can barely get the words out. I'm going higher and higher and I need him inside me now.

"Tell me what you want."

He's so quiet.

"Please..." I cry out as he continues to suck. "Please come up here."

I put my hands down and try to pull his head up to mine.

He kisses my body the entire way and stops to suck each nipple. He withdraws his fingers and puts his hands on the side of my waist. My legs are wide open waiting for him. He kisses me and in one swift move, he is inside me.

"Aaahhhh!" I scream in surprise.

The peace ripples through me again. He pulls out. He bites my neck and moves down to my breasts. I try to pull him up to my mouth. He kisses me and stabs me again.

"Aaahhhh," I cry out and he slides back.

He tries to move down, but I won't let him go. He sucks on my lower lip, but still won't push back in. He leans back and looks into my eyes.

"Are you ready? I don't know if I can hold back any longer," he says quietly into my ear.

Yes, I'm ready. I'm freaking out here. I nod, but instead he starts all over again, kisses at my knees and over my thighs. I dig my head back and close my eyes, trying to control myself. My legs begin to twitch when he palms my clitoris. I'm going to come. He hops off the bed and refills our glasses. *No, wait!* I'm panting, trembling, longing for his body. He smiles down at me and I just stare at him. His body is driving me wild. He knows exactly what he's doing. He likes teasing me.

He traces his finger from my ankle up my leg, over my naval, and down my other leg. He turns around and comes back up and stops at my opening, spreading the wetness just like before. He inserts a finger and takes a sip of the freshly poured cold glass of wine. He takes a small ice cube and puts it in his mouth. It stays on the end of his tongue and melts between us as he sucks my clitoris.

"Please Aidan," I moan and scream and lift my hips.

He rests his forehead on my stomach for a second. When he lifts his head he is smiling. He loves this. I pull his lips to mine. He pushes himself inside me with a quick hard thrust. When he pulls out, I grab his hips and pull him back inside.

This time he doesn't come out, he thrusts in and out in a perfect rhythm. He thrusts faster, and I meet him for each one. Faster and even faster. I close my eyes and want to scream. He slows and kisses me. I can feel every inch of him as he moves. My heart is beating out of my chest. He looks at me with his hooded eyes. I feel his smooth behind and pull him as he comes down. I love feeling the muscles while he moves. I am going to explode.

"Are you ready baby?"

"Come on," I scream as he starts to thrust faster.

He pounds so hard and strong. I come around him on his second hit. We groan back and forth as he comes with me.

"Oh baby."

He falls to my side and holds me close.

"That was amazing."

He's propped on one elbow smiling down at me.

"You consume me. I can't think about anything else."

He's taking my words again.

"I feel the same way. I'm glad I'm here."

I made the right decision. Aidan is the one for me. I will not turn back. This feels so right.

"You are so beautiful, breathtakingly beautiful, Gabriella."

He kisses my nose. I take a deep breath and look around the room.

"I do have one question."

He looks nervous.

"Why did I have to close my eyes while you carried me up here?"

He lets out a laugh or a sigh of relief, I can't tell.

"I wanted to get you to my bed as soon as possible. I didn't want anything to distract you. I saw your face when we pulled up to the door."

"Why didn't you tell me about your house? It's huge, and you have staff."

I stop. I don't know what else to say. I haven't had a moment to let this all sink in.

"Yes. I do. They take good care of me."

A man that needs to be taken care of. No surprise. I snicker to myself.

"I just don't understand. You own a consulting company. Right? But this..." I wave my hand around the room, "this is too much."

I sit up and take in the room.

His bedroom is very simple and modern. The oversized bed is lifted high off the floor by a wooden frame that connects to shelving behind it. The frame has large, abstract art pieces underneath. It's very different and creative. The shelves hold small decorative art pieces, a few books, two sculptures, and two small pictures. There is a wall of windows from floor to ceiling with a door leading to a balcony with white plush chairs and a table. I can see the ocean beyond the balcony. It's the bluest water I've ever seen. I close my eyes and imagine the mornings waking up here. The light must fill up the room. It is very peaceful and calming. I lie back down and shake my head.

"We can talk about the house and work later." He bends down to kiss me. "You have made me so happy. You said yes. That's what you said at the restaurant." He kisses my cheeks, moving towards my ear. He whispers, "You've agreed to be mine." Shivers run down my back. I nod. He squeezes me so tight and he traces his fingers around my nipples. "Are you hungry?"

"Starving." I flash a big grin.

While we get dressed, I watch his beautiful body. He keeps checking the clock. It hasn't been quite an hour yet. We have a little time, but he seems rushed. He puts on jeans. They look much more comfortable than what he had on at dinner. We went to Simply Fondue twice and we didn't stay or eat either time. I laugh out loud.

"You're not laughing at me, are you?"

He squints his eyes and smiles at the same time. Oh those dimples. I can see both sets at the same time. *Can't we just stay in bed?*

"Can you believe we have been to Simply Fondue twice, but have no idea what their food tastes like?"

We laugh out loud together and he picks me up and twirls me around.

"You're right," he pauses and sets me down. "That's a very emotional place for me. The first time I was devastated..." he does a fake frown, "and the second time overjoyed."

There's that smile.

"We should go back sometime."

"Yes, that would please me."

He pulls my hand, opens the door, and leads me downstairs. I can see the door where we came in. Everywhere I look is more breathtaking than the next. When we get to the bottom of the staircase, I still and squeeze his hand.

"Give me a minute."

I look around with my mouth hanging open again. The entry way is so inviting. It has a gracious foyer with dark wooden floors, a stylized metal chandelier, and an exquisite sitting bench. I see a large oval red and cream rug in front of it with a table the same color as the floors. It holds a single vase full of dendros. *My favorite flowers?* This is too weird. There is a thick red silk ribbon tied around the vase. I turn and see the wide staircase that we just came down. The stairs are white, with dark wood tops that match the floor and table. It looks to go up forever. He squeezes my hand and I close my mouth.

"See what I mean," he lifts his eyebrows. "I didn't want you to get distracted."

I nod in understanding. He pulls my hand again.

We go through a set of double doors that lead outside. There is a table all set up for dinner. Candles, wine bucket, plates with silver covers, white linen napkins, the whole works. He pulls a chair out for me to sit and I'm in awe again. *Is this the South Lawn he referred to with Alan?* I have a lump in my throat. I don't know if I can eat. I've never been somewhere so beautiful. And this is someone's home.

The back of the house looks taller than the front did. It has old fashioned faded copper plated roofing with copper spouts. There are windows everywhere. The double paned patio doors have iron railings that lead to a balcony on the second floor. Is that his bedroom balcony? Oh I'm so turned around. Above the doors are two candle lit sconces. There is a half-moon shaped window. We are on a huge white concrete patio with several vintage iron love seats. They have plush red cushions. There are individual iron chairs with matching creamy cushions under the balcony. How many people can sit out here? There are three large flower pots around the love seats with coned shaped bushes on each side of the door.

"Hey. I'm over here."

He snaps me back.

"I can't help it. I'm in shock over here. I don't know if I can eat. I can't swallow as it is."

"Don't be silly."

He lifts the silver cover off my plate. I'm nervous to see what's under it. I burst out laughing. It's a hamburger with some fancy fries and vegetables. He looks up at me and winks and laughs out loud.

"This couldn't be more perfect."

I am so relieved it's not some fancy dancy dinner with a sauce I can't pronounce. I really just need regular old food right now.

"I agree," he giggles.

"I called and let Alan know what to make after we arrived."

He did? When? That's not possible.

"You did?"

I don't understand. My eyes weren't closed that long and I didn't hear him say anything. He nods and winks at me.

"Eat up."

I am famished. This hamburger is delicious. I am still looking around at the love seats, the windows, the house.

Aidan raises his glass of wine and points it towards me. I take mine and clink his. He takes a long drink and watches me the whole time.

"Gabriella," he swallows. "I want you to stay all weekend here with me."

He does? My heart beats out of my chest. I want to do cartwheels. I want to leap across the table and jump in his arms. I'd really like to ride him on that chair.

"I don't have anything here. I need my..."

He is shaking his head so I stop talking.

"Go up to my room and change out of those clothes. There is a robe on the back of the bathroom door. Put that on. Call Lucca and let him know you won't be home. Have him pack a bag for you for the weekend and we will pick it up in the morning."

His demands are making me wet.

"You won't need any more than the robe tonight. And you won't have that on very long either."

He is staring me down with those dark eyes. I am melting on the spot. Neither of us is speaking. He points to the doors with his head. I can't move and he is still staring. I slowly stand up and push my chair back. He nods and closes his eyes.

I close the doors behind me when I enter the house and lean back on them for support. *What just happened out there?* That was so hot. My heart is still beating out of my chest, even harder than it was before. I want to look around the house some more, but decide not to. I run up the stairs two at a time, my skirt almost rips. I fumble around for my purse and find my phone. I ignore all messages blinking at me. I am out of breath. I find Lucca's picture and press it.

He answers on the first ring.

"Gaby. I've been dying over here. Where are you? Who are you with? Are you ok?"

He's breathing and talking so fast, he is hard to understand.

"Lucca. Calm down."

I listen for a second while he catches his breath.

"Gaby. Just tell me. Who. Are. You. With?" he says each word as its own sentence. That's all he really wants to know. Who did I choose?

"I am at..." I pause and I hear him hold his breath, "Aidan's palace."

"Wwaaaaaaaaaaaaaa," he is screaming. "Oh my God. Oh my God. Gaby, don't mess with me right now. Are you really with Aidan? And did you say palace?"

I'm holding the phone away from my ear.

"Yes. I am with Aidan. This is where I belong. I listened to what you said."

"This is so exciting, Gaby!"

"Yes it is. Listen, I don't have long. I will explain later. Aidan has asked me to stay here all weekend. I will only be home in the morning to pick up a few things. Will you please pack me a small bag?"

"For you to stay with Aidan. Yes I will."

"Thank you, Lucca. I will see you in the morning."

"Have fuuunnnn."

I hear his chuckle.

"Goodnight Lucca."

I sit on the edge of the bed and lean back on my hands. I am here with Aidan. He is falling for me. We made sweet love. Right here on this beautiful bed. The ocean is right there. He says I feel like home. I could call this place home, call him home. I do feel comfortable here.

Shit, he's waiting for me downstairs! I drop my clothes to the floor and run to the bathroom naked. There is a white plush robe on the back of the bathroom door, right where he said it would be. I hope Alan or Marie don't see me on my way outside. How embarrassing. I don't even know them. I close my eyes tight and take a deep breath. *Here I go.*

Aidan is sitting exactly how I left him. I ease the door open and go back to my seat. He smiles. I smile back and notice he has covered our plates with the silver covers. He stands and takes them off. He waited for me. He is so sweet.

"Gabriella, you are stunning in white. You should wear that color more often. Your skin is glowing."

"Thank you."

I never know what to say after all his compliments.

"Let's finish eating. I'd like to show you the rest of the grounds, and the pool."

There's a pool? Another evening walk? Our last one was a lot of fun. I smile, but it turns into a frown.

"What's wrong, Gabriella?"

"I can't wait to see the pool. But I..."

I look around wondering if anyone is watching.

"I feel uncomfortable in this robe knowing Alan or Marie is close by."

He looks confused so I keep talking.

"I mean. Are they watching for when we are done? Or..."

He is rubbing his hair forward. I love when he does that.

"No one is watching us, Gabriella. My staff respects my privacy. I will let them know when we are done. And there is a lot more staff here than just Alan and Marie. Don't worry."

"More staff? What? What on earth do they do?"

I feel like I'm stuttering. *What does he mean they respect his privacy? Does he have lots of women here and they just know to mind their own business?* I'm frowning again.

"What now?" he asks.

"Why are they so scarce then? Are they used to seeing you here with different women?"

I regret that question the second I say it. I try to stay strong and look him in the eye. His eyes widen.

He stands and yells.

"I haven't had a woman here since...." he stops himself and sits back down.

He takes a breath to calm himself and then lowers his voice.

"No, I don't have different women here. I have been alone in this house for the past five years. Well except for the staff of course."

I'm trying to process what he just said. Alone here for the last five years. No women here. They must wonder what's wrong with him. They must wonder who I am.

"I'm sorry Aidan."

I put my hands out on the table like he did to me in the restaurant. I see his dimples now. I'm not going to ask any more questions.

"Let's go for that walk?"

He stands and grabs my hand.

There is a stone trail leading off of the South Lawn. It goes underneath some more fruit trees. Everything is perfectly manicured, and there is not one stray piece of fruit on the ground. It's now dark, but the trail is lit by candle sconces on tall poles. The moon is bright tonight. We are walking hand in hand. It's very romantic. I see the end of the trail and a large, beautiful, perfect pool area. There are four lounge chairs with bright red cushions. There is a U-shaped retaining wall with chocolate brown mulch holding flowers and six round bushes. Five candle lit steps lead us down to another level with a bar, four stools, and a table with a large white umbrella in the middle.

And there it is. The pool. It's breathtaking. Clear blue water glistens in the moonlight. Four steps lead into the water and it looks like it gets deeper at the other end. We stop at the edge.

He pulls me so we are facing each other and he hugs me close. He kisses me lightly on the lips. I stand on my tip toes to kiss him deeper. He stops and closes his eyes. He pushes all of my hair behind my shoulders and trails his finger along the edge of my robe between my breasts. He kisses my neck as one breast comes free and he squeezes it gently. He begins to untie the robe and I take a step forward so we are as close as we can be. He pushes his groin into mine, and the hard erection in my stomach makes me moan. I want to feel him. I put my head back as he finishes and now my robe is hanging open. His hands move up to my shoulders and he opens my robe just a little so both of my breasts are exposed. I stand here breathless. I knot my hands in the bottom of his t-shirt. I go on my tip toes again to kiss him. I cup his erection through his jeans and I feel tingles spread throughout my entire body. I kiss him as I slowly lift his shirt over his head and go right back to his mouth again. I am feeling his warm hard chest with both hands. We are panting together looking in each other's eyes. I need his body.

"I need you, Gabriella," he says determined.

He keeps reading my mind.

He circles my nipples twice with his fingers and trails them up to my shoulders. He moves his fingers behind my arms so that my robe falls to the ground. I undo the button of his jeans. I move the zipper down and push his jeans to the ground. He steps out of them and leads me into the pool.

We enter the warm water together, taking one slow step at a time. When we reach the bottom he grabs my other hand. He kisses my lips one time, then my neck, then to my ears. We are in water up to our navels. I want to touch him. He takes a few steps and pushes my body against the wall. He pins me with his hips and I can't move. He still won't let my hands go, but he is teasing me with his erection. It's so close I want to scream. He bends down and takes a nipple in his mouth. I moan as he tugs it with his teeth. He bites it and swirls his tongue round and round. He lets go and repeats with the other one and I lean my head back and whimper. He pushes his knee between my legs and they part. I am in flames, longing for his touch. He moves my hand to the other and he holds both of mine with one of his. His free hand goes between my thighs and hovers over my entrance. I cry out and push forward. *Touch me. Touch me.* He spreads my juices under the warm water and I open my legs wider. He inserts a finger and slowly massages my inside wall. My heart is pounding. I need this. His touch. *Him.* He inserts another finger and my hips sway along with his movements. He pulls out and I groan. As soon as he lets go of my hands, I grab his erection.

He closes his eyes and puts his head back. I slowly move him back to the stairs and push him to sit down while stroking up and down. I sit next to him on the first step. He leans back on his elbows and I take his full length in my mouth.

He grumbles.

"Fuck."

I suck as hard as I can, timing my breathing, taking him as deep as I possibly can. He tastes so good. When I feel him hit the back of my throat, I wrap my hands on the bottom where my mouth doesn't reach and squeeze hard. I move up and down, not letting go. I feel him push forward. I curl my tongue and swirl it around the tip. His hands are fisted in my hair. I take a few more long slow strokes with my mouth and I let up. I kiss him and he opens his eyes.

"Let's move down a step or two," I whisper while nibbling his ear.

He moves down two. I put my arms around the back of his neck and sit on his lap straddling him. I rub myself on his erection and circle his navel with my finger. I kiss and bite his neck as he pushes on my behind giving me more pressure. I whine in his ear and he lets out a deep groan. I kiss his lips and he parts them. Our tongues begin to swirl. He bites my lower lip and I whimper. He sucks it gently. I push harder, but the pressure is at its max. I need him inside me now.

I back up and aim his erection towards my opening. I go up on my knees just a little bit and slide slowly onto him.

"Aaaahhhhhhhhhhhh Aidan."

He pushes on my behind. I move back and tighten my muscles around his tip. I still to take in the look on his face. I slide down again so hard. His breath is raspy and he tightens his grip. He pushes me back and down so hard I cry out. I stop. He can't get any deeper. I feel him hit the top, into my stomach, and my whole body clenches around him. I wrap my arms and my legs as tight as I can and just squeeze him. I'm scratching at his back and he squeezes back. I don't back up, I just circle round and round.

"Baby. Do that again."

He is panting.

I squeeze him with every single muscle in my body and circle, getting faster. He pushes my behind as I move. When he hits that sweet spot, I still and fall forward. My body is almost uncontrollable. My heart is like a hammer in my chest and I can't calm down. I bite his neck and he groans. I slide on and off of his erection with every ounce of energy I have and he lets go of my behind. I look into his eyes while holding his neck. We blink together. His fingers grab each nipple and squeeze. I swallow and put my head back and move back and forth as hard as I can. Up. Down. Around and around. Hitting so hard against him.

"Come on baby," he shouts, "that's it."

I clench one last time and surrender. I come all around him and hold on tight as he comes with me.

"Oh baby."

I hug him as we calm down together and our breathing slows. I move and sit on the step next to him and rest my head on his shoulder.

He stands and grabs towels from underneath the bar. We dry off and wrap them around our bodies. He stretches out on a lounge chair. He pats next to him and I sit down.

"I want to hold you for a while under the moonlight," he says while stroking my hair. *How does he know that stroking my hair calms me?*

He wakes me by whispering in my ear.

"Let's go up to bed."

I must have fallen asleep. I don't know how long it's been. He puts on my robe and we stroll inside, holding hands again. I admire the candle sconces the whole walk back. These are my favorite thing about the whole house. He leads me to the kitchen and we have some water. I am exhausted. He pulls me up the stairs and into his bedroom. He takes my robe off and gestures to the bed. I climb in. It's so plush and comfortable and these sheets are so soft. I could sleep here forever. His middle finger strokes my face as he smoothes my hair off of it. I close my eyes and smile. I am drifting in and out of sleep. This has been a long crazy emotional day. I can't stay awake. I think I hear him whispering to me.

"Everything you do is right."

I drift off.

"I would be lost without you. You are mine."

I blink my eyes but don't respond. The final whisper I hear is, "I love you."

He falls asleep behind me, spooning me, holding my hand.

Chapter 7

The sun is shining in. I open my eyes and close them again. I blink a few times to get used to the light. I can really see the ocean view from here and I haven't even moved. Aidan is still holding my hand. We didn't budge at all last night.

I start to remember the hamburgers. That was funny. I remember when he told me to go change, and to call Lucca, and the pool. *Oh, the pool.* I smile and wonder how beautiful it must look in the daytime. I try to recall what he was whispering when we went to sleep, but I can't. I look back and Aidan's eyes are still closed. He is in a deep sleep, breathing heavily.

I close my eyes again and wonder what we will do today. I'd like a tour of the rest of this big house. It still blows my mind that I'm here. He needs to tell me more about his job and how he has all this money. *Did he tell me that he has been alone here for five years?* I'm sure that didn't mean he hasn't had any friends over. Just that no one has lived here? I'll have to ask him. All these questions are building up. I look at the clock and it's only nine.

I stay in his embrace, but turn to face him. I want to study his features and engrain them in my memory. He has such a strong jaw line and cheek bones. I reach up and put my finger in his dimple. You can even see them while he sleeps. I trace my finger over his eyebrows and he furrows. I giggle and do it again. I trace the muscle lines on his bicep and on his chiseled chest. As my hand gets lower, his eyes open.

"Good morning, beautiful."

He smiles and both dimples pronounce. I touch them.

"Good morning, handsome."

"What were you doing while I was sleeping?"

"Nothing."

"Uh huh."

He smiles and moves the hair from my face.

"You are so lovely in the morning. I love waking up next to you. I love having you in my bed."

He kisses my shoulder.

"I love those things too. You make me smile."

"How long have you been awake?"

He looks over my shoulder at the clock.

"Not long. You're pretty good looking in the morning too."

He pulls my body to his. Our legs are straight and I feel his morning erection. We are forehead to forehead looking into each other's eyes. He sticks his lips out to kiss me. I kiss him back.

He leans back.

"What do you want to do today?"

He pushes against me harder.

"I know how I'd like to start the day."

He lifts his eyebrows.

"Aidan," I scold with a big smile.

"Turn around baby."

He grabs my bottom arm and turns me over.

I do as he says and put my back to him, so we are in the spooning position again. He kisses my shoulder and his hand runs down the back of my thigh. When he reaches my knee, he lifts and my legs part. His body slides down. I feel his finger find his way and I am ready for him. I grab one of his pillows and hug it tightly and bite on the corner. His erection finds my opening and he smoothes the tip in and around. He surges in all the way and I bite down on the pillow and grunt loudly. Holding my leg up, he slides in and out too gently. He comes all the way out, rubs the tip around, and slides in again and again. He lets my leg fall so my knees are together but he is still inside me. He puts one hand on each shoulder and thrusts hard. I whimper and he slows. I want to open my legs but I don't have the strength. He doesn't stop moving and when my muscles relax, he speeds up, building me up again quickly. He tries to slow again, but this time I let go. I bite the pillow as hard as I can. He makes me come so easily. I lose all will when he's inside me. He moves me to my stomach and pounds over and over, harder and harder, and he comes. So. Hard. He pounds again.

"Oh baby," he whispers in my ear. His body relaxes as he wraps his arms around me and eases out from between my legs. He turns me to face him.

"Your body, Gabriella," his breathing is coming back to normal. "It's incredible. You drive me wild. I can't control myself when you're naked in my bed."

I see that hurt in his eyes again. He is smiling trying to hide it, but I see it deep in there. *What is it about?* I smile shyly and kiss his lips.

"Your body drives me wild too. It responds so quickly to your touch, your voice, your scent."

I'm trying to build him up and take that hurt away.

"Our bodies were made for each other. We fit together perfectly."

His eyes are getting the light back.

"Yes, they do."

I kiss his nose.

I close my eyes and think about what I was doing two weeks ago. I would have never imagined I'd be where I am today. I was having constant fights with Zach. He made me feel insecure. He never gave me compliments anymore. He didn't take care of me like he said he would. Yes, he brought me down when I spiraled and had an attack, but it's not like he came running every time I needed him. He didn't give me that safe secure feeling. He didn't live for me like I lived for him. It didn't feel that we both put in the equal effort into the relationship. He brought down my confidence. Aidan builds it up. I can't think about Zach anymore. He is out of my life. *Would I be here if he hadn't broken up with me last Friday? Would I be in this palace of a house with a palace of a man?* Aidan doesn't know me yet. He doesn't know the deep down real crazy me. He won't want me. *Can you love someone after only a week? Did he say he loves me? Was I dreaming?* I squeeze my eyes tighter.

"Hey." He shakes me out of my thoughts. "What's going on?"

"Nothing."

A tear falls down from my eye onto the pillow.

"I'm just so lucky to be here with you." I take a deep breath. "I feel like you saved me. I need that."

"Gabriella, don't cry," he kisses away my tears from my eyes. "You are the one who saved me." I did? *What did I save him from?*

"I feel so safe in your arms."

I ignore his saving comment.

He gives me a tight hug and whispers in my ear.

"And I feel safe in yours."

He lets go and opens the balcony door. He waves his finger.

"Come here baby."

He is still naked, so I stay naked when I get out of bed. He pulls me onto the balcony. We have our hands on the railing in front of us as we watch the waves crash to the shore. I close my eyes and listen and let the breeze blow my hair back. Deep breaths while I tell myself I'm really here. He puts his arm around my waist and closes his eyes.

"This is home, Gabriella. Me and you exactly where we are right this second."

I peek at him and he still has his eyes closed. *Does he want me to live here? What am I saving him from?* He is confusing.

"I want to stay like this forever, Gabriella. Stay with me."

He opens his eyes and looks at me. I turn and he bends down, picks me up and kisses me. He kisses me deep. His tongue is swirling around my mouth. I wrap my legs around his waist, and he kisses deeper. We really do fit together perfectly. He sits back on the lounge chair. He overtakes me with his passion and we are panting again. I have my fists in his hair.

"We. Need. To. Get. Ready. Baby," he says between kisses on my lips. "I still have that goodie."

Oh, I forgot about that. He rubs my behind with his hands. He wants me to get ready but he won't stop kissing me. I don't stop either. I want him to carry me to the bed with my legs wrapped around him. I want to stay in bed all day. I want to stay like this forever. Just like that as my thoughts mirror what he said, I remember. *He did say he loved me last night.* It wasn't a dream. I pull back, and ease myself back onto his knees.

"What is it baby?"

He tries to lean into kiss me again.

"Aidan..." I put both hands up on his cheeks. "I love you too."

His eyes broaden as his smile takes over his face. My hands are still on his cheeks and I sink a fingertip in each dimple.

He stands so quickly that I let out a little yelp. I wrap my legs around him tighter and hold behind his neck. He brings me to the bed and leaves the balcony door open. The sun is shining in and the breeze is so strong that the drapes are blowing all around. The waves are crashing extra loud. He sets me on the edge of the bed. I let go of his neck and fall back and put my hands above my head. I keep my legs wrapped. He touches my face and trails his hands down my shoulders, under my arms, over each breast, to my stomach, and grabs my hips abruptly. *Yes.* This is exactly what I want. He backs just enough so he can slip his erection inside me. He pulls my hips down and slides in. I dig my head back against the bed and cry out. I am warm and wet and already trembling. He pulls out and pushes in as hard as he can. *Yes, Aidan.* I cry out each time he hits. I thrust my breasts up and make an arch over the bed. I am going to explode. He won't slow down. There is no stopping. He thrusts over and over harder each time. He hits the sweet spot and I stiffen. He thrusts even harder. I didn't know it could get harder. He reaches up and grabs each nipple, and just like that I let go, crying out. He tugs each nipple and my orgasm keeps going as he continues to thrust. When I look up at him he explodes inside me.

"Oh baby," he whispers.

I love how he looks when he comes.

I am getting my clothes back on and start wondering what the surprise could be. I finish my hair and makeup and look into the mirror.

"Same old me again today."

Yep, I'm the same. I'm in love, but I'm the same old me. I hope he loves the real me back. A knock at the door interrupts my thoughts.

"Ready baby?" Aidan asks through door.

I open it and he's leaning on the wall with one hand. *Fuck he's sexy.* He's dressed and ready for the day.

"Yes, I am. Don't forget I need to get my bag at home."

I can't wait to change.

"I didn't forget. We will stop there first."

He grabs my hand and pulls me outside. He's excited about something. He's pulling me at almost a running pace. I don't see his car, only a white BMW SUV limousine. A man dressed in a tuxedo is standing and holding the back door open for us. I turn to Aidan.

"What's going on? This isn't for us, is it?"

My voice is squeaking again.

"Gabriella, I told you I had a goodie."

He looks serious with a little grin on his face.

"Oh wow!"

I do a little jump and climb in.

He gets in behind me and tuxedo man shuts the door. *If the girls could see me now.* The inside is bigger than my bedroom. It has glass all around with several small screen TVs and illuminating lights along the top with dark tinted windows. There is one long bench seat that takes up one whole side and curves around the front underneath the window to the driver. All the seats are white leather. It smells brand new. There is a fully loaded bar with another seat next to that. The floors are black and white wood. I hear loud music playing, sounds like soft rock. It's very romantic.

"This is incredible, Aidan. How did you? When did you?"

He's laughing at me as I stutter.

"I made some calls."

He smirks at me. *When does he do all these secret calls?*

"You are full of surprises."

"So are you," he whispers.

He pulls the cover off of a tray on the bar. It's full of fresh fruit, croissants, rolls, and breads. I grin. *Has he thought of absolutely everything*?

"Mimosa?" he asks. *Yep, he has thought of everything.*

"Yes please."

I do a silent clap with my hands. He mixes the drink and hands it to me. I hold mine until he mixes his.

"To a wonderful day with my perfect woman."

He holds his drink up. I hold mine up too.

"This looks delicious, Aidan. I've worked up quite an appetite because of you."

I squeeze his knee.

"Then you'll be ravenous by tonight baby." He raises an eyebrow.

Holy shit. What does he have in mind?

"Tell me what you have planned."

I squint.

"I will. Let's get your bag first."

He makes me a plate with a little bit of everything on it. I drape my legs across his. He feeds me taking bites of his own between each of mine. We eat the whole way to my house.

I wait for tuxedo man to open my door.

I step out and turn to Aidan.

"I won't be long."

I kiss him quickly on the lips.

"Hurry back baby."

He sits back in the seat and closes his eyes. Lucca isn't home when I go in, but I see my roller suitcase waiting for me by the door. Lucca is the best. I see a note on top of my case.

Have fun Gaby!
You deserve this!
Call me later, Lucca.

I don't go in past the door. I pull up the handle on my case and wheel it out and lock the door. When I turn around, Zach is standing in my face. I didn't see or hear him pull up. *Where is his car? Where is Aidan? He didn't see or hear anything either?*

"Aahhhh!" I let out a quick scream.

My heart is pounding. I feel scared. He is inches from me.

"Zach. Um, what are you doing here?"

I look over his shoulder. I try to stay calm.

"Where is your car?"

"Gaby, I have been here for almost twelve hours waiting for you. Where have you been?"

He is glaring at me.

"I can't do this."

I shake my head and try to go past him, but he puts his arm out. He holds it out firm and backs me up against the door.

He puts both hands on the door next to my ears, pinning me. I can't move. I am trapped. *Where the fuck is Aidan?*

"Where were you last night? You said you would meet me at seven!"

He's yelling in my face, staring me down.

"Why didn't you come? Where have you been?"

He is scaring me. He is so close to me. *Please don't hit me.*

"Zach. Please back up."

I start to cry and put my head down.

"I am not backing up. I am not going anywhere. You tell me now. And look at me."

He's spitting on my face as he yells. He lifts my chin with his fist.

"Zach. Please. Please back up," I plead.

"You don't stand me up and then expect me to be all calm and quiet."

"Please."

I'm begging him.

"I stayed out of your hair all week, just like you asked, I sent you flowers. Fuck! That's not me. But I did it anyway to please you. There is no pleasing you, Gaby. No matter what I do, you are never fucking happy."

He's breathing harder and yelling louder.

"And did you see the damn balloon?"

"I can't marry you, Zach."

I shake my head and look down again.

"Marry him?"

Aidan's voice is loud and forceful. He pulls the back of Zach's collar and backs him off of me. I fall to the ground trying to catch my breath.

"There is no way she is going to marry you!"

Aidan is yelling at Zach now.

"You bitch. You've been with this guy?"

Zach is pointing and shaking his finger at me.

"Don't call her that."

Aidan pushes Zach's shoulder.

"She's been with you? She left me for you? What the fuck? Who are you anyway?" Zach yells.

They look like they're going to fight again.

"I didn't leave you," I'm screaming, sobbing. "You left me. You crushed me. You dumped me and made me feel like garbage."

I'm getting louder.

"AGAIN!"

I try to get up but I can't.

"Why didn't you tell me he asked you to marry him?"

Aidan is yelling at me?

My lump in my throat is back and I can't swallow. I am in shock. Zach is yelling at me. Aidan is yelling at me. Just ten minutes ago I was over the moon in love. I'm spiraling down, down. I can't stop it. I put my head on the ground.

"She's a bitch."

Zach looks at Aidan.

"I told you to stop saying that."

Aidan punches Zach. Again. I close my eyes. I can't watch this. I can't listen to this. I rub my face and cover my ears. They are fighting. No one is holding me.

"Luuucccccccccccccccaaaaaaaaaaaaaaaa," I scream, and go in and out of consciousness.

"Good luck with her. She's a handful."

That's Zach's voice.

"I stuck by you. Look at you. How can anyone love you when you're like this? He will never take care of you like I did. He will never bring you back down. He will hate you."

I black out with Zach yelling at me. He is really out of my life now. *I could have had... Aidan won't know how to control me, how to help me...he will hate me...*

I open my eyes and I'm in Aidan's arms. We are in the limo. I am on Aidan's lap and his arms are tight around me with his head down on my shoulder. *What have I done?* Zach is right. Aidan will hate me eventually. He has seen me spiral twice. He will think I'm crazy and won't want me anymore. He won't be able to handle me. He will get sick of me.

Where are we going? I look out the window and see the ocean alongside of us. I don't hear Aidan, but I feel his upper body shake. *Is he crying? What's going on?* I'm disoriented. Tears stream down my face. I can't hold them in. I try to keep silent. A tear drops off my chin and onto his neck. His face flies up to mine and our eyes meet.

"Oh baby. You are awake."

His eyes are wide. He looks relieved.

"I'm so sorry Aidan."

I put my head down. I feel ashamed.

"I love you. Don't be sorry," he says softly and I shake my head.

"I need my phone." I look around for my purse. "Please, where is my phone?"

I hold out my hand.

"Gabriella. Let me hold you."

I want him to hold me. I don't want to lose him, but I'm scared to let him in. He will hate me soon. I try to push off his lap and he squeezes me tighter.

"Gabriella, what's wrong? Why are you moving away from me?"

His brow is furrowed. He doesn't understand. I can't let him love me. I can't get any closer to him. We will both get hurt.

"Aidan. I need my phone. Please bring me home."

"Why? Who are you going to call?" He won't let go of me. "I will not bring you home."

"I need to call Lucca. I can't do this. You can't..." I shake my head. "You won't..."

"No. Just this morning we said we were home with each other. We said we loved each other. We made love. I held you in my arms. You looked in my eyes and told me you love me."

I know. I'm sorry.

"Did you mean that?"

"Yes I did. But..."

I try to push again. He lets me out of his grip slightly, and when I move back a little, he pulls me on top of his lap, so I'm straddling him. He laces his fingers in mine so tight I can't move. He leans back and looks deeply into my eyes.

"Listen to me. There is nothing to be sorry for. I am the one who is sorry for not getting out of the car sooner. I was reliving our morning together, and when I looked out, Zach had you pinned against the door. That will never happen again. Ever."

He's getting louder.

"I said I wanted to take care of you, and I meant it. I will protect you and guard you no matter what," he's almost yelling.

"But you will hate me," I try to get a word in.

"And whatever that was about. I will not hate you. Zach is fucked up."

Aidan shakes his head.

"He should not be speaking to you like that. And I don't give a fuck why he thinks...or you think I will hate you. That will not happen. And you are not to speak to him again."

"But..."

He holds my fingers tighter and presses them against the seat.

"I will never let you out of my sight again. It doesn't fucking matter why he said that," he says firmly.

He kisses me hard on my mouth and I kiss him back.

"Now, I had a nice day planned, but we will reschedule again."

I can tell he has calmed after the kiss.

He has me in his trance. I can't look away. I just nod.

"I really wanted to make love to you in here."

He looks around the limo.

"I was going to get you silly drunk at a wine tasting, and make love to you again on the way home."

I smile at him. I'm nervous that Zach will try something again. I'm nervous that Aidan won't be able to handle me for long. I try to put that out of my mind. He was holding me. He saved me the first time last weekend, and he just did it again. *Can I let him into my madness? Into my darkness?*

"We are going back home to have a bath. Do you understand?"

"Yes."

I nod again.

"Good girl. Now come here."

He pats the seat next to him.

I sit with my back to him and he wraps his arms around me. He pushes a button and tells the driver to turn around. I hear his breathing slow. He holds me in his arms, while stroking my hair and rocking slightly. *How does he know this is what relaxes me?* This is how Lucca brings me down. *Shit, I was going to call him.*

The rest of the drive back is quiet. He holds me tight like he will never let go. I feel lucky to be in his arms. I feel safe. *Please don't let me go, Aidan. I love you too.* I close my eyes tightly as if to transfer my thoughts to his head. He has mirrored my thoughts before. I smile but he can't see me. I lean my head back so I'm under his chin. He releases his arm so I can lie across his chest. He looks sad, or worried, I'm not sure. We gaze into each other's eyes and he doesn't move. I lift up slightly to kiss him. I want him to know I'm sorry and I trust him and thank him for holding me, and for not bringing me home. We hold our lips together. I part mine in hopes that he will respond. He doesn't. I lick his lips and he backs up.

"I'm sorry."

He closes his eyes.

"Hey," I whisper.

He opens his eyes slowly and bends down to kiss me. His lips are open and his tongue takes over. It's like he's glad I'm back to normal. I don't want to dwell on the morning. I want to move past it and enjoy our weekend together. I move my hands to his biceps and slowly up to his neck. I sit up on my knees and straddle him again. We don't stop kissing as I push myself into his erection, and he lets out a gasp. I lick his lips and our tongues touch. I bite his neck. I like this game. I lick his lips again and push even harder on his erection. I repeat with his lips, tongue, neck, each time grinding harder. His hands are fisted in my hair and mine are behind his neck.

"Can you close the divider so he can't see us?"

I nod towards the driver. The glass is closed, but I want the solid divider closed. He lifts his eyebrows and leans forward. The divider closes.

"Perfect," I whisper as I swirl my tongue around. "So, what was that about making love in here?"

He lets out a laugh as I circle my fingers around his naval. I love his laugh.

"Is that your signal that you want me?"

He looks down to my fingers and smiles. I guess it is. I had no idea I did that. He stands slightly and lays me on my back on the long bench seat. He kneels to the side of me.

He strokes my face with his fingers.

"Baby, I love you."

"And I love you."

He laughs again. He looks so happy. He leans down and licks my lips.

"You haven't changed your clothes yet. I could assist you with that."

He starts to unzip my skirt.

"Yes, please."

I nod a little too excitingly.

He pulls my skirt down and kisses the line where my panties meet my leg. He pulls it past my feet and trails kisses the entire way. I just watch him. My skirt lands on the floor. He looks me in the eyes as his middle finger circles my ankle. It slowly moves up my calf, to my knee, and slows way down at my thighs. I try to spread my legs, but his stomach is at my side. He shakes his head. He traces around my panties. *Please touch me.* I arch up and he shakes his head again. His finger moves to my opening, but he doesn't go underneath. He slowly strokes up and down. My stomach is aching. I push up one more time with want. *Fuck. I need him now.* I feel a little more pressure and I shove my head back in the seat.

He rests his upper body across the middle of my thighs. I can't move. I can't bend or spread my legs. He is holding me down. He continues stroking up and down. The feeling is so light. It's making my whole body sensitive. When I reach for him, he tucks my hands behind his shoulder so they are against the seat too. Now I am totally trapped and he continues to torment me. He loves this. He doesn't stop the stroking, still looking into my eyes.

I mouth "please" to him.

He smiles and mouths back.

"Please what?"

He won't stop. The pressure stays light and the slow up and down motion is killing me. He doesn't take his eyes off of mine. I start to close my eyes and his fingers move my panties over. My heart is pounding. He spreads my wetness. I am trapped and going to explode. He bites my nipple through my shirt. I am going crazy. I want to spread my legs. I want to bed my knees, anything to distract this torture. He bites harder and the very tip of his finger goes inside. I gasp. He circles it around and around, and I build even higher. I'm throbbing as the waves of orgasm begin. He lets my hands go free and I fist them in his hair.

"Aidan, please," I beg.

"Sir, we have arrived."

I hear over the speaker.

Chapter 8

As we approach the door, Alan greets us.

"Good afternoon sir, ma'am."

Same ol' routine for Alan. Aidan pulls me through the door, up the stairs, and to his bedroom. The door slams and he has a determined look in his eye.

"Get in the bath."

The bathtub is up a small staircase off his bedroom. There is a tall fireplace in the wall that his bedroom and the bath share. While I undress, I see the fire start. He comes up and starts the water. I watch as he takes off his shirt. He pulls matches from his pocket and lights the two candles on the vanity. He unbuttons his pants and winks at me as his boxers and pants fall to the floor. My heart pounds. His wink. His erection. My lump has returned. I close my eyes and inhale the scent as he pours bath oil in the water. It smells like lavender. He reaches his hand out and I take it. We step into the warm water together and sit down facing each other.

"Let's start today over," he says. "Let's forget about the last couple hours."

"That's the best idea I've ever heard."

I can't wait any longer for him to be inside me. I am still swollen from the limo ride. I move across the water to kiss him and grab his throbbing erection at the same time. He is so hard and ready. I stroke him up and down under the water and we kiss harder. I can't hold back anymore. I push his legs together so I can sit on his lap. I line up his erection to my opening with my hand, and he grabs my hips and turns me around. I'm so frustrated. No! He opens his legs wide, and pushes me down between them. I feel him hard against my back and he pulls me so I lean against him.

"Open your legs baby."

I open them as wide as I possibly can.

"Put both feet up on the sides." I lean back all the way and put one foot up on each side of the bathtub.

"Give me your hands."

He tucks each hand under his knees against the tub.

"Now sit still." He nibbles at my ear.

Tingles spread like wildfire. His hands grab my breasts and he squeezes and tugs at each nipple. He circles them between his fingers and I arch back.

"Aaaahhhhhhh!" I scream out.

"Feel it baby," he says in my ear.

His hand moves down my body, over my stomach, and a finger slides right inside. It swirls around the succulence and he squeezes one nipple even harder. His finger moves in and out, faster and faster and then withdrawals. I try to move my body along with his fingers' rhythm, but I can't.

"Absorb the pleasure."

His finger slowly circles my clitoris, and then inside and back out to my clitoris, then two fingers go in. I try to arch back. I feel his erection get harder. All fingers stop what they are doing, and he switches hands. *No.* I can't sit still. He circles my other nipple. With no break, he pushes two fingers back inside and palms my clitoris around and around. I push my head into his chest. My heart is pounding. His heart is pounding. Each time I moan, he moans back. He's driving me wild. His fingers push hard on my front wall and my knees start to tremble.

"Please don't stop, Aidan."

He pushes harder and my knees are knocking against the side of the tub. I can't control it. Water is sloshing around and onto the bathroom floor. With one light nibble on my ear, I stiffen my legs, and I come like I've never come before. He keeps both fingers inside until I come down from my orgasm.

"I love that feeling on my fingers."

I lean back to kiss him and he hugs me close. I feel safe in his arms. We lay in the bath for close to a half hour. I drift off for a few minutes as he holds me against his chest. I turn to face him and reach behind his back and open the plug. The water starts to drain and I nuzzle his chest until it's all gone.

"Let's get out."

He says in his deep scratchy voice. He stands and holds his hand out to me. I grab it and step over the side.

"Put your hands on the side."

He demands. I look in his eyes and he doesn't blink. Oh shit. I turn around and put my hands on the side of the bathtub and bend over.

"Spread your legs."

I spread my legs. He grabs my hips and is inside me in no time. He slams into me and I whimper. I bend my legs slightly and put my head down. He starts again and slams hard and fast. There is no break. I might fall forward.

"I'm going to come Gabriella, hold on."

Fuck. I brace myself and close my eyes tight. I put my arms straight to help support. He pounds repeatedly, getting harder each time. The intensity is building and I come again, knowing he is on the brink.

As my muscles start to contract around him, he yells.

"That's it!"

He explodes inside me.

He pulls out half way and thrusts again, and doesn't stop until he's empty.

"Are you hungry baby? It's already four and we never had lunch. I can call down to Marie."

He is nodding as he asks, he must be hungry.

"Yes, I am. Starving actually. I can't believe it's this late already."

I smile back to him.

He calls Marie and tells her to make his favorite. I wonder what that is. He says we will dine in the Court Yard in one hour, and appetizers should be served in a half hour. I watch him. He is so alluring and in control. I wonder how much he pays his staff and if they live here full time. We are both on the edge of the bed holding hands, naked. He squeezes my hand as he directs the staff what kind of wine should be served and what to prepare for dessert. *Fuck, I forgot about my car.* It's still at Simply Fondue. I squeeze his hand to get his attention.

"What is it baby?"

"My car is still at Simply Fondue. I don't want it to sit there overnight again."

"Got it."

He smiles back.

Got it? What does that mean?

He continues his conversation with Marie. They discuss the menu for tomorrow. It's Sunday tomorrow and I wish I could skip over next week at work and fast forward to the weekend. Next week is going to suck with the conference.

"Let's go down for dinner," he says softly, "and put the robes on."

He winks.

"Ok. What is your favorite?"

"Favorite what?"

"I heard you tell Marie to make that for us."

He laughs.

"My favorite is Shepherd's Pie. She makes it once a month. It's my comfort food. I thought we could use something like that today."

I laugh inside. He's like a big kid asking mommy for his favorite meal on his birthday.

"That does sound good," I say as he hands me my robe.

He pulls my hand. When we get to the bottom of the staircase, I see my car parked on the brick road out front. I double take and step back.

"Is that my car? How did it get here? When did you do that?"

I didn't see the car parked outside when we came in from the limo.

"I had Geoff go get it when we returned," he says it like I should have known that already.

"Who the hell is Geoff?" I'm confused.

Aidan continues to amaze me.

"He's my assistant."

His assistant? He didn't ask for my keys. He works with his staff so secretly.

He pulls my hand. *Wait, I want to talk about my car.* We pass through the kitchen, through the TV room, through the back porch, and out to what I assume is the Court Yard. That's what he called it on the phone with Marie. I stop his pull and look around. The landscaping is similar to the South Lawn. It's manicured perfectly. This is like a private retreat back here. It is absolutely beautiful and tranquil with lush greenery. This patio is stone, very elegant and old fashioned. The stone is polished and refined. There is a short wall surrounding us that is rustic and natural. It has a seating area and a dining area with matching furniture of light wood with red cushions. He loves those red cushions. I snicker to myself. Every time I pass through a room or a new outside area I say it's my favorite, but this is definitely my favorite. It even has a stone fire place. It is so secluded and detached. This is a perfect place to come and relax.

"Ready to eat? Marie is on her way out."

How does he know that? This is so weird. He sits at the dining table and pulls me to his lap. We kiss softly. It's so romantic sitting on his lap while we are each in our soft robes.

"Sir."

I look up and a beautiful young woman is holding a tray of food. She looks younger than I do. *She's the chef?*

"Yes Marie. Set it here," He points to the table. "Marie, this is Gabriella."

"Nice to meet you ma'am."

She extends her hand to mine and we shake.

"Nice to meet you too Marie," I say.

She smiles and removes the items from the tray. We are having white wine, baguette with cheese, sliced fresh veggies and a colorful mixture of berries. She sets a small plate at each place, with the food in the middle and pours two glasses of wine.

"Please let me know if you need anything else sir."

She smiles at me. She looks really familiar. *Where do I know her from?*

Marie returns to the house and we finish our dinner. The shepherd's pie was very good. The ocean is directly behind us from this end of the house. It's a stunning view, but the sound of the waves crashing into the beach is making me sleepy. Well, that along with the wine and full stomach. I really would like to go lay down but it's too early to go to sleep.

Aidan tells me more about Geoff and what his duties are. He talks about the upcoming week and what he has to finish for work. I say there is a concert coming that I want to go to, but I just found out that Lucca will be out of town. He reminds me again that he doesn't like my kind of music. *Yes, I know.* I tell him about my big conference, but not about my night time responsibilities. I can't let him know about that. Not yet. I hate that part, but I have to do it.

"You look exhausted," Aidan says in the middle of work talk.

"I am."

I want to go to sleep in his arms, tight and safe.

"Let's go lay down for a little while, then for a moonlight swim later."

He leads me to the TV room. He has the biggest TV I have ever seen. It's a widescreen and it hangs over a huge fireplace. There are bookshelves to each side. They are so high that he has a wooden ladder to reach the top shelf. There is a mirror as big as the TV that hangs over the entry to the room. Another bookcase is at the side wall and it's filled with different art pieces and vases. The top shelf has a huge wooden A and the second shelf down has a huge wooden S.

His initials?

He fidgets with one of his hundred remotes and an old black and white movie starts on the screen. He sits in the corner of the plush red couch and I snuggle in beside him against the oversized pillows. I rest my head on his chest and close my eyes. So much has happened since last night. Our meeting at Simply Fondue was perfect. I loved the look on his face when he saw me. It made me feel so special. I hug myself. Last night was intense. He is a remarkable lover. Each time he makes me come harder than the time before. No one has ever done that for me. Our bodies were made for each other. This morning in bed and then on the balcony. All those sweet things he said to me. We professed our love. I need his love. I'm hungry for it.

Then the craziness with Zach. He scared me. Aidan saved me and said he would always be there for me. *Am I crazy? How did we fall in love so fast? Is this the love at first sight that I was thinking about last weekend?* He makes me feel loved, and in such a short time. I already feel more loved by him that I ever did with Zach. I need this. *Can his love cut through my darkness?* I put my arms around him and hug him extra hard. He kisses the top of my head. His legs are stretched out on the couch and crossed at the ankles. He looks so relaxed. That's exactly how I feel. This house is incredible. This is too good to be true. I close my eyes again and drift off to sleep.

"Gabriella, wake up."
He shakes my shoulder a little and I open my eyes.
"Hey."
How long have I been sleeping?
"What about that swim?" he whispers in my ear.
"Can we go up to bed?" I ask as I look into his eyes.
I hope he can tell I mean not to sleep. I want to make love and fall asleep in his arms. *Put your hand out and take me upstairs.*
"As you wish," he whispers in my ear.
I gasp as he lifts me from the couch and carries me in his arms. He has one arm behind my back and the other under my knees. I start to nibble his neck. He tries to back away, but I keep nibbling and licking his neck, then his ears.
"Oh no you don't."
He pretends to drop me and I let out a yelp.
We make it out of the TV room and into the kitchen. I wrap one arm around his neck to hold on, and touch his bare chest with my other hand. I open the robe slightly and trace my fingers over his muscles and around his nipples, then down to his naval. *I guess this is my sign I want him.* He stops in the entry way and stands next to the oval table. He licks my lips. I part them and our tongues are entwined. He moves from my lips to my neck. I keep my hand on his chest and bend my neck back. My heart starts to speed up and I can feel the moistness growing between my legs. He is back at my lips and I kiss him hard. I suck his bottom lip and I feel his knees buckle a little. His answering groans are making me melt in his arms. He stands up straight as though to regain his strength, and he takes the first step up the stair case. It feels like he is going to drop me. *Do I make his knees weak like he does mine?*
I take my hand off of his chest and move it behind my back so I can stroke his erection underneath. I part his robe so I can touch him. He is so hard and ready. I let go of him as he sets me on the stairs. He kisses me and lets out a long groan that is

so erotic. My legs are trembling and I need him inside me. I need the peace. He takes my nipple in his mouth and sucks. I rest my head on the stairs and open my legs. *Please don't make me wait anymore*. He stops sucking and circles my nipple with his tongue. His gentleness is unbearable. I push forward to feel his erection but he backs up.

He looks deep into my eyes while standing between my legs and supporting his hands on the stair next to my head.

"Hold on baby," he whispers as he unties my robe the rest of the way.

I can't even think straight. I tear my gaze away from his and close my eyes while putting my head back on the stair again. *Fuck.*

"Please Aidan."

I look at him as he unties his robe. We both still have them on, but they are open, ties hanging to the side. This is so sultry. He kneels between my legs, and puts his hands on my knees. Slowly they move up the top of my thighs then down to my opening and two fingers from one hand slide in while the thumb on his other hand presses on my clitoris. I struggle to open my legs wider for him. *Please push harder. Please go deeper.*

"Aaaaahhhhhhhhhhhh Aidan!" I scream.

He removes his fingers and puts them both in his mouth. He sucks them slowly in and out. I just stare at him. This is so fucking carnal. Still sucking, he pushes inside me. I cry out.

Finally!

I close my eyes as he whispers, "Next time you will suck my fingers as you come."

Holy shit. He licks and sucks my earlobes while he picks up momentum. I can't hold on anymore. I unleash and come all around him on the stairs. I dig my fingers into his back. He slows and drags his movements making my orgasm last longer and longer. Feeling every inch of his erection is so powerful. When my fingers loosen their grip, he pushes up on his arms and pounds into me, again and again.

He collapses on top of me as he comes.

"Oh baby."

I hug him tight until he is ready to get up. We lay and let our breathing slow together. I love this man. *I love this man.*

He carries me up the rest of the stairs and puts me in bed. He removes my robe and I lay down. He holds me from behind and I feel his robe is off too. I hope no one saw us on the stairs. *Did they hear me*? And an even more pressing question, *where do I know Marie from?* I'm glad today is over.

"I love you baby," Aidan says softly in my ear.

"I love you too Aidan."

He laces his fingers in mine and we hold hands all night.

When I wake up Aidan is still holding me. I turn my head back and his eyes are open. He is looking at me.

"Good morning handsome."

I smile.

"Hi baby." I turn to face him.

"It's almost nine. Are you going to brunch today?"

Shit, I forgot. I've been sidetracked by this gorgeous man and our love affair.

"Yes, I should go. They will be expecting me."

I don't want to leave this safe haven, but I have to eventually I convince myself.

"I will drop you at brunch and get you when you are done, and then you will be all mine for the rest of the day."

He has a wicked look in his eye.

"Oh really?" I lift my eyebrows. "I do have to go home tonight though remember."

"I don't want you to go, baby."

"I don't want to go, but I have to. I have the busiest week of the year at work this week."

"Fine, but you're mine until after dinner."

I nod.

"But I hope you're mine a lot longer than that."

Me too. He pulls me close to his body. After a bone crushing hug he moves to his back. I slide right up next to him and wrap my upper leg around his and begin to ride it. The pressure feels so good on my clitoris. I tighten my legs and ride harder.

"I'd like that," I whisper in his ear.

"Good girl."

He hits my behind.

"I want you baby."

I lick his ears while I increase pressure. He turns on his side so I can't ride anymore. He parts my legs with his knee and his fingers start to explore.

"You're so wet. This pleases me."

He spreads the wetness up and down and inserts just a small fingertip inside.

"Please, please, please Aidan," I'm begging.

"Do you like that baby?"

"Please."

"Please what?" He pushes his finger a little bit deeper. "Like that?"

"Oohhh yes." He keeps up the pace of pushing in and out so lightly, and kisses me on my lips.

"You need to get ready."

He pushes a little harder.

"No."

I shake my head back and forth. He withdraws his finger and licks it.

"You taste so good. I'll finish that when we get home."

He stands up goes to the bathroom. He leaves me on the bed breathless, naked, wide open for him. I don't want to go. I want to stay in bed all day with him.

"Come on baby."

He yells for me from the bathroom. I can barely move. I struggle to get up. He has all my clothes laid out from my bag.

"Can I help you get dressed?" he asks.

"Can we shower?"

I need a cold shower. His teasing almost pushed me over the edge. Maybe I can get him to respond in there. He smiles and starts the water. I wonder if he knows what I'm thinking.

"After you."

He motions to get in the water.

I step in. It's so hot and steamy. *Holy shit.* I stand still while I adjust to the temperature. He stands in front of me and starts washing his hair. He looks even sexier when he's wet. I admire his body. He is so beautiful. I reach to touch his chest and he closes his eyes. I trace every single muscle with my fingers. I slide down his body, circle his naval, and grab onto his erection. He opens his eyes and shakes his finger at me.

"No, no."

As he says no, he pushes a finger inside me. I am soaked, swollen, sore. I can't leave like this. I tilt my head back and he withdraws. *No. Don't stop.* He kisses me quick on the lips and gets out. *What the hell?*

I finish my shower and get dressed. I don't know where Aidan is. I don't hear him.

"Same old me again today."

I pack up my bag, but leave it in the bathroom corner. He's not in the bedroom. As I start down the stairs, I can hear him yelling. I can't make out the words or see who he is with. I sit down and try to listen. Everything is muffled. It sounds like it's coming from the kitchen. *Is it Marie?*

"Are you ready to go?"

He startles me. He is smiling but something is bothering him.

"Yes."

I stand and walk down the rest of the staircase. He puts out his elbow and I take it.

"Let's go then. The sooner you get there the sooner we can come home."

I see the smile tugging at the corner of his mouth. I feel the exact same way. He opens my door and away we go. I can't wait to get back here.

"What time would you like me to come back for you?"

"Give me an hour. That should be enough time."

I grab his knee.

He drops me at Sweet Elle at exactly ten o'clock. The girls are seated and waiting for me. They all smile when they see me.

"Look at you. You're glowing," Sam gushes.

"Hi Sam."

I flush beat red.

"What have you been doing? Tell us everything. I mean everything."

Kelly leans forward and smiles like she's listening intently.

I start at the beginning. I tell them about the flowers last week, the email marriage proposal, the Thursday kiss in the bar, the Friday dinner where I had to choose, the lovemaking, the house, the ocean, the yard, the pool, the incident with Zach, how scared I was, how Aidan took care of me. They all have their elbows on the table resting their chins in their hands. I am the only one speaking until I spill the last sentence.

"He said he loves me."

"What?" Simone yells across the table and slams her hand down.

"And I said I love him back," I murmur.

"Gaby, tell me you're kidding."

Simone is scolding me. I remind myself that she doesn't believe in love.

"I'm not kidding, Simone."

I try to stay strong in my voice.

"This soon?"

She sounds like it's a ridiculous possibility. She is rolling her eyes. Kelly and Sam are keeping quiet.

"Yes, Simone. Haven't you ever heard of love at first sight? Haven't you ever felt that pull towards someone? Haven't you ever felt so safe with someone that what your friends think doesn't matter? He does all of that for me, Simone. He saved me. He makes me feel safe and takes my stress away. He is my nirvana, Simone."

I'm getting angry. I only look at her when I talk.

"I feel special. I feel loved. I've not felt this happy in years. I'm so..."

I stop talking. She is squinting at me. I look to Kelly. She shrugs her shoulders. Sam does the same thing when I look at her.

"Neither of you have anything to say?" I look at Kelly and Sam again and put my hands up.

"We are happy for you Gaby, but..." Sam looks around the table.

"But what?" I take a deep breath. "You know what?"

I look down and pick up my phone and call Aidan.

"Forget this. What is wrong with you guys?"

Before anyone can answer, I say to Aidan, "I need you" and I hang up.

I dig in my purse and pull out two twenty dollar bills. I throw them on the table and stand up.

"Gaby, I'm sorry." Kelly looks at me.

She mouths "I'm sorry" again. I shake my head and walk out the front door.

Aidan is waiting for me. *How did he get here so fast?* He opens my door and I get in and slam it shut before he can.

"Please let's go," I say and he peels away from the curb.

"What happened, Gabriella? What's wrong?"

He sounds concerned.

"Nothing, I don't want to talk about it."

I turn to look at him.

"I want you to take me home and make love to me. I want to get lost in you. I need to escape from all this."

I point at my head.

"Please Aidan."

He squeezes my hand.

"Thank you for coming."

"I will do whatever you need, Gabriella. I'm here for you."

See? The girls *are* crazy. He loves me. He takes care of me. I lose all thought and will when he's inside me. I just want to get back.

What is wrong with Simone? She never supports me. She is so selfish. *And how could Kelly and Sam just sit there?* No one takes my side or sticks up for me. I need to call Lucca. He was ecstatic for me when he knew where I was. I should tell him about yesterday when I went to pick up my bag. I'm getting overwhelmed. How can I possibly get through the next few days at work? My breathing increases. I need to lie down. I lean forward and rub my face. *Can I just get through one day without all the bullshit?*

"Aaaahhhhhh!" I shriek.

"Gabriella, stop," Aidan scolds.

I look up to his face. His face looks stern.

"What the fuck happened back there?" he shouts.

I shake my head and start to cry.

"Look at me, Gabriella."

He grabs under my chin and I can't turn my head away. I open my eyes.

"Stop, I said."

He looks at me intently.

Is he mad? He puts up one finger and lifts his eyebrows. I sit silent and my tears stop. He lets go of my head but I don't move. He leans out the window to open the gates. I look straight ahead and he drives up to the door. I try to wipe my face. I don't want Alan to see I've been crying. *What is wrong with Aidan? Who was he yelling at earlier?* He parks and opens my door. He doesn't put his hand out. He squats down next to me and looks me in the eyes.

"I am going to take you inside and make love to you just like you asked. And trust me, you will get lost. You will escape. I will create a world for you so astonishing, so mind-boggling. You won't know what to do. And remember what I said you were going to do next time you come."

Yes, I remember. I sit and watch him with wide eyes. I am speechless. He puts his hand out and I take it. He pulls strongly and is one step ahead of me.

Alan opens the door just as we get to it but doesn't speak. We rush through it, up the stairs, and down the hall to his bedroom. He doesn't let go of my hand as he shuts the door and leads me to the end of the bed. He releases my hand and I just stand frozen in place.

"You will do exactly what I tell you. Do you understand?" he asks firmly.

"Yes."

I nod.

Oh my God. What is he going to do? What is he going to have me do?

He steps back.

"Take off your shoes, then your pants, then your shirt. Put them on the edge of the bed."

His face is stoic. I do exactly as he instructs in that order. I swallow to get rid of the lump in my throat. It's not working. My stomach is burning deep down.

"Good. Now remove your bra and put it there."

He points to the edge of the bed. I reach behind to unclasp my bra and add it to the pile. I stand and wait while he stares at me.

"Put your hands behind your head."

I clasp my hands behind my head and hold my arms up. He walks towards me and lifts my breast and takes my nipple into his mouth. He sucks hard. I put my arms down and grab his hair.

"I did not tell you to put your hands down, Gabriella."

Fuck.

I put my hands back behind my head. He hasn't let go of my breast. He sucks my nipple again with more pressure and I try not to move. He moves to my other nipple and sucks harder than he did before. He stops and circles it with his tongue, around and around as it grows harder.

"Aaaahhhhh!" I scream out.

He looks at me and shakes his head. *I'm not supposed to make any noises either?* He steps back.

"Take off your panties."

I put my hands down slowly. I hope I can use my hands to take them off. I drop them to the floor and step out of them. He points to the bed, and I bend down to pick them up. When I turn around to put them with the rest of my clothes, he slams against me and my body falls. The top of the bed is just below my breasts. I extend my arms forward to support myself.

"Spread your legs."

I open them.

"More, Gabriella."

I spread them wider. He reaches between my legs from behind and swirls his fingers, stretching and pulling.

"You are soaking, Gabriella. This pleases me very much."

He inserts his finger all the way. He holds it there for a moment as I push back against his hand. He withdraws and puts two fingers inside. They move in and out too slowly, and his thumb grazes my clitoris. I jerk in surprise. His thumb teases softly. He turns his hand so his fingers push on the front wall and I nearly collapse.

"Oh Aidan."

"If you make another sound, we will start over."

He removes his hand and my knees buckle.

"Turn around."

I stand and turn slowly to face him.

"Watch me while I remove my clothes. Do not close your eyes."

He starts with his shirt. He grabs the bottom and slowly starts to lift it. My knees are weakening. I need the bed to hold me up. As the shirt moves up his body, I see his rippled muscles. I want to touch him. He drops it to the floor. He stands staring in my eyes. He undoes the button of his pants and lowers the zipper. They slowly slide down his legs along with his boxers. My eyes widen at his erection. He is so large and solid. I want to reach out and taste it. He steps out of his pants and takes a step closer towards me. He puts his hand around his length and uses his thumb to spread the bead of moisture around the tip. My heart just skipped a beat. He lets go and grazes that thumb along my bottom lip.

"Lick your lips."

I lick my lips. He tastes so good. He bends down to kiss me. Our lips are caressing and our tongues are swirling. He isn't touching me anywhere else, only kissing me. I want to wrap my arms around him, but he hasn't told me to.

"On the bed."

He lifts me under my arms and helps me on the bed.

"Lean back on your elbows and bend your knees."

He pauses while I bend my knees.

"Now drop your knees to the side."

I am so exposed right now.

"Keep your head up, Gabriella."

He hops up on the bed next to me, and slides a vibrator from my knees down to my ankles. It slides back up to my knees, down my thighs, over my opening, and up the other leg. I try to control my breathing. He inches it closer to my opening and my breathing quickens. He caresses the lips and parts them with it. He rubs it up and down, over the clitoris, and then hovers over my opening. *Fuck. Push it in.* The vibration is making my knees quiver. I can't sit still. He moves his body closer and rests his erection on top of my thigh. It's in full view and throbbing. I feel myself open further to draw him in, but he doesn't move.

He slides the tip of the vibrator in and out of me, each time getting a little deeper. The deeper it goes, the slower he gets. My whole body feels swollen, my lips, my breasts, everything. He rocks and moves his hips back and forth, his erection rubbing my leg. He takes my nipple in his mouth. I put my head back and cry out. This is the best feeling I've ever known.

"Aidan, please."

I am breathing so fast. I can't swallow. He lets go of my nipple and stops rocking.

"I told you to keep your head up and to keep quiet."

He doesn't stop the movement of the vibrator. He clasps his hand around it with enough sticking out from his grip that it will fill me up. He withdraws it totally, and slams it into me. It stops with his hand hitting my clitoris and he drags it back. He slams it again, and again, and again. I am tearing at the blanket underneath me.

"You will not come right now, Gabriella."

He stops and moves his body between my legs.

I can't breathe or hold my body up anymore. I straighten my arms and lay my head back on the bed. I close my eyes and turn my head to the side. He leans down, puts his hand behind my neck and turns my head towards his. He kisses me deeply and I try to kiss him back.

"Turn over. Up on your knees."

Do I have the strength? He backs up and I turn and get on my hands and knees.

"Hold yourself up."

I want to lie down. I keep my arms straight.

"Open your legs more."

I open them enough that I can hold myself up without falling.

"That's it."

He grabs my hips and teases me with the tip of his erection sliding all around, up and down. He reaches underneath and grabs both breasts at the same time while his erection is floating over my opening. *Put it in. Put it in.* He squeezes each nipple so hard, at the same time he inserts just the head of his erection. I cry out. Before I can push back onto him, he backs up, still squeezing my nipples. The ache in my stomach is unbearable. He lets go and glides two fingers inside me. I cry out again. He withdraws them.

"Hold yourself up, Gabriella," he says sternly.

I can't. He reaches in front of me and I feel the vibrator tickling my clitoris.

"Aaaahhhhhh. Aidan, please."

I am gasping for air. I want to come. I need to let go. *Push me over, Aidan.* The tickling

stops.

"Remember what I said. You will not come."

The tickling starts again. It's too light. My entire body is full of sensation. He kisses and blows up and down my back. I want to fall forward. I feel the tip of his erection teasing me again. It pushes in and out, each time going a little deeper. I push back hard and engulf the entire length. I scream. This is too much. I stop and hold it at its deepest point. He bucks forward and thrusts in and pulls all the way out.

"Noooooo. Don't stop," I beg.

It slides in again painfully slow. It feels so hard. I squeeze myself around him. He pulls out. I shape my mouth in a tight circle and take deep breaths. My chest is pounding. He pounds it in, backs up and pounds again. *Don't stop. Don't stop.* He increases pressure with the vibrator and I yell out louder than ever before. He is still pounding and the vibrator stops. I hear it drop to the floor. His hands move from my hips and graze my breasts. One hand grabs my shoulder while he picks up speed. Two fingers from his other hand go into my mouth.

"Come Gabriella. Come now."

I suck his fingers hard, I close my eyes as tight as I can, and with one more thrust, I come strong and collapse to the bed. He slows and I enjoy the aftershocks of my orgasm, as he comes with me. I can't move. He falls next to me. His breathing is still fast.

"You are my princess, Gabriella."

Chapter 9

I wake a few hours later with Aidan holding me. *What time is it?* I am starving. That was absolutely insane. He was right. That was the best escape I could have ever imagined. *What is this man doing to me?* He has taken over my mind and body, making it do things, and taking it places I didn't think I could go. This is exactly what I want and need. He has uncovered desires beyond my imagination.

Is his body what I need to stop from spiraling? He said stop and I stopped. That is not the reaction I thought I would have. Something about him. I can't describe it. I hear him stirring. He squeezes me and I look back at him.

"How are you feeling, Gabriella?"

"I feel glorious, ecstatic, on top of the world."

I turn and hug him.

"I feel the exact same way."

He is so sweet.

"I do hope I helped you escape. And next time I say we are going to start over if you make another sound, I won't let you off so easy."

He smirks at me. Oh my God. *What does that mean?* He speaks so slow and sensual.   I smile back. I don't comment on what he just said. He is so beautiful. His eyes are so deep. *Is that hurt I saw before going away?* He strokes my face with his fingers and kisses me lightly on my lips.

"We only have a few hours. Let's go down and eat."

"I wish I could stay in your arms forever," I whisper and close my eyes.

"I'll see what I can do about that," he whispers back while kissing my forehead. "Lunch is waiting by the pool. Come on."

He sits up and looks down at me. How does he know lunch is by the pool? Weren't we just sleeping? He has some weird communication thing with his staff. I can't figure it out. Are they that in tune with his needs?

"It is? How do you know that?"

I squint my eyes. He winks back and pulls me off of the bed. Holding my hand he opens his bedroom door, and we are in the hallway totally naked. I pull back but he doesn't let go.

"Hey. We need robes or clothes or something."

I point back to the bedroom.

"No we don't."

He yanks my hand and I jerk forward.

We are walking down the stairs naked. I am looking to the sides of the staircase, down the hall, behind me, all over. Can anyone see us? He has a staff of I don't know how many people. He thinks I am going to believe that no one will ever see us.

"Please. This is uncomfortable," I whine a little.

He stops. *Shit.*

"I told you already that no one will see us. Our privacy is one hundred percent respected. You need to trust me. Don't worry about this again."

He is so serious. I feel nervous.

We hold hands all the way to the pool and he doesn't say anything else until we get there. I hope he's not mad. There is a large tray with a silver cover on the table. The places are set and the wine is poured. Did Marie set this up? Aidan pulls out my chair and I sit down. He moves his chair so he is right next to me. He moves his place setting over and his wine too. He lifts the cover and he smiles. There are fresh veggies, fruit, and finger sandwiches. They are still warm. I touch my wine glass, and it is ice cold. How is everything the temperature it should be when we were in bed ten minutes ago? I shake my head. This man is so puzzling.

He places food on his plate but not mine. What is he doing? He takes a piece of pineapple with his fork and brings it to my mouth. I lean forward and take it. He wants to feed me? *Ok.* He continues with veggies and more fruit. He takes bites for himself between mine. I really want a sandwich. I wait. There is one on the plate. I hope that's next. He must be angry. Why isn't he talking to me? I'm so confused. Should I say something? I choose not to.

We finish eating and he stands up.

"Finish your wine."

I swallow what is left in my glass and set it on the table. He puts his hand out and I take it. He is leading us to the pool. We slowly walk down the four steps into the warm water. It feels so nice. We walk a little farther and he stops when the water is just under my breasts. He kisses my lips lightly. He puts one hand behind my neck and leans me back into the water, submerging my hair. His other hand moves my hair around under the water and gently brushes it back by my forehead. All of my hair is wet now, but not my face. He stands me up and I watch as he does the same thing.

"You look amazing when you're wet."

He winks at me and flashes a smile. I've missed those dimples. I smile back feeling bashful all of a sudden. He wraps his arms around me and kisses me deep. I want to jump into his arms and wrap my legs around him, but he releases me.

"I want to show you something."

He pulls me out of the water. We start walking a path the opposite direction of the house. I hadn't seen this before. The cobblestone is surrounded by beautiful greenery and flower gardens. In the distance, I see a large cream colored hammock between two trees. It looks so high, like we need a ladder to climb into it.

Aidan turns to me and I raise my arm quickly to block the sun from shining in my eyes. Suddenly he squeezes his eyes closed, puts both hands over his face and bends forward.

"Please don't," he screams loudly.

I stare down at him. *Oh my God*. What is he doing? Please don't what?

"Aidan, what's wrong? Look at me," I plead.

He is shaking.

"Please don't hurt me."

He won't look up. His voice is high. He is scared.

"Aidan, I am not going to hurt you. What is wrong with you?"

I'm screaming. *Look at me damn it!* My hand is on his shoulder trying to shake him from this.

"Aidan," I scold, but he doesn't come out of his hiding.

I take a couple deep breaths. What is going on? Why is he doing this? Why would I hurt him? I realize that screaming is not the solution. I can't handle being screamed at when I'm spiraling.

I bend down and whisper in his ear.

"Baby, I will not hurt you. Please look at me."

I feel his muscles relax and he takes his hands away from his face. His eyes are wide looking at me, like he can't believe I'm here. He blinks like he doesn't recognize me. I take his hand while he stares.

"Gabriella," he whispers while closing his eyes.

"Yes."

We are both whispering. He stands up straight and hugs me so tight, I can't move.

"Thank God, Gabriella. I'm so glad you're here."

What? I'm confused.

"Tell me what's going on. Why did you cover your face? Why did you scream? Who do you think is going to hurt you?"

He better tell me. We are on the trail still naked. He looks around to the pool and over to the hammock. He must remember what we were doing. He puts his hand out for me to take. I hesitate. I want to talk about this.

"Tell me," I say before putting my hand in his.

"Let's relax in the hammock. I need to hold you. I will tell you there."

He points.

I take a deep breath and we begin to walk. He pushes the hammock back so I can slide on. I am in position and he gets on and lies next to me. His arm is under my neck and the other one around my waist. He hugs me tight again and kisses my head.

I peek up at him. *What isn't he telling me? What happened back there?* He looks into my eyes and shakes his head, closes his eyes and kisses my head again. He doesn't want to tell me. But after a scene like that, he has to. I need to know. Who has hurt him before? This is that hurt in his eyes I could see the first time I met him. He holds me tight like he will never let go. I wait until he is ready to speak. I tickle and caress his legs and chest. I love him and want to touch him lightly, lovingly.

We sway in the hammock listening to the ocean waves and the birds chirping. Work is taking over my thoughts. I can't think about that right now. These next few days are going to be hell. Maybe I shouldn't go home tonight if Aidan is like this? Should I stay? Would he want me to? Will I be able to get my work done?

He lets go and puts his hand behind his head and lies on his back. His other hand is still under my neck. As he moves, I turn my body to his. There is that magnet again. I hug him.

"Gabriella," he pauses and I look to him.

He has his eyes closed.

"Do you remember when I said I've been alone here for five years?"

He turns so we are facing each other and we are looking in each other's eyes. I nod. He swallows.

"I have not had a woman here in five years. I used to live with someone. But she..." he shakes his head like he doesn't want to continue. "She used to hurt me, Gabriella."

What? A woman used to hurt him? Hurt him how?

"What did she do to you?"

My lump in my throat has returned. His eyes look so sad.

"I don't want to talk about the details, Gabriella. I just wanted you to know why I responded the way I did back there. When you raised your arm like that..."

He looks like tears are forming.

"When you raised your arm it brought back memories, very bad memories. I'm sorry."

He is whispering. I want to know more and ask questions. I am trying to process all of this.

"I'm sorry that I can't say anymore."

He hugs me tight to his body.

I feel my own tears forming. What has happened to him? Who did this to him? How could he just let some woman beat him? *I don't understand.*

He shakes me from my thoughts when he speaks again.

"My world has been very lonely since then. I've withdrawn. It's been very repetitive. I was just getting through one day at a time. But then, I saw you in Lucca's truck. You were just sitting there in the middle of all your friends. You looked so quiet and sad. They were all hanging out the windows, but there you were. Something about you. Something was pulling me towards you. I felt like you were someone I could try to trust with again. You looked so beautiful that night," he pauses.

I thought I looked so plain that night.

"You brought me out of my shell. I had to meet you. And now. Now my world is in disarray because of you. I can't sleep. I can't work. I can't think of anything else."

He touches my nose and whispers, "Just you."

I smile and my tears are forming, but for his love, not his fear.

"I love you so much. I don't want to be without you, Gabriella. You and your disarray is exactly what I need. I will protect you forever if you let me. My love for you has taken over."

He kisses me and adds, "Disarray love."

"I love you too."

A single tear drops down my cheek. He kisses it away.

"Come here baby."

He pulls me off of the hammock and leads us to the sandy beach. We are walking towards the waves. I turn back to look at the house. His property is so impressive. There isn't another house in sight.

"Do you remember our first walk on the beach?" he asks as his fingers graze over my stomach.

Tingles spread like wildfire throughout my body.

"Yes I do," I say with a big smile.

"I liked that."

"So did I. I wanted you so bad that night," I say softly.

Is he trying to get my mind off of the beatings? It's working. But the hurt in his eyes reminds me.

"Come on."

He yanks my hand and sprints over to the solid part of the sand. It's wet but not squishy to walk in. He lets go of my hand and falls to his knees. He traces his finger spelling something in the sand. The sky is getting darker above us. We should go in soon before it rains. I can't believe he just said all those things. I turn back to him and he has written in huge letters DISARRY LOVE with a big heart around it. He puts his hand out and pulls me down. I smile. He makes me so happy. He is so romantic. I lean forward on my hands and knees.

He slaps my behind and I yelp.

"Hey!"

He laughs. I'm so glad to see him laugh. I hope he is feeling himself again. I will wait to discuss that other woman. I lean forward again and trace a big "A" with a slash and a big "G" next to it. I draw a heart around and put an arrow through it. He smiles and pulls me to hug him.

He leans over to whisper in my ear.

"Love letters in the sand baby."

I melt all over.

"Let's go back."

We arrive at the table where we had lunch. There is a new bottle of chilled wine waiting. I shake my head and laugh. It always shocks me that everything is ready for him. How does the staff have his food perfectly hot and his drinks perfectly cold at the exact moment he needs them? Is that what all his money buys? Servants to anticipate your every need? I laugh out loud and think about that crazy boss lady in The Devil Wears Prada.

"What's so funny?"

He looks to me.

"Nothing, you're just so amazing Aidan."

"You amaze me too."

"Thank you."

I'm feeling very naked right now. I really need to get home and get some work done. And I can't wait to tell Lucca everything.

"Put your hands back on that stool."

He points. What? Why? I turn and see a bar stool behind me. *Was that there before?* I reach behind and put my hands on it.

"Take a step forward and lean back."

What does that mean? I try to do as he says.

"I mean arch your back so your breasts are out."

Oh. I push my breasts forward and put my head back. What is he going to do?

"Close your eyes."

They close and I feel a freezing sensation over my nipples, and I squeak in surprise as shocks spread. The sensation stops and starts again. I open my eyes and see him pouring cold wine over my breasts. He takes a nipple in his mouth and swirls his tongue licking up the wine. He sucks hard and releases when I cry out. He repeats with the other nipple. The cold to warm sensation is exquisite. He teases and tugs at each while tickling my thighs. I want to lean back on the stool. He slides a finger between my legs and plays in my heat too lightly. He stops and moves his body closer while pushing my legs together. He stands directly in front of me and I feel his erection at my stomach. He steps back and slides it between my thighs. He rocks slowly as it glides around in my juices. I arch my back which puts my breasts almost in his mouth. He doesn't touch them, just continues playing.

When he backs up, he grazes my clitoris and my whole body shudders. Each time I moan, he stops and backs away. I am panting. *Where is he going?*

He turns and slides a finger inside of me and massages.

"Let's go inside."

My eyes widen. I want him to make love to me like he did before lunch. I can handle that again.

We walk to the TV room. He sits down on the couch and pulls me next to him. He finds a football game and smiles at me. I try to push his back to the couch, but he shakes his head. What is he doing? What is his game? I sit back and close my eyes. I try to catch my breath. *He is so frustrating.* I'm taking loud breaths to get his attention. He squeezes my knee and smiles. He must know he is driving me crazy. I close my eyes and let out a loud sigh.

His lips are on mine and I startle. He licks lightly and circles his tongue around my mouth. I reach to touch him, but he backs to the floor. He positions himself between my knees and pulls me forward. He licks my inner thighs and up to my opening. I'm throbbing and dripping. His tongue touches so lightly that my knees quiver. He sucks my clitoris gently, and then pushes his tongue inside. It's too light, too soft. He stands up. *No, where is he going?*

He pulls me up and we walk through the foyer. I see my car out of the window. *Shit.* I need to get home. I don't want to leave this naked beautiful man, but I have to. I look down. He stops and lifts my head with his finger under my chin. I watch him as he looks out to my car. He knows I need to go too. He kisses me again deeper this time, as his fingers linger between my legs. He bends and picks me up and I squeal. He carries me up the staircase, and kisses me the whole way. His tongue licks my lips, then sucks them and enters my mouth. It is so slow and sensual. I don't want him to stop. He has me under his spell again.

He shuts the door with his foot and lowers me to his bed, but he doesn't get up here with me. He just stands to the side and tickles me with his fingertips. I reach for him.

"I know you need to leave," he says.

"I know. I don't want to though."

"You could stay."

He winks.

"I have so much work to do before the morning. I'm afraid if I stay here, I won't get much done. Then I will be more stressed than I already am."

"You know I can take your stress away. Stay."

"Please make love to me."

I close my eyes. My body is full of sensation. His fingers are still tickling up and down my body.

"If you're not staying, then I want you on the edge until I can see you again."

My eyes fly open. *What?* I am going to explode. Thunder crackles outside and he stops tickling me. He looks in my eyes, and I see the hurt returning.

"You should go baby."

I pack my bag and check my phone. I have texts from Sam and Kelly asking if I'm all right. I text them back quickly and say I'm fine. I have nothing else to say to them right now. When I come out of the bathroom, the bedroom door is open. Aidan is waiting for me at the bottom of the staircase. What's the hurry? He wants me to leave? He didn't try very hard to make me stay. I surely could have been convinced. I shake my thoughts. I should get home before the storm hits.

When I get to the bottom stair, his hand is extended for me. I take it and we walk to the door.

"I will pick you up Friday evening, Gabriella."

"Yes."

"I will call you in the morning."

"OK."

"Disarray love," he whispers as he hugs me goodbye.

I kiss his lips.

When I get home, I stop at the door. Last time I was here Zach had me pinned against this door. I haven't thought about him since. I want to go back to my happy place. I want to go back to Aidan's house and be safe in his arms. He said he will protect me forever if I let him. I close my eyes and smile and unlock the door. Lucca is waiting for me on the couch. He jumps up.

"Gaby! I've been dying for you to get home. I couldn't wait to see you so you can tell me everything."

He hugs me.

"You are glowing, Gaby. You look so happy."

He holds me back at arm's length and looks at me.

"I am?"

Wow. Aidan's spell stays with me even now.

"You were so weird on the phone. I am so glad you were with Aidan. I mean look at you. You're simply radiant."

I feel radiant. I feel happy.

We each take a corner of the couch and put our feet up next to each other. I start by telling him how I felt when I left here and had to choose which restaurant to go to Friday night. I tell him my anguish in the car. Was I making the right decision? I said that we didn't even stay for dinner and about the limo the next day, and what happened when we got here with Zach.

"Ah! I hate him so much. I am so glad you didn't decide to marry Zach."

"Me too. Aidan is so sweet. I miss him already."

I do miss him.

I continue with how I fell to the ground and woke up in Aidan's arms. I discuss my worries that Aidan will hate me eventually and what Zach said before he left. I briefly tell him about my escape from reality in Aidan's bedroom, and how he's so weird with his staff, and the ocean, the house, the pool, the sand, the disarray love, how he makes me feel, all the sweet things he's said to me about protection and watching over me, everything. Well not about the other woman. I want to know more about that before I talk to Lucca about it. I gush about my perfect weekend.

"Wait, I forgot to tell you about brunch this morning."

I roll my eyes.

"I'm surprised you went to brunch today."

"Well I shouldn't have. The girls weren't very supportive. They think it's too soon, that I haven't known Aidan long enough."

I smile.

"I actually walked out on them."

I laugh. *Simone's face was priceless*.

"What did you do when you left?" Lucca asks.

"Aidan was waiting for me outside."

"He was? He waited the whole time you were in there?"

"No," I shake my head. "I called and said I needed him, and he was there within minutes. Now that you say that, he did get there rather quickly. It's like I say I need him and he's just there."

"Remember what I told you Gaby? Thursday night when you went to sleep?"

"I think so."

Tell me again.

"True love always wins. Your stories about love letters in the sand and the disarray love, and the holding hands all night."

He leans in and whispers, "That sounds like true love."

I close my eyes and hug myself. I go to sleep happy in my bed listening to the relaxing thunderstorm.

When I get to work, Lexi is waiting with my coffee. She smiles as I walk in and hands it to me.

"Thank you, Lexi. How was your weekend?" I ask.

"It was fine. You look different today Ms. Woods."

I do?

"What does that mean, Lexi?"

Does she mean good different or bad different? Do I look like I've had the best sex of my life, all weekend long?

"You just look happy. You had a smile on your face as soon as you walked in."

I guess that would be different. I'm not usually smiling on a Monday morning entering work I suppose. I smile back at her.

"Yes, I feel happy."

Why can't I stop smiling?

"Mr. Nathan is here already and waiting in your office."

Mr. Nathan is our biggest client. I do whatever I need to keep his business with us. If he took his business away, we would fold. We've been preparing for his arrival.

"Shit. What? He's early."

Damn, I was hoping for an hour to prepare.

"Yes, he is. He insisted on waiting in there and not in the conference room as I suggested. I hope that's ok."

She looks down. Does she think I will be mad at her? I know how persistent and demanding Mr. Nathan can be. Of course she had no choice but to do as he asked.

"It's fine. Thank you."

I close my office door behind me and set my bag and coffee on my side table. My flowers are still covering my desk. I smile and flush. If I sit in my chair he won't be able to see me.

"Good morning Mr. Nathan. Nice to see you again."

I try to sound pleasant even though I am annoyed he is here before me.

"Gaby."

"Give me one moment."

I put up my finger and pick up the phone.

"Lexi, the dendros in here, get rid of them. Now."

I slam the phone down. I don't want Zach's flowers in here. My cell phone rings. It's Aidan. Mr. Nathan looks frustrated that I am not giving him my full attention. Well what does he expect? I need to get settled in on a Monday morning and he is here staring at me. I answer.

"Good morning sweetheart," Aidan says with glee in his voice.

He sounds so happy. My heart is beating out of my chest just at the sound of his voice.

"Good morning."

I want to be back in his bed and not at work. Lexi knocks at the door and sneaks in to remove the flowers.

"How was your night?"

It was lonely without you.

"It was nice to catch up with Lucca."

Lucca is on my side, unlike the girls.

"Good. I was thinking. I cannot wait until Friday to see you again."

I don't want to wait until then either. Mr. Nathan stands up and looks in my eyes.

"Um, Aidan? Could I call you back at lunchtime? I have a client in my office."

Fuck.

"Fine," he sighs and we hang up.

"Sorry about that. Are you ready for the conference today?"

Mr. Nathan has my attention now.

"I'm more concerned with tonight's activities, Gaby."

I knew that's what he was going to say.

"Yes sir. I have everything arranged just like last year."

Mr. Nathan flies in once a year for this. I arrange his nighttime schedule as well while he's here. He gives me a lot of responsibility which is very stressful. If something doesn't go perfectly as planned, he gets very angry. We can't lose his business.

"I hope so."

He nods and gives me a stern look. I smile. He is so intimidating.

"The schedule for the day ends at five-thirty, sir. Dinner is at six-thirty, and I will drop you at The Shut Eye at nine. Everything is arranged."

"Is she available again this year?"

"Yes."

He requested the same girl he had last year, Maggie. She was hard to book, but I did it. It took weeks of convincing, but I pulled it off.

"Good. You will be accompanying me this year."

What? I will not go into The Shut Eye. No way.

"Um."

I'm at a loss for words.

"You will not drop me at nine. You will get me at eight-thirty from dinner and then escort me into The Shut Eye."

He is giving me the stare down. I can't say no, but I can't go there. I've heard crazy stories about that place.

"I would like you to watch, Gaby."

Watch? Watch what exactly? *I can't do this.*

"Um."

I still don't know what to say to him.

"Got it?"

He won't break eye contact. I can't have him angry at me. *Fuck.* My heart is pounding.

"Yes, sir," I murmur.

"Excellent. I will see you at five-thirty."

He claps his hands together, and turns to leave. When the door closes, I sink in my chair to catch my breath. What did I just agree to? What have I done? I want to call Aidan back, but I can't tell him about tonight. I haven't even told him that I arrange evenings like this, and now I have to attend one? I am horrified. I need to do as Mr. Nathan asks, or I will lose my job. I love my job. I've worked so hard to get where I am.

"Aaaahhhhhh!"

This is nuts.

The rest of the day is full of meetings and sessions. Lexi comes in and out to update me on the progress of each. She brings me lunch and I take a five minute break to inhale my food. We work through the schedule for tomorrow, and where the dinners are for each night. I look at the time in the corner of my computer and it's five-fifteen.

"Fuck!"

I jump out of my chair. I intercom Lexi.

"Lexi are you still here?"

"Yes ma'am."

"I need to go now for Mr. Nathan. Can you finish up?"

"Yes, I will see you in the morning."

She is the best assistant anyone could ask for. She is helpful and so discreet with Mr. Nathan's preferences. We never discuss unless in the walls of my office. No one else knows what we do for him, which is demanding, but we have each other to vent to.

I pick up Mr. Nathan at the end of the sessions. I have to wait while he showers and dresses for dinner. He asks me to stay in the sitting area of his suite. I prefer to wait in the hall, but he insisted. I look around his room and see his suit laid out for the evening. Mr. Nathan is probably in his upper forties, with salt and pepper hair, very tall and muscular. He has the face of a younger man, but his hair makes him look his age. He is very powerful and arrogant, and acts so deserving. I roll my eyes and laugh to myself. How is a man so good looking and powerful needing to arrange dates like Maggie? I wonder if he has a girlfriend or wife back home. *Oh, I hope not.* I don't want to be part of his straying.

He makes me sit through dinner with him. I am the only woman and everyone is probably wondering what I'm doing here. I listen as they discuss deals they are working on. I don't want to be here, and I really don't want to go to The Shut Eye. I'm getting nervous. My stomach is aching and I want to go back to yesterday and escape again with Aidan.

Aidan! Shit! I didn't call him back. I pull out my cell phone and Mr. Nathan taps my hand with his index finger. I look to him and he shakes his head. *Fuck.* I need to hear Aidan's calming voice. I want to tell him where I'm going. He could get me out of this couldn't he? I put my phone back in my purse. I didn't even have a second to see if I had any missed calls or texts.

Mr. Nathan leans in and whispers.

"Turn your phone off for the night."

No. I don't want to. I nod and reach in and push the power button.

Dinner ends promptly at eight-thirty. We are waiting outside for the car to bring us to The Shut Eye. The driver pulls up and we both get in the back. I look down to my hands. My breathing increases and I lean forward putting my head in them. I start to rub my face, but Mr. Nathan interrupts me.

"Gaby, are you ready for tonight?"

Ready? What does he mean?

"Yes."

I nod. I feel like all blood has left my face. I am anxious.

"Excellent."

He smiles at me. I want to ask him why I'm going, but decide against it.

It's a short ride. We don't speak the rest of the way. As we get closer, my stomach ache increases. I'm starting to panic. I listen to Mr. Nathan take different phone calls, which sound so boring. I wish he didn't come in for the conference anymore.

The driver opens my door and I get out. The Shut Eye looks like a big white house from the outside. There is no sign indicating it's a business. It just looks like some rich guy's mansion. I've dropped Mr. Nathan off here before but have never gone in. He nods with his head towards the door and we make our way up the walk and knock. A woman wearing black leather shorts with a black leather bra with white thigh high silky stockings answers the door. *Holy shit.* I must look so out of place here. I look down at what I'm wearing. Mr. Nathan and this woman nod at each other and she gestures to come in with her hand. She shuts the door behind us. I can't swallow.

Straight ahead is a long hallway with multiple doors on each side. Some are open and some are closed. The lighting is soft, and there is instrumental music playing. The music is kind of loud, but not so loud that you can't hold a conversation. It smells of sex and sweat, with a hint of air freshener, like they try to spray something to mask the scents. I might be sick.

"Maggie will be upstairs and ready in twenty minutes," the woman says to Mr. Nathan.

He nods and walks to the first room. I follow slowly behind him. He stops at the door and looks in and I stand next to him. *Oh my God.* My stomach sinks. What kind of place is this? There are ten people in there. Five couples having sex at the same time. I can't breathe. I back up, but he pulls my arm.

"Give it a minute and you won't be able to look away if you try," he whispers to me.

There is moaning from all of them. My knees feel weak. I scan the room. The first man I see has something tied around his scrotum and something in his mouth. The woman in front of him looks like she is pumping air through a tube to whatever it is. It's some sort of gag I think. She is stroking his erection, and then scratches his underside with her nails. It looks like he screams, but I don't hear it. She drops to her knees and pulls on the tie. His eyes squeeze shut. She applies lubricant to a vibrator and slides it between his legs.

There is a woman next to them sitting on a table with her feet flat and her knees bent. She leans back against the wall and spreads her thighs. She is fully exposed. A man plays between her legs and she shrieks as her legs tremble. She grips the edges of the table and a long moan escapes as she comes. I can see her labia pulsating. The man strokes himself and grins. He gets on the table and starts to enter her. I can't watch this. I try to look away. There is another woman wearing a belt of some kind. It looks like brass and has a lock and keyhole on its side. She is fucking a man with her mouth. A woman dressed in a short maid's uniform is walking around this room with her hard breasts exposed. She is taking orders and she squeezes some of the women's nipples as she walks by them. This is *crazy*. I can't be here.

My heart is pounding. I can't believe what I'm seeing. There are some other people in the halls too that just move from room to room. Mr. Nathan pulls my arm. I close my eyes and look down as he pulls me to the next room. This is too much. I want to leave. Why does he come here? He nudges me. I open my eyes and we are looking into the room across the hall from the first one. There is a woman with a cuff around her ankle and she is chained to a big ring in the floor. She has a bar between her ankles that holds her legs wide open. She is bent forward with both hands on the floor. A man behind her has a paddle. He hits her behind and she cries out.

"May I have another please?"

He plays between her legs and she grunts and purrs. I shake my head and look to Mr. Nathan. He smiles out of the side of his mouth. That looks interesting. I feel a pain deep in my stomach. I am becoming aroused by the spanking. I look away. I see a whipping post in the corner. There are three wooden posts that meet at the top. A woman is tying a man's hands in front of him and she instructs him to lean back. She lifts his bound hands and ties them to where the posts meet at the top. She opens his legs and ties them to the other posts. His eyes are unfocused, but he doesn't look at all scared. I swallow over the lump in my throat. I need to go home.

The next room has a woman with knee high leather boots on, and a short black leather skirt with the bottom cut out of the back of it. It's the weirdest thing I've ever seen. A tall man directs her to lean over what looks like a massage table. She leans forward and he ties her hands to the end. He doesn't hesitate for a second, and he spanks her hard. I see her tuck her head under and she lets out a muffled cry. He spanks her again and again and again. Her cries get louder, but he doesn't slow down. When he does stop, he reaches between her legs.

He withdraws his hand and says "good girl" as he rubs his wet fingers together. He spanks her again one time, then his hand goes between her legs and she moans. Another spank, another touch. He repeats it a few more times. I actually see her entire body relax and now she moans even as he spanks. She raises her behind up to his hand. She is enjoying this. *I am enjoying this.* He instructs her not to come until he commands her to. To come on command? Aidan did that to me. Mr. Nathan was right, I can't look away. I feel excited watching this. I don't know if I could endure any of it, though.

I hear a deep man's voice coming from the next room. There is a couple in the middle and a man in the corner. The man in the corner is narrating the entire scene.

"She rubs his erection with the cane up and down. He puts his head back and breathes deep. She pushes him down to the couch as she stands in front of him. She takes him in her mouth one time. He moans loudly. He is throbbing, needing more. She moves the cane between her legs and uses both hands to circle it in her arousal. Her breath is quickening. She tells him he cannot move from the couch. He is only to watch her. She removes the cane and sways it beneath his nose. He inhales her scent and he stiffens even more. She slides it back between her legs and puts one leg up on the couch next to him so he can see everything. Her labia are beginning to quiver. She moves back and forth against it while increasing pressure. She squeezes her nipple with one hand and moves faster with the other as she gets closer to climax. She closes her eyes and focuses on coming. She screams loudly, throws the cane to the floor and leans forward so he can reach her. She tells him to put his two fingers inside so he can feel her come. His eyes roll back as he drives himself to orgasm. She arches her back and rides it out."

The man's voice is so slow and sensual. It's kind of hot.

The maid from the first room tells Mr. Nathan that Maggie is ready for him.

He mumbles in my ear.

"You take the car home. You've seen enough for tonight. I'll see you in the morning and we will do this again tomorrow."

He walks away before I can respond. I swallow and take a deep breath. I walk the long hallway to the door. I don't look in any rooms as I pass them. But I hear the sounds, the music, the screaming, the pleasure, the moaning. I try to block them out. *Get me out of here!*

The driver is waiting outside. I shut the door and give him my address. What was I doing in there? I shouldn't have come. This is what Mr. Nathan does every year when he comes into town? This is what I arrange for him? I had no idea. That woman getting spanked. She was enjoying herself. Who are those women back there? And that man on the post? *Holy shit.*

It's storming out again tonight. I am exhausted. I need to go to sleep.

Lucca is in bed when I get home. I leave him a quick note on the fridge saying that we need to talk. He will be gone in the morning when I get up. Has he heard of The Shut Eye? I can't even think straight. This has been the longest day. I don't want to do this again tomorrow, or ever.

I wake feeling like I'm hung-over. I did not get enough sleep last night. I don't want to go to work. I miss Aidan.

"Aidan."

Shit!

I find my purse on the floor and grab my phone. I hug it to me as it powers on. I have two voice mails and five texts. Simone texted me once. It says:

IM SORRY

Wow. That probably took all of her strength to say that. I will call her later.

The rest are from Aidan.

Lunch – you didn't call me
Dinner – still no call
Where R U
I will be waiting for you when

you get home

Waiting for me? He wasn't here last night when I got here. What happened? I find his name and call him and it goes directly to voice mail. Why is his phone off? Why did he say he would be here but he wasn't? Oh I wish he had been here to hold me all night. Should I tell him what I did? Will he be angry?

That woman raising her behind to get spanked, I can't get her out of my mind. I was getting aroused watching her. For a moment, I wished I was in her position. It looked so enjoyable. I wanted to trade places. Why isn't Aidan answering his phone? My mind is racing. This woman lingers in my thoughts.

I hope Aidan is all right. Maybe he is embarrassed about the woman that hurt him. He doesn't want to talk about it. How did she hurt him and why did he let her? *I want to get spanked, and play with a cane.*

"Stop."

I can't focus. I take a hot shower and submerge my face under the water. I don't want to see Mr. Nathan again. I hope he doesn't discuss anything today. I will tell him that I can't go tonight. He will have to accept that. I feel dirty. I should have showered last night. I probably smell like that place. I close my eyes and imagine myself leaning over the massage table. I shudder. I get dressed and finish my hair and makeup.

"Same old me again today," I mumble and I'm out the door with five minutes to spare.

Lexi is waiting with my coffee. She is squinting at me. Does she know what I've been fantasizing about? *No of course not.* I shake my head and laugh.

"Good morning, Lexi."

I smile.

"Good morning, Ms. Woods. Mr. Nathan is waiting in your office again this morning."

What?

"He is? How long has he been here?" *Why is he here already?*

"About twenty minutes ma'am."

Fuck!

"Thank you, Lexi."

I close my office door behind me. He doesn't stand to greet me. He is sitting and smiling at me with a devilish grin.

"Good morning, Mr. Nathan."

Why are you here?

"Gaby. Good morning."

He's still grinning. I look down at my watch.

"Sir. Did you need something before the day starts?"

"Just wanted to report that Maggie came through again. She is quite a trooper. Make sure she is available again tonight. Same time."

He winks. *Trooper? What did he do to her?*

"Um. I'll see what I can do."

Lexi will have to call.

"See what you can do?"

He is crinkling his forehead.

"You will ensure that Maggie is available at nine. You will join me for dinner and escort me there."

I put my finger up, but he won't let me speak.

"Otherwise, next year I will not be attending your conference. Do you know what that means Gaby?"

Yes, that means he will take his business elsewhere. I can't let that happen.

"She will be ready at nine."

He needs to get out of my office so I can start working.

"Excellent."

He claps his hands together. I hate when he does that. He always gets his way and he knows it. *Asshole.* I smile and he leaves. My cell phone rings. It's Aidan. *Yes!*

"Hi."

I'm so glad he called.

"Hey baby. I've been trying to…"

"Hold on."

I interrupt him. Mr. Nathan comes back into my office without knocking. *What now?*

"I'm sorry Aidan. I need to call you back."

I can't wait until Mr. Nathan flies home.

"Listen to me. You need to get rid of that job," Aidan says angrily and hangs up.

Shit.

I throw my phone to my desk. He is mad at me. I need to talk to him. I put my head between my hands and take a deep breath. I look up and smile to Mr. Nathan.

"Yes, Mr. Nathan?"

I'm trying to not look annoyed.

"Gaby, wear something more fitting for tonight, will ya?"

Fitting? Does he mean tight or fit for the venue or?

"Sir, I can't..."

"Gaby," he shakes his head, "come with me."

He crooks his finger. He leads me to the first session of the day. He is making me sit through this. I know all this. I organized it. This is doing me no good to sit here. He is punishing me. I haven't arranged Maggie yet.

"I need my..." he cuts me off again by putting his finger to his lips.

I need my phone to make arrangements for Maggie, or have Lexi do it, and call Aidan back. He wants me to quit my job?

"You will be spending the day with me," Mr. Nathan whispers.

No!

I sit through the morning sessions and his working lunch. I start to daydream during the afternoon sessions. *Oh Aidan.* May I have another please? I'm lifting my behind for him to spank me again. It feels so good. His fingers exploring between my legs amid each strike. I close my eyes and put my head back. Mr. Nathan nudges me with his elbow. It's break time. The only time I can use the restroom. He brings me to my office at five-thirty when the day is done.

"I've had Lexi get you something to wear after dinner."

He did what? He hands me a small bag.

"You will change after we eat."

My stomach falls. How can I get out of this?

"Let's go. I'm hungry."

I carry the small bag and my purse out to the car. We have the same driver as last night. I haven't arranged for Maggie or called Aidan back. Today is a disaster. I sit forward and lean my head on my hands. I hear Mr. Nathan laugh quietly. *I hate him.*

Dinner is all about his business and deals again but with different people this time. I peek in my purse and see my phone. I know if I take it out, I'll get the look of death again. I feel sick. I don't want to go back. I might throw up. I stand to use the restroom but Mr. Nathan pulls me back down.

"Sir, I need to use the restroom," I whisper.

"You can wait till we get there. You will change then too."

He glares at me.

We finish dinner and he shakes his head when he sees I didn't eat hardly anything. I can't swallow so there is no way I will keep any food down. He leads me to the car and we get in.

"Gaby, you will change when we arrive. We will be early so I can see you before I meet Maggie."

Fuck, Maggie. I didn't call. He didn't give me a chance to. Did he do this on purpose?

The same woman answers the door. She looks confused. I assume because she isn't expecting us this time. She gestures us to come in and closes the door. Same smell, same sounds, same music. I lean on the wall for support. Mr. Nathan looks at me out of the corner of his eye.

"Maggie at nine!" he directs the woman.

"She is not available sir."

His head whips around to me. His eyes are wide. He looks furious.

"What?" he asks with clenched teeth.

"You didn't give me a cha..." I try to explain.

He gives her a fake smile and pulls me by my elbow to the corner of the foyer.

"You assured me that Maggie would be available. I am not pleased. I saw your face flush last night when you were watching the woman with the spanking skirt. It's your turn. Go change. Now!" he demands, still through clenched teeth.

My eyes widen. I can't breathe. I just nod and he directs me to the bathroom. I close the door behind me and sink to the floor. Thankfully, it's only big enough for one person. I want to cry. I want to scream. My heart is pounding. I sit up, only far enough to throw up in the toilet next to me. I breathe heavily through my mouth, trying to settle myself. What does he want to do to me? What will he make me do? Why is he doing this? I open the small bag and pull out a short sleeve white button up blouse. It's so short. It may not even cover my breasts. No way am I putting this on. I reach in again and see black. I sit back. I can't take it out of the bag. I know what it is before I even pull it out. It's a spanking skirt, just like that other woman. *Oh my God...* I rub my face and tears start to fall. I'm sweating. I start to rock and there is a loud knock on the door which makes me jump.

"Now!" Mr. Nathan yells through the door.

"One minute."

I change quickly. I leave my panties in the bag. I look ridiculous. I can't do this. How can I get out of this? Mr. Nathan scares me in more ways than one. I'm starting to spiral, as an attack begins. The smells and sounds are taking over. The music is even louder in here. I can't concentrate. I see my phone in my purse. *I need to call Aidan.* My hands are so sweaty, I almost drop the phone. I find his name and push it.

"I. Said. Now."

Mr. Nathan bangs on the door. I don't respond to him.

"Gabriella. What the fuck is..?"

Aidan is yelling too. I can hardly hear him over my heart throbbing in my ears.

"I need you," I say softly.

"Where?" He snaps.

"The Shut Eye," I whisper.

I squeeze my eyes as tight as I can. *Don't be mad. Don't be mad.*

"What the fu..? I'm coming for you."

He hangs up.

I stand but my knees are shaking. I lean against the wall and take one final breath before opening the door. Mr. Nathan has a hand on each side of the door frame. I jump and almost fall back. He grabs my elbow and pulls me into the hallway.

"About fucking time," he snaps, "give me that."

He grabs the small bag and my purse. He pulls me to the last door on the left side of the hall. This door was closed last night. He shoves me inside and slams the door behind us.

Chapter 10

"Face the wall in the corner," Mr. Nathan points, "and do not look at me."

I look down and go to the corner. It smells like wet wood and sex in here. I need to throw up again. I listen closely. He is mumbling something to himself, but I can't make out what he is saying. I hear the door open and then close slowly. So slowly like someone turned the knob and placed it shut. The door is on the opposite side of where I hear Mr. Nathan. Someone else must be in the room. The lump in my throat is present. *What is he going to do to me?* I'm sweating. I can't do this. The person who entered shuffles their feet along the floor. My heart is bursting out of my chest. I lean forward so my head can rest against the wall.

"Up straight," he commands.

I straighten. I hear chains or metal clinking together. I can't tell what it is. It sounds like a key unlocking something. I cringe at the sound.

"Nice ass on that one," another man's voice says. It's deeper than Mr. Nathan's voice. I am so ashamed in this skirt. I want to die.

"I know."

"So firm too. This will bounce off nicely."

"Ha, yep."

"And look at those tits. You sure can pick'em."

"I've had my eyes on her for years." *What?!*

"I can't wait to suck them. Pointing right at me. Mmmmm. Mmmmmm."

I lean forward again and something hits my behind. I cry out. It stings so badly.

"I said up straight bitch."

I stand up. I can't do this. I can't listen to this. What are they going to do? Why? What? Who is that? I'm becoming disoriented. I take a few deep breaths and concentrate on standing. I need some water. I might fall over.

One of them trails their fingers up both of my arms. It feels so gross. They go back down and grab my wrists abruptly. They place one on top of the other and I hear handcuffs clink into place, and my stomach falls and I stop breathing. They are too tight. I try to wriggle out of them, but I can't move.

"You're not going anywhere," he breathes into my ear. My head falls forward.

"Remember, you will not look at me and you will not look at him. You will do what we say."

I feel faint. I can't respond.

The other voice says, "There's a couch over there. Walk to it while looking at the floor. Get on it, on your knees and face that way." I can see a hand point to the left.

"Lean down and face the inside and stick your ass up in the air. Knees at the end and your feet up. Go."

The other one demands, "Now!"

I can't tell who is who anymore. They are talking so slowly. I start to walk towards the couch. I try to peek at them, but they are positioned behind me. I trip and fall to the ground. I am too weak, too scared, too lightheaded. They pick me up at my waist.

"Now," they yell and someone slaps my behind.

I make it to the couch and get into position. I lean on the back of it as my tears leak out. This is too hard without my hands free. My wrists hurt as I try to pull out of them. I am bent over and feeling exposed. My hands are bound behind me. This couch smells of old sex and sweat. It's so rough against my face, I'm gagging.

I hear them whisper between each other. They have moved back and I can't hear them clearly. The clinking of their belts startles me. I turn to look out and they both have their pants off. One of them is stroking themselves up and down. I hear the other one hit something on the palm of his hand. I scream and they laugh at me.

"Please don't," I whimper.

"Look, she's begging already," one says.

I close my eyes tightly and face the inside of the couch. I'm starting to spiral more. I want to rub my face but I can't move. I hear muffled voices and laughing and cheering, then moaning. Are there more people in the room? The music has gotten louder and the other sounds trail off. I'm drifting. I want to plug my ears. Zach's words come back to me. *She's a bitch, he will never bring you back down, he will hate you*. His last words circling through my mind. *He will hate you, he will hate you, he will hate you.* It won't stop. *How can anyone love you when you're like this? He will hate you.*

I'm almost out, when I hear a door slam. I turn my head and open my eyes. The door is flat on the floor.

"Get the fuck away from her."

"Who the fuck are you?"

"Get the fuck away from her I said."

Aidan is here. He came for me just like he said he would. I close my eyes and I feel safe instantly. I'm going to be ok. My muscles relax and I drift in and out. I switch between memories of drawing in the sand with Aidan when I close my eyes, and when I open them, I see fighting and punching. I close them and I'm in Aidan's bed watching the waves.

Then I hear, "Fucking unlock her now." I feel my hands release from the handcuffs and my arms drop to my sides like dead weight.

"Maggie, this is the fucker you see every year? You are done. Look what he's doing to her." That's Aidan's voice.

"Mr. Scott. I had no idea." *Mr. Scott? How do they know his name?* I'm struggling to keep my eyes open. That is the last thing I hear. My eyes close.

The loud thunder wakes me. I sit up and look around and I'm in Aidan's bedroom. I lay back and let out a big sigh and breathe deeply. I am safe. Thank God. Wait, I don't remember getting here. Where is Aidan? What time is it? What happened last night? Why am I naked?

I sit up and try to regain my senses. I rest my elbows on my knees and put my head between my hands. Mr. Scott? That woman's voice. She knew his name. All the memories of last night flood my mind and shivers run through me. I look at my arms and legs. My wrists have some bruises, but otherwise I look fine. I have to find Aidan. The bedroom door is closed. I get the white robe from the bathroom, and put it on. I peek out the door and the house is dark. I don't see or hear anything. He wouldn't leave me here all alone, would he? I look out on the balcony, but no one is there. I don't see my purse or my clothes. I walk into the hall and slowly down the staircase. Still no light or sounds. I go through the kitchen where there is a small night light on above the sink. He's not in the TV room either. This house is so big I don't know where else to look. I've only been in a few rooms on the way outside.

I wander back through the foyer and down a long hallway that I haven't been down before. I've never seen this side of the house. There are so many doors and connecting hallways. It looks to go on forever. I lean on the first door on the right, trying to decide where to go. I am determined to find him. I start walking and look in each room. Some of the doors are closed, and some are open. Some of the closed ones are locked, and others aren't. The rooms are different bedrooms and bathrooms. There's an office that's bigger than his bedroom. There's a beautiful wooden wine cellar with probably two thousand bottles and another TV media room which must seat at least thirty people.

The next room is huge and decorated for Christmas. Wait, it's September. I go in. It's beautiful in here. If I listen very closely, I can hear Christmas carols playing, but it's so faint. There are four trees of all different heights and sizes. They are all decorated differently with multi colored lights and ornaments. There's a sleigh in the corner with six reindeer pulling it. There is a ledge all around the room about eye height. It is lined with hundreds of different Santa figures. Huge colorful bells are hanging from the ceiling, and there's a red velvet high backed chair in the corner. Like one that Santa would sit in and listen to kids ask for what they want. This is a happy room. I can't help but smile. I touch the beards on some of the Santa's as I make my way around. I close the door behind me. That was weird.

I try a couple more doors, but they are locked. I lean outside of the last one and put my head against it. When my head hits, it sounds strange. This is not how it should sound. I touch the door and it feels so thick. This is not a normal bedroom or bathroom door. This is a heavy duty door. I don't know what it's made of. I hear a distant sound coming from inside. I put my ear to the door and it sounds like glass breaking. I try the knob and it opens. It's very heavy to push open and it closes behind me on its own.

I'm standing in a totally empty room. It seems so huge. The ceilings are high and nothing is on the walls. It is very cold and creepy in here. As I turn the knob to go back out, I hear the glass breaking sound again. *What the hell?* I follow it to the opposite side of the room, and I see a small handle coming out of the wall. I didn't see it before. Now that I'm close I can see the cut out of a door so I pull the handle.

Aidan is grunting loudly. He is all sweaty and swinging a baseball bat at a stack of dishes. They crash to the floor and shatter. The lights are dim. It's very hot and the air is so thick. It smells of heat and sweat. I close my eyes. *What is going on?*

I am looking through the door, but it's only cracked enough so I can see. He moves down a table filled with different office equipment and hits each and every one of them with the bat. There are many tables filled with dishes, vases, TVs, telephones, printers, lamps, and mirrors. What is he doing in here? His eyes look so angry and more hurt than I've ever seen. I don't want him to see me. I don't want to go in when he's like this. This is scary. He lifts a chair from the floor and throws it across the room and screams as he lets go.

"Fuck!" he yells and I jump.

He throws individual dishes at the wall and they explode. He is spitting, then growling and hitting everything in his sight. Sweat is spraying off his body as he moves. He is panting and out of breath. He puts his arms straight out and rests his hands on a table. His eyes close and he takes some deep breaths, then looks up. I try to close the door so it's only open a hair of a crack so I can still see with one eye. He turns his head and looks at the door. *Oh my God.* My heart pounds harder and I gasp. *Shit.* He squints and starts walking towards the door. *Fuck.*

I let it go and run as fast as I can across the empty room. The heavy door is hard to open from this side. I use my body weight to pull it open.

I'm running down the hallway. I don't know which way to go. How do I get back to the foyer? It's so dark and I don't remember how I got all the way down here. I see the Christmas lights from underneath the Christmas room's door. I run past and see the foyer ahead of me.

"Gabriella!" he yells from behind me. *Fuck, he saw me.* "Gabriella, stop!"

I don't stop. I run faster. I run up the stairs two at a time and turn down the hallway to his bedroom. I look over and see him below starting the stairs. My legs are burning and my stomach is aching. I am panting. I slam the bedroom door behind me and fall to the floor in front of his bed. I'm on my hands and knees with my head down trying to catch my breath.

"Gabriella."

He bursts through the door. He is beside me with his hand on my back.

"Why are you running from me?"

He pulls me to him. I push him away and fall so I'm sitting on my behind.

"Don't touch me," I scream. I'm sobbing uncontrollably. I need to get out of here.

"What? Come here," he screams back and puts his hand out.

"No. I can't do…. I need to go."

"You're not going anywhere."

"Don't say that to me!" I'm screaming at the top of my lungs. "Don't! Don't come near me. That. That fucker last night said that in my ear right after he fucking hand cuffed me. Aaaaaahhhhhhhhh! He was going to. He almost. The other guy." I can't get my words out. *Get me out of here.*

"They almost. Aaahhhh. Then that bitch knew your name. What the fuck was that about? Who are you? I trusted you."

I pause to catch my breath and gather my thoughts.

"Then I wake up alone and naked. I just want to wrap myself up in a million blankets and cover myself forever. You left me alone after what I went through? And I find you. I find you in that room."

I stop screaming and start to rub my face.

"What were you doing in that room? You should have been here holding me, protecting me like you promised. You were hitting, throwing. You were. You were scaring me." I'm going out of control. My worst fear is being out of control. I stand up before I start to spiral. "I need to get out of here!"

That's my final scream.

"Gabriella, let me hold you," he says more calmly now.

I put my hands at my sides and hold them steady.

"Where is my purse?"

"Please Gabriella. I will do…"

"Where is my purse Aidan?" I ask with my eyes closed.
I am leaving. There is no more discussion.

He stands up and brings me my purse from the bathroom. I pull out my phone and find Lucca's picture and press it. I have no idea what time it is. The storm has let up and it's still dark out. He answers on the second ring.

"Gaby, what's wrong?" Lucca asks nervously.

"Oh Lucca." I start sobbing again.

"What's wrong? Where are you?"

"Please come get me Lucca."

I give him the address and we hang up. I gather the rest of my things from the bathroom. I throw the clothes from last night in the trash can. I never want to see those again. I see a few papers fall from my purse onto the bathroom floor, but I don't pick them up. I don't care what they are and I want to leave as fast as I can. I hang the robe on the hook behind the door and get dressed.

Aidan is sitting on the bedroom floor when I come out. I walk right past him and into the hallway and down the stairs. I wait at the front door. I put my head down and the tears begin to fall. I was trying so hard to be strong up there. I really don't want to go, but I can't breathe here. I knew I shouldn't have let someone new in. I knew this was too good to be true. I do love him, but I can't get hurt again. I know in my heart that he'd never hurt me, but I've also never seen that look in his eye. He looked like he was going to kill someone. I'm so confused. I need Lucca.

Aidan comes down the stairs and stands in front of me. He doesn't touch me. I open my eyes and see his feet. My tears flow faster.

"I'm sorry," he whispers. "Please don't go. I will do whatever it takes Gabriella."

"I'm sorry too. But, I have to go."

I don't want to go. But I also want him to do as he promised.

He leans and rests his head on mine and we stand together, face down. He reaches for my hand, but the buzzer interrupts us. He pushes the button to open the gates for Lucca. I see Lucca's head lights through the window and I open the door. My chest is going to explode. *Am I doing the right thing?* As I turn to walk out, Aidan grabs my hand.

"Disarray love Gabriella," he whispers and kisses the top of my hand.

I can't look him in the eyes. I don't respond. I pull my hand back and shut the door behind me.

The drive home is quiet. My sobs finally begin to subside and Lucca holds my hand the whole way. He doesn't probe me with tons of questions, which I knew he wouldn't. As we walk in the house, my phone vibrates. It's a text from Aidan. It says:

Come back to me

I turn my phone off. I need to get through the night. I need to talk about things with Lucca. He soothes me.

"Can we scissor on the couch?" I ask him.

I love when we lay on opposite ends of the couch and scissor our legs and talk. That's the best. He probably needs to go back to sleep though.

"Of course, Gaby."

He smiles and squeezes my hand. I lock the door behind us and change into shorts and a t-shirt. Lucca does the same and we meet on the couch and get comfortable.

"What's going on?" he starts.

"These past two weeks have been crazy, especially the last two days."

"You came home last night, right?"

"Yes, but you were asleep. Today was the worst day of all."

"Your client was in town. Does that have something to do with it?"

I take a deep breath, "Have you heard of The Shut Eye?"

"Um yes. Why?"

He sits up a little bit.

I start by telling him about last night and how it wasn't that bad. We just moved from room to room watching. I admitted to him that the spanking and cane intrigued me and he agreed. He said he's been there before to watch, but it's been a while. I tell him about my day of hell with Mr. Nathan and how he made me sit in the meetings and meals. I tell him my humiliation in the bathroom changing into that stupid skirt. I was so scared. I didn't know what he was going to do to me.

"Why didn't you call me Gaby?"

"I don't know. I should have. Then I wouldn't have seen..." I trail off.

"Seen what?"

"Wait, let me finish."

I tell him about the handcuffs, and Mr. Nathan and the other guy directing me to the couch. I say how they made me lean forward and how it smelled and felt on my face. They were whispering and my thoughts were going back and forth, in and out. I couldn't control them. I thought about Zach's last words. As I tell Lucca his face changes from horrified to sad and back to horrified. He doesn't interrupt but lets me get the whole story out. I explain how deep down I knew and trusted that Aidan would get there before something bad happened. I don't know how I knew that, I just felt it. I wasn't as scared as I probably should have been.

"But then the woman knew his name. She called him Mr. Scott. I was shocked."

"How does she know him?"

"I have no idea. I didn't stay at Aidan's long enough to talk about anything."

"What happened at his house? Why did you call me?"

"I woke up and couldn't find him, so I wandered the house looking for him in the dark. He has a Christmas room."

I go on and on about trying all of the doors and some were locked and some weren't, and the confusing hallways. I give details of what I saw in each, especially the Christmas room and the huge office. Then I recount the heavy door with the empty room and the glass breaking.

"He was breaking stuff with a baseball bat and throwing plates and chairs across the room. It was so creepy and chilling. He stopped and I stilled outside the door. He turned towards the door and I ran and he ran after me."

"Did he hurt you?"

"No, but he scared the shit out of me. He said that I wasn't going anywhere, which is what they said to me after they handcuffed me, and I freaked."

"Gaby. I'm so sorry."

"I yelled and screamed at him not to touch me. I had to get out of that house. I don't understand what he was doing in that room. Why did he leave me alone in his bed after what I just went through?"

"That sounds like some sort of break room or anger room."

"I'm so mixed up. I do love him. Remember what I told you about disarray love?"

"Yes."

"There was one thing I left out."

"What?"

"Right before he said all that to me, he told me that some woman used to hurt him. He has been alone in his house for five years. I raised my arm and he flinched. He asked me not to hurt him. I think she used to beat him."

"Oh my God Gaby. You need to talk to him and find out more about all of this."

"I know. He didn't tell me much else, but I can tell he is hurting."

"What are you going to do?"

"I have so much to think about. I'm exhausted."

"From what you've told me now and on Sunday when you got home, he loves you. He drops everything and comes for you. He did it again tonight. I believe in true love," he pauses.

"True love wins, remember?" he whispers. "You sound like two imperfect people finding love."

And with Lucca's final thought in my head, we hug tightly as he tucks me in. I look at the clock and see it's two-thirty in the morning. I set my alarm for seven and fall asleep as soon as my head hits the pillow.

I arrive at work, but Lexi is not waiting with my coffee. *Where is she?* I check her desk, but it doesn't look like she's here yet. I shut the door to my office and sink in my chair closing my eyes. I haven't had a moment to think about all this. I don't even know what happened to Mr. Nathan. Will I lose my job if his company's business goes away?

My thoughts immediately switch to Aidan. *Aidan.* I do miss him. I do love him. We had such a lovely weekend together. I want to stay with him and trust that he means what he says. He said I brought him out of his shell and he could trust with me again. He doesn't want to be without me. The security and attention he gives me is an incredible feeling. The way he helps me escape from my life and my thoughts is even more incredible. When I'm with him I don't have to worry about controlling anything or having any responsibility. He gives me the freedom to do that, that's how I can escape. I'm just so relaxed in his presence. *But that woman*. What did she do to him? She hurt him and now I left. I feel terrible. But that woman last night knew his name. And the room with the shattered glass. I'm getting worked up again. I open my eyes. I need to start working and focus on something else.

There is a knock at the door.

"Ms. Woods." Lexi glances around the door.

"Yes Lexi. Come in." I wave her in.

"How are you doing? I understand Mr. Nathan is in the hospital."

"He is? Which one?"

"HBH, ma'am."

Huntington Beach Hospital?

"Ok. And I'm fine. Thank you, Lexi."

"I also wanted to remind you that Beth is starting today."

Fuck, I forgot.

"Yes. Please show her around and get her settled. Make a lunch reservation for us at noon."

"Will do." She nods and leaves my office.

Why is Mr. Nathan in the hospital? Did Aidan hurt him last night? Why did Mr. Nathan put me through that at The Shut Eye? What was he thinking? Should I go confront him? He won't be able to hurt me in a hospital. I need to see for myself how bad he looks and ask him some questions.

I check the clock on my computer and it's only a quarter after nine. I could be back from the hospital in time for lunch. But I have to help train Beth. *Fuck.* I totally forgot she was coming today. Why is she starting on a Wednesday?

I can't train someone now. I still need to catch up from Monday and Tuesday. Mr. Nathan kept me so occupied. I shouldn't go out to lunch either, but I have to. It's Beth's first day. It would be rude not to. My mind is racing, I need to go.

I ask the Information Desk lady for Mr. Nathan's room number. He is on the fourth floor in the ICU. *ICU? What the hell?*

I find the elevator and get in. Should I do this? Should I just let this go? Should I beg that he keeps his business with us? I need to know why he involved me at that house and why he and that man did that to me. The elevator pings open and interrupts my thoughts. I find his room number on the sign. The rooms are all in a circle around a nurse's desk in the middle. I close my eyes and take a deep breath. I open them and start to walk around the backside of the desk. I see his room and my heart skips a beat. My hands feel sweaty. I'm so nervous. What should I say?

The door is half closed, but I see the blinds are open. I look through the window and see a man in bed. Tubes are coming out of his body from every direction. I lean back to double check the name on the door. It says Mr. Nathan. I look back to the man and he is unrecognizable. Is that really him? His face is so swollen and discolored with deep cuts and dried blood. I take a step back. *Holy shit!* Is that all from Aidan? Did he do this to him? Did he do this for me? I am in shock. I turn and look through the window again. I step to the side and through the door. There are so many beeping machines and wires. I get a closer look at his face and a woman's voice startles me.

"He almost died."

I turn and a woman in blue scrubs is in the room.

"He is in critical condition. Someone just dropped him at the Emergency door last night. He wasn't breathing and his heartbeat was faint. We've been working on him all night."

Holy shit.

"Is he going to make it?" I ask.

"We're not sure. The next few days will tell. Do you know him?"

"Yes I do," I say as I put my head down.

"There was another woman here this morning to see him."

Another woman?

"Do you know who she was?"

"No, I didn't speak to her. I just saw her in here. She didn't stay long."

A girlfriend? I wonder who the other woman could be.

"Oh. What did she look like?" I inquire.

"She was taller, with big blonde hair. She was extremely thin and she had chicken legs."

Oh my God. That sounds exactly like Lexi. She's the one that told me Mr. Nathan is here. Is that why she was late this morning? How did I not put this together? I have chills. What does Lexi have to do with this?

"I don't know who that was. I do need to get back to work. Thank you."

I excuse myself from the room.

As the doors of the elevator close, the elevator doors across the hall open. A man is looking right at me. *Is that Aidan?* My heart pounds as I try to push the Door Open button, but it doesn't work. What would he be doing here? Was that him? I don't know. He looked right into my eyes. He saw me too. He looked exhausted. Maybe it was just someone who looked like him? He wouldn't come here to see Mr. Nathan. *Would he?*

When the doors finally open again, I push the fourth floor to go back up. I need to see if it was Aidan. The ride up is taking forever. I get off and walk around the circle of rooms. I don't see Aidan anywhere. I look back in at Mr. Nathan as I pass by his room, and he is alone. I let out a sigh. Ok, that wasn't Aidan. It couldn't have been.

I can't believe Mr. Nathan is in the ICU. He looked terrible. Did Aidan hurt him to protect me? No one has ever done that for me before. I want to see him. I have so many questions, but it's too soon.

I hear Maggie call him Mr. Scott. Her voice is sticking with me. He hurt another man to protect me. I am so confused. I knew he would come for me. He is there for me like he said he would be. I need him.

"Fuck!" I yell in the elevator. I can't do this right now. I need to get back and confront Lexi. Was she here too? Why?

I drive as fast as I can back to the office. Lexi is at her desk and looks up when she sees me walk in. I look sternly in her eyes and point to my office. I see the blood fall from her face. I walk in my office and hear the door close behind me. I turn and she is standing with her head down.

"Lexi. Sit down." I point to the chair in front of my desk. "What is your relationship with Mr. Nathan?"

"I don't know what you're talking abo..."

I cut her off.

"Don't fuck with me Lexi. Not right now. I'm not stupid."

I watch as her eyes widen.

"I know you were at the hospital this morning. I know you bought that stupid skirt. We arrange things for Mr. Nathan every year. You and I are the only ones who know about that," I pause and stare at her. She doesn't move.

"I'm sorry." She is crying now.

"Sorry? Sorry for what? Do you have any idea what he put me through last night? He and some slimy fucker handcuffed me and..."

I'm yelling at her but she interrupts me with her sobs.

"Ms. Woods. I had no idea he was going to do that to you. He asked me to buy that skirt. I didn't know it was for you. I'm so sorry."

She puts her head down.

"Have you been talking with Mr. Nathan on your own?"

"Yes."

"What about Lexi?" I'm trying to stay firm. I really want to cry with her.

"The Shut Eye." She still won't look up at me.

"What about The Shut Eye? Lexi? Answer me." I'm getting louder.

"I suggested that he take you to watch." *What?*

"Why?" I slam my hand down on my desk and she looks up to me.

"I thought you would enjoy it. All that you've been going through with Zach. I thought it would... I had no idea he would try to hurt you."

"Enjoy it?" *Ok I did enjoy the first night a little bit.* "Why Lexi?"

"I don't know!" she screams.

"Have you been there before?"

"Yes."

"When?"

She hesitates, deciding whether or not to answer. After a brief pause, she whispers her answer to my question.

"I used to work there."

I am speechless. I shake my head to let this sink in. She used to work there? When?

"What?"

"That's how I met Mr. Nathan ma'am. He used to hire me before Maggie."

She looks ashamed.

"Enough with the ma'am crap. Mr. Nathan strongly recommended I hire you. Now I know why!"

"I'm sorry." She keeps saying that. *This is unacceptable.*

"Stop saying that. I heard you. Do you know who the other man was?"

"I had no idea there was another man," she squeaks.

I didn't see him in the ICU either. What happened to him?

"Give me a minute. Stay put."

I step outside my office door. I lean back and close my eyes, taking a deep breath. What should I do? Within seconds, it hits me and I go back in.

"Lexi, you will ensure that XPlod Marketing stays with us," I demand. XPlod is Mr. Nathan's company. She looks up.

"Ma'am that is already taken care of. They called this morning and signed on to stay with us for another ten years of support."

My jaw drops.

"Good."

I can't let her see that this news has taken me by surprise. *How did this happen?*

"Have you arranged lunch?"

"Yes. The reservation is for noon at Matsu."

"Perfect," I pause. "I can't have you work here anymore, Lexi. Please go."

I can't look in her eyes.

"But ma'am," she whispers.

I close my eyes and shake my head. She stands and leaves.

I sink to the floor in the corner and I break as tears fall down my face. The stress takes over. I start rubbing my face. *Lexi was involved.* I can't believe it. After all these years, and I never knew. Why would she have him take me there? That doesn't make sense. Was she trying to hurt me?

I don't believe that she didn't know the skirt was for me. I need her to go. I can't look at her ever again. She can go visit Mr. Nathan and stay with him for all I care. I need to call XPlod. What is the new contract about? Does he still work there? Was this because he feels bad? I'm so mixed up again.

His face was so swollen. I can't get that picture out of my mind. *And Aidan did that to him.* This constant stress is driving me crazy. My mind is all over the place. I put my head between my knees and start to rock. Suddenly I feel a hand patting my back. It's a familiar rhythm. I look up.

Zach is standing over me.

Chapter 11

Zach kneels beside me, comforting me like he used to do when I was upset. He leans over and wraps his arms around me. He strokes my hair as we rock. It feels nice. For one minute, I forget my problems and let him hold me. My tears flow freely and he doesn't let go. That was the one thing he did for me.

Wait. Zach is here? What? I don't want this anymore. I want Aidan. I want Aidan to help me escape. I sit back and break his hold.

"Hey," he says, smiling.

"Zach, what are you doing here?" I wipe my face.

"I want you Gaby. I miss you."

Memories of him pinning me against the door come rushing back to me.

"Get out Zach." I point to the door.

"Fuck! I was just holding you and now you are kicking me out?"

"Zach. Go." I point again. There is a knock at my door.

"Come in," I say loudly. I'm thankful for the interruption.

"Hi, Ms. Woods. Lexi left and we need to leave for our reservation," Beth says quietly.

"Thank you, Beth. Stay right there." She nods and smiles.

I grab my purse and motion for both of them to step out of my office. I close my door and we all ride down in the elevator.

"I'll be back, Gaby. I'm not letting go," Zach says. *What does that mean?*

When the doors open, Zach turns to the right and leaves. Beth and I turn to the left to go to the employee parking lot.

"Beth, I'm sorry for all the commotion this morning. Would you mind driving? I need to make a call."

"Of course not ma'am." I shake my head and laugh.

"Please call me Gaby."

"Ok ma'am. I mean, Gaby." We both laugh.

Beth is about my height with sandy blonde hair. She has bright blue eyes and a small scar on her cheek. I wonder how that happened. She has an athletic build, but dresses very sophisticated. While she drives to Matsu, I call XPlod. I talk to the CEO but he won't give out much information about the new contract. I push for more answers, but all he will tell me is that their largest investor insists on it. I thank him for his business over and over. I feel relieved.

I look up XPlod's website on my phone and see their top investor is some company called Nationwide Consulting. Why would they be interested in XPlod's software needs?

I text the girls and Lucca. Simone and I are back to normal. I'm still surprised she said she was sorry.

Over lunch, I tell Beth that Lexi won't be returning. I don't tell her why, but say that she is now my number one assistant. She was going to be helping Lexi, but I need her to step it up. We talk through my calendar and the schedule for the rest of the week. She appears so eager to learn and do a good job.

We work hard and train Wednesday and Thursday into the evening hours. Beth is a quick learner and is very helpful. I actually enjoy working so closely with her. She is someone I could see myself being friends with. We have a lot in common and she likes my music too. Maybe I will ask her to go to the concert with me. Yes, she is my assistant, but I'd like to work on a more friendly level. I hate that ma'am and Ms. Woods crap, especially now that Lexi is gone.

Friday morning comes all too quickly. I feel sad today. I've been so wrapped up in work the last couple days. All I've been doing is working and sleeping. I miss Aidan. I am so stressed. I need him to escape. I lie in bed and imagine him next to me. I need his touch. Yes, he scared me, but I don't believe he would hurt me. He is probably waiting for me to contact him. His last communication I totally ignored. His text said *Come Back to Me* and I haven't replied.

I decide to get through one more busy day and I will call him tomorrow morning. I shuffle to the shower and get ready.

"Same old me again today." I look at myself. *Yep, same old me.*

"There has been a delivery for you. A man just dropped these off at the front desk." Beth peeks her head into my office.

"A man?" I ask as she hands me my coffee.

"Yes, he asked if we would give them to you." *He?*

I stand and take two boxes from her hands.

"Thank you Beth." She leaves.

The boxes are wrapped in white silk with bright red ribbons around them. I know they are from Aidan. There is one small box and one extra-large box. I set them in front of me on my desk. I untie the ribbon and remove the silk from the top one. It's a small wood box. It's very smooth and looks like something someone made. I sit in my chair and stare at it. I'm nervous to look inside. A lump begins to form in my throat. I take a few deep breaths and grab the small knob on the front and open it.

Inside the cover it says "Come Back to Me" just like his text. It's engraved in the wood. He must have made this. I swallow. I look in and see a stunning glass red heart. It fits perfectly in the palm of my hand. I pull out two pictures of our love letters in the sand. DISARRAY LOVE and A/G with hearts around them. I hug them to my chest. *Oh Aidan. I miss you. I love you.*

There is a small folded piece of paper in the corner. It's the card he sent to me with the flowers. It's from the day of our first dinner together. The first night when he swept me off my feet.

Happy Thursday Gabriella
One dozen roses for the
one that I'm falling for.
See you tonight.
xo Aidan xo

He was falling for me then. It seems like so long ago, so much has happened. This must have fallen out of my purse back at Aidan's house. I'd been carrying it with me.

There is one more piece of paper in the box. I take it and lean back in my chair.

My Princess Gabriella.
You have made me laugh again.
You have given me feelings that I didn't think I could feel.
I need you, I want you.
I am lost without you.
I want to hold your hand every single night.
You belong with me – You are mine.
I will explain everything, and answer any questions you have.
I am giving you my heart.
It was broken, but you put it back together for me.
You are my dream come true.
I live for your smile, and die for your kiss.
I will do whatever it takes.
xo Aidan xo

I kiss the note and tears stream down my face. This man is so sweet. I have so many questions for him. *I do belong with him.* I want him to hold my hand. I am his. I sit up and take the red heart in my hand and squeeze it as hard as I can. He is giving me his heart. I put the papers back in the box and close it, careful to set the heart on top. I unknot the bow and silk of the large box. *What could this possibly be?* I slowly lift the cover and I gasp.

He has taken my breath away yet again. It's the most stunning silk red gown I have ever seen in my life. I hug it to my body. It's floor length with straps off the shoulder and it dips down between the breasts. It's absolutely beautiful. It's perfect.

My thoughts are racing. I check the tag. *It's my size.* I am in awe. How does he know my size? What is this for? I will never do this dress justice. It's so lovely. I sit down still hugging it to my body. I see a note on the bottom of the box. It says:

Join me tonight

Tonight? Shit. I set the dress on my chair and open my office door. Beth is at her desk.

"Beth." She looks up. "The man that dropped this off. How did he look?"

"How did he look? What do you mean?"

"I don't know. How did he look?" I laugh. I don't know how to describe what I mean.

"Hold on."

She picks up the phone and calls the front desk. I watch as she listens to them tell her what he looked like.

"She said he looked nervous, like he was in a hurry. He just dropped the boxes on the desk and said to give them to you, and he turned and left."

"That's it?"

"He looked exhausted. His hair was all messy." Exhausted? Has he not slept? I should have responded sooner.

"Thank you Beth." I go back in my office and find my phone to call Aidan, but am interrupted by Beth over the intercom.

"Our ten o'clock is here Gaby." *Fuck.*

"OK."

The day is back to back meetings. I daydream about Aidan. I want to go back and relive last weekend. I want his arms around me. I want to go to his house and surrender to his care. I need him inside me. I need to feel his body around mine. I need to call him about tonight.

The afternoon is spent placing our clients on flights home. I'm so glad they are gone. We even used our lunch as an informal meeting to get them on their way early. It's a weight off my shoulders that this week is over.

"Let's go home," I say to Beth.

She looks thankful. Her first three days have been crazy.

"It's five and I'm done for today. I couldn't do any more work if I tried. I'll see you Monday morning. Have a nice weekend."

"You too, Gaby."

The elevator ride down is relaxing. I am finally not rushing somewhere or worrying about something. I run my fingers through my hair in relief. When I step out of the elevator, I see Aidan and I stop breathing. He's about ten feet in front of me. *Holy shit*. He is looking right at me. My hands are instantly sweaty and time has stopped again. How long has he been waiting there?

He looks so debonair. He has never looked so desirable. He is wearing a black suit with a crisp white shirt, and a bright red tie and red handkerchief. His hair is combed to one side. He is absolutely gorgeous. How is a man so magnificent waiting for me?

He is holding a single red rose in one hand, and a pair of red shoes in the other. He smiles but doesn't move. I stop in my tracks. I feel the pull. I set the two silk boxes down on the floor with my purse. I can't breathe. I smile back and he takes one step forward and stops. The second he stops, my body takes over and I run to him as the magnet kicks in. I watch him set down the items he's holding. It's the slow motion thing again. *I want him. I need him.* My body crashes into his and he hugs me so tight he lifts me off of the ground. Tingles run through me. I have my arms crossed behind his head and I kiss his neck over and over and over. *He smells heavenly.* I've missed him. I've missed his touch.

"Oh Gabriella! I love you so much."

We each hug tighter and he sets me on my feet, but keeps his arms around me.

"I've been lost these last couple of days. Come back to me. I need you," he whispers.

"Aidan. I need you too."

"I don't want to ever be without you again. Join me this evening."

He kisses my lips and I feel the zing. I close my eyes. I've been yearning for this feeling.

"Yes, Aidan," I pause and meet his eyes, "but I want to make it clear that we have a lot to discuss."

"Yes, I know we do. I am ready to answer any questions. I told you. I will do whatever it takes. I need you to come back to me."

His eyes look so sincere.

"I want to come back, Aidan." I kiss his lips. "And I love you too."

He smiles and picks up the rose.

"For you, my love."

"It's lovely. Thank you." I smell it.

"Let's go."

He picks up the red shoes and takes my hand. He pulls me to where I set my boxes. He hands me the shoes and purse while he bends to pick up the boxes. He holds them under his arm and pulls my hand.

When we get outside my building, I see the same limo we had before. He looks back to me and I blush. I remember the last thing we did in there and I'd like to finish where we left off. Tuxedo man opens the door and both he and Aidan gesture with their hands for me to get in. I sit down and watch Aidan slide the boxes onto the seat and then he slides in. I look around and there are red roses everywhere. This man continues to amaze me.

"Where are we going?" I ask.

"We are stopping at your place so you can change into this." He taps on the large box. "And these." He holds up the red shoes.

They are red silk pumps with one rhinestone on the outside of the toes.

"My place? Why not your place?"

"We will not go back there until you agree to be mine again."

Oh.

"We need to get through your questions. I am ready and will be completely honest with you, Gabriella. I need you to trust me. Trust is not to be abused. I don't want to scare you."

I move the boxes behind me and scoot next to him. I put both hands on his cheeks and kiss his lips. They feel so soft. I feel the sparks starting. I keep my hands on his face and look into his eyes. Is the hurt still in there or is it starting to fade away? I need him to tell me everything.

I kiss him again and our lips part. My heartbeat is picking up. He reaches for my hand and holds it, while his other hand rests on my leg. Our kisses get deeper and he squeezes my hand. I want to run my hands all over his body, but I resist. His grip is getting tighter. I put my hand over it and he loosens.

"I can't help it Gabriella. I want to feel your body everywhere but I'm fighting my urges. I don't want you to..."

I put my finger to his mouth.

"I want that too."

"I need your body. It does something to me."

"And yours to mine," I whisper back.

He pulls me to his lap and we wrap our arms around each other the rest of the ride. Here I am again, relaxing in the safety of Aidan's arms. I close my eyes tightly and smile.

Tuxedo man opens the door for us. Aidan gets out and points to the boxes. I hand them to him and he extends his hand to mine. I grab my purse and the red pumps and take it. He puts his elbow out.

"You're coming in with me this time I see," I tease.

"Hell yes I am." He walks faster.

When we get inside, Aidan pushes my body against the door with his. His lips are hovering over mine. I feel his erection at my stomach. We are panting together as the passion surges through my blood. He bends and kisses me deeply. My knees buckle and he backs away.

I see Lucca in the kitchen. He smiles at me, and then to Aidan. He lifts his eyebrows and smiles even bigger back at me. I do the same look back with the eyebrows and the smile.

"Wait here. I'm going to change." I take the boxes from Aidan and leave the shoes.

"Ok baby," he says as he sits down on the couch.

I love when he calls me baby. I take the boxes to my bedroom and close the door. I sit on my bed and take some deep breaths. I'm going out tonight with Aidan. I have to change into a silk gown and shoes. He has given me his heart. He wants me to be his. Again. *Deep breaths, Gaby.* That suit. That tie. He looks amazing.

I set the wood box on my dresser. I open it slowly and see his words "Come Back to Me" inside the cover. The butterflies are fluttering around in my stomach. I find my small black clutch and transfer my wallet and lipstick into it along with the note and the red heart. *He has given me his heart*, I tell myself again. I take the big box, a clean pair of panties and bra to the bathroom. When I'm done changing, there is a knock at the door.

"Come in."

"Ho- Ly-Shit Gaby! How hot is Aidan tonight?" Lucca asks with his eyes popping out of his head.

"I know." I blush again. "Will you zip me up?"

"Yes. He was just telling me how much he loves you, and how he has been going through hell missing you."

Lucca starts to fix my makeup and I hand him the note. We both stop and read it together. I melt again at Aidan's kind words.

"Wow. Can I have him for myself?" Lucca sticks his lower lip out to pout.

I take out the red heart.

"He gave this to you too?"

I nod.

"This is like a dream, Gaby. He says you're his dream come true, but he sounds like any girls dream come true to me. Any girl would kill for this attention. Shit, I would kill to be treated like this by a man." We laugh together.

"Lucca, remember when I was really bad about a year ago? I told you I wished something bad happened to me just to get some attention from Zach?"

"Yes." He nods. "Why?"

"It's like a fantasy. It comes so easily from Aidan. Where before I would beg to have Zach rush to my side and he never did. But Aidan. He just does that so effortlessly. Something about him makes me trust him completely. I feel so lucky."

"Don't cry. You will ruin your makeup that I just fixed."

We laugh again.

I do trust Aidan. He makes me feel so safe, protected, needed, like no one else ever has.

"Ok, how do I look?" I step back.

"Perfect," he says while kissing my cheek.

"Thank you Lucca. I'm lucky to have you too."

He smiles.

"Give me a minute."

Lucca steps out and closes the door. *I can do this.* I have my questions ready for Aidan. I might hear some things I don't want to hear. I need to hear them though. *I can do this.* I love him.

When I come out of the bathroom, Aidan is standing in front of the couch. He looks to me and puts his hand behind him as he sits down.

"Gabriella, you are absolutely radiant."

I smile my biggest smile ever. He makes me feel so confident.

"I knew you would be beautiful in red, but this is so much more. May I?"

He holds the shoes out. I walk to him and twirl my hair. While holding my ankle, he slides them on my feet one at a time. *This is so hot.* They fit perfectly, of course.

"Thank you Aidan," I say.

Lucca is grinning from ear to ear.

"Let's go."

Aidan puts his elbow out and I take it. Lucca grabs my arm and kisses my cheek.

"Have fun, Gaby. Keep your mind open," he whispers in my ear.

He wants me to be positive and not think the worst about the answers I might get from Aidan. He likes Aidan and wants to see me happy.

"Where are we going?" I ask once we are in the limo.

"The Ballet Club. Have you been there before?"

"No. What type of place is it?"

I've definitely never heard of it.

"It's a black tie restaurant with private tables. They have ballet shows every hour that we can see from our seats."

"I've never seen a real ballet before. That sounds fun."

He reaches for my hand and holds it the rest of the ride. I don't ask any more questions. I don't want to be interrupted once I start asking the hard questions. I rest my head on his shoulder and enjoy his warmth.

The limo stops in front of The Ballet Club and I see a line forming outside. The door opens and I take Aidan's elbow. He leads us up the stairs and into the club. We don't wait in line and no one stops us. The hostess spots Aidan and they do some sort of weird nonverbal communication thing and she leads us to our table without anyone saying a word. *How does he do that?* I'm impressed.

Our table is elevated right in the center of the club. It's very private and partially enclosed. We have to take three steps up to it and we can see the stage perfectly. He nods at the hostess and she leaves us alone. He extends his arms on the table with his palms up. I love when he does that. I put my hands in his and we look deep into each other's eyes.

"I want to start by saying thank you. Thank you for joining me tonight. I am honored to have such a beautiful woman at my side."

I smile and look down.

"Gabriella, I want more than anything for this to work."

One of his hands points back and forth from me to him.

"I will be completely honest. I want us to communicate our wants, needs, desires, everything. We should be totally open with each other. It kills me that I scared you. That I hurt you." He closes his eyes. "When you left that night." He stops and opens them. "When you left I was scared too. I was scared you would never return."

A woman dressed in a black cocktail dress brings us a bottle of wine and sets one red rose beside my glass. I smile at her as she leaves.

"I'm sor..." I try to say I'm sorry, but he doesn't let me finish.

"You have nothing to be sorry for, Gabriella. You didn't do anything wrong. I understand why you left. I should have..."

Now it's my turn to interrupt him.

"I want you to tell me about the wood box you sent me."

I want to get started on my list of questions.

"What about it?"

"Did you make it?"

"Yes. I stayed up all night. Actually I haven't slept much since you left."

"Oh. I'm..."

He cuts me off mid-apology.

"Having my arms around you, holding you all night, that's the best feeling I've ever felt. I miss it. I need you. I need you in my bed."

"I miss that too, Aidan. Thank you for the box. Thank you for the pictures and the letter. And for this dress, for this night. For everything."

I can't believe he made that for me. And he dropped it off himself!

"Gab..."

I interrupt again, needing the answer to the question that's been in the back of my mind all day.

"Were you at the hospital on Wednesday?"

"Yes."

"Did you see me in the elevator?" *I knew I saw him when I was leaving!*

"Yes."

"Where did you go?"

"I stayed in the elevator and went to a different floor. It had only been a few hours since you left. I assumed you..."

"Why were you there?"

"I told you, Gabriella. I will protect you forever if you let me. I had to see that fucker. I had to make sure he was not going to hurt you again. Ever."

"I see."

Wow. He did hurt Mr. Nathan to protect me.

"Do you know how he is doing?"

"No. I don't. I was planning to check this weekend. He's not going anywhere anytime soon."

He smirks. Ok, question answered. *Which one should I ask next?*

"Tell me about the woman that used to hurt you."

He lets go of my hands and sits back.

"What do you want to know?"

"For starters, what's her name?"

"Liz."

"How long were you with her?"

"Two years."

That's a significant amount of time. *Did she hurt him the whole time?*

"How did she hurt you?" I'm proud of myself for getting right to the point.

The woman in the cocktail dress drops another rose near my glass.

"Let's have some wine," he says as he slams almost his whole glass. He's trying to change the subject, but I don't miss a beat.

"How did she hurt you Aidan?"

He closes his eyes. *Should I back off?* This must be hard for him. But I need to know the answer if we are going to continue our relationship.

His eyes slowly open and I see the hurt again. This is the worst I've ever seen his eyes look. The rest of his face falls. He looks shattered. In an instant, it seems as though I've brought him back to a dark place and I feel terrible. I promise myself I will never bring this up again, but I need to hear what happened. *I need to know.*

"I don't want to hide anymore. I will tell you."

He swallows.

"She used to beat me. She would hit my face, my chest, my legs. She would raise her hand just to scare me. She would..."

I can't hear anymore.

"Why did she hurt you?"

"I don't know. She just started hitting me one day six months into our relationship. I didn't hit her back. I couldn't hit her back. I thought it was a onetime thing, but it wasn't."

"How often did she do this?"

"Every time it stormed outside."

I gasp.

What? That's why he acted so weird when it thundered. It stormed the first night I met him and he disappeared to the car. It stormed last weekend when I had to go home for work. It happened Monday night when I got home and he said he was waiting for me at my house.

"Is that why you weren't waiting for me Monday night?"

"Yes. I was waiting but I had to leave."

I wish he would have been there.

"What did she do when it stormed?" He shakes his head.

"As soon as it started thundering, she would blast this music through the house. Then I would know. I hated that fucking music." He looks down.

"Music?"

"Some kind of death metal rock music or something. It was horrid. I don't know. She said it made her hyper. I would cringe every time it came on."

Is that why he doesn't like my music?

"You don't know why she did this?"

"I don't. I assume it was her way of control. Her family always picked at her and said she wasn't good enough."

"That's not a reason to hurt you."

I feel so bad for him. *Why did he allow this to go on?*

"I know that. I let her do it."

"You never hurt her back?"

He sits back, crosses his arms, and closes his eyes. *Oh no.* He sits like this for what seems like forever. When he opens his eyes, they look glossy.

He finally speaks.

"I did once. I couldn't take it anymore. This particular night it was so bad. It just wouldn't stop. She wouldn't let up and I snapped."

He takes a deep breath and says, "I hit her back. I hurt her face. I saw blood and it shocked me. I stopped immediately. She left and we haven't seen each other since."

I move next to him and hug him tight.

"I'm so sorry, Aidan. I'm sorry you had to go through that."

"I'm sorry I hurt her. I felt awful. I've been dealing with that ever since."

I hug him tighter. *Poor Aidan.* He's sorry he hurt her. *She deserved to be hurt!* I feel so sad for him. I kiss the top of his head.

"I buried myself in work. I've kept busy every minute of the day. Like I said, the past five years have been very repetitive. One day at a time. I don't need to work. I just did it."

"It helped you get through."

"Yes it did. But now I don't want to anymore. I want to spend every minute spoiling you. I want to give you goodies every day."

Spoiling me? Goodies?

I kiss his head again and I can feel the tears forming. He is hurting inside and talking about how he can spoil me. *Who is this man?* I love him so much, and my heart is aching for him. The waitress interrupts us with another rose by my glass and a shrimp appetizer. He sits back.

"Let's continue," he says.

"Aidan, I'm sorry. I will stop asking questions."

I should stop now.

"No. I need to do this. I need to tell you. I will keep us together above anything else, Gabriella. I don't want to hold this in anymore."

I'm not sure where to go from here. I will ask him about work.

"What is the name of your company again?"

He might have already told me, but I don't remember.

"Nationwide Consulting."

"And you say you don't need to work? I don't understand."

"I have a President and a CEO. I'm the owner. They do all the work. Actually, Nicholas is the President."

Oh.

"Your brother, Nicholas?"

"Yes, we started the company together from nothing. We were determined to put ourselves through college after our parents died and we were living on the streets."

"Is that what you speak about?"

I remember him telling me about his motivational speaking.

"Yes. We do it together sometimes. We even travel."

The name of Aidan's company triggers a foggy memory. *Why does that sound familiar?* I close my eyes and put my hand to my head. *Where do I know that name?*

"What's wrong?" he asks.

"You own Nationwide Consulting?"

"Yes. I just said that."

I inhale sharply as I realize where I've heard the name.

"You are an investor in XPlod?"

His eyes widen.

"Yes, how do you know that?"

"Did you have them sign with my company for ten years?"

"Yes, but how do you...?"

"Why Aidan?"

"Again, I told you I would protect you forever," he says quietly.

Holy shit. He saved XPlod from leaving my company. He saved my job. I am astounded by this man over and over.

I shake my head.

"I did what I thought you needed," he says firmly. *Fuck.*

"Aidan, I don't know what to say."

And I really don't. He leans forward and grabs my hand and looks in my eyes.

"Gabriella, I will do anything for you. You give me purpose, a reason to... I see you and I instantly feel better."

Another rose arrives and a lobster dinner. I can't eat. Not now. I have knots in my stomach.

"What do you do now when it storms out?"

"Now? Now I go to that room you found me in."

"The hidden room? Where you were breaking stuff?"

"Yes."

"Why?"

"It's just a way to get through the storm. A way for me to get out of my head, to forget, to hurt something, to control the situation, to release."

He looks sad again.

"You've been doing that for five years every time it storms?"

"Well no."

A tear streams down his face. *Fuck, I should have stopped.*

"I used to go to The Shut Eye."

"The what?"

Did I hear him correctly?

"The Shut Eye," he whispers.

"Oh my God Aidan!" *Fuck, I did not want to hear that.* "What would you do there?"

"I own it, Gabriella. That is how Maggie knew my name. I'm so sorry."

He puts his head in his hands. *He owns it?* Did he do anything there? Did he sleep with a different woman every time he went?

I might be sick. I can't eat. I push my plate away from me.

"Did you?" I can't even say it. "Did you participate?"

"Yes, sometimes."

"Sometimes?"

"Yes."

"What do you mean sometimes?"

"It's not what you think. For me it was about control. It was about the joy. The joy watching women's bodies react to my control. The Shut Eye is about being erotic, not sexual."

So he didn't sleep with the women? But what does he mean?

"So you didn't have sex with them?"

"No."

"You just pleasured them?"

"Yes, for the most part."

"Answer the question Aidan."

"Yes, I pleasured them. But I didn't..." He stops.

"Didn't what?"

"I didn't always allow them to come."

"Allow them?" *What the fuck?!*

"It's a control thing. Some would beg to come and I wouldn't let them."

"Why not?"

"Liz did that to me. Before she would beat me, she would build me higher and higher sexually, and then deny me."

Who was this crazy bitch?

"Why do you own it?"

"Liz asked me to buy it. I kept it after she left."

"Oh," I say, processing his rationale. "I want to you to sell it."

I don't want him going there.

"I sold it yesterday."

"You did?"

"Yes, I knew you would want that. I want that." His sadness is fading away in front of my eyes.

"Oh. Wow. Ok."

I'm stuttering.

"Gabriella. Is there anything else?" he asks.

My mind is overloaded with information. There is only one more question that comes to mind, and I hope he is ok with it.

"What about when it rains?"

He laughs a little.

"Rain is fine. I love the rain and the rainbows that follow. They bring hope."

"Me too."

We smile together.

"Let's eat."

He points to my plate.

Cocktail girl drops another rose at my glass and asks if we need anything else before the show starts. That's the first time she's spoken. We didn't even get menus. She just brought food and wine. *Did he have all of this pre-planned? And what are these roses for?*

We eat our lobster while the lights dim. He moves in next to me putting his arm around my back. I snuggle on his shoulder and the ballet begins. It is so peaceful to watch. I find myself thinking about Aidan's pain. *How could he let her hurt him? Who could do that?* He feels bad that he retaliated.

Does he think he will hurt me? What will happen if I am with him and it storms? Will he just leave me and go to that room?

I can't think about this anymore. I just want to move forward and be his again. I want him to be happy. He makes me happy. I want to please him. He is still fighting for me. No one has ever loved me like this before.

One more red rose is dropped while our dinner plates are cleared away. The lights come back on as soft music fills the room.

"That was just lovely. Those dancers are so graceful."

"Let's dance baby." He stands. "We can't waste that dress. Let me show you off."

My heart flutters.

"Thank you sir," I say as I grab his hand to stand up.

He puts his arms around my waist and I put mine behind his neck. He holds me close as we sway to the music. I feel the sparks. He steps back and holds my hand up in the air. *What does that mean?* He makes a twirling motion with his other hand. I flush and turn around under has hand. This is so romantic.

He kisses my ears and whispers softly.

"I love you baby. Say you'll be mine."

He kisses my lips.

"Stay with me tonight."

I want to stay with him. I want to be his. I want his protection and his security. I want him.

I lean back.

"What were the roses for at the table?"

"I thought you'd never ask."

He kisses me and whispers once more.

"One rose for each time you've said you loved me. That is my favorite sound in the whole world."

My body melts. He says the sweetest things. He does the sweetest things. *And didn't I just say I love him at work tonight?* How did he? When did he?

I squeeze him tighter than ever before and with his hands behind my back, he lifts me off of the ground. He kisses me and slowly turns around to the music and kisses me deeper. I am so happy right now. *I am in love.* I have his heart. I am jumping up and down inside. The song comes to an end and he sets me down.

I touch his cheeks.

"Yes Aidan."

"Yes what?"

"Yes I will be yours. Yes I will stay with you tonight. Yes to everything."

I would do anything for him. I see his body relax. I think I hear a sigh of relief.

"You are my destiny," he says before kissing my lips. He licks them. Zing!

"Let's go. I have a goodie."

He pulls my hand and he grabs the roses from the table and leads us out the front door. Did he pay? Should we tell the waitress we are leaving?

The limo is waiting and the door is open. Tuxedo man also is under his command I see. Things ready the exact moment he needs them. I giggle inside. Aidan pulls me on his lap and I sit across his legs.

"I'd like to finish where we left off in here," he says lifting his eyebrows.

"I wanted to do that on the way here." I lift my eyebrows back.

He puts both hands in my hair and pulls my lips to his. I feel like he's going to kiss me hard, but he doesn't, he touches my lips softly. My heart starts to race. He is so gentle. His lips move from my mouth to my neck, trailing kisses the entire way. It's so soft and I can feel his hot breath as he moves. I want to peel this dress off. His body starts taking over mine. I love this feeling.

Chapter 12

We stop at the London Hotel. I thought we were going to his house. The door opens and he gets out. He must see the confused look on my face because he waves his hand for me to get out too. *A hotel?* I don't have any clothes to change. He holds my hand as we pass through the lobby and get in the elevator. He doesn't stop to check in or get a key. He pushes me against the side wall with his groin as soon as the elevator doors close. His hands are holding mine at the side of my head. This is so carnal. He bites my lower lip and I tilt my hips towards him. The gentleness is driving me wild. I moan and he rubs harder. I am aching. I am throbbing. I have missed this feeling he gives me.

"Come on baby."

Wait, come back! I look and the doors have opened right into the room. This is more than a room. This is a suite, or a penthouse, or something. There is soft music playing. I see candles, probably hundreds, all around. How romantic. *Who did this?*

I look down and see a trail of red rose petals on the floor in front of us and he pulls me to follow them. The petals lead to a lavish bed covered in more petals. I am in complete awe. How does he keep surprising me?

There is a long red silk nightgown at the end of the bed. I swallow. The ache in my stomach is back. I want him. I need him now. I turn to look at him and he smiles. I jump in his arms and we kiss.

"I love you Aidan. Please make love to me," I say in between kisses.

"I love you more. Let's fuse," he whispers.

He sets me down and turns me away from him. He brushes my hair to one side and he slowly unzips my zipper. I am trembling at his touch. I can't breathe. The warmth from his hands is consuming me. He lowers my dress down my body while trailing his fingers. It's too light. I close my eyes and feel tingles between my legs. He gives me the chills.

I step out of the dress and he lays it across the couch next to the bed. He turns me around and brushes the hair away from my face. He reaches behind my back and unhooks my bra. His lips are hovering over mine the whole time. The ache between my legs is becoming unbearable. I lean to touch my lips to his, but he steps back and puts my bra with the dress. His fingertips start at my cheek and tickle past my shoulders and down my arms. He has one finger under my panty line at my stomach and moves it back and forth from hip to hip. I am having trouble standing. My knees weaken.

He bends his knees and kisses the panty line softly as he pulls them down. He kisses my hip and trails kisses to my knee as they come off. I run my fingers through his hair. His middle finger runs up my thigh and past my stomach and he circles my naval as he stands. I need him to slide it between my legs to relieve this pain. He stops and touches his nose to mine and rests his forehead on me. He still won't kiss me. I am panting. *I am losing my mind.*

He steps back and picks up the nightgown. He raises my hands above my head. I hold them up as he moves behind me. He is breathing on my shoulders and neck as he moves around and it's driving me wild. I can't stand in these shoes. I might collapse. He takes a breast in each hand, licks my ear and I quiver. He squeezes each nipple between his thumb and finger and my knees give out. I fall back against him and whimper.

"Yes baby," he whispers in my ear, "I've got you."

"Aidan. Aidan, please," I beg.

"Keep your hands up baby."

He lets go of my nipples and kneels in front of me. He takes one shoe off and then the other. He brushes my nipple softly with his lips as he stands and holds the nightgown above my head. It slips over my hands, then my head, then down my body. The silk feels luxurious next to my skin. He circles my hard nipples over the fabric and I put my arms around his neck. He swoops down and picks me up under my knees, my favorite way he holds me, and lowers me to the bed.

"You are so beautiful," he says as he backs away and looks in my eyes.

I watch his every move as he starts to undress. *Oh, how I want this man.* I am craving for him. As he lays his jacket on the couch, I put my head back and close my eyes. I love him. I want to give myself to him completely.

We gaze at each other while he undoes his shirt buttons too slowly. One button, then the next. *Hurry up!* He is directly in front of me. I sit up. I want to help him. He smiles and shakes his finger back and forth. I lie back on the pillow and watch him take his shirt off and he puts his hands to his tie.

"Leave the tie on baby," I say and he grins.

His pants and boxers lower to the floor. His naked body is hard everywhere I look. The tie hanging between the defined muscles of his chest is a welcome sight. I am trembling. He steps towards the bed and I lean forward, knees bent. I grab the tie, wrap it around my wrist, and pull him down between my legs. His body is flawless. He rubs his erection between my thighs and I squirm beneath him, still holding his tie.

He stops and leans to one side so my leg and arm are both trapped beneath him. His arm is under my neck and he raises my other arm to his and holds my wrist tight. He slides the nightgown up my legs and pushes them wide open. His hand rests on my inner thigh and he kisses me. He starts with light licks and then sucks my lips. When his tongue enters my mouth, his fingers circle my opening. I gasp. I can't move. I can't push my hips up or use my hands. Sensations are building everywhere. I can't lie still. I need him inside.

"Do you like that? Tell me baby," he whispers.

"Yes....Aidan.....please....."

My body is shaking in need.

His fingertip slides inside and I cry out. It slowly spreads the moisture to my clitoris. He kisses me so intensely and teases with his fingers, tantalizing me. I can't hold on. I'm building quickly. He knows my body so well. It's as though he's memorized my reactions. This is so welcome and frustrating at the same time. He needs to relieve this ache, he needs to go deeper, he needs to.... I shake my head back and forth. I'm going to explode. I'm on the tasty edge. He slows and I dig my head back into the pillow.

"Aidan, please."

"I could kiss you all night baby."

"Please. Fuse. Fuse," I'm almost weeping. *Please come inside of me. Please!*

"Your body Gabriella. I need your body like I need to breathe."

And in that second, he turns and pushes his erection inside of me.

"Aaaahhhhhhhhhhhhhh!" I scream out loud.

Fuck. The moment he's inside, I feel the peace come over me. It's astonishing. I need him too. I want to give him what he needs. I run my hands over his hard body and push up to meet him. He thrusts again slowly and I feel every perfect inch. I am tingling everywhere from my head to my toes. I grip around him with every stroke. We kiss, tongues swirling, massaging together, while he pushes and moves his hips, grinding in every direction, like he can't get enough. I wrap my legs around him and my feet under his knees, so we are one big pretzel moving as one, our bodies in sync. I am making sweet, tender love to the man I love. We are cheek to cheek, and I am absorbing every one of his moans. I want to melt into him. He picks up speed pushing deeper, with more force, and I am building up higher. I tighten around him.

"Come for me baby."

His scratchy voice pushes me over. He drags gently in and out, drawings out my orgasm even longer.

"Oh Aiddddaaaannn!" I scream his name.

My body relaxes and he thrusts extra hard and he screams as he comes.

"Gabriella. Oh baby. Fuck. Gabri...." he groans as he collapses on top of me.

I am in his trance floating back down to earth.

Our breathing slows and he lies at my side. I touch his cheek as we catch our breath. I look around the room at the peaceful candlelight. This night couldn't have been more perfect. Our love is perfect. He is so charming, and sweet, and thoughtful, and beautiful. The five red roses, the petals, the nightgown. He is absolute perfection.

I still feel sad for him. We saved each other, I can see that now. Love heals. It's healed both of us. I feel filled with sunshine. I move to my side and he turns his body behind mine. I've missed the magnet. I've missed our mesmerizing pulling force. I've missed the spooning.

He laces his fingers in mine and I tighten my eyes. I've never been happier than I am right now. I love him. He is my love of a lifeti...

He interrupts my thoughts and whispers in my ear.

"You are my love of a lifetime. Goodnight baby."

He has mirrored my words. I fall asleep knowing we are in each other's spell again.

I wake up to Aidan breathing heavily and kissing my ear. I open my eyes and see the candles still lit, but almost out. The music is still playing. I feel his erection at my back. He circles his hips. My breath is quickening and I push back on him. He moves down and without letting go of my hand, he slides inside me. Our hands tighten as my body reacts to his passion, his lust. We make love again in the middle of the night without saying one single word.

A light knock awakens me. I open my eyes and see Aidan in a robe walking around the room. He hands something out the door. I can't see who he is talking to. I sit up. I'm still wearing the silk nightgown. I lay back on the pillow and can't help but smile. Last night was so magical. Shocks run through me as I remember his words. *I need your body like I need to breathe. You are my love of a lifetime.*

His love makes my life easier. Aidan is moving around the table. It looks to be set up for breakfast. I slide out of bed and stand in the doorway and watch him. He has put the roses from the Club in a vase in the center of the table. Two places are made up and the food is covered with silver covers, just like the ones at his house. Large goblets are filled with orange juice. I take a few steps towards the table and he sees me.

"Good morning beautiful," he says softly.

"Good morning handsome." I smile and start to twirl my hair.

He reaches his hand out.

"I love you how look in the morning, so natural, I love it."

He pulls my chair out and I sit down. He sits across from me. I see he still has the red tie on underneath his robe. I am immediately aroused. He looks so cute right now.

I smile.

"What's so funny?"

"Nice tie," I say.

He looks down and then up to my eyes.

He lifts his eyebrows.

"Do you like that?"

"Yes, you look cute." I'm still twirling my hair.

"Cute?" He laughs out loud. "I haven't been called that since I was a little boy."

"Well you are."

He shakes his head.

"Did you sleep well?

"Yes, the best I've slept since last time you held me like that."

"Me too. I hope you're hungry."

He lifts the covers at the same time. It's a full plate with eggs, French toast, potatoes, bacon and fruit.

"It looks delicious." I look over to the bar. "Is there any coffee?"

"Shit!" he says loudly. He looks disappointed in himself. He stands and picks up the phone.

He mumbles into the phone.

"Coffee. Vanilla cream." He hangs up.

"Aidan, it's ok."

"No, it's not." He shakes his head.

Geez, it's really not that big of a deal.

"Aidan. Last night you said we should be totally open and honest with each other."

"Yes." He squints at me.

"There is something I want to tell you." I'm nervous.

"Go ahead." He sits back. I take a deep breath.

"I had to fire Lexi yesterday. She told Mr. Nathan to take me to The Shut Eye. She used to work there. Before Maggie."

I'm trying to gauge the reaction on his face.

"Ok. Why are you tel...?"

"Do you know Lexi?" I cut him off.

"No, Gabriella, I don't know Lexi," he says firmly. I hope he's not mad.

"I just wanted to know."

"Anything else you want to know?"

"Yes."

"What?"

"Why do you have a Christmas room in your house?"

He laughs out loud.

"You were in the Christmas room?"

"Yes. It was nice. But, it's September. Do you have it set up all year?"

"Yes, I do. It's my happy room."

"Why do you need a happy room?"

"I go in there after the break room. That's where I come back to reality."

He keeps talking while he answers the door and brings me my coffee.

"Oh." I shouldn't have said anything. This should be a romantic breakfast, not like this.

"Gabriella. It's just where I go to be happy, that's all. Christmas was my favorite time as a child. It was like a fairy-tale. I put that in as soon as I bought the house. Nicholas goes in when he visits. Our parents made Christmas over the top for us. It brings back my happiest memories."

"Oh."

"Life has been tough since they passed away. Nicholas and I connect in there."

"You're right. It was fairy-tale like." It really was.

"Eat up Gabriella."

Is he annoyed with my questioning?

"Zach came to see me this week."

The words spill out of my mouth. I had to get if off my chest.

Aidan nearly spits out his breakfast.

"What? Where the fuck did that come from?"

"He came right after I fired Lexi. I was crying."

I stop and look down.

"I was starting to-- I was-- He comforted me." I glance up at Aidan. He looks angry.

"He did what?" His eyes are blazing.

"He…"

"What did he do? How did he comfort you?" he asks through clenched teeth.

My heart is pounding. *Why did I bring this up?*

I'm still looking down.

"He hugged me and stroked my hair."

Aidan stands so fast that his chair almost falls back.

"I wanted you to help me escape. I don't want him anymore."

"Well I should hope not."

He's standing with his hands on the table yelling at me.

"He said he would be back and he's not letting go."

I regret saying that. But I have to get everything out.

"Not letting go? He's not letting go?"

Aidan steps away from the table and turns back and looks at me.

"I'm the one not letting go Gabriella. I am not losing you." He's getting louder.

"Don't be angry."

"Angry?"

"You are very sexy when you're angry," I say quietly. I don't want any more yelling. He looks so sensual right now.

That robe. That tie. His forcefulness. He blinks his eyes a couple times. Finally his body relaxes and he smiles.

"Oh really?"

"Yes."

I nod and don't break his stare. He sits back down in his chair and starts eating again. I seemed to have calmed him down. I'm waiting for him to say something and finish what's on my plate.

"Let's go back," he says.

"Back?"

"Back to the part where you said you wanted me to help you escape. What did you mean?" *Oh shit.*

"I mean. When you."

I stop and start twirling my hair again. Why am I like this right now?

"I mean how you helped me. When you picked me up from brunch."

I can't look him in the eyes. I feel embarrassed saying this out loud. I see a big grin come across his entire face.

"I remember that well." His grin is distracting. "Are you embarrassed, Gabriella? Nothing we do or say is uncomfortable. Nothing is hidden. We will have no secrets. Ok?"

I nod.

"As long as we are being honest and open, are there any fantasies you want to share with me?" he asks.

His eyes are smoldering. I'm feeling the zing he gives me, but he's not even touching me. He starts to loosen the knot in his tie. My mouth falls open so I can breathe. He undoes his tie and lets it hang to the sides. My heartbeat picks up.

"No. I just like when you help me escape. Escape what's in here."

I use both hands and circle them above my head.

"No fantasies then?"

He hasn't blinked. I'm tingling everywhere. He stands and puts his hand out to me. I take it and he leads me to a loveseat across the room. I sit down and he stands directly in front of me and removes his robe. The tie is still dangling from each side of his neck. He is hard all over. My lump is back. He sits down next to me.

He leans in and licks my ear and whispers.

"Fantasies Gabriella. Tell me yours."

He doesn't stop licking and nibbling. His warm breath is making me squirm.

"Tell me."

"I wish you would help me escape like that again."

I can't go into details. I feel silly.

"Be careful what you wish for baby."

He lifts his eyebrows. *Oh my God.* What does that mean?

He leans back on the arm of the loveseat and rests his hand on the top of it. He sits naked with the tie hanging, his erection solid. I can't concentrate. I can't just sit here. I turn my body towards him and put my arm up by his. I bend forward to kiss him, to touch him, to take him in my mouth, something, but he shakes his head.

"No, no. Tell me," he says.

I bend again and circle the tip of his erection with my tongue. He groans and puts his head back. I turn my swirls into a light sucking, but I don't go past the tip. I want to make love. I don't want to talk. I want to sit on his lap and ride him until we scream. I want to...

I feel his hands in my hair. He pulls my chin and I look up to him.

"Lie back baby," he says quietly.

He lifts my nightgown to my waist with one hand and positions himself between my legs. The tip of his erection is teasing my opening spreading my succulence. I dig my head into the pillow behind me and I feel myself open to draw him in.

"Tell me," he says pushing all the way in.

I cry out and he withdraws totally.

"Now." he demands. He repeats and withdraws again.

"Aidan, please."

"Please what?"

"Please..."

I can't say it. My breath is ragged.

"Tell me then."

He pushes in again. He is so hard.

"I can't."

"Can't what?" He hovers over my opening, tantalizing me.

"I feel silly."

He thrusts in three times and I dig my nails into his back. *Don't stop. Please.* He pulls all the way out and holds his body above mine, but his erection is too far away. He looks into my eyes as I reach to touch his chest. I want to say it. I should just say it. I close my eyes and take a deep breath. When I open them, he hasn't moved. He's still too far. *Fuck I can't say it.* I take a deep breath. *Fuck it.*

"I want you to spank me," I say softly.

His eyes open wider and his mouth opens as he gasps. He kisses me hard. His tongue takes over my mouth. He thrusts in harder than before and I moan on his lips. He pushes my legs up and they are both over his shoulders. He's grunting as he gets deeper.

He stops kissing me and groans between each thrust.

"Where. Did. That. Come. From?"

"I saw it at. At The Shut Eye."

I'm building. He feels amazing. He slows and looks into my eyes.

"Tell me what you saw."

"Ok, but don't look at me."

He nuzzles by my ear, and mine is by his. He's still moving in and out slowly. I wrap my arms around his neck.

I lick his ear and lower my voice seductively.

"I want you to throw me over your lap and caress my bottom. I want you to spank me like you're showing me who's boss." I stop and swirl my tongue. "Tell me I've been a bad girl. Make me scream and beg for mercy."

"Holy fuck, Gabriella!"

His voice is scratchy. The room is spinning. I'm shaking, quivering around him. He pushes in so fast, but drags out too slow. Over and over. He slows and circles his hips.

"What else?" he moans.

"They. Aaahhhh. They had a...."

"A what?" he moans again.

His circles stay the same pace. I'm soaring. *Please. Oh please.*

I suck his ear one last time.

"A cane."

I feel his entire body stiffen.

"Fuck. Hold on," he stays sternly.

This is it. The zing goes right to my groin and he pounds. Pounds. Pounds as I tense and cling to him. I can't think straight. The waves of orgasm are crashing around me. *Fuck! Don't stop. Don't stop.* I scratch my nails down his back and my muscles contract and we come together.

We have caught our breath and are sitting at opposite ends of the loveseat. Our legs are entwined, kind of like how Lucca and I scissor. His body is glistening with sweat. He looks amazing. I tilt and grab an end of the tie that's still hanging from his neck. I pull it and watch as one end goes up behind his neck and comes out the other side, and slides down his body. I fold it so it fits in my hand.

"I'm going to keep this."

I see the smile at the corner of his mouth.

"I couldn't hold on. I was losing my mind. Where did all that talk come from?"

I feel the blood fall from my face. It was easier to talk about this when he wasn't looking at me.

"I told you. I saw some things at The Shut Eye that looked intriguing."

I lift my eyebrows.

He smiles.

"You will tell me more later. I can't manage any more right now. Fuck Gabriella." He shakes his head. "Is there any more? Anything else?"

"No."

"Ok."

He blows out a long breath and puts his head back on the pillow. I watch his chest go up and down.

He lifts his head.

"Just so you know I am going to extract every single ounce of sexual pleasure you have."

He jumps up and kisses my nose and walks to the bathroom. *Oh the back dimples!* Glistening back dimples. I sink down on my pillow and squeeze my eyes. Every ounce? *Wow!*

"Gabriella!"

Aidan is hollering from the bathroom. I jerk awake from my doze.

"Gabriella, come in here."

Was I sleeping? That really tired me out. When I step into the bathroom, he is holding the red glass heart he gave me in his hand.

"I saw this in your purse," he says smiling.

"Yes. I put it in there."

Obviously.

"You did?"

"I want to carry it with me."

"Not only have you put my heart back together, you have also filled it up," he says softly.

He is absolutely the sweetest man. He has filled my heart up too. He has taken away my doubts. His words always make me melt. A tear streams down my face.

He wipes it away with the back of his hand and kisses me.

"Let's shower."

He starts the water and puts his hand out. I love how he does that. It gives me such a reassuring and caring feeling. I cross my arms at the bottom of the nightgown and slowly lift it up my body. He watches my every move and I see his mouth open farther the higher I get. I giggle inside. I lift it over my head and drop it to the floor. He stands still with his mouth hanging. I give his behind a little tap and get in the water. He steps in with me and he taps my behind. We laugh together and take turns washing our hair.

"You have made me so happy. When I look at you," he pauses, "when I look at you I see all of my wishes and dreams coming true."

I beam. He has made me so happy too. I was worried the first night he stayed with me that he would leave the next morning, but look at us now.

"Aidan, I never wonder if you will be there for me. It's like you are my guardian."

"That's the disarray love baby."

"Yes."

I smile and look down. He hugs me tight and we let the water wash over our bodies. I love this man. His love makes all the difference. What did I ever do to deserve this? I feel so lucky.

He steps out while I finish my hair. I hear the door open and close. A minute later I hear it open and close again. *What's he up to?* I look and see a small bag on the floor. I turn the water off and wrap in a towel. I peek inside the bag. It looks like clothes from the gift shop. I forgot I don't have any clothes here and I'm not wearing the gown home.

Who bought these? When did he call someone and tell them to shop?

I close my eyes and laugh. I dry off and slip on the jeans that look way too expensive. As I pull the shirt from the bag, I see a small box in the bottom. I put the shirt on and take out the box. *What could this be?* I open the cover and see a beautiful necklace with a red heart pendant. It's a smaller version of the one that's in my purse. It's shimmering. It's glass or crystal, I'm not sure which. But it's absolutely gorgeous. There is a small note pressed into the cover. I unfold it and it says:

My heart around your neck.
An easier way to carry it with you.

DL

I fall back. I have to lean on the vanity. *What the?* Five minutes ago we talked about the heart in my purse. How does he do that? How did he? I shake my head.

"Same old me again today."

I'm the same old me, but I sure am happier.

When I open the door, I see that Aidan has packed up our things and is waiting for me by the bed. I have the necklace on and am clutching it in my hand. He looks up to me and smiles.

"How did you? When did you?"

I'm stuttering. He laughs and picks me up under my legs and spins around.

He kisses my lips and says, "Let's go home."

Alan opens the door as we approach.

"Good afternoon sir, ma'am," he says with a smile on his face.

"Hi Alan," I say.

"Alan." Aidan nods. "Have Marie serve lunch in the kitchen in half an hour."

"In the kitchen sir?" Alan asks. *Why is he asking that?*

"That's what I said Alan," Aidan responds.

What's that about? Does he never eat in the kitchen?

"Of course sir."

Aidan carries our things up to the bedroom and I follow behind him. I've missed being here. Something looks different in his bedroom. I stand in the doorway and look around. What is it? He's watching me.

There is a new wardrobe chest in the corner. It's light wood and very tall, with two double doors on the top and three drawers beneath. I point to it and he smiles and pushes his hair forward. He's so cute when he does that. *Ok, what's going on?*

He sets the things on the bed, and we walk towards it together. I'm nervous to open the doors. I use both hands and open them at the same time. One side has my clothes hanging and the other has three shelves. Each shelf has something on it. The top one has a wooden G, just like the ones he has for himself downstairs, but smaller. The next shelf has the pictures of our love letters in the sand in little frames. *How did he get those?* The next has the wood box he made me. I lift the cover and the flower card is inside.

I put my hands on my cheeks and gather my thoughts. How did my clothes get here? How did that box get here? Every time I turn around, he does something that blows me away. I open the drawers and they are filled with my bras and panties. The bottom one has shoes. I shake my head. I finger through the hanging clothes, and there are also some new red silk items. I blush. There is a long red nightgown with a ruffled train. It's so elegant and romantic. I look to him and he rubs his hair down again. I put my hand under his chin and kiss his lips softly. I point to the wooden G and he grins as his dimples pronounce.

"I want to get you a big one for downstairs. I started with this," he says quietly.

"What do you mean?"

"Gabriella. I want you to stay here with me."

"I'm here, Aidan."

"I mean forever."

My heart skips a beat. Forever? What is he saying?

"I don't want you to leave."

"Aidan. I. You. You want me to live here?"

Is that what he's saying?

"Yes."

He touches my cheek. I don't know what to say. What about Lucca? I need to think about this. I can't answer right now.

"How did my stuff get here?"

"Lucca helped," he says. *He did?*

"I had Lucca bring some of your things for the weekend, and the box. Stay."

"Aidan. I."

I stop. I don't want to disappoint him. I want to please him. But moving in? I get the red heart and tie from my purse and put it on the shelf next to the G.

"I love you Aidan."

"Stay."

He's not giving up. He wants an answer. I'm not ready to answer.

"I need time to think about this."

I want to stay. The thought of him holding me every night is captivating. I did wish I could stay in his arms forever. I remember him saying he would see what he could do about that. I smile. *Is this what he meant?*

"Stay," he persists.

"I will stay the weekend Aidan."

He picks me up below my waist and I yelp. I wrap my legs around him as he carries me to the bed. We fall to it and laugh.

"What do you want to do today baby?" he asks while kissing me.

I think for a moment.

"I'd love to have a relaxing day here. Can we watch movies? Maybe swim?" I sit up. "I know. I want you to show me the rest of your house. I could sit on your lap in the Christmas room."

I lift my eyebrows.

"Oh baby."

He kisses and rubs against me. I feel the tingles.

"Let's go eat."

Marie serves us lunch at the table in the kitchen. I watch her. She looks so familiar, and she is so young. It's driving me nuts that I can't place where I've seen her before.

"What's wrong?" Aidan asks.

"What do you mean?"

"You're squinting. You're staring at Marie. Has she done something?"

"Oh. I didn't realize. I'm sorry. She just looks so familiar."

His eyes widen. *Shit.*

"Why do you look like that?" I ask.

"I hadn't thought about it until you just said that. But."

"But, what?" *Do I want to hear what he's going to say?*

"She knows Maggie," he stops, "and Maggie knows Lexi, right?"

Oh my God. Yes. Now it's all coming together. Marie came to the office once to visit Lexi. I wonder if they are still friends. *I hope not.* That would be awkward.

"Right. How do they know each other?"

I'm confused.

He swallows.

"Marie used to work at The Shut Eye."

"What?"

I'm getting angry. I push my plate away. I don't want to talk about The fucking Shut Eye anymore. *Ever.* Why does this keep coming up with him? I need to get some fresh air. It's suffocating in here. I walk out the door towards the South Lawn.

What the fuck just happened in there? Why is a girl that used to work at The Shut Eye here, working in Aidan's kitchen? Has he fucked her? Has he seen her naked? Has he done things to her? Did he pleasure her? *Oh my God!* I'm going to be sick. Does this have something to do with why he was yelling at her before? I think he was yelling at her. I don't know. I DON'T KNOW. I'm starting to spiral. *Fuck.*

I continue walking without looking back. I need to sit down. Where is Aidan? He asked me to live here. I can't live here with her. I can't look at her ever again. I start rubbing my face. I fall to the ground and look back to the door. Aidan is talking to her. He's holding his finger up. It looks like he's scolding her. Is he telling her not to say anything to me? I want to go home. I can't live here. I can't stay here. I'm rocking and rubbing my face. I close my eyes and slowly lower my head to the ground.

Aidan catches my head before it hits. He lifts my body so I'm sitting up straight. My head falls forward and he lifts it under my chin.

"Gabriella, stop this." he says sternly. "Look at me. Open your eyes."

I can't. I don't. I will not talk about this anymore.

"Gabriella. I said look at me."

The firmness of his voice snaps in my head. I open my eyes and tears fall.

"Gabriella. Listen to me very carefully."

Each time he says my name, I focus a little more.

"Gabriella. Keep your eyes open. Look into my eyes."

I look in his eyes. They look sincere.

"I know what you are thinking. You need to stop. I hired Marie to cook for me. That's all. She needed help, and I helped her." He presses his forehead to mine. "I have not slept with her."

He backs up.

"I went there one evening and I saw her working. She was young, too young to be there. She was homeless too. Her parents had just died and she had no one. She wasn't as lucky as I was to have a brother to lean on. Are you listening to me?"

I nod.

"I was just giving her a chance, a chance to get out of there. I had to get her out of that life."

I'm concentrating on what he's telling me. So he helped her. That's what he said. That was nice. *I guess.*

"You haven't slept with her? You've never fucked her?" I ask.

"No," he gasps.

"Have you seen her naked?"

"No."

"Have you pleasured her? Have you touched her? Have you anything?"

My tears fall harder. Am I nervous of what he might say or mad at myself for doubting him?

"No Gabriella. Nothing. Stop this," he's almost yelling.

Ok. It's ok. I feel better. I'm catching my breath. I close my eyes with relief of his answer.

"Were you yelling at her last week?"

"When?"

"When I was on the stairs waiting for you. Before you dropped me at brunch."

"Yes."

"Why?"

"I heard her on the phone. She was talking to Maggie." *Maggie?*

"What about?"

"I don't know. I don't fucking care. I told her that is unacceptable. She is not to talk to her again. She said Maggie called her."

"Oh." I'm starting to calm down now.

"They didn't have a chance to talk. I made her hang up. She knows the rules." *Rules?*

"Oh."

"Ok Gabriella. Are you ok now?"

"Yes." I nod.

"Good. We are going in."

He leads us to the TV room and he plays an old black and white movie. I snuggle in next to him on the couch and close my eyes. He is holding me tight. I don't like these movies. Does he find them relaxing?

One minute he's asking me to live with him and the next I'm spiraling. This emotional ride is getting to me. He's right. Our worlds are in disarray. *Because of each other.*

I was so worried if he would be able to handle me and my attacks. So far, he is. He can. But will he hate me eventually? If I did live here, he would see the real me, the raw me. Somehow he makes it easier to be me though. I like that he takes care of me and tells me what to do. But will he hate me? Aaahhh! *Why can't I stop asking myself that?*

Zach has fucked with my head so much. He has made me insecure and I can't stand that. He better leave me alone. Will Aidan and I make it or won't we?

My thoughts suddenly change course. I think of Lucca and I smile at the thought of him sneaking my clothes over to Aidan's house. I love the little chest Aidan bought for me. I love the shelves. I love the silk. I love the G. I love how thoughtful he is. *Could I live here?* I don't know. I need to call Lucca. I'm starting to day dream about the first walk on the beach I had with Aidan. That seems like so long ago. My heartbeat picks up. Why am I feeling like this? What's happening?

Out of nowhere, a loud crackle of thunder shakes the house. My eyes fly open.

Chapter 13

Aidan's entire body stiffens beneath me. I turn to him and he looks scared. His eyes are as big as saucers and he's still. *Fuck. What should I do?* It's going to storm and I'm here. I shake my head back and forth. I know he wants to go to that room. I start to cry. I don't want him to go. I can get him through this myself. He can't run there every time it storms. I can do this. *I will do this.*

I look him in the eyes.

"Don't go. Don't go," I'm pleading.

He sits forward and pushes me to his side as he stands up. I grab his arm and try to pull him back down. I'm determined to do this. He looks down.

"Aidan, please don't go. I know you won't hurt me if you stay. Please," I'm almost whining.

He stares at me, like he's processing what I just said. I know he won't hurt me, but does he know that? I hold eye contact with him. I can't breathe. *What's he going to do?*

He holds his glare and suddenly snaps his fingers and points towards his bedroom. I swallow over the lump in my throat. His eyes are blazing. I slowly stand and walk towards his room. I look out the window before I go up the stairs. It looks dark and lightning flashes through the clouds. My stomach is burning. Am I making the right decision? *Be brave. Be brave.*

What will he do up there? Should I just let him go to the room? Let him do what he needs to do until it passes? *No*. I can do this. I will do this for him. I will let him use my body to get through this. I love him. He won't hurt me. I'm reassuring myself while trying to control my breathing up the stairs.

He slams the door behind us. I stop. Do I hear faint music playing? I have to strain to hear it, and I know I didn't see him turn it on.

He stands to my side and puts his hand on my shoulder. He moves it to the back of my neck and then into my hair. I am trembling. He closes his fingers tightly around my hair and slowly pulls my head back. An extraordinary feeling is taking over my whole body. I don't know what's happening to me. My knees are weak and I can't breathe. I close my eyes and a moan escapes my lips.

"There it is," Aidan says as he puts my head up.

I feel dizzy. There what is? Why is his voice so deep? It doesn't even sound like him. He pulls out a small bottle from one of my new drawers. He sprays something on my neck. It's some weird perfume. I'm standing here as still as I can as I watch him put it back. It smells musky.

"Slip your clothes off Ella."

His voice is distracting. *Why did he call me Ella?* That's just part of Gabriella? I drop my clothes on the floor next to me. He snaps his fingers again.

He points to the end of the bed.

"Stand".

Stand? I am standing. I walk slowly to the end and stand as still as I can. I can do this. My ears are throbbing with my heartbeat.

"Feet shoulder width apart," he demands and I respond instinctively.

"Back straight. Head forward. Hands behind your back." I follow each of his commands.

"No. Present stand."

I hesitate. I don't know what that means and I'm not sure what to do next. I stand still and swallow. *He won't hurt me*. I close my eyes and wait for his command.

"Hands behind your neck."

That's what present stand means. I do as he commands.

He sits on the edge of the bed and looks at me. When I make eye contact, he takes his two fingers and touches my forehead and runs them down my eyelids and they close. My world goes dark.

"Keep your eyes closed."

My breathing is picking up. I can't think anymore. This feeling reminds me of when I spiral. I'm standing, waiting, wet in anticipation, wondering what his next move will be. I hear the zipper of his pants. He must be undressing. The thunder is getting louder. I feel like I'm going to fall over. All of a sudden he grabs my arm and puts me across his lap. *Oh my God*. This is it. Am I ready for this? He caresses my bottom all over with his hand. The touch is so light, it becomes more sensitive. I am trying to relax my muscles and focus on this new sensation. I am getting so aroused by this. *Yes*. This is what I need. I hope this is helping him and he doesn't want to leave me here and go to that room.

His caressing turns into little hand spanks. It feels good. The sensations are indescribable. I am getting lost in them. Chills run through me as I realize I am completely under his control. His other hand moves between my legs. *Yes, touch me Aidan.* I arch my hips in need. He places one finger on each side of my clitoris and spanks my bottom harder than before. I cry out in surprise and squirm beneath him. *This is what I want.* When my muscles relax, he does it again and again. The stinging on my bottom mixed with the tingles between my legs is so sublime. The switch between stroking and stinging, from pain to arousal is so intense.

Another hard spank. The vibration from the spanking is beyond exciting. I'm focusing on his next one, insane with anticipation. I can't think. Within minutes he has taken me to some weird space, like I drop out of reality and thoughts are impossible. He hits again. And again. Between each hit he squeezes my clitoris. Everything is melting together now. He slows and caresses softly, savoring the heat he's created. He lifts his leg, and my bottom goes higher in the air.

"Who's bottom is this?" he asks is his deep scratchy voice.

"Yours." My voice is quiet and soft.

"Yes. Mine Ella. Who do belong to?"

"You."

He spanks again hard. *Yes.*

"Ouch!" I squeal.

His hits are now lower, near where my legs meet. One more time. And again. Still squeezing, he hits again, getting harder each time.

"Ouch!" I scream. This is the best pain I've ever felt.

"Take it for me baby," he demands.

And with those words, he drives me even deeper into the space. All that exists are his commands and the sensations he's creating. I want more. *Do it again Aidan. Spank harder.* He hits again, squeezes his fingers, and hits again. My head is spinning. The jolts from pleasure to pain are so powerful. I am in a place way beyond pain. He stops and sets me on the bed. I feel him spread my legs wide and ice being rubbed over my bottom. He spreads it all around as it melts on my burning cheeks. He slips a finger inside my opening.

"You are so wet. This pleases me."

He teases his finger in and out, spreading my juices. I'm shivering, soaring higher and higher. He continues circling and putting extra pressure on my clitoris.

"Ella. You will live here with me."

"Yes."

I barely slip out a whisper.

"Good girl."

He rubs the ice between my legs, runs it along my swollen lips, and slips it inside. My body is limp, in oblivion. He pulls my hips up and slams his erection into me from behind. I cry out. He pushes hard on my clitoris with his finger and slams. Slams in and out. In and out. I'm in endorphin paradise. Now he switches between slams and spanks. I'm teetering on the edge.

He whispers so softly, I can barely hear him.

"Come for me Ella."

I feel an immediate quickening between my legs and his voice pushes me over. I come instantly when he says to. My body moves on its own, almost coming off of the bed.

"That's it. Yes." He stops moving. "Yes, keep going."

His words drag my orgasm out longer and longer. I now lay completely still as he pounds furiously and empties inside. He collapses next to me. I'm unable to move. My body is heavy and so full of emotions. I feel like I might cry. I drift in and out of sleep, on the edge of incoherence. I don't hear thunder anymore.

He whispers in my ear.

"Sleep baby."

I feel him pull a blanket over my body.

"We will discuss your moving in when you wake."

He kisses my cheek.

I wake a few hours later alone. I look around, but I don't see Aidan. The bedroom door is propped open. I let out a loud sigh as my head hits the pillow. *What the hell? How did he do that?* I close my eyes and jolts race up and down my body as I remember his voice, his touch, his commands. That's the control he was talking about. That was--that was more than exotic. The mind control. It's pure ecstasy. His control is my fuel, totally intoxicating. He can do that again any time. Our fantasies are aligning.

I touch my behind and it's a little sore. I like that. I liked falling asleep with it stinging. He can use my body when it storms out. I gasp and sit up. *Aidan.* Where is he? Was I not enough for him? Did I not hold out long enough? He told me to come, didn't he? Did he go to that room? I need to find him. I jump out of bed and put on the robe. I run down the stairs and turn towards the break room.

"Gabriella."

I hear from behind me. I stop and turn. Aidan is in the kitchen looking at me. He's not in that room. But did he go there? I need to know.

"Gabriella, where are you going?"

I run towards him as he walks to the foyer. He catches me and kisses the top of my head.

"Gabriella, what's wrong? Where were you going?"

"Oh Aidan."

I feel like I might cry. He sets me down and looks in my eyes.

"Tell me what's wrong."

"I thought you were in that room. You left. I thought you..."

Just please say you weren't in there.

"I was just instructing Marie regarding dinner this evening and tomorrow evening."

He looks confused.

"So you didn't go to the. To the break room?" I ask quietly.

"No. Why do you think that?"

"I thought that maybe I-- I thought that maybe I--"

I look over his shoulder. I don't want to talk about this here.

"Maybe you what?" he asks firmly. *Don't be mad.*

"Will you please come back upstairs with me?" I whisper.

He scoops me up in his arms and carries me up the stairs quickly. He slams the door with his foot and sets me on the bed.

"Maybe you what Gabriella?"

Now his teeth are clenched. *Ok, I better tell him.*

"I thought that maybe I wasn't enough for you. You know when it was storming. Maybe I didn't last long enough and you still needed to go in there. Maybe my body wasn't...."

Why am I still whispering?

"Your body? What have I told you about your body?"

"Um."

"What have I told you? I told you that I need it. I need it more than anything. You will never think it isn't enough again."

His jaw is loosening a bit.

"Look at me." He points to his eyes.

"I did not go to that room. After what we just did," he laughs, "I might never need to go in there again."

He's laughing. I did it. *I knew I could do it.* I'm mentally patting myself on the back. I smile and he kisses my lips.

"Even though I let you off easy this time."

He winks. I gulp. *Fuck.* What does that mean?

"Let's go down. I want you to rest. I will start a movie for you while we wait for dinner. I have some things to arrange for tomorrow. And some things to discuss with you."

Tomorrow? What's tomorrow? What does he want to discuss? The conversations that we've had in the last twenty four hours are about all I can handle right now.

He must see the nervous look in my eyes because his next words are assuring.

"It's ok baby. Come on."

He waits while I get dressed and I put my phone in my pocket. We hold hands to the TV room. I sit on the couch and he hands me the remote.

"Give me about an hour. I want you to rest. Then we will eat and talk."

He kisses my nose and leaves the room.

What does he want to talk about? I can't imagine what it could be. I flip through the channels on the TV, but nothing is keeping my attention. I take out my phone and text Lucca. He tells me Geoff contacted him about getting my clothes and the wood box from my room. I remind him of the things that looked intriguing at The Shut Eye that we talked about and told him Aidan spanked me and I absolutely loved it. Should I not tell people that? I don't care. It's Lucca. He won't tell anyone. And he's been there too.

I decide I won't tell anyone else. I tell him about the Ballet Club and the hotel. It's nice to catch up with him. *Wait.* Did I agree to move in here? That thought just hit me like a ton of bricks? Did I say yes while he was? When he? Is that what Aidan is going to talk to me about?

I can't tell Lucca that now. What time is it? I don't want to wait in here anymore. I text Simone, Sam, and Kelly at the same time to pass the rest of this hour. We are having brunch again tomorrow. I can't tell them I am moving in with Aidan, not after last week when I walked out. What am I going to do?

I throw my phone to the table and let out a long sigh. I turn the TV off and lay back. I close my eyes and memorize the endorphin paradise. I float between all the different sensations in my mind. *Yes, I could live here.*

"Hey, are you sleeping again?"

Aidan startles me.

"No."

I really wasn't.

"Were you dreaming? You had a pretty big smile on your face."

He's smiling down at me.

"You make me smile. That's all."

He told me that after our first night together.

Dinner is served by the pool. The sky has cleared up and the sun is shining. Marie is nowhere to be seen. I wonder if Aidan told her that I know about her past. She must have recognized me too from the visit at my office. I don't know. I don't really want to see her now anyway. I guess it bothers me that Maggie called her. Aidan sold that place. *Why would she call?* Aidan is watching me. I don't want him to know what I'm thinking. He would be angry. Maybe we will swim. I've been looking forward to that.

"Gabriella. We need to discuss a few things," he starts.

A few things?

"Ok."

"I have a business dinner tomorrow evening. I know it's a Sunday, but I need to go. You will accompany me."

He's looking in my eyes like I don't have a choice. He didn't ask, he's telling me.

"Ok. But..."

"Nicholas will be here at four tomorrow afternoon and he will be joining us."

Why do I have to go?

"Reservations are at six tomorrow evening for four."

"Four?"

Who is the fourth?

"Yes. We are meeting an associate who is in town. He leaves Monday morning."

"Ok."

He isn't giving me any options here.

"Great. Now about your things."

"What things?" I ask.

"From your house. Geoff will be moving the rest tomorrow."

That's so soon. *Too soon.*

"Tomorrow?" I spit the question out in shock.

"Is there a problem?"

His eyes look scorching. I can't back out. I don't want to back out. I am avoiding the talk with Lucca.

Marie interrupts us by bringing a tray with a glass pitcher and two short ball glasses on it. It's filled with ice and something white. *What is that?* She sets the glasses on the table and fills them. She doesn't say a word and disappears through the trail.

"Drink up baby."

He's back to 'baby' now. I'm thankful for the interruption.

"What is this?"

I ask as I smell it. It smells sweet.

"Oh, I can't say."

He squints at me and smiles. *Why is he being so weird?*

"Please."

I stick my lower lip out.

"I love when you beg." He stops and lifts his eyebrows.

"I will reward you later." Tremors run through me. *How does he do that?* He lifts his glass and looks at it.

"This is a love potion made special for me and you," he says.

"Love potion?"

"Yes. It has milk, wine, nutmeg, sugar, ginger, and lemon juice. Try it."

He motions to my glass. *Love potion?* He's trying to get me in the mood again? I don't need a potion for that. I giggle to myself and take a sip. It's actually very good. It's sweet and smooth.

I set the glass on the table as he leans forwards.

"I'm still waiting to hear more about that cane."

He winks and slams the rest of his glass. My jaw falls open. My heart is pounding in my chest and the wetness between my legs is saturating my pants. He sits back and smiles at me. It's all I can do to lift my jaw up.

"There is one more thing Gabriella."

I hesitate, wondering what else we need to cover after this long day.

"Yes?"

"Your job."

My job? What about my job?

"Earlier this week when I contacted you and you ignored me. I was not pleased."

"That's because--"

"No excuses. I was not pleased."

He's repeating himself. What is he trying to say?

"I told you. You need to get rid of it."

"I don't want to get rid of it," I snap. *I love my job.*

"Why not?"

"It's just part of me. I've been there my whole adult career. It's who I am."

In an odd way, I guess it's my form of control. I'm in charge. I'm the strong one there. Maybe I'm tired of being the strong one. I like that Aidan does that. Could I handle that full time though? I'm confused. Why are we talking about this?

"I want to enable you to be who you are Gabriella, but this is just a job. You are very smart and talented. You can do better."

Now he's being complimentary. I'm not sure exactly what he's telling me.

"I have to go back on Monday Aidan." I can't *not* go back.

"Fine. Next weekend we are going out of town. We will finish this topic then."

Out of town? He's all over the place tonight. Jumping from one topic to the next. This love potion isn't working. I roll my eyes.

"Out of town?"

"Yes," he says firmly and stands up.

"But I--"

I'm supposed to visit my parents with Sebastian. He puts his finger up and shakes his head. I stop talking.

He reaches for my hand and I reluctantly take it. He's done this before when I wanted to continue talking. He's so maddening sometimes. He walks towards the pool and lets go of my hand. He gestures with his head towards the water. *He wants to swim?* I shake my head no. I want to talk more about going out of town. He nods his head yes and steps out of his shoes. He lifts his shirt over his head and puts his hands on my waist. I don't move. His bare chest is so distracting. I want to taste it. I want to run my fingers down it.

I leave my hands at my side. I'm remaining firm in my decision to not let him distract me with a swimming session. He steps back. I assume he's reading my body language, and a small laugh escapes his lips. *This isn't funny*. He unbuttons his jeans and lowers them. He doesn't have anything on underneath. My eyes perk up and he kicks them off and they fly about ten feet. I shake my head and laugh. He's putting on quite a show. I watch his erection as he walks towards me. I want to drop to my knees and take him in my mouth, but I decide to keep playing this stubborn game. I close my eyes. I can't concentrate with *that* coming at me. I smile and he's at my neck nibbling on it.

"What's so funny?" he asks.

I lift my shoulders to spread the tingles he gives me. "Nothing."

He leans back and grins. His hands are underneath my shirt tickling my naval. He's using my trick. He lifts my shirt and I hold my arms up so he can take it off.

"I knew it."

"Knew what?" I ask.

"Nothing. I can be very convincing." *Yes he can. When he's naked.*

I put my head back to give him better access to my neck. He licks it and nibbles as he tries to unbutton my pants. He's struggling with them.

"What the fuck is wrong with these pants?"

He's laughing as he fumbles with the button.

"I don't know. You bought them." We laugh together.

I can't stay mad at him. We manage to get them undone and slip them off. We are both naked walking down the stairs into the pool. The water is so warm and soft. It feels nice on my bottom. Well the ice felt nice too. I look to him and he is watching me.

"I love seeing you smile so much today. I hope it has something to do with me."

His finger slides down slowly between my legs. He parts the lips and massages my opening. His eyes fly up to meet mine. He can feel how wet I am.

"Of course Aidan."

I take his face in my hands and kiss his lips while his fingers explore. Our tongues entwine and I feel him grow harder against my stomach. Memories of this afternoon flood back again.

I pull him close to whisper in his ear.

"When you do this to me… when you take me with you and we escape together… I'm helpless. I will let you have it all, whatever you want."

He abruptly removes his fingers and slaps both sides of my behind at the same time with his hands.

"Ouch!" I cry out. He lifts me and slides me onto his erection.

"Oh. Aaaahhhhh. Aidan."

I wrap my legs behind his back to hold on. He strides across to the side of the pool and pushes me against the wall. He grinds his hips so deep, I bite his shoulder. With the sting still on my behind, and him squeezing it now to push himself deeper, and his hard erection pushing and stretching me wider, I can't control myself. He circles and I tighten my legs and bite harder.

"I love seeing you like this. I can't."

He pauses as I bend my knees up and pull him in deeper.

"I can't get enough of you, Gabriella."

His breathing is ragged. He's grunting between each word. He bends his knees and thrusts up. Each time he hits that sweet spot I moan and he growls back. Back and forth, louder and louder. *Don't stop Aidan.* My inside muscles grip around him and he stiffens and stops. But, I almost. Why is he stopping? He is so hard inside me.

"You drive me absolutely wild. I love you with my whole body and soul. You are what's been missing. You are the missing piece to my soul."

He's panting. I squeeze my legs. I want him to keep going. His hardness lingering inside is unbearable.

"We are going inside," he says as he lets go of me.

What? Why are we going inside? He grabs my hand and pulls me to the end of the pool. As we get shallower in the water, my knees and legs feel weaker. They are jelly. I splash him from behind and get his back and hair wet. He stops and lets go of my hand. *Oh shit.* He turns around smiling from ear to ear.

"Did you just splash me?" he asks.

"Yes," I squeak.

"Now you're in trouble."

He splashes me back. We both laugh as we splash each other back and forth. We tickle and dash, and giggle and dunk. We play and have fun all while seducing one another in the pool.

Aidan pulls me towards the house. So much is going through my mind right now. I got him through the storm which I'm still pretty proud of. I also got through the spankings. I'm beaming inside. Thinking of the fear and excitement he created give me chills down my spine. The euphoria trip was off the charts. I love Aidan so much. My deepest desire is to please him. It was love at first sight. It's as if once he held my hand that first night, he has never let go. I don't want him to let go. I trust him completely. Somehow he makes me feel beautiful.

In some way he knows how to build my confidence. He surprises me constantly with his words. With his actions. He wants me to quit my job. I can't do that. I still don't know what happened to Mr. Nathan, or the other guy. I have brunch tomorrow. I need to tell Lucca I'm moving, and inside I'm missing him already.

We have dinner with Nicholas and some business associate. *Why am I going to that*? I told Aidan that Zach came to see me. Marie used to work at The Shut Eye. Aidan owns it. Well, used to own it. Lucca. Brunch. Spankings. Lucca. Moving. Zach. Work. Mr. Nathan. Dinner. *'Aaaaahhhhhhhhhhhhhhh!'* I scream inside my head. Why do I build myself up and get all stressed? I have to stop doing this. As we arrive at the top of the stairs I squeeze Aidan's hand. He squeezes back and lets go.

"What is it?" he asks. I look down.

He repeats himself.

"I said. What is it?"

I glance up at him with a lump in my throat. I circle both of my hands over my head. I hope he remembers what that means. I need an escape from my mind. He doesn't ask any questions. He nods, snaps his fingers, and points to the bedroom. I put my head down and walk past him to the end of his bed. The door slams behind us.

"Remember, you will do exactly as I say. Do you understand?" he asks from behind me.

I nod as shivers run through me. My loins are already burning.

"Clothes on the floor. Shoulders and knees on the bed."

Shoulders and knees? I follow his command and drop my clothes to the floor. I climb on the bed and sit on my knees. *What does he mean shoulders?* I slowly lean forward, turn my head and rest on my shoulders.

"Bottom up."

I push my feet back so my bottom is in the air.

"Arms over your head."

I do as he says and entwine my hands together. I hope this is ok.

"Very Good. Good girl."

Was he going to tell me to do this with my hands? I smile inside.

"Legs apart."

I open my legs so they are shoulder width apart. That's how he told me to do it this afternoon.

I finally feel him. He slowly runs his fingers over my back, and my body arches wherever he touches. The touches are so light, so soft, my heart starts to flutter. Fingers from both hands tickle the cheeks on my bottom. They are still sore, but this feels so good. I feel the moisture build between my legs. The fire is burning deep inside. His fingers slip between my thighs and they caress my swollen lips. They are so sensitive right now. They glide through my heat and when he finally hits my clitoris, I cry out.

"Yes, baby," he whispers while circling his fingers. He increases pressure and I push back against his hand. I want him to go inside.

He stops.

"Bottom up."

I lift back up. He spreads my lips with two of his fingers and another one slips inside. All. The. Way.

"Aaahhhhhh," I moan.

He withdraws. I hear him undress and get on the bed behind me. His hands are on my hips and he slides his erection between my lips. He teases with the tip, hovering over my opening. My heart is pounding and I try to rub against him. He backs up. He bends down so his chest is covering my back. He squeezes both nipples and I moan again.

He continues the sweet torment with the tip of his erection, and whispers in my ear.

"You will not make another sound. If you do, I will stop."

He pushes the tip a little deeper, and pinches the nipples a little harder. I'm losing my focus.

"I've said that before, and didn't comply, but this time. Oh baby. This time I mean it."

He is grinding against me as I feel myself open more to suck him inside. I push back on him and try to spread my legs farther.

"And if you move in any way, I will spank you," he growls.

I gulp. *Fuck.* He lets go of one nipple and tickles my bottom.

"I'm sure you're still stinging from earlier."

He licks my ears and lifts up. He taunts me, teasing me with his hard body. Waves of pleasure are running through me. I predict how my body will react, and am not disappointed. I can't hold myself up anymore. I can't breathe. I can't move. His fingers are tickling up and down my thighs as he plays. I'm concentrating on not holding my breath. I need to relax and take in these sensations. I feel the vibrator tickle my clitoris and I almost let a moan squeak out but I catch it. I realize how total his control is. I don't know if I can keep all this inside much longer. I want to beg. I want to scream. I want to lie down. The vibrator moves back and forth over the most sensitive part of my entire body and my knees start to buckle. They are quivering.

Without stopping, he bends down again and whispers.

"I can't wait to bury myself inside you."

My whole body shudders at his words. That's it. I can't fight it anymore. I'm fighting for control, gasping for breath. He pushes hard with the vibrator and I'm on the edge, climbing into the most intense state of exhilaration. The pressure lightens and eventually stops. *What? Why? Wait. Please Aidan.*

"Turn over," he commands.

Oh finally. Put it in. Fuck me. Fuck me hard.

I turn and lie on my back, relieved to not have to hold my body up anymore. His body is on top of mine.

He kisses my lips.

"No sounds," he reminds me.

Within one second, he slides down and with both hands he spreads my legs and takes my clitoris in his mouth. *Holy fuck.* I can't do this. He sucks it away from my body, and it grows harder. I've been craving this sensation of constant arousal, but I don't know if I can. I don't think I can. *Aaaahhhhh!* Sensation washes over me. I'm trying to be still like he said. He sucks harder, swirls his tongue, and sucks again. I'm on the edge again and he stops. The edge is so delicious.

He is at my face, kissing me, biting my lips. I can taste myself. He slams into me and I cry out. I have to. This is so fucking intense. He bites my neck and I cry out again.

"Yes baby, scream for me," he grunts as he slams harder.

He's not letting up. I scream every time he hits.

"Come for me Gabriella," he demands.

One final thrust and I'm gone. I'm shattered. I come hard around him at his command.

"Yes," he screams and comes with me.

"My princess," he says as we merge our bodies into our spooning position and he holds my hand.

Chapter 14

"We will stop at the hospital before I drop you at brunch," Aidan says to me while I'm showering.

The hospital? I don't want to go.

"Did you hear me?"

"Yes."

Can't he go while I'm at brunch and then come back for me? I'm not going to argue with him. I really don't want to see Mr. Nathan. He creeps me out now.

"Good."

Aidan shuts the door.

I finish washing my hair while dreaming of yesterday. I am in total bliss. Aidan, the man of my dreams, my love, my destiny. His body, my body, his control, the effects. I throb just thinking about it. I step out of the shower and wrap my hair in a towel. Today is going to be a long day. I need to see Lucca before Geoff just shows up there to move my things. I need some alone time with him.

I open the door and see Aidan sitting on the bed. He is dressed for the day and looks so happy. His dimples make me smile. I am naked with only the towel in my hair. He has my clothes laid out for me next to him. I start to dress and feel shy as he watches my every move.

"Aidan. I'd like some time with Lucca today."

I need this time. I need him to understand.

"What do you mean?" He looks confused.

"I need to talk to him alone. I need to tell him I'm moving."

Aidan's face lights up.

"Hell yes you do!"

He pulls me to him and he hugs me.

"I'm going to have him pick me up from brunch and he can drop me here after. Ok?"

"You must be here by four o'clock."

"That's plenty of time Aidan."

He takes his wallet out of his pocket and hands me a credit card.

"Take this."

"What's this for?" *Why is he giving me his credit card?*

"Lucca picked out the black dress you wore on our first date, right?" he asks.

How does he know that?

"Um, yes." *Why?*

"You looked so delectable that night," he grins. "Take him to get a dress for this evening."

"Um, er- ok."

I sound stupid. I hate when I stutter in front of him.

"Actually, get a couple. Come back here with your hands full of bags. Buy the store out for all I care."

He smiles.

"But be here by four," he says more seriously.

Yes, I get it. He's talking like he's up here on cloud nine with me.

I finish my hair and makeup. I grab my purse and practically skip to meet Aidan by the front door. I smile at him. *He is my paradise.*

I text Lucca from the car and arrange for him to pick me up from brunch for our day of fun. I tell him we get to shop for dresses and I can mentally see him jumping up and down while he's texting me back. He's probably more excited than I am. I've missed him. I'm not looking forward to discussing the move, but I know out of everyone, he will be the one that understands.

Aidan goes over the plan again for tonight on the drive to the hospital. Nicholas is coming at four. We have reservations. I'm rolling my eyes inside. He has told me this already. I still don't understand why I have to go. I guess it doesn't really matter as long as I can be with him.

We park outside the hospital and my stomach drops. I don't want to go in. Aidan opens my door and puts his hand out. I'm looking down and don't reach for it. He squats next to me.

"Gabriella. Come in with me."

"Why?"

"Now." He shakes his head like he's frustrated with me.

"But--"

"I know this is what's best. You need to see him, confront him, something."

He puts his hand out again and I take it.

We don't speak as we walk inside. I trust that he knows what's best. The ride to the fourth floor is taking forever. I can't swallow. *What if Mr. Nathan's awake?* I don't want to go. When the elevator opens, Aidan steps out, but I stand still. Our arms are extended between us. He looks back to me and pulls his hand and I jerk forward.

He drags me around the desk and we stand in front of Mr. Nathan's room. The blinds are closed, but the door is halfway open. I'm looking at the floor. I can't make eye contact with him, not after what he put me through. Aidan goes in first and I follow behind him. I hear him let out a loud sigh and I look up. Mr. Nathan looks exactly the same way he did when I was here. He's still hooked up to the same machines, and his face doesn't look any better. Has he woken up at all? Aidan and I look at each other. A nurse interrupts us before we can speak.

"Do you know Mr. Nathan?" she asks.

"Yes, I was here earlier this week. We were just looking for an update on his progress."

I speak before Aidan.

We aren't family so I didn't know if the nurse would give out any information or not. I want her to know I was here before. Aidan squeezes my hand.

"I see. Well, nothing has changed. He is no better and no worse. We still don't know what happened to him, but at this point we aren't sure if he will come out of his coma."

Aidan squeezes my hand again. We know what happened to him.

"Thank you ma'am," Aidan says and leads us out of the room, around the desk, and into the elevator.

This time I am keeping up the pace with him. It seems like we both want to get out of here as fast as possible. When the doors close, he pulls me into his arms. We hug tightly and I feel tears forming as I rest my head on his shoulder. I am deeply relieved that Mr. Nathan hasn't woken up, that he can't hurt me. Is that wrong of me? Is it wrong that it's a total turn on that Aidan fought for me, to protect me? He leans me back and looks in my eyes.

"I will never let anything happen to you," he says firmly and holds me tight until the doors open.

Aidan drops me at Sweet Elle at exactly ten on the dot. He kisses my cheek and I remind him I will be home, as requested, by four this afternoon. He smiles and watches me walk in.

It feels like forever since I've been here. The girls are all at the table waiting for me and smile as I approach. Kelly, Sam, and even Simone stand up to hug me.

I tell them about my crazy week at work with Mr. Nathan and The Shut Eye, and how Aidan came to rescue me. I explain how I had to fire Lexi but hired Beth. The only details I leave out are about the break room at Aidan's house and the thundering activities. My stomach burns deep down as I think about it. I enlighten them with my favorite story of the whole week, the red dress.

"He sent you a dress?" Kelly asks.

"Yes." I'm beaming.

"To your work?"

"Yes." I'm nodding with glee.

"And then you didn't expect him to be there, but he was, and you ran to him and he picked you up in his arms?" Sam asks.

"Yes."

"And put your shoes on for you, and had five roses dropped at the table," Sam pauses, "all for how many times you said you loved him. He kept track?"

She sounds surprised, impressed, I can't tell.

"And got you a limo and hotel room that was full with candles and rose petals?"

Simone speaks. Is she impressed too? I nod.

"Gaby, this is love?" Simone asks. I nod again.

"I'm very happy for you. You deserve this."

She stands and comes to hug me. She really is trying. I hated arguing with her.

"Thank you, Simone. That means a lot."

We go back and forth with the rest of the story. Simone tells us about her new job and her new car. Kelly and Sam talk about the matching outfits they found online. We all laugh. It feels so good for the four of us to giggle together again. Simone asks about next week and I say that I will be out of town with Aidan. She smiles like she understands, but I wonder if she really does. She wants to plan a slumber party for the following weekend for the four of us. I'm sure that will be fine.

I look up and Lucca is at the table. I stand immediately and throw my arms around his neck.

"Lucca! Thank you for coming." I hug him tight.

"Of course, Gaby."

I let go as he turns to motion at our server.

"Oh, and the waitress told me to tell you the table has been paid for."

What? Who? Did Aidan pay again? I didn't see him. I hug myself inside.

"Of course it has," Simone says. Did that sound a bit sarcastic?

We all hug goodbye and promise to text later this week before I go out of town.

Lucca drives us to the mall. My hands are getting sweaty. I don't want to have this conversation with him. I will miss our late night talks, scissoring on the couch, him taking care of me, tucking me in. Maybe it will be a relief for him not to deal with my spiraling anymore. Maybe he will...

"Gaby, I have something to tell you."

He interrupts my inner dialogue. What is he going to say? I look to him as we step out of the car and shut our doors. He stops us at the back of the car and leans on it.

"Gaby, remember I told you I'm going out of town this week so I can't go to our concert?"

"Yes." *I'm nervous.*

"Well, I need to be away for a bit longer," he says as he holds my hand.

"How much longer?" I ask.

"A few weeks. I'm not exactly sure how long yet. My mother is ill and I need to fly home to take care of her." *Oh no.*

"Ok." I feel sad for him.

"I will work from there, but I am worried about you. I wish you wouldn't stay at the house by yourself. What if Za..?"

I shake my head and he stops.

"Lucca, Aidan has asked me to move in with him," I say quietly.

He looks relieved at first, then disappointed, then back to relieved.

"Move in?"

"Yes."

He looks like he is thinking through a plan.

"This is good. I'm glad you won't be at the house alone. I need to get through this with my mother. But when I get back..."

He stops and shakes his finger at me and smiles.

"When I get back, you might just have to come home." We laugh together.

"I will miss you, Lucca." I will miss him more than anything.

"I will miss you more, Gaby." He squeezes my hand.

We hit all of his favorite stores and laugh and giggle as I try on things that I would never buy. We joke that Sam would buy these things, and that Kelly would too now that they dress alike. He picks out eight stunning dresses, and I am going to buy them all. He knows my body and what fits, so I have to get all of them. Who knows when we will shop again? The thought makes me sad.

I end up with three black dresses, one navy, one charcoal, and three red. I run my fingers over the red ones while the cashier rings them up. Aidan loves red. I hope he loves me in these. I close my eyes and smile. It's only been a few hours and I miss him. I can feel him even when we aren't together. I check the time on my phone and it's only just shy of three o'clock.

"Lucca," I whisper in his ear.

"Gaby," he whispers back. I smirk.

"I have an hour. Let's go to..."

I stop and look behind me and whisper, "...the naughty store."

"Gaby! What has Aidan done to my best friend?" He lifts his eyebrows.

What has he done to me? I relish in the memories.

Lucca leads me to the store where they sell nighties, teddys, panties, anything you can think of.

I whisper again.

"Whatever I buy, it has to be red."

"Oh my! A red man?" He lifts his eyebrows again and I blush.

We look around, hold things up, and I try things on. I have a knee length red nightie, a red bra with matching panties, and a red teddy in my hand. I set them at the register. As the cashier is scanning them, something else red catches my eye. It's set at the far end of the counter. I pick it up and it's a red leather sleeping mask. I bring it to my nose and smell it as I close my eyes. The scent immediately arouses me. Sensations flood my body. *What's happening to me?* I put my hand on the counter to hold on. My head is spinning. I open my eyes and look around. I feel dizzy. I have to buy this. I hand it to the cashier as Lucca approaches.

"Oh Gaby! You are a naughty girl."

As those words slip out of his mouth, I imagine Aidan saying them to me in that voice. The voice he had during the storm.

As we approach the gates to Aidan's house, my stomach is unsettled. I don't want to say goodbye to Lucca. He's always been in the next room, or just a few miles away. I smile thinking about the pep talks he's given me, the times he's tucked me into bed after a bad day, the cruising and singing at the top of our lungs. He is the best friend I could ask for. He pushes the button and the gates open. I hold his arm and a tear falls down my face. My pulse quickens. What am I going to do without him? He stops in front of the house and looks to me.

"I love you, Gaby."

"I love you too, Lucca."

My face is getting all tingly. I can't hold back the tears.

"I will only be gone a couple of weeks," he says. But I feel like it will be much longer.

"When are you leaving?"

"In the morning." *The morning?! That's too soon*. He wipes my tears with the back of his hands.

"I'm sorry to hear about your mom."

"Thank you. Remember I am only a phone call away. We can still text all day like usual. It's not like you work in your office anyway."

He smiles.

We laugh out loud together and hug tightly for several minutes. My head is resting on his shoulder. I don't want him to go. I don't want to say goodbye. He kisses my hand as I get out of the car. I carry all my bags up towards the door and Alan opens it for me. I turn to look back at Lucca and wave. He blows me a kiss and drives away. I watch him make his way back through the gardens and tears stream down my face uncontrollably. *I will miss you Lucca.*

I wipe my face and catch my breath before going in. Alan is still standing in the doorway. I step in and he closes the door behind me.

"Mr. Scott has been waiting for you ma'am," Alan says.

"Thank you Alan," I reply and he disappears down the hallway.

I set my bags down on the floor next to my feet and stand between them. I see Aidan and Nicholas in the kitchen. Nicholas is wearing a dark suit. He is dressed for dinner. I watch them talk and laugh back and forth. Aidan is so good looking and poised. I could watch him all day. I've really missed him today. He looks up from his conversation and we make eye contact. His face fills with delight. When I smile back, his face falls. He must be able to tell something's wrong. I'm not crying anymore, but I'm sure my face looks like I have been. He walks swiftly over to me while holding my gaze.

He holds my face in his hands.

"Baby, what's wrong?"

I wait a moment to compose myself before I can reply.

"Lucca is flying home for a while to help his mother. I'll miss him. That's all."

"I'm so sorry baby. Of course you will."

He kisses my forehead and hugs me. I'm back in Aidan's arms. I feel better already.

"I'll be ok. It was unexpected. He told me before I could tell him I was moving. He didn't want me to stay there alone."

"That was very kind of him. He's a good friend."

"The best." I smile.

"Speaking of. All your things are upstairs. Geoff brought them today."

It's all here? Already?

"What have you done with my brother?"

Nicholas interrupts us. I forgot he was here for a moment.

"Hi Nicholas. Nice to see you again."

I extend my hand. He grabs it and pulls me into a hug.

"Look at you. All lovey dovey." Nicholas is pointing to Aidan.

"I thought he was unchangeable. I don't know what you've done to him. He's been telling me about all his goodies for you."

Nicholas is talking to me now. I smile. *Goodies?* They must have gotten that word from their parents.

"Very funny."

Aidan punches Nicholas on the shoulder and they play fight back and forth. They are very cute together.

Aidan picks up my bags and turns to Nicholas.

"Give us a minute. We'll be right back."

He winks at him and gestures with his head for me to go upstairs. I follow behind him as he carries all the things I purchased today. I can't wait to show him what Lucca picked out. I'm sure he will be pleased. He throws the bags on the bed and wraps his arms around me.

"I missed you today, Gabriella," he says while kissing my neck. His touch sends shivers down my back.

"I really missed you too. I thought about you while I was shopping."

"I want to throw you on that bed and make passionate love to you." His hands are in my hair and he's licking my lips. "But we need to get ready for dinner." He's not letting go.

"Can I show you what I got today?"

"Yes." He presses his groin into mine and I feel his erection.

"Ok. Sit down." I'm trying to push him back to sit on the bed, but he's so strong.

"Let me show you!" I laugh in protest.

He releases his grip and sits on the bed. I can still see the erection through his jeans. I shake my head to bring myself back to reality. His body is so distracting. He leans back on his elbows and grins at me. I'd love to sit on his lap right now. I'd love to ride... I shake my head again. *Stop it.*

I take out each of the dresses one by one. When I hold up the last one, it's a knee length strapless red dress, and his eyes broaden. He grabs it and sets it next to him.

He mouths the word "tonight" to me.

I nod and he winks. I slowly pull out the red nightie and he puts his hand over his heart and moves it up and down like his heart is fluttering. I laugh inside. I set the red bra and panties on top of the red dress he wants me to wear, and he falls back to the bed still fluttering his heart. He's so funny. I remove the red teddy and let the bag drop to the floor below it. I hold it up to me and he lifts just his head to look. His eyes broaden even more as he presses his head into the bed beneath him. Now he's extending his arms the entire way doing the heart flutter thing with both hands. I bend down to take the red leather sleeping mask out of the bag and hold it discretely in my hand. I have a lump in my throat. I don't know what he will think about it. I quietly climb up on the bed and straddle his hips. I hold it behind my back as he looks up at me. I kiss his lips softly holding myself up with my free hand. He kisses me back and reaches to my shoulders. His hands run down my arms.

He stops the kiss abruptly.

"What's behind your back?"

"Nothing," I whisper and shake my head.

"Gabriella."

He gives me a stern look. *Oh, calm down.*

I bring my hand in front of me and open it, holding the mask up so he can see it. His eyes look like they are going to pop out of his head. *Shit.* What does that mean? Is this a good look or a bad look?

I see a smirk form in the corner of his mouth. I hold it to my nose and smell it again. I inhale deeply and lean back on his bent legs while closing my eyes. The smell is so erotic. I feel the dampness between my legs. I look to him and hold it under his nose to smell. He closes his eyes and in one second, he has flipped me onto my back. He's kissing me, grinding against me, biting my neck.

"You... You..." He's trying to say something between his ragged breaths. "You are going to wear that later."

I wrap my legs around his back. I wish we didn't have any clothes between us.

"You said I could. Could have it all, whatever I want," he whispers.

"Yes."

Now my breathing is ragged too. He does this to me so quickly.

"Tonight. I'm taking it. Be ready."

He's grunting, biting my breasts over my shirt. I cry out. He stops and stands at the end of the bed, leaving me breathless, panting for him.   .

"Get ready. Meet me downstairs."

He leaves the room and shuts the door. My head falls to the bed as I calm down. What just happened? I take it he likes the mask? I hug myself and close my legs. We need this dinner to get over with. I want to be naked in this bed. I run my hands over his sheets. *Oh Aidan. I love you so much. You take me places only love can go. Places I've only dreamed of.*

I change into the new red bra and panties and step into the dress. I look in the mirror and find that it does fit nicely. Lucca has come through again! The red heart necklace looks nice with it too. I find the red shoes from Friday night that Aidan bought. They are on the floor in front of the chest where my clothes are. I open the doors but my clothes are gone. The only things hanging are the red silk items. Where is my stuff? Where are the things Geoff brought?

I open Aidan's closet door and have to step back. I've never been in his closet. It's as big as his bedroom. All of my things are hung around one side, with his along the other. My shoes are stacked neatly on the shelves in the middle of the wall. This is incredible. His side is full with different suits, ties, shirts, sweaters, all arranged by color. He has just as many shoes as I do. There is a chandelier in the middle of the ceiling. This is unbelievable. How have I never been in here? I walk around and feel the different material of his suits and shoes. Drawers in the middle hold socks, his boxers, and my bras and panties. It's so organized. How did all this happen in a couple hours?

I go back to the chest. The pictures, the wood box, and the G are still on the shelves. I smile. I would like a big G for downstairs someday. I hang the nightie and feel chills as I remember Aidan's fluttering heart.

I leave the teddy and mask on the end of the bed for when we get home. I hang the rest of my new dresses and close the closet door. I walk down the stairs feeling sexy and confident. Aidan has done this to me. Lucca asked what happened to his best friend. *Well look at me, better than ever!* Aidan and Nicholas walk out of the kitchen as I hit the bottom of the staircase. Aidan has changed and is also in a dark suit and tie. When did he do that? They really do look like twins today.

"You look fabulous. We've been waiting for you."

Aidan holds out his hand. Waiting for me? Doesn't he remember what just happened upstairs? I needed a moment to recover.

"Aidan said we couldn't go in there without you." Nicholas smiles at me. *In where?*

"Come on baby."

The three of us walk down the hallway and into the Christmas room. I remember that Aidan told me Nicholas likes to come in here whenever he comes over. They both walk slowly around touching the beards of the Santa's and humming to the music. I smile. That's what I did when I found this room.

Aidan follows Nicholas and I follow Aidan. They reach their hands up and clink the bells together above their heads. They stop at the trees and move their hands between the different ornaments and lights. They pause at some ornaments like they are reliving a memory when they received it. It's heartwarming to watch them do this together. It must have been devastating to have your parents die at such a young age. Aidan sits down in the high backed red velvet chair and pats his leg for me to sit down. I sit on his lap as Nicholas inspects one of the reindeers. No one is talking. It's weird. Aidan takes my hand and moves it between his legs. I feel his erection and my eyes fly to his. He smiles and moves my hand back to my lap.

"I told you this was a happy room," he whispers in my ear.

I look at Nicholas to make sure he's not looking at us. I'm so embarrassed. I shake my head and Aidan taps my bottom as we leave the room.

Tuxedo man is waiting with the doors open to the limo to take us to dinner. I listen as Aidan and Nicholas discuss business. I hear Aidan say he might not be in the office as much going forward. He says he is considering doing 'The Talk' next weekend. *What's 'The Talk'?* He hasn't said anything to me, just that we are going out of town. I have no idea where we are going. They both agree they are happy Mr. Blake is flying back tomorrow. Mr. Blake must be the associate we are meeting for dinner. I'm bored already sitting here listening to this. I wish I could have had more time with Lucca instead of go to dinner. I am excited to get home though and try on some new things. I smile to myself and Aidan catches me. He squints and smiles back. Those dimples make me melt.

I walk into The Waterfront Hotel lobby holding Aidan's arm. Nicholas checks in with the hostess while Aidan leads me to the bar. He orders us each a glass of white wine. I excuse myself to use the restroom while we wait. I touch up my lipstick and text Lucca while he's packing. He says the house is lonely without me. I tell him Aidan loved the sleeping mask. We go back and forth and end with him saying he is going to text me before he leaves in the morning.

When I walk towards the bar, Nicholas and Aidan are talking to a man in a suit. That must be Mr. Blake. As I get closer, the man looks back at me over his shoulder and smirks. Why did he smirk? I look down at my dress to see if I've spilled or torn something. Why did he do that? It's bothering me. Does he know me? He doesn't look at all familiar. Aidan turns and introduces me to him.

"Nice to meet you Mr. Blake," I say as I extend my hand.

He shakes it and nods. There is that smirk again. It's almost rude, arrogant. And he can't even say nice to meet you? This is going to be a long dinner.

The hostess finally comes to lead us to our table. I sit between Nicholas and Aidan, and Mr. Blake is across from me. He is looking at me. I feel uncomfortable.

"Your waitress will be right over," the hostess says while opening the menus.

"Fine," Mr. Blake says.

In an instant all of the hairs on my arms stand on end. My hands are tingling and my lump in my throat is so big it's blocking my air. *That voice.* How do I know his voice? I immediately feel sick. Something is wrong. I don't want to ruin their business dinner. I don't know if I can leave gracefully. I can't move. Mr. Blake is watching me, making me more nervous. I slowly reach for Aidan and almost knock his glass of wine on his lap. He's not paying attention. He's looking at his phone. I manage to tap his arm with my fingers.

"Excuse me," Mr. Blake says as he stands and walks away from the table. My entire body stiffens and my eyes fly open. I feel like I'm going to pee my pants. I'm holding my breath, wanting to throw up all over the table.

"Gabriella. What the fuck?"

Aidan sounds mad. I can't tell him what's wrong. I don't know what's wrong.

"I…"

I can't say anything else. I am freezing. I am weak. I'm trying to breathe.

"Nice ass on that one." That's it. That's how I know him. A wave of fear takes over my body and tears begin to stream down my face.

"Fuck Gabriella. What's wrong with you?"

Aidan is getting louder. I can't answer him. I can't speak. I'm starting to spiral. I lean forward and rub my face. I look through my fingers and Nicholas is just staring at me. I'm screaming inside. I don't want to make a scene. I shake my head back and forth and I remember. That voice. At The Shut Eye. Mr. Blake is the other man. The man in the room with Mr. Nathan. *Oh my God. Oh my God.*

"Tell me!" Aidan hits his hand on the table so hard, the glasses jump up. "Now!"

I run my hands down my face and look in his eyes. He looks so angry and concerned at the same time.

"Aidan I'm so sorry." I'm sobbing.

His eyes are burning.

"That man," I'm wiping my tears as I talk. "That man was in the room with Mr. Nathan. When I was…"

Aidan's eyes get bigger. He looks like he wants to kill someone. He's looking around the room, but Mr. Blake is nowhere to be seen.

"You watch her," Aidan says to Nicholas.

"Aidan, please don't go. Please don't leave me here," I'm pleading. I need him to take me in his arms and bring me back down.

"Please don't go."

"Do not fucking leave her side Nicholas."

He's talking through gritted teeth while he stands up scanning the room.

"Aidan, please don't leave, please don't go. I need you. Please," I'm begging.

I will get on my knees if I have to. I need him to hold me. I reach for his hand, but he moves it away.

He gets right in front of my face.

"Gabriella I love you more than anything. There is nothing you can do to stop me."

He gives Nicholas a stern look and leaves the table.

No. No. No. No. No. Nooooooooooooooooooooooo. Aaaaiiiddddaannnnnnnnnnnnnnnn. Don't leave! I'm losing my thoughts. I'm spiraling down. Nicholas is still looking at me. He must think I'm crazy. I'm rubbing my face resting my elbows on the table. I need to lie down. What is going to happen to Aidan? Where is Mr. Blake? They are business associates. How does he know Mr. Nathan? What if he hurts Aidan?

No! I cry harder. *Please don't let anything happen to him. Please!* I'm pulling at my hair. I can't lose him. I can't do this. Didn't Aidan see Mr. Blake when he came to get me that night? Why haven't I thought of this before? Did he let Mr. Blake leave because he knew him? Was Aidan in on it*? Please don't hurt Aidan.* I will be lost without him. Please. My mind is on overload. I drop my hands to the table and put my head down. I feel a hand at my back. That's the last thing I remember.

I'm naked in front of Aidan and he's holding my hand. It's dark out, and there is one single candle flickering in his room. My body jerks as I realize where I am. I look down to Aidan's hand. It's holding mine. His arm. It's on top of me. *He's here. He's ok.*

I turn and face him. He is sleeping, breathing heavily. His face has a few cuts on it. I touch them with my fingers, and he doesn't flinch. He's in a deep sleep. I have no idea how we got here or what time we got home. *Oh Aidan.* My savior, my protector, my guardian, my world, my escape, my divine love, my home. He's safe. He promised that nothing would happen to me. I kiss his nose and turn over. As my eyes close tightly, tears leak out. I feel safe. I fall asleep in my favorite position, our bodies molded together, on a wet pillow from tears of pure bliss.

"Wake up baby."

Aidan is caressing my cheeks and moving the hair off of my face. He's looking down at me smiling. What a perfect way to wake up.

"Hi."

I peek at him. The cuts on his face look worse than they did in the middle of the night. I reach to touch his eyebrow.

"Aidan, tell me what happened."

He closes his eyes.

"Not now baby. I'm just checking if you are going into work today."

I don't want to go to work. Is this what he meant about getting rid of my job? I want to be in his arms all day. I pull him down and hug him with all my might. I'm so glad nothing happened to him and I didn't lose him. I can't lose him. I don't want to be without him. *Ever.* He is my light. I have a desire in my heart to be united to him. It's like he's guiding me to a perfect life on a leash of love. I can't let go. I am more than content to let him lead. *Hold me forever Aidan.*

"Hey, are you ok?" He backs up and looks in my eyes.

"I'm so relieved that you're here Aidan. That we are here together. I was so scared when you left the table. I didn't know what would happen to..."

I'm talking too fast and starting to get worked up.

"I am fine. You are fine."

He's whispering. I assume to calm me down.

"What did I tell you when we left the hospital?"

"That you would never let anything happen to me," I squeak.

"Exactly. I meant that Gabriella. You are my most treasured..," he pauses, "when I look at you. When I look in your eyes. I see forever Gabriella."

How does he do that? He says what I'm thinking. I want to be with him forever.

"I see that too," I whisper back. "I want that too."

"When I'm with you. All of my pain. All of my fear. It all disappears," he says.

His eyes look glossy. My heart sinks. This is how I saved him? His pain and fear for the past five years. He said I was someone who he could trust with again. *Do I make him feel safe too? Do I serve as his rock as he does mine?*

"You have set me free Gabriella." His words melt my heart.

I don't even want to talk about last night. I don't care. I trust him completely. He protected me like he promised. Mr. Nathan and Mr. Blake are his concern. I can't worry about it. My need for his love is so much more powerful than the need to understand. His love is of infinite perfection, so much that the unknowing doesn't matter. Our love is sacred. I just know he did what he did for me. He is here. I am here. We are together. We are in love. We want forever. I pull him to me again and his lips touch mine. All that matters right now is that I am his.

His fingertips tickle my naval and slowly move over my breasts. My nipples harden at his touch. I feel the sparks as our bodies take over. My need for his and his need for mine. His teeth sink into my bottom lip and I tremble. I cling to him as he moves his trailing fingers down my stomach and between my thighs. They don't go where I want them to. My fingers linger up and down his back and onto his bottom. Our kissing gets deeper as our tongues swirl, but the touches stay light. His body is so hard, so smooth, so irresistible, pressed against mine. I feel him grow harder, which only increases my excitement. I dig my head back into the pillow and he bites my neck. I moan and he shifts so he's centered between my legs. He drags his erection between my lips, but doesn't push inside. I spread my legs wider but he plays with his tip spreading the moisture. I can't sit still. I wrap my legs around his back hoping he will sink every inch inside of me. I feel him smile against my cheek.

"You know, I take my protective duty very seriously." His deep voice in my ear sends shocks through me.

"Yes, Aidan." I'm breathless.

Stop talking. Push it in. I tilt my hips in hopes he will slam himself into me. The gentleness and slowness is making my head spin. I need him to soothe my sting, satisfy my burning desire. He won't push in, he won't increase pressure.

"Please, Aidan." I'm panting and pulling his hips towards me.

He is so strong, holding himself up above me. The tip drags slower. *No!* I want to scream. Don't slow down. My heart is pounding. I want to flip him so I can ride this out. I need him now. I'm grabbing at the sheets beneath me, trying to pull him with my legs. He is watching me with his hooded eyes.

"Let's fuse," he whispers. *Yes. Fuse Aidan.*

Slowly the tip enters, and he takes it out. He pushes it in again, and withdraws. I lick my upper lip and then the lower while we gaze at each other. Each time he enters, he gets a little deeper, and the peace spreads. *Yes, this is it. This is what I need. Please Aidan.* He picks up rhythm the deeper he goes, and I dig my nails into his back. Don't stop. I feel him in my stomach. He circles his hips and I tighten around him. I lift my hips off the bed and he pounds in fast and drags out slow. Every part of my body is responding. Up, down, left, right. I'm teetering on the edge already as I soar higher and higher. He bends down and overtakes me with his mouth. Our tongues are entwined moving with the rhythm of his thrusts.

"I should stop. You need to get to work." He's pounding, grunting between hits.

I can't take this. I'm grabbing for the sheets again, a pillow to bite on, anything, shaking my head back and forth, crying out each time. There is nothing in my reach. I'm going to explode. *Don't stop Aidan.* His pace stays the same, driving me higher by the second. Heat rushes through my body. It starts at my heart and spreads everywhere. My body is on fire. My breathing is out of control. My eyes are unfocused. My head is spinning. I'm swollen. I'm aching. I am totally consumed by him. I need to release.

"Aidaaaann!" I scream and move my body up the bed.

"Oh no you don't. Get back down here," he growls and puts his hand behind my neck.

He pushes my knees up next to my ears and pushes deeper, biting my neck and pinching my nipples. Every time I move up the bed, he follows me. I can't hold on anymore. I'm shattered. I convulse as my eyes roll back and come all around him. All tension and worries fly out of my body. One final hit and he collapses on top of me and empties inside. We are panting, catching our breath together as I enjoy the aftershocks of my orgasm. He hugs his arms to mine and my trembling slows.

"I love to watch you come." He licks my lips softly and rolls onto his back.

Chapter 15

"I don't want to go to work today." I really don't.

"I told you to get rid of it," Aidan says as he plays with the heart around my neck.

"I feel nervous. I…"

"What about?" he interrupts.

"I have a call this morning with the new guy at XPlod. I don't want to do the call. I don't want to talk about…"

"Hey," he puts his hand under my chin. "You can do this. You are strong."

"And Beth is so new. It's just stressful having to train her myself. I'm sorry. I don't mean to unload on you. I just have such a busy day today."

"You will get through. I'm sure Beth is capable. And I know you are a good boss."

He's so encouraging. He might have to be my new pep talk person.

"I'm here for you Gabriella. Remember that always. I want you to be who you are for me. If this job is who you are, then so be it. But I don't want you to go either."

"Yes, I know." I kiss his lips and get up for a shower.

The hot water pours down my face. I don't want to go today, but I can't quit my job. I can't not work. It's just a rough patch right now. It will pass. Beth will step up. Aidan is right. I will get through my call and work closer with Beth. I really like her. We had a productive first three days and I see her potential. I can do this. When I step out of the shower, my clothes are hanging on the back of the door. I didn't hear Aidan come in here. I shake my head. Will he do whatever he can to make my life easier? I smile at myself in the mirror and finish getting ready.

"Good morning, Beth," I say as she hands me my coffee.

"Good morning, Gaby. Did you have a nice weekend?"

"Yes thank you. Did you?"

"Yes I did. You have a full schedule today. Shall we go through it?"

"Sure, come on in."

I wave her into my office. She sits down and goes through my morning as my computer powers on.

"The new representative from XPlod is calling at eleven. She sounded pleasant when she set up the appointment."

A woman? That's good to hear.

"How long is that scheduled for?"

I hope not long. I don't want to discuss or think about Mr. Nathan. I can't answer any questions.

"It's for a half hour. Then a Mr. Scott is booked just before noon."

Mr. Scott? *Aidan?*

"Did you say Mr. Scott?"

"Yes."

"When was that added to my calendar Beth?" Aidan didn't say anything to me.

"Just before you arrived this morning. His assistant called."

"Thank you. Can we finish up in fifteen minutes? I need to get organized for the day."

I really want to be alone with my thoughts.

"Of course." She nods and leaves my office.

Aidan is coming for lunch. I sink in my chair and close my eyes. I need to process everything that has happened. My tough guy. My Aidan. He called and put himself on my calendar. He's so structured and full of guidelines. I laugh to myself. This will be a perfect time for him to meet Beth. She and I have a lot in common and I think he will like her. I can't wait to see him. I wish I could have stayed home with him today.

I feel that when I wish for something with him, he makes it happen. His romance and his unexpected actions are so hot. He's constantly surprising me, taking extreme care of my every need. I believe that as long as I love him, he will take care of everything else. His love makes all of my fears fade away. He put me to bed last night after I ruined his business dinner. This is my perfect man. My dream come true. My love at first sight. I felt it on our first date. My dark knight who gave me his heart.

I text Lucca. He is on his way to the airport to be with his mother. I wish him a safe trip. I am so sad to see him go. I text the girls to check in with them. I'm just passing time now and avoiding work. *Focus Gaby. Focus.* I check my email and my calendar again. And there it is – just before noon I see "Mr. Scott" on my appointment book. My heart flutters.

"Gaby. Are you ready?" Beth knocks on the door. Has it been fifteen minutes already?

"Beth sit down." I point to the chair in front of my desk.

"Have you ever been in love?" I ask her.

"Yes."

"Sorry if that was too personal. It's just that I have fallen in love with someone that is beyond words. He's so perfect, I can't even describe it."

"That's very lucky when you find someone like that."

"I know. I just can't believe it. I think I'm going to wake up one morning and this was all a dream."

"I know exactly what you mean, Gaby." She smiles warmly at me.

"Ok. Back to work. I need to focus." We laugh together.

"Ok," she says as she shows me the schedule again.

"Wait, do you have plans Wednesday evening?"

I want to ask her to go the concert with me. I loved that song that was playing at her desk this morning. We would have such a fun time. I decide not to. I'd rather be home with Aidan.

"No."

She probably thinks I want her to work late.

"Forget it." I smile.

I show her the different programs on the computer, and tell her which one is for each task. I explain that my calendar is of utmost importance, and is never to be changed without my knowledge. Added to yes, but changed no. Lexi used to change things around so much. I never knew what I was doing next and it drove me absolutely crazy. I also need to see all changes and requests that come in from our clients. They have to be presented to me in an organized fashion and discussed one by one in order of importance. Beth will have to learn the order. I remind myself that I will need to be understanding as she learns that.

"Fuck!" I yell.

"What?" Beth jumps.

"Sorry. I forgot to call my brother."

I need to call Sebastian and have him reschedule with our parents this weekend. The following weekend won't work either. Simone asked that we have a slumber party. I'm getting stressed.

"I'll be outside Gaby. Call me when you're ready."

Beth leaves. I hope I didn't startle her. *What's going on with me?* I'm just nervous for the call with Xplod. I need to get that over with.

I text Sebastian and tell him we need to reschedule for a few weeks out. He responds and says he's in a meeting, but he needs to reschedule too. He and Victoria and doing some procedure or something to get pregnant, so he wants to wait. That's a relief for me. I told him he can tell mom and dad, he's older. We tease back and forth and he gives in. I quickly tell him about Aidan, but he doesn't write back. I want Aidan to meet him. I want Aidan to meet my parents.

"Gaby," Beth says through the intercom. I jump out of my seat.

"Yes."

"Miss Lisa for you. Your eleven o'clock is on the phone."

Fuck! Here we go.

"Thank you, Beth."

My heart is pounding. Beth managed to scare the shit out of me. *Deep breaths, Gaby. You can do this. You are strong.* I remind myself of Aidan's words from this morning. I pick up my phone with sweaty hands.

"Good morning Miss Lisa," I start.

We have the most pleasant conversation. We go through the new contract, pricing, and products. She only mentions Mr. Nathan once, but doesn't ask me any questions. I am so grateful. She sounds like she will be a great client and easy to communicate with. The whole time she is talking, I close my eyes and hope that I won't have any more night time activities to arrange. That part of my job is over and is a weight off my shoulders. My muscles relax just thinking about it. We end the call on a positive note. She may fly in a few months from now to meet and get acquainted with me. She also offers to fly me out sooner, if I think that would be helpful. Aidan and I could go somewhere. That would be so fun.

The call runs over and it's already a quarter to noon. I have a text from Aidan. It says:

DL

DL? It's from an hour ago. Disarray Love. *He is so cute!* Another text comes through. It says:

Get your savory ass down here. Let the afternoon begin!

I want him to come up here and meet Beth. I look out and she is not at her desk. What does he mean afternoon? I check my calendar quick on my computer and Mr. Scott is now from just before noon until five, not just the lunch hour. *What's going on?* I grab my purse and slam my office door. I'm kind of mad, but happy at the same time. I hate when my schedule gets changed. I didn't want to do all that stuff this afternoon anyway, but now I'll just have to do it another time. I like to get shit over with. I'm trying to remember exactly what was on the calendar for today before the change. It's been barely an hour since I told Beth not to change my schedule, and she did it anyway. I will have to talk to her when I get back.

When I get outside, I see the limo, tuxedo man holding the door open, and Aidan. He is leaning with one hand on the side of the limo, his feet crossed, and his other hand on his hip. He looks like a model doing a pose. It's so natural for him to look like this. He is so strikingly handsome. And he's waiting for me. Will I ever get past that? *I'm his.* That thought alone sends flames racing through my body. How could I possibly stay mad? I shake my head and smile as I walk towards him. Just the sight of him is so distracting.

His smile is as big as can be. He reaches for my hand and kisses the top of it before I get in. There is a huge picnic basket on the seat. *He planned a picnic?* Surely that won't take all afternoon. *What's he up to?* I squint at him as the door shuts behind him. He scoots next to me almost knocking me over, and his face is at mine. His lips hover as I try to swallow. He consumes me so quickly.

"Hi," he says.

"Hi yourself."

"How was your call?"

"It went very well," I say. He's still hovering. I can feel the heat from his body.

"See. I knew you could do it." He's so reassuring.

"Yes, you were right as usual." I want to kiss him.

"I've booked you for the afternoon."

I close my eyes.

"I know." *I'm not mad. I'm not mad.*

"Don't make me get you naked right here right now Gabriella."

My eyes fly open. He wouldn't.

"Aidan."

He starts unbuttoning my shirt.

"Don't be mad at Beth. Geoff can be very convincing."

He lifts his eyebrows. I'm sure Geoff didn't convince Beth the same way Aidan convinces me.

"I just…"

He won't let me talk. His tongue is taking over my mouth. His power builds a fire inside of me. *Ok, I give up. The zing wins.*

The door opens and we are at Charming Park. I haven't been here in years. How does Aidan even know about this place? Lucca and I used to… Lucca! I look at Aidan and he's smiling. Lucca and him set this up didn't they? Lucca and I would have picnics here, and swing, and just be goofy together. I look around and it looks exactly the same. Two huge swing sets, the yellow spiral slide, the see saw, the green picnic table, it's all still here. I can't believe it. Aidan carries the basket over to the green picnic table and sets it down. He's watching me look around. That's the table Lucca and I would sit at. It's perfectly placed in the middle. We liked to play with the kids. There is no one here now though. Aidan is so sweet. A picnic. I do a little jump and skip over to him. I throw my hands behind his neck and kiss him.

"Thank you. You are so sweet." I kiss him again.

"My goodie for today."

He smiles and sits down. He pats the spot next to him and I sit so our legs are touching. He shakes his head and laughs as he opens the picnic basket. He takes out a tray of cheese and crackers, veggies and dip, a huge bunch of grapes, and cubed ham with toothpicks sticking out. This isn't exactly the food Lucca and I would eat. I laugh to myself. Aidan makes us a plate and he starts to feed me. I lean forward and take the ham off of the toothpick with my teeth. It tastes delicious.

"Tell me your wishes, Gabriella."

Whoa, where did that come from? I don't know how to answer. I pause and think for a moment.

"You know what I wish? I wish that every single night, I could come home, and focus on me and you. I want to relax and enjoy each other. That sounds like paradise."

"You are my paradise," he whispers in my ear.

I remember I said that about him not so long ago. He's mirroring my words again. We have some mind reading connection that's beyond words.

"Without your love, nothing else matters," he says and kisses my cheek.

He stands and holds his hand out. I take it and he pulls me towards the swings. I am so excited. I want to run to them. I love swinging. He lets go and I sit in the middle swing. The middle swing is always mine. He sits next to me.

I look at him and raise my eyebrows.

"Ready?"

"Oh yeah."

He smiles with his deep dimples and that makes me giggle. That's what Lucca would say.

I stand back as far as I can, and lift my legs as I swing forward. Back and forth, pumping my legs strong. Aidan is keeping up with me. We are going so high, that our heads are higher than the top of the swing set. I put my head back and feel my body flow through the air. This is so much fun. It's such a liberating feeling, a release almost. I love being goofy. I love that Aidan is here with me. My Aidan, still surprising me every day. When I look over to him, he is smiling, laughing, head back, free as a bird. It's so refreshing to see him happy and stress free. I feel the exact same way.

I jump off and land on my feet. I run for the spiral slide. I look back and Aidan is right behind me. *Shit!* He's chasing me, so I run faster and grab the side of the slide to hold on. I spin around it and Aidan slams into me from the other side. We laugh and giggle and fall to the sand together. He's tickling me on my ribs, under my arms, my neck. I can't sit still.

"Aidan. Aahhh!"

"What?" He tickles harder. I can't stop laughing.

"Aidan." I try and wriggle away, but he's so strong.

"What's so funny?"

"I can't. I can't."

I can't talk. Tears are streaming down my face from laughing so hard.

"What is it?"

He's trying to be so serious. He lets up and I catch my breath. I'm still laughing as I wipe my face dry. This is the best picnic ever. I love his goodies. He is a goodie all on his own.

My hair is in the sand and he's next to me on his side. I see him look around. No one is here. We are alone. He moves the hair from my face that was sticking with my tears, and he bends down to kiss my lips. My cheeks hurt from laughing so hard. He kisses me again and stands up extending his hand.

"Slide now?"

He points.

"Of course."

We climb the spiral stairs to get to the top. I go first and he kisses my bottom from behind me. I wait while he finishes the last couple stairs and he walks in front of me. He sits down and pats the spot between his legs. *Aren't we too big for this?* We might get stuck. I sit and he pulls me back and kisses my head. He pushes off with his arms and we are sliding down together. We are going so fast around the turns that we slide up the side a little bit. When we reach the bottom, we stop like dead weight. We laugh again and he tickles my ribs. I yelp and stand up.

"Hey!" I pretend scold him.

"Hey what?" He puts his hands up and smiles.

"Nothing. I'm just having so much fun with you. Thank you."

I kiss his lips as he stands up.

"Good, cause there's more." He lifts his eyebrows.

"There is?" I'm squeaking. I sound like a little girl.

He nods and pulls me to the see saw. He lowers my side and holds it steady while I get on. He looks so cute today in his tight jeans and t-shirt. I watch him and his muscles walk to his side and climb on. He puts his feet up and his side falls to the ground as mine flies into the air. I shriek and hold on tight. I'm stuck up here. *Don't get off Aidan.*

My hands are sweating. I hurt my ankles on a see saw when I was younger when the bottom person suddenly got off and sent me tumbling to the ground. I will never forget that. I'm nervous and I don't like being up here. He's looking at me smiling. *Can't he see the fear in my eyes?*

"Gabriella. Don't you trust me?" he asks still smiling.

"Yes, of course I do." *I do. I really do.*

"Then why do you look so scared? You don't actually believe I would drop you, do you?"

"No."

"Look into my eyes. Trust me, Gabriella."

With his reassuring words, a rush of relief washes over me. I do trust him. More than anyone.

"Ok. Now, what are you going to do with me?" I ask.

"Oh baby, don't tempt me. I can think of a million things I'd like to do with you right now." He gives me a wicked grin.

His feet touch the sand and he pushes so he goes up and I come down. We can only do this a few times. He is a lot heavier than me and it just doesn't work. I put my feet up and lean back as far as I can, trying to get him off the ground. We laugh together, and he does the same thing, so I'm up in the air again. This was so much easier with Lucca. Aidan stands so the see saw is level, and I climb off.

He pulls me back to the green picnic table, and takes a small container out of the picnic basket. He takes the cover off and tilts it so I can see inside. *Is that? Is that what I think it is?*

"Do you remember?" he asks.

"Yes, of course I remember." I smile.

It's the chocolate cake we had on our first date. It was so good, but I ate it too quickly so we could go for our walk on the beach. He gets a bite on the fork and holds it up.

"May I?"

I close my eyes while leaning forward to take the bite. It's so delicious, and it brings warm memories. The first time my body was begging for his touch. What will he think of next? We take turns taking bites until it's gone.

"So, do we get to repeat what we did on our walk too?" I ask.

"That was a magical night, wasn't it?" He lifts his eyebrows.

We gather our things and pack up the basket. I take one last look around the park before climbing in the limo. I picture

Lucca and Aidan making plans together. Each day with Aidan is better than the one before.

A song comes over the speakers and Aidan bolts to turn it off. He shakes his head. That's the same song Beth was playing this morning. Why did Aidan do that?

I am interrupted with a text from Sebastian saying that he's told our parents that we aren't coming. We will have to make a trip up there in three weeks and stay an extra day. Our parents always make sure we make up the time. I can't complain. I am lucky to have them, and they are still alive. I can't wait for them to meet Aidan. I need to tell him, but I'll wait. They will love him. How could they not?

The limo stops in front of the Hollywood Theater. I look out the window and the marquee says A/G in red. I look at Aidan and back to the marquee, moving to the window to get a closer look. *What is going on? Why does it say A/G? Is that a movie name? Is that our initials the same way I drew them in the sand?*

Tuxedo man opens the door, and Aidan gets out. I'm still staring out the window in awe.

"Gabriella," Aidan says.

I'm speechless, confused, baffled.

"Gabriella," he says more firmly.

I look and see his hand extended in the limo, but I don't see his body. I scoot over towards the door and take his hand. He kisses my cheek and pulls me inside. There is a woman holding the door open. There is no one else here, not even other employees. He leads us into the theater and at the exact moment we enter, the movie starts to play. There is no one in here either.

"For you my love."

Aidan gestures to the empty theater.

"What have you done?" I can't stop smiling.

"You said your last movie was ruined."

He remembers that? We talked about movies for two seconds.

"So I thought we'd try it this way."

His smile is as big as can be. He is spoiling me, just like he said.

He points to the two seats that are in the exact center of the theater. As we get closer, I see a small A and a small G made out of red ribbon on the seats. I shake my head. The letters on the marquee were our initials. I am truly stunned. I asked myself what he would think of next and then here we are. At an empty theater with our initials outside, and embroidered on the best seats in the house.

The previews end and the lights go out. Aidan puts his arm around me and holds his other hand on his lap palm up. I put my hand in his and he squeezes it. I sit up and look at the "A" above his head. I close my eyes tight. *This man.* He is making all of my wishes and dreams come true. He's right. Our disarray love is all that matters. *Don't cry. Don't cry.*

Gunfire takes over the screen. It's the new Transformers movie. *Well I won't cry during this!* I laugh inside as I think that Lucca must have told him I wanted to see this.

When the movie ends, Aidan whispers in my ear.

"Let's go home and focus on you and me."

The next morning is not welcome. My calendar is full and I still have to finish what I should have done yesterday. My computer clock says "9:15" and my first meeting is in fifteen minutes. I have to do a presentation to another department recapping the conference and I don't feel prepared.

"Good morning, Gaby," Beth says as she enters my office. She has hesitation in her voice and looks nervous.

"Good morning, Beth."

I'm trying to shake the angry look off my face. I'm still upset at her about changing my calendar yesterday, right after I told her not to. Aidan told me not to say anything, so I won't. It was a wonderful afternoon, and an ideal evening. Chills run down my arms as I remember our hours of lovemaking, the giggling, the pillow talk.

"Are you ready? What can I do to help?" Beth asks.

"I'll need you to do the second half. You went through it, right?"

Beth is looking over my shoulder out the window. *What is she looking at?*

"What is it Beth?"

I turn around, and the sky is getting black. I can't take my eyes off of it as I walk to the window. I look from left to right around the sky. It wasn't like this on my drive in. I hear small crackles of thunder through the thick glass, and see lightning in the distance. My body tenses and my lump returns. *Aidan.* I need to get out of here. I need to get home for him.

"I need to go. You do the presentation."

I grab my keys and run out of my office. The elevator is taking too long, but I'm on the twentieth floor, so it will still be faster than the stairs. It pings open, and as the doors close I see Beth in the hallway.

She's holding up her finger as I mouth "I'm sorry" in her direction.

She wouldn't understand why I have to leave, and it's really none of her business. I push the button for the first floor over and over. *Hurry up!* The elevator opens on the first floor and I burst out, running through the lobby to the employee parking lot.

I start the car and I take off. I'm racing, driving as fast as I can. Aidan's house is ten minutes away. I can see the sky is worse in that direction. The thunder is getting louder. *Oh Aidan. Wait for me.* Is he in that room? I don't know. I want to be the one to help him, the one to get him over his pain during storms. I want him to not need that break room anymore. *My body is his. I can get him through.*

My heart is racing while I fly through yellow lights and hit each curb as I turn. The rain is pounding down. Puddles are already forming. It's slippery and I can barely see past the windshield. The wipers can't go any faster. OK, I see his gates. I roll down my window and the rain takes over. I'm getting soaked while I try to push the button. I don't know how to get in. I can't get in.

"Fuck! Aidan! I'm coming!"

I'm pushing the button as fast as I can. I don't know how to use this box. I've never had to. The gates always open automatically when I pull in from work.

"Open the fucking gate!"

I'm yelling at the box. *Can't anyone see me? Can they hear me?* I try to call Aidan from my cell phone, but the gates open slowly. I roll up my window and speed up to the house.

Fruit is falling from the trees hitting my car, from the forcefulness of the storm.

I slam my door and run as fast as I can to the front door. Alan is holding it open. Where is Aidan? Should I ask Alan? Does he know about the room? I look left to the kitchen, straight up the stairs, and right to the maze of hallways. I don't see him. I choose the maze and run. I don't remember which way to go. I would try to listen for the Christmas music, but my heart is pounding too hard in my ears. When I turn the third hallway, I see the heavy door. I notice it's slightly a different color that the others. I use my body weight to push it open.

Aidan is pacing back and forth in the cold room.

"Ella. I need you. Elllllllaaaaaaaaaaaaaaaaaaaaaaaaaa!"

He's screaming with his head back, like a wolf howling at the moon.

"I'm here. I'm here. I'm here Aidan," I repeat until he finally looks at me.

He closes his eyes. I stare at him for what seems like forever. *What's he going to do?* Last time he said he let me off easy. But how far will he push me? I trust him to know how much I can take. So many emotions are flowing, but I know he won't hurt me. The lump is growing in my throat while I wait for his eyes to open. He snaps his fingers and points upstairs. My breathing stops. I turn around slowly without saying a word.

He is behind me while we walk through the hallways. I turn back and I see him take the red ribbon off of the vase of flowers in the foyer. I can hear his heavy breathing while we walk up the stairs. He slams the bedroom door, and I stop.

"Present stand," he says in that voice. The same voice he used during the last storm.

I quickly remove my clothes and stand at the end of the bed, feet shoulder width apart with my hands behind my neck. My eyes are closed. I am focusing on my breathing and what's next. The thunder is getting louder, and I can hear the raindrops hitting hard against the balcony door. I think I hear that soft music again.

I see him open the drawer in my wardrobe chest. He grabs the perfume and sprays some on his finger. He rubs it on my neck and leans in to smell it. I can hear his intake of breath, and shocks run through me as I recall what we did last time I wore this perfume.

"On the bed, Ella."

His voice startles me. He pinches my nipples and I climb to the center of the bed. He stands at the side, and he closes my hands together. He lifts them over my head and I see him take the red ribbon out of his shirt pocket. I can't breathe. I watch him tie it around my wrists and then to the bed. *Why is he tying me up?*

His fingers start at my neck, and trail between my breasts. He pinches both nipples again and then slides his fingers to the side swells of my breasts. I am shaking, shivering, trembling at his light touches. They lightly flow all the way down my legs and to my ankles. He stops and grabs them and pulls me down, so my arms are extended above me. *Fuck.* I have fear and excitement running through me at the same time. *I trust him.* I pull with my arms, but they are stuck. I'm helpless.

He holds up the red leather sleeping mask. *Where did that come from?* I gulp and dig my head back. *I can do this.* I see a small smile form in the corner of his mouth. He places it over my eyes and I slip into total darkness.

I hear him light some candles, and I actually feel the room get warmer. I hear him undress and his footsteps as he walks across the floor. Then they stop. *Where is he?*

"Do as you're told. Obey!"

I shudder as he whispers in my ear.

His fingers touch between my legs, and I wince. I don't know where he's going to touch next. He traces my swollen lips up and down with two fingers and massages them. He parts them and glides his finger between my opening and my clitoris. One slips inside and he twirls it around. He withdraws and his fingertip is at my mouth. He's stroking my mouth back and forth.

"Taste how wet you are Ella."

I lick my lips and put my head back. I can taste my tangy arousal. I am tingling everywhere. The thunder is constant now, and something slaps the inside of my thigh. I jump in surprise. I spread my legs wider and feel a rush of air as my legs open. I'm going to that space, the space where the only thing that exists is his touch and my imagination.

I hear the humming of a vibrator and it touches my clitoris lightly. I arch towards it, but he pulls it away. I settle back to the bed, and I feel the vibrator again. I arch and he pulls it away. I settle again. This is so frustrating. The vibrator tickles but I don't move. I understand. He's in control. He's rewarding me by not pulling away this time. He decides how high and how fast I go. My anticipation is building as I drop out of reality. My sensations are slowly rising and getting more intense.

Suddenly I feel his warm breath at my neck. He takes over my mouth with his tongue. The pressure increases with the tickling, and I'm trying so hard to sit still. I want to push up, but I don't want it to stop. My heart is thumping in my ears. This darkness is amplifying every touch. I slowly push up with my hips. *I have to...* And in one second, the vibrator is gone, and I'm turned onto my stomach. *No. No!*

He pulls on my hair to control the angle of my head, and I instinctively move any way he guides me. Out of nowhere, he spanks me so hard, and I cry out. He spanks again, and again with his hand. I'm breathing steadily, trying to focus on the sensation, and take my mind off of everything else. He puts his hand in the small of my back and hits again. He picks up a steady pace and switches from cheek to cheek. I'm trying to twist away, but he's holding me down. The harder I struggle, the faster he hits.

"Ouch!" I scream.

"Yes, Ella. This is all mine." He strokes the heat he just created.

He hits again, but they are slower this time. There are more seconds between each spank. I don't know if I can do this.

"Ouch!" I scream again.

The spanks slowly speed up, over and over, and I feel the sweet feeling of relaxation take over. *Yes, this is it. I did it.*

"Good girl." He is stroking my hair. "You are so beautiful, Ella."

He pushes a finger inside and spreads the wetness. Another spank. I am drifting as he alternates between touching and spanking. Everything is melting together as my bottom warms. He hits again. I feel myself lift to the spanks.

"May I have another please?" I can barely manage a whisper.

He hits again three times extra hard. *Yes!*

Every touch from him is pure pleasure. I'm back in endorphin paradise. This is my space of acceptance, where I surrender to his touch.

He flips me onto my back again. Another hit on my inner thighs and my legs spread open wide for him. The vibrator starts at my ankles and moves up my legs, past my knees, up my thighs. It barely brushes my clitoris, and I gasp. He passes it too quickly and goes down the other leg. It starts up again, and when it gets to my clitoris, he circles it lightly. I think he's touching it. I can't tell, it's too light. Or is this my imagination?

"Tell me what you want." His voice echoes.

"Aidan, please."

"No, Ella. Not good enough."

"Please."

He takes it away. I feel a vibrator go inside of me. It feels like a vibrating egg. I can't breathe. I'm climbing. He leaves the egg inside, and a second vibrator starts on my stomach. My insides are quivering. I can feel the vibration in my spine and my heartbeat in my clitoris. It moves down past my naval and up and over each lip. He spreads them with his fingers, and grazes my clitoris again and again. I moan each time while trying to control the tremors. I'm going to explode. He stops.

He's licking my neck, flicking soft licks all the way down to my nipples. He sucks each of them and they are harder than they've ever been. *I'm almost there. Don't stop.*

"Keep your nipples hard Ella."

I'm trying to focus. The vibrator circles my clitoris, and mixed with the one inside me, I am soaring higher than ever. I can't hold on.

"Please Aidan. Please don't stop," I beg.

"No Ella."

Everything stops. I feel the bed lift as he gets off. *No!*

Something is rubbing up and down my legs. It's too light. I don't know what it is. It goes up and over my stomach, and grazes my nipples. I moan. It moves up each arm, all the way to my wrists, and back down again. He hits it on the swollen lips covering my clitoris and a shock of electricity shoots through me. I cry out. He hits again, and another shock spreads.

"Aidan," I'm panting, "please."

"Not yet."

It feels like the bristles of a hairbrush. It's running up one leg, and his tongue up the other. I'm controlling my breathing, keeping my nipples hard. When he reaches my clitoris, he sucks it. I scream. He reaches up and pinches my nipples, rolling them between his fingers as he sucks harder. My hips rise. I can't breathe. I can't think. I shake my head back and forth, struggling to move. I need to release. I'm starting to cry. I can feel the mask getting wet. He stops.

He hits my lips again and my body jerks. He stops. Something soft grazes my throbbing nipples. It feels like fur. It's circling them both at the same time. He stops. His tongue is taking over my mouth, and the vibrator circles my clitoris with more pressure this time. I'm pulling at my restraint, I'm almost choking. *Can I do this?* It feels different now. I'm dizzy.

"Don't you dare come until I tell you," he whispers in my ear.

His hot breath shoots through me. *I can't. I can't.* I rub against him, against the bed, anything. I need some relief. I try to rub my legs together, but he pushes my thighs down.

"Please Aidan. Push me over," I'm pleading.

The pressure gets harder, and the circling keeps at a steady pace. I am building. I am soaring. I am shattering beneath him and the explosions are starting. *Please Aidan. Please!*

"Now!" he growls in my ear, and I blast into the most thunderous orgasm.

I'm trembling everywhere as he pushes my knees up. I feel limp, I can't move. He yanks the egg out and throws it to the floor. My orgasm is still going and he thrusts inside me.

"Yes. That's it," he yells as he pounds against me.

My muscles contract, sucking him in. He pushes one leg up more and gets deeper, absorbing my vibrations. There is no stopping. He pushes and pounds with his perfect control. Our bodies in perfect harmony.

"Again," he demands, and I convulse beneath him at his command, with an orgasm that shakes me to the core, over and over.

He slows his movements and whispers.

"Good girl. Let's see how many times you can do that."

Chapter 16

When I get out of the shower, I see my clothes hanging on the back of the door like every other day. Today, Aidan has set out my favorite jeans and a plain black t-shirt. *Where are my work clothes?* I can't wear this to work. I get dressed and do my hair and makeup. I look and smile at myself in the mirror. Aidan is on the phone in the kitchen when I get downstairs so I can't ask him what's going on.

I kiss his cheek and mouth "goodbye" to him.

He squeezes my hand and mouths "I love you" back.

He doesn't let go. I'm standing here listening to some work conversation I know nothing about. I trace my middle finger up his thigh. I stop at the top of his leg and he doesn't flinch. I move between his legs and caress him up and down. His eyes fly to mine, and I don't break his stare. He turns his body away, so I stop. He grips my other hand tighter. I put my hand on his hip and trail my fingers towards his navel. I circle it slowly and stop at the button of his jeans. I pretend like I'm going to undo them, and he faces me. I look down and his erection is bursting out of his pants. I affect him as quickly as he affects me. I should leave now when he's like this. He's always teasing me. This is my chance while he's distracted on the phone.

I cup his erection and squeeze it hard. He closes his eyes and grips my hand so tight that it feels like it's going to break. He either has to let go of my hand or drop the phone. This is perfect. I press harder between his legs and I hear his voice shake into the phone. This is so much fun. I stroke him and bend down and breathe hot air over his jeans onto his hardness. His knees buckle. I stand and drag my finger around his back, over his shoulders, up his neck, and into his hair. I kiss and nibble at his neck and ears. He moves to sit down on the stool. I swirl my tongue and pull at his hair. He lets go of my hand and reaches for me. I slowly walk backwards out of the kitchen as he watches me with his hooded eyes. *That was very amusing.*

I call Lucca on the drive to work, but he doesn't answer. Tonight is our concert. We were supposed to go together. The Foo Fighters are our favorite band and we go every time they come to town. I really want to go, but I want to be with Aidan more. I try to put the concert out of my mind. *Oh Aidan.* He's making me start to love thunderstorms. I knew I could trust him. He pushes my limits into unknown territories. He knew how far he could push me and how much I could take. The balance of fear and trust is so powerful. It was beyond thrilling. My phone rings.

"Hello."

"Hi baby."

"Hi."

What's he going to say?

"Tomorrow I am going to pick you up at work and we are leaving for out of town," Aidan says.

Tomorrow? Tomorrow is only Thursday.

"What about work on Friday?" I ask.

"We are leaving tomorrow night," he says firmly. I guess that's not up for discussion.

"Where are we going?

"I've agreed to do 'The Talk' this weekend. You will come with me."

"Where?"

"We will fly to Little Palm Island."

"Ok. What is 'The Talk'?"

I can't believe he hasn't said anything about what just happened in the kitchen.

"I have done it for the past four years. I wasn't sure about going this year, but I think it's for the best. It's an annual speaking engagement I do."

"Will I get to hear you speak?"

"I would like that."

I can hear the happiness in his voice. Did he think I wouldn't want to hear his speech?

"Ok good."

I would love to hear him talk about overcoming his obstacles. He said he discusses how he and Nicholas put themselves through college after living on the streets when their parents died.

"I will see you tonight when you get home. I love you."

He hangs up. Well that was short and sweet. He didn't let me say much. I will have to ask him more about the trip tonight.

Work is long and boring. Beth doesn't ask me about yesterday when I ran out of here. I'm so glad she is respecting our boundaries. She had my coffee ready and today is just a normal day. I let her know I'll be out on Friday. I meet Simone for lunch. She is happy at her new job and has had a few dates with Matt, but nothing has really come out of it. I tell her again that I won't be around this weekend and she rolls her eyes. I laugh inside. That was totally expected. She reminds me that we are having a slumber party the following weekend. I fill her in on the details regarding Lucca and his mother. She is mad that she didn't get to go shopping with us after brunch. Why didn't she say something that day? *Oh well.* It was nice to catch up with her.

When I get off the elevator at five, Aidan is waiting for me. *What is he doing here?* He said he would see me tonight at home. He's running in place, throwing punches, like he's getting ready for a boxing match. He's wearing jeans, a black t-shirt, and tennis shoes. I've never seen him in tennis shoes. I look down and that's what he set out for me to wear today. I watch him throw a few more punches, and he looks up to me and smiles. I smile back and shake my head.

He walks toward me.

"Hey baby. Are you ready?"

Ready? Did I miss something?

"Ready for what, Aidan?"

"The Foo Fighters."

He puts his hands up above his head like a touchdown sign.

"What are you talking about?" I'm confused.

He hates my music because of Liz. He's told me repeatedly.

"My goodie for today." He winks.

Wait, he's going to the concert with me?

"What do you mean?"

I'm so excited to go, but don't want him to be miserable.

"Just come on."

He pulls me through the lobby to outside where his BMW is waiting. We get in and when the doors shut, Aidan pulls me to his lips. His heart is pounding. I can feel it through his shirt. Is it from the boxing match I just witnessed or because he's nervous?

"Aidan, I'm..."

He pulls away from the curb and starts talking.

"Lucca sent me your tickets. I talked to him yesterday, and a couple times today."

I just look at him in shock. He did this for me? *He arranged everything with Lucca. For me.* My face feels tingly like I might cry. I can't believe this.

"He told me some of the songs, and I listened to them online. He assured me I would like them, and it wasn't the kind of music I thought it was."

I'm still watching him in awe. I'm speechless.

"I actually know a few songs, and the guitar and drums are fine. I realize it's the voice and the screaming that affected me with that other music. Gabriella, are you listening?"

Yes, I'm listening. I'm just... I'm just... I don't know what I am right now.

"Yes."

"Good. I've been listening all day and I really like it."

He's talking so fast. He sounds excited. I'm thrilled that he's going with me and that he's opened his mind for me, like I have for him.

"I really like Lucca. He recommended a place for dinner."

Aidan leans forward and hits a switch, and The Foo Fighters take over the sound system. He rolls down the windows, turns the music all the way up, and cruises. I am singing along word for word at the top of my lungs. This is so incredible. I peek over at Aidan, and I can see him sing to the songs he knows. We don't hit any stoplights and we cruise all the way to The Red Chair. My heart almost stops. The Red Chair. Lucca's favorite place. *Did Lucca help recreate this night as though he was home with me?* Aidan and Lucca are in cahoots to take care of me. I squeeze my eyes shut.

He pulls me to a little booth in the back corner by the kitchen. This is Lucca's booth. I squint at him. He orders our wine, dinner, and a kamikaze shot for each of us.

"That was fun," Aidan says, "singing along with you. I'm glad I reached out to Lucca."

He's smiling with those deep dimples.

"Yes it was. Thank you, Aidan. You're spoiling me with all your goodies."

"That's the point."

He is spoiling me. He puts his palms up on the table and I put my hands in his.

"Tell me about yesterday," he says. "Is there anything you want to say? Anything you didn't enjoy, hated, loved? I need to know."

"Aidan. It was staggering. I have no words."

"Are you absolutely positive?"

"Yes Aidan."

I feel the blood drain from my face. Our wine and shot arrive at the table. He holds up the shot and we clink them together and slam them.

"What is it?" he asks.

I feel embarrassed. Even though he told me nothing is uncomfortable between us. I still feel it inside sometimes.

"Gabriella." He's giving me his blazing eyes, squeezing my wrists.

"To be honest," I pause and think how I want to word this. "I didn't know what would win. The endorphin paradise or the waves of orgasm."

His mouth drops open.

"Endorphin paradise?" he whispers.

"Yes." I nod back.

"Waves of orgasm?" he asks.

"Yes."

"Well, we shall play that game more often. You never know what will win."

Oh those eyes. Zing!

He lifts his glass and says, "To two souls in sync. To matching desires." He winks at me.

We do have matching desires. This is what I was talking about with our fantasies aligning. Some days are emotional and raw, even difficult. But at the end of the day, love wins. Just like Lucca told me. Our dinner arrives. We finish our wine and dinner without saying a word. I'm reliving the storm from yesterday in my mind. I hope Aidan is too.

"I'm So In Love With You" begins to play softly in the background and Aidan points to himself and then to me as he sings along.

I might melt on the spot. He is so cute. He stands and puts out his hand. I take it and he leads us to the dance floor. He holds me close to his body, and I can feel every hard muscle through his t-shirt. When the song comes to an end, he takes a step back and holds my hand up in the air. He does a twirling motion with his other hand and I flush again, turning around under his hand.

As we arrive at the concert, Aidan pulls us through crowds of people, so we are directly in front of the stage. I don't know how he did it, but he does his weird body language thing with one of the security guys, and here we are front row. There's no assigned seating, everyone has to stand. Our arms are actually hanging on the stage. This is unreal. There must be thousands of people here. We are watching the set be prepared between the opening band and The Foo Fighters. This is so exciting. I've never been this close before.

The band starts, and we fist pump singing along to every song. We are high fiving the people next to us, having the time of our lives. I glance over to Aidan a few times, and he is smiling and enjoying himself. This is such a relief. I snap a picture and text it to Lucca. He will be so jealous. I reach my arms back and start to twirl my hair to put it up. I am so hot in here.

I feel Aidan's hands at my hips.

"Leave your hair down baby."

The songs are slowing and Aidan's hands circle my waist as he stands behind me. I still.

He leans down to whisper in my ear.

"Did you enjoy teasing me this morning? You didn't think I was going to let you get away with that did you?"

The hair on my arms stand on end. I feel his erection at my back. He is grinding it against me slowly. His voice is rippling throughout my body.

"See what you do to me. Feel how hard I am?"

I close my eyes at his words. He's pressing himself into me. I'm holding on to the stage for support.

"Can you feel this moving in and out of you?"

My knees buckle. *Yes I can feel it.* I can feel every single inch. I can't hear the music anymore. Time has stopped.

"I'm going to show you who's boss," he growls.

I gasp. He's using my fantasy words. He grinds harder and faster.

"I'm going to fuck you like I hate you." His tongue is swirling in my ear. "And you're going to beg me to do it again." My body falls against his. "You won't be able to walk tomorrow."

My heart is pounding. I reach my arm back to touch him, feel him, something. I will take him in my mouth right here if I have to.

His hand grabs my wrist and puts it to my side.

"No," he says sternly.

The guy next to us starts talking to him. They are yelling to hear each other. Aidan lets go of my waist and leaves me panting, wanting more. I try to compose myself and stand up straight. He looks over to me and smiles. I am so overly aroused, and he's so frustrating. I'm sure he loves every minute of this. At least when I did it, we were at home. I run my fingers through my hair and he's back at my waist.

"I wasn't done," he snarls in my ear, and the shocks fly through me.

"I am going to lick every single inch of you. Especially the parts that make you scream my name. I will look in your eyes as you beg."

My lump returns as my heart skips a beat. I want to get out of here.

He pulls my shirt up and slips his hand down the front of my jeans. My eyes fly open. *Holy shit.* I look around and no one is watching us. The stage covers the front of my body and so many people are squished together. I still feel nervous, which just heightens my arousal. His finger slips inside so easily. He swirls the succulence around, and I can't move. I'm pinned between him, the stage, and my jeans. Again, he has me helpless. I try to push back and a small moan escapes my lips. It's so loud in here, I'm sure no one can hear me.

"Stay quiet." He stops moving his fingers. He starts again. "Is this what you want? Does it feel good?"

"Yes."

He stops.

"Quiet."

His control is evident. I must be quiet to accept pleasure.

His fingers circle and with gritted teeth he says, "I'm going to push you over so hard. So mother fucking far over, you're going to come all over me."

Then he lowers his voice and adds, "I love when you come all over me."

My heart skips a beat. My knees give out and he has to hold me up. He pushes hard on my clitoris as I put my head back on his shoulder. He kisses my ear and removes his hand from my jeans.

My body is limp. I reach for him, and he starts fist pumping to the music again after licking his finger. I need to focus. Concentrate on my favorite band in front of me. They play four more songs, and Aidan has us stay till the very end. He doesn't say anything else.

We are both on an adrenaline high the whole drive home, so he blasts the music again and we let the cool moonlit breeze blow in our hair. I sing along, but I want to reach for him. I want to touch his leg. I can see his erection through his jeans, but I don't want him to say no again. I must wait.

When we get home, we fuck fast and hard. And he is right. I do beg him to do it again. And again. And again. And again.

Today at work is busy and the day is flying by. Aidan is taking me out of town tonight. He wouldn't let me pack this morning. He said that will be taken care of. I'm so excited to be totally alone with him. No staff, no assistants, no one. Just me and him. Naked. I laugh to myself as I move around my office. I am so sore from last night. So pleasantly sore. He wasn't kidding about not being able to walk. I still need to tell him about visiting my parents. I hope he will come with me. I don't want to be away from him for that long. I remind Beth that I am out tomorrow and give her a to-do list.

"Gaby." Beth startles me over the intercom.

"Yes."

"Mr. Scott is on the line for you."

"Thank you." I pick up the phone.

"Aidan. Is everything ok?"

"Hi baby. Yes. Look out your window right now. What do you see?"

I look out and see the other tall buildings and people walking down below. There is not a cloud in the sky. The sun is shining and off in the distance I see a hint of a rainbow.

"Do you see it?" he asks.

"Yes, Aidan. I see it."

I know exactly what he's talking about. He loves rainbows. He said they bring hope.

"Good. It's the first one I've seen since we met, and I wanted us to look at it together. I saw one during the day before I met you, and made a wish. Hope pulled through that day."

Is he talking about me? He wished for me?

"Let's make a wish together. Close your eyes."

I close my eyes. He stays silent and I make my wish. I wish to be connected to Aidan until the end of time.

"Did you make a wish?" he asks.

"Yes Aidan."

"I will see you in a half hour. I love you." He hangs up.

I finish my emails and arrange my desk so it's ready for me on Monday. We will be back by then, won't we? Aidan never said when we were returning. I look at my computer clock and Aidan will be here soon. I gather my purse and briefcase and lock my office door behind me. Beth isn't at her desk.

While I wait for the elevator, my phone vibrates with a text from Aidan. He is here. This is perfect timing. We really are in sync. When the elevator pings open, Zach is waiting inside. I jump back and almost choke on my breath. He is alone. *What is he doing here?* He has a weird look on his face. I can't move. He takes a step out and grabs my arm, pulling me inside. When the doors close, and we begin to move, he pushes the 'Stop' button. I can't breathe.

"Gaby. You can't ignore me."

"Zach, why are you here?"

"I have come to take you back."

"Take me? Zach, what do you want?" I'm trying hard to stay strong.

"You have to take me back. I'm miserable. I miss you."

"That's not going to happen." I roll my eyes.

"Yes it is. I'm taking you home with me." He looks so angry.

"No, you're not."

"Yes. I. Am." He gets right in front of my face.

"Push the button Zach." I want the elevator to move.

"No Gaby. You need to take me back. You will take me back. Please marry me."

I'm watching him as he runs his hands up and down his thighs. He's trying to be strong and in control, but he can't do it.

"I will do all the promises I made. I will follow through. I will," he says.

It's like he's trying to convince himself, not me. I don't care. I don't want him. I'm getting claustrophobic. The air is so still and thick.

"Please push the button Zach." *Please get me out of here. Please get me downstairs where Aidan is waiting for me.*

"I'm not pushing the button. I'm not. Not until you say you'll marry me."

"I will not marry you."

His eyes change. He's getting that look. The look like he's going to hit me.

"I told you. I told you. You are such a bitch!"

He's yelling pointing his finger in my face. I'm beginning to cry. I put my head down to my chest. It's starting.

"Don't go down Gaby. I can't handle that anymore!"

His screaming increases. As I look up, tears stream down my face. I have to hold onto the back wall so I don't fall down. *Stay strong, Gaby. Stay strong.*

"Gaby I'm so sorry. I didn't mean it."

He steps back. He's crying and pulling at his hair. He is out of control.

"Please marry me. Please. Please take me back."

Now he's crying harder, begging. I've seen him like this before. *Am I the one who brought him back down all these years, when I thought he did that for me?*

"Please Gaby." He's on his knees.

I look at him and shake my head.

"Bitch!"

He spits at my feet. He is constantly going up and down, on his emotional roller coaster. He's back in my face with his finger.

"You disgust me. I'm so sick and tired of you. I'm going to hurt you as much as you've hurt me."

He's pulling at the hair by my face. That look is back. *Please don't hit me. Please don't hurt me.* I can't swallow. I start to rub my face. I'm spiraling down. It's slow motion as I slowly sink to the floor.

Aidan. I need you. I need your control. It keeps me level. I need your firmness and forcefulness. It balances me. I need your power and your confidence! I'm yelling in my head. *Aidan, I need your disarray love.*

"Get the fuck up!" Zach screams.

He is pulling at my arms screaming. I can't stand. I'm limp. He's pulling between my arms and my hair, but I can't move. He continues to yell and shout and I don't even hear the words. I lean my head on the back wall and just let him go. I can't watch him. If he hits me, he hits me. I don't have the strength to fight. I close my eyes and start to sob. I need to lie down.

As my head slides towards the floor, I feel my phone vibrate on my hip. *Aidan.* I can hear his voice in the back of my head. Somehow it's louder than Zach's yelling. Aidan is saying the things he's said to me in the past when I start to spiral. He's talking in his firm voice with absolute control.

I hear him say, *"Gabriella stop. Stop I said. You will do exactly as I say. Do you understand?"* I squeeze my eyes tighter with each word. I'm focusing on his voice and his voice alone. *"Gabriella stop this. Look at me. Open your eyes."* I hear Aidan's fingers snap. It's with the same level of intensity as when he points to the bedroom. My eyes fly open. The echoing sound of

Aidan snapping his fingers in my head gives me immediate strength.

I sit up and watch Zach go ballistic in front of me. I stand and push the button and the elevator begins to move. He is sweating and pacing back and forth. He stops and puts his hands on my shoulders and pushes me back to the wall. My head hits with a loud thud and it bounces off. I fall forward and close my eyes. Zach catches me. I don't know if he knows we are moving. I put my hand on top of my head. It is throbbing and hurts just to touch it. My ears are ringing and I'm disoriented. I feel like I'm going to throw up. Zach's arms are around me holding me up as I slouch. I can't stand.

The elevator finally pings and my eyes open and close. My strength is gone. Zach lets go of me and I drop to the floor. My head falls back, hitting in the same spot. My headache instantly amplifies. Aidan is here now. Calmness takes over my body. I see him holding Zach under his neck against the opposite wall. I can't hear anything with the pounding in my ears. Aidan's lips are moving, but there is no sound. My eyes continue to open and close. I want to get up and jump in his arms but I can't move.

Aidan and I finally make eye contact. I hold his gaze for a few seconds. With his two fingers, he points to his eyes, and then to mine.

He mouths "stay awake" to me.

He punches Zach and I turn my head. I can't look. I can't hear. I'm struggling to keep my eyes open and not slip under. I try to hear Aidan's voice or fingers snapping in my head again, but it's not working. *Pound! Pound! Pound!* All I can hear is the blood pumping through my ears. *Stay awake Gaby. Don't spiral. Happy thoughts.* My eyes close and I see the rainbow in the sky. I wish to be connected to Aidan until the end of time. I repeat my wish over and over, clutching the red heart around my neck. I'm living in a perfect world that he has created for me, where I surrender to his care. In that moment, as I realize exactly what that means, I give up and slip under.

Chapter 17

I wake in my favorite position. I'm in Aidan's arms safe and sound. This is exactly how I believed it would be when I was in the elevator, living under his arm of protection. We are in a hospital room. It's dark, but the light is shining through the window of the door. I see people passing by. I look down and I'm wearing his jacket. I turn my head and look to Aidan. He is looking at me. I move onto my back to look at him more comfortably. He has such a content look on his face. He smiles and kisses my lips softly. He provides the most tranquil feeling. We gaze into each other's eyes without speaking. I feel our intense connection. I don't see the hurt in his eyes anymore. It's almost as though I can see my reflection in them. He is my twin flame. We are two hearts beating as one. I close my eyes tightly and tears leak out. He has saved me every day since I met him. His content feeling is radiating through me.

"Are you ready?" Aidan whispers and I open my eyes.

"I'm ready for anything with you Aidan."

And I am. I will go anywhere and do anything for him.

"Are you sure you feel ok?" he asks.

"Yes." My headache is dull, but I'm fine.

"Good. They said we could leave as soon as you wake up."

"Take me with you Aidan. Let's go back to our paradise. Take me home."

He laughs quietly.

"It's the middle of the night baby. The plane is waiting for us. Remember?"

Yes, I remember now. I'm so exhausted. How long have I been sleeping? They said I was good to leave, good to fly? I'm confident Aidan has made sure of that. I am worry free. I have no questions for him because I know he's taken care of it all, and his love takes over.

"Yes."

I will be in paradise as long as I'm with him.

He stands and puts his arms under my knees and behind my back. He lifts me off of the bed and carries me out the door. I put my arms behind his neck and nuzzle his warm chest. I watch as he does the silent communication thing he is so good at with the nurse at the desk. I fall asleep in his strong arms.

I feel him buckle me in the car and I rest my head on his lap as he drives.

He carries me up a small flight of stairs onto a plane that is waiting for us. I wake only for a second to peek at it.

Waves are crashing and birds are singing. *Are we home in bed?* My head feels heavy. I'm awake but haven't opened my eyes yet. I feel Aidan's arm around me with his fingers laced in mine, breathing heavily behind me. My eyes slowly open and I see a white canopy above us. I jerk as I sit up. We are on the biggest bed I've ever seen, right in the center of the room. I look forward, and two balcony doors are open and all I can see is water. Pure blue water in every direction. *Am I dreaming?* This is just like my dream from when I was little. The beach house suspended over water. I can't believe he remembered! I didn't even describe it to him in detail, but this is exactly it. I unlace our fingers and sneak out of his hold. I walk to the doors and look out. We are about ten feet above the ocean. This is incredible. I put my hands out to my sides like I'm flying, and let the breeze blow my hair back. My eyes are closed, my head is back, and I'm soaking in the sun, the air, the sounds. This is so peaceful and exactly what we need.

"Aahhh!" I scream as Aidan scoops me up into his arms and spins us around.

"Good morning beautiful." He kisses my nose.

"Good morning handsome." We are both smiling as big as can be.

"Come here."

He carries me back to the bed and we flop down together. He lightly tickles my ribs and I try to squirm away.

"Aid...A... Aid!"

I can't get his name out I'm laughing so hard. His arm is under me holding my hands down. He tickles under my arms and I squirm harder.

"I love your laugh."

He stops the torture and moves the hair away from my face as I catch my breath.

He reaches in his back pocket and pulls out his cell phone. He tilts his head so it's right next to mine, and holds his phone at arm's length above us.

"Smile."

He giggles and starts taking pictures of us. He turns his phone to the left and to the right, every angle he can manage and snaps picture after picture. Every time he turns the phone, I make a different face. I smile with big teeth and then no teeth. I stick my tongue out and then in his dimple. I can see he is changing his expressions too.

Suddenly he tickles me again on my stomach and I squeal. Of course he snaps some more pictures. We are laughing so hard. He turns to me and we can't keep a straight face. He sticks his lips out and we try to kiss while laughing, and he snaps more.

He scrolls through the pictures. Most have both of us in them. Some have my head cut off. Some are of just our mouths. We look so ridiculously happy. My smile couldn't go away if I tried.

"Hey, go back!" I say.

"This one?"

He stops on one of just him. He looks so serious. He looks like such a bad boy. *My bad boy.*

"Yes. Send that to me please."

"Why?"

"I don't have any pictures of you. I need this in my phone so I can press it when I call you."

"Hell yes you do!"

He tickles lightly and I circle my fingers around his naval. He sits back and looks in my eyes. I run my fingers through his hair. I want him to make love to me. He shakes his head no. I stick my lower lip out and he smiles.

"Gabriella, you need to rest today," he says quietly.

I stick it out again. *Fine.* I nod in agreement.

"Let's unpack and then we'll eat. We will walk the grounds and then rest some more."

"The grounds?" I ask.

I almost forgot where we were.

"Ok. This place is amazing. This room is amazing. You are amazing," I pause, "we really do have matching desires, don't we? In every way."

"Yep. I've eyed this house for some time. It's been my dream to stay here. When you mentioned it on our first date, I knew we would come here. I felt it."

"I didn't even describe it. But look." I point out the doors. "This is exactly how I envisioned it."

"I know," he whispers.

I circle his naval again with my fingers. He stops my hand with his and pulls me to his body. I can feel his erection in my stomach. We push our bodies together but don't move. I close my eyes as the shocks make their way through me.

"Let's unpack. You need your rest for tonight," he says slowly and sensually in my ear as he pushes harder against me.

Zing! *I can't wait for tonight.*

He gets up and lifts a suitcase onto the end of the bed. He unzips it while watching me. I sit up on my elbows and admire his body. He pulls out the long red nightgown, the romantic one with the train. My heart stops. Then the red teddy. *He packed them.* I immediately smile. I've been waiting to wear those. He sets them next to the case.

He taps the teddy with his fingers and mouths "tonight". He does the heart fluttering thing with his hands over his heart. He gets cuter by the second.

He pulls out a black dress and sets it on top of the teddy. He taps it with his fingers while still looking in my eyes. He wants me to wear the dress tonight with the teddy underneath to his speech. I nod. I know exactly what he's telling me.

I watch as he moves around the room putting our items away. He doesn't let me do anything, and takes care of my every need. He extends his hand and leads us outside. We walk around the deck that surrounds the entire house. I have to hold onto his elbow so I don't fall over. I am in awe at the size of it. Glass windows and doors envelop every inch. There is a deep veranda that takes up one whole side. As I peek through the windows, I see banana trees growing out of the floors. This is a place of fantasies. I might have to pinch myself. We are actually here. We even have a private beach!

We spend the day admiring the rest of the property, walking the shoreline, eating fruits from the island, laughing and playing. Aidan takes more pictures of us running in the sand and posing in front of the palm trees. He carries me, twisting around, kissing me deeply. He gives me a piggy back ride and I hug him tight with my arms and legs. His body in front of mine, in my arms, feels so soothing. I hope he can feel my love radiate through him, like I do when he holds me. We have so much fun together. We even recreate our love letters in the sand. DISSARAY LOVE and A/G. After a late lunch, he leads us onto the veranda and to the oversized couch. He lies down and holds both arms up to me. I smile and get into position. He holds me tight while we drift off together to the peaceful sounds of the waves.

I get dressed with the red teddy underneath the black dress Aidan has picked for me to wear. I do my makeup a little bit more dramatic than I normally do, and I curl my hair. I feel pretty. I want to look nice for his big night.

Aidan whistles when I come out of the room, and I flush. He lifts his hand and does the twirling motion as I walk towards him. I stop and turn around, feeling shy. He is wearing a black suit, crisp white shirt, and a black silk tie. He looks so beautiful. He has his hair to the side. The same way it was when he surprised me at work the night we went to the ballet. *Can't we just stay here and make love?* I need his body. He hugs me and I circle his naval with my fingers over his suit coat. I hear him laugh under his breath. He grabs my hand and leads us outside.

Tuxedo man is waiting with the door open to the limo. *How did he get here? Where did he come from?* That's not our normal limo. I shake my head as I realize that's not possible. We are on an island far from home. He tells us our ride is only going to be about fifteen minutes.

Aidan pulls me to his lap and I sit with my legs over his. We don't speak. I wonder if he's anxious about his speech. He's twisting my hair with his finger, which makes me smile. I have no idea what to expect when we get there. I'm trying not to be nervous or think about it. I want to be free not having the butterflies flying around.

We arrive at what appears to be a back door to the Conference Center. Aidan gets out of the limo and extends his hand to mine. I take it and he leads us inside. There are a few people walking around in suits. We are in a weird area, almost like being behind a stage. We walk a long hallway, and I see a poster with Aidan's smiling face on it. I stop his pull. It says *Welcome Back Aidan Scott*. I feel the lump in my throat grow. He pulls and we start walking again.

There is a set of double doors ahead of us. It looks like he is walking towards them. As we get closer, I can hear chanting. *They aren't saying Aidan, are they?* He stops right in front of the doors. They *are* chanting Aidan. *Holy shit.* I look down, and he puts his fist under my chin and lifts my head so I look at him. He lifts his eyebrows.

"Are you ready for this?" he asks.

Ready for what? He didn't give me any warnings. The people are chanting his name. I'm confused. *Have they heard him speak before?*

"For what?"

"To come out there with me." He's smiling. He looks excited.

"Out there with you?" My throat is growing shut. I can't go on the stage.

"Yes."

Before I can answer, the double doors whisk open from the other side. I look and see thousands of people as they stand to cheer and clap for Aidan. He squeezes my hand tight and leads us out. I am a step behind him. I feel like I might die right now. He is waving to the crowd. We walk the entire length of the stage and he sits me down on a chair that's on the opposite side. He bends to kiss my lips and walks back to the middle. I am so happy to be sitting right now. There is my Aidan, still amazing me. He's in the middle of a stage with people cheering for him. I am in shock. I had no idea it would be like this. His popularity shouldn't be so surprising, but for some reason it is.

He stands under a spotlight with his beauty and confidence beaming off of him. He is waiting for the crowd to die down. He starts speaking and the people silence immediately as if they couldn't bear to miss one single word. I glance out to them and they are all in his trance. I try to focus on what he's saying, but I'm entranced too. He owns the stage, walking back and forth engaging everyone. Just watching his poise and assurance make all my nerves disappear.

I hear him mention Nicholas and his parents. He talks about living on the streets with his brother and that they made a pact when they were fifteen to stick together and make a life for themselves. They refused to stay in foster homes so they got jobs and finished high school. They were sleeping outside, but they had each other. That's all that mattered to them. They finally saved enough money and got a studio apartment and applied for college grants.

I feel so sad for him. My mind drifts back to our first date when he told me. I must have sounded so heartless. I can't even begin to imagine what they went through. And how he helped Marie. He is such a good man, with a big heart. I bring the red heart from my neck to my lips and kiss it. When I look up, I see Aidan looking and smiling at me. There he is, comforting me while he is giving a speech. I smile back and he continues to captivate the audience. He looks from person to person like he is talking directly to them. I need to call Lucca and tell him where I am. He won't believe this.

When I hear him say the word abuse, I snap out of my thoughts. Is he talking about what Liz did to him?

"Most of you recall my stories about thunderstorms, don't you?" Aidan asks the crowd.

They all answer "yes" in unison. They must have heard him speak before.

"Well, meet the woman who has saved me every day since I met her."

He points in my direction. My jaw drops and I can't breathe. That's exactly what I said about him. He is slowing walking towards me, still speaking to the crowd.

"We complement each other. The sense of completion she gives me is like no other. She... She is my twin flame."

He's standing above me now, holding out his hand. My legs are liquid. I can't stand. He is mirroring my words, like two souls with one thought. I look to him with tears welding in my eyes. He closes his and nods to me as he slowly opens them. It's as if he knows exactly what I'm thinking. I manage to stand and take his elbow. We walk to the center of the stage and he waves at the crowd. I lift my hand slightly and wave too.

"Thank you all for coming. See you next year."

As he turns and leads us to the double doors, I hear thunderous applause and whistles. They cheer for Aidan like they want more. He doesn't flinch, but walks out with his complete control.

The ride back has more energy than the ride there. Aidan's heart is racing. I can feel it through his shirt as he pulls me to his lap again.

"Gabriella, you have given me a new energy. Nicholas was right. What have you done to me?" He is smiling and running his hands through my hair.

"I mean that was incredible! That was such a rush. It was so much better than ever before," he pauses.

When I open my mouth to speak, he interrupts.

"Because I could share it with you."

He leans in and kisses me deeply, more passionate than ever. His hands are fisting my hair like he can't get me close enough. I'm trying to keep up with the pace of his tongue taking over. I am shaking, insane with need. He called me his twin flame. My body quakes at the thought. We are connected, we are complements, we are now complete.

"Sir, it's starting to rain," Tuxedo man says over the speaker.

My heart skips a beat. Aidan stops kissing me and looks out the window. It's very dark out. I don't hear any thunder or see lightning. It's just trickling. He looks in my eyes.

"It's just a little rain baby," he whispers licking my lips.

We are catching our breaths as we pull up to the beach house. Tuxedo man opens our door and we get out. I stop and put my head back, letting the rain hit my face. Aidan pulls me to his body and I yelp.

"I have an idea," he says in a wicked tone. "Kick your shoes off."

He takes them and sets them against the door. *What is he thinking?*

We walk down to the beach. He stops and takes both of my hands in his and we look into each other's eyes. The clouds are covering the moon. There is a smoky haze in the air. The atmosphere is so sensual right now. It matches the look in his hooded eyes. I gulp as he leans in and touches my lips with his. I feel his lips part and I follow. Our tongues begin to swirl, and he doesn't let go of my hands. He takes one step closer so our bodies are pressing together. He is consuming me in an instant. One of his hands lets go and makes its way down my thigh. He touches just below my dress line. I smile against him as memories of our first walk on the beach flood back to me. I was begging him in my head to go higher and touch me. His hand moves up and grazes between my legs.

The rain is picking up and large raindrops are hitting our faces. He leans back to look at me and we both laugh out loud. He shakes his head like he knows exactly why I'm laughing. He starts to kiss my neck and ears. His fingers are still exploring. I want him to move my panties over and slide around. *My panties. Wait. I have the teddy on.*

"Aidan," I say quietly. My breath is ragged.

"Yes, baby." He looks at me and I slide the strap of my dress off my shoulder so he can see the teddy. His entire face lightens up.

He stops what he's doing and turns me away from him. He unzips my dress and slides it down my body, kissing and breathing his hot breath on my back all the way down. The rain is so cold. My nipples are achingly hard.

Aidan throws my dress up away from the water. The waves are starting to get closer to us. My hair is hanging by my face, completely drenched from the rain. I am standing in the red teddy and he steps back and nods his approval. I roll my eyes. He smiles and falls to his knees. He kisses the top of my thighs and my knees give out. He pulls me down and we are both lying in the sand. I'm on my back and he's at my side leading the way. He unsnaps between my legs and touches my skin.

I'm not wearing any panties. I don't think he was expecting that because he bites my neck and squeezes my swollen lips. My body jerks in surprise. In one second, he has two fingers inside of me and his palm at my clitoris. I moan loudly against his cheeks. He moves in perfect circles and my legs begin to twitch. I wrap my arms around his neck and close my eyes tight. Rain is hitting my face. This is so salacious. He doesn't stop his painfully slow movements and I hear him unzip his pants. He moves his body between my legs and I feel the tip of his erection hovering over my opening. When I arch up, he backs away.

Fine. I'll stay still. He pushes the tip in, and I tense around him. He waits. My heart is picking up along with my breathing. I want to pull him in deep. He pushes in the tiniest bit more and I tense. He waits. *Come on. Please Aidan*. He is on his elbows holding himself above me. Rain is pounding on us and the waves are at our feet. Another tiny bit goes in and I tense again. I'm trying to suck him inside. I circle my mouth to control my breathing. *Ok, I'll try to relax*. If I do, I'll swallow the entire length. I put my arms to my side and let my knees fall apart.

"Yes baby. Feel it," Aidan says as he inches himself all the way in.

He pushes as deep as he can and I feel it in my stomach. I immediately wrap my legs around him holding him close. He circles his hips and I bite his shoulder. He stops. He drags in and out and I dig my nails into his back.

"Remember. Absorb the pleasure."

I remove my nails and teeth from his body and push my head back into the sand. He circles and thrusts in every direction. I'm flying. He's hitting that sweet spot inside over and over again. When I start to twitch again, he slows. I want to go on top. I tap the side of his hip. *Will he know what that means?*

"Are you sure?" he asks.

I nod. He does know what I want. He withdraws and I skip a breath. He lies in the sand and I climb on top of him. I slide slowly onto his erection. I bend my knees up so they are under my arms, and position my feet underneath his shoulders. I swallow at his depth. He has never been as deep inside of me as he is right now. I open my eyes for a second to see him fold his hands behind his head. I flip my soaked hair back and let the raindrops hit my face. I push and pull and grind and scream, riding orgasm after orgasm.

I decide to ask some questions over breakfast. We are almost done eating, so I think now is a good time.

"Aidan. Tell me about the people last night."

"People?"

"Yes, who you spoke to. They've heard you before haven't they?"

"Most of them have. I did see some new faces in the audience." He's smiling.

"I was stunned at how many people were there. They were chanting your name." I stop.

"I guess I've grown a following in the last four years."

He smiles his big teeth smile. He looks so proud of himself.

"People fly in to hear me speak. Nicholas and I used to come here in the summer. Some are my friends were in the audience that have known me since the beginning. It was nice to see them. Nicholas has come with me before. But this year."

He rubs his hair forward.

"This year I wanted it to be just you and me."

He rubs his hair again.

"I wanted to show you off," he whispers.

Show me off? No one has ever wanted to do that before.

"Oh."

Now I'm twirling my hair. I feel like we're on our first date here.

"And to top it all off. I love the rain even more than I did before."

He smiles out of the corner of his mouth. Oh that naughty look. I shake my head and throw my napkin at him.

"Did you just throw your napkin at me?" He squints.

"No." *Oh shit.*

"You don't want me to get up do you?"

He looks like he's going to pounce on me. I'm ready to run if he does. I shake my head back and forth trying to stifle my smile. He's smirking and leaning towards me. We stare each other down. My heart is pounding and my hands are getting sweaty. He puts his hands on the arms of his chair, like he's going to use them to push himself up. His eyes are blazing.

"Tonight you will wear the nightgown. We are going to try something new. I am certain you will approve."

Ok good he's talking. *Something new?* He looks so serious now.

"Ok Aidan."

"We have a topic to finish discussing Gabriella."

Fuck. What could it be?

"What?"

"Your job."

My throat immediately closes. Why is he bringing this up right now? He jumps from his speech to the nightgown to my job. I can't keep up this morning.

"What about my job?"

"I told you to get rid of it." He looks angry.

"I know, but..."

"Do I need to bring up what happened in the elevator?"

"No."

I put my head down. I feel tears forming.

"Aidan. I'm sorry."

I meant to tell him that Zach said he wanted to hurt me. I've been avoiding telling him.

"For what, Gabriella?"

"For not telling you."

His eyes widen.

"Not telling me what?" His teeth are clenched.

"Zach said he is going to hurt me."

I close my eyes. I can't look at Aidan's face. He will be furious that I've kept this to myself. He slams his fist on the table and my eyes fly open.

"Why am I mad, Gabriella?"

"Because I... Because he..."

I can't speak. I'm squeaking like a little girl.

"I told you to leave your fucking job. Zach knows where you work."

Aidan is right.

I move to sit on my knees in front of him. I kiss his hand. When I look up into his eyes, my tears fall.

"I will leave. You are right. I need a month."

"Unless I say otherwise, you will not return alone."

I knew he would say that.

"I know."

"Do you have any idea how much I love you? The lengths I would go to, to protect you? No matter what the price. No matter what harm it caused me. I will protect you, Gabriella."

I kiss his knee. A rush runs through me as my acceptance takes over. Aidan loves me and is putting me first. I give myself to him completely. He pulls me onto his lap.

"I want to tell you my wish," he says nuzzling my neck.

"What wish?"

"When we wished on that rainbow."

"Ok."

"I wish to be connected with you until the end of time."

My whole body goes limp. I feel boneless. *That was my wish*.

"I wished the exact same thing," I manage barely a whisper.

"I know. I heard you. You are my twin flame, remember?" he whispers back.

"Yes."

I gather some strength and reach for his face. He takes my hand in his and laces our fingers together.

"I love you. Fuck. I more than love you. I adore you," he says.

"I should be put away for love insanity." He smiles, screaming it to the world.

"Let's make a promise till the end of time."

"I promise, Aidan."

"I promise, Gabriella."

We love play and tease all day long. When he is on the phone, I open my robe and flash him. We have a naked pillow fight and almost pass out from laughing so hard. We press our naked bodies up against the window and make funny faces at the birds. We take a naked nap together on a lounge chair in the middle of the veranda. It's pretty much a naked day. I ask him to come with me to meet my parents and he rubs his hair down, but agrees.

He giggles and points to a tire swing we see below. We raise our eyebrows together and walk down to it. He sinks in the middle and I sit across him. We talk and kiss and laugh some more while he explores my wetness.

"Dinner will be ready in ten minutes baby," Aidan says.

How does he know that? He hasn't talked to anyone but me. I roll my eyes inside. I will never understand the secret communication thing he does.

"Let's go up and you can change into your nightgown."

He bites my lip.

"Ouch!"

Aidan stays outside while I change. I slip the supple silk down my body and feel immediately alluring. It fits perfectly, and lands where it should land on the floor. The ruffled train is so striking. I walk in a circle and watch as it trails behind me, following me around each corner. I turn my body quickly and see it land in front of me. I bend down to feel it. The smooth material is soft and sensual.

I look up and Aidan is standing in front of me. He is still naked and has both of his hands balancing on a black cane in front of him. I gasp. *Where did that come from*? I try to stand with my shaky legs. Arousal floods through me like a bolt of lightning. I close my eyes and put my head back. That extraordinary feeling has returned. I'm trembling. He taps it two times on the floor and I snap back to reality. My breathing and time has stopped. We gaze at each other for what feels like an eternity.

He takes a step forward and sets the cane at the edge of the bed. He walks towards me with his hand extended. I slowly raise my hand and my jaw at the same time. He leads us outside where dinner is set up. We eat in complete silence like we don't want to waste any time talking, but know we need our energy. The sun is starting to set. We watch it go down together slowly over the horizon.

Aidan puts his arms on the table with his palms up. I set my hands in his and he squeezes them. We rise together and walk to the bedroom. He opens the balcony doors and the breeze fills the room. He kneels on the end of the bed and taps next to him. I swallow hard and climb up.

He makes a motion with his hand like he's cutting the bed in half. He wants me to lie across, not up and down. He slides the cane between my legs and it hits my most sensitive spot. I rest my hands at the side of my body. I'm taking deep breaths. I'm starting to feel dizzy but nothing's happened yet. He is kneeling next to my chest. He traces his finger up my thigh and I follow it, bending my knees. His finger moves down my thigh and my knees drop to my side so I'm wide open.

His hand is holding the cane up straight, and he bends down and kisses me. I feel the cane push against my clitoris and I moan against his lips. He backs up and I see his hand moving the top of the cane in a circular motion. The bottom doesn't move, but when he circles, it puts pressure in exactly the right place. Every time he comes around, I cry out. My heart is racing, as his speed picks up.

My body is settling into this new sensation. The cane is so hard. My whole body jumps every time it slides off my clitoris. He is watching my face intently. Looking into his eyes as he drives me to climax is so sensual. He licks his lips and my knees start to twitch. He pushes harder and I squirm beneath him. I see him nod slightly.

He takes my hand and wraps it around the cane. I look to him and he nods again. He lifts my other hand and I grab on. As he slides off of the bed near my head, I straighten my legs. He is standing above me. Fingers from both hands touch my shoulders and skim down my arms. He pinches each nipple and rolls them between his fingers. I move up the bed an inch so my head is almost hanging off. He rubs the tip of his erection between my lips. My tongue swirls and begins to suck. As he pushes deeper in my mouth, I wrap my legs tighter around the cane. I time my breaths with his thrusts. When I feel him hit the back of my throat, I circle the cane myself. I push and drive and force and steer it exactly where I need it to go. This is the feeling I've been craving. This is my fantasy he is fulfilling. I'm on the mouthwatering edge and I scream over him. He holds himself still inside my mouth, and withdraws slowly. He pushes in again and leans forward flicking his tongue over my nipples. I can't fight anymore, it feels too good. He must know I'm close because he stands up straight and backs away. I stop my motions and drop the cane. I'm grabbing at the blanket. My total body is swollen.

Aidan walks around the bed and is at my feet. He lifts the cane to his nose. He closes his eyes as he inhales my scent. He starts to flutter his tongue against it and I fist my hair. He grabs both of my ankles and lifts one over the other. He turns me onto my stomach. He climbs next to me and drags his fingers down my back. I am slowly coming back down to earth. He tickles his fingers on the lower part of my bottom.

"I know the sweet spot," he whispers in my ear and I shudder, almost violently. I'm shaking, trembling, spinning.

He starts to massage my shoulders one at a time, while still tickling with his other hand. Then everything stops. Suddenly I feel the cane hit my bottom, and an electric current sends shock waves to every single swollen area in my body. I scream. It's like a vibrator. It stings, but my entire body fills with an inconceivable sensitivity that I've never felt. He hits again near where my bottom meets my thigh, and I can't control myself. I'm moaning and weeping at the same time and shoot into the most shuddering orgasm. I'm writhing against the bed, screaming Aidan's name, reaching for something to bite onto.

He turns me onto my back and holds my arms down. He looks into my eyes, but I can't hold his gaze. I shake my head back and forth as the shocks continue to jolt me. He watches me as my breathing slows. I finally make eye contact and we breathe together in unison. He is enchanting me with his hooded eyes. He presses his forehead to mine and moves between my legs. He pushes his erection inside and I wrap my legs around his back. We make sweet, slow, tender love and watch each other come.

Chapter 18

We are flying home today. Aidan is holding me tight as he watches out the window. I am resting my head on his shoulder trying to grasp all that has happened since we met. One day I was begging for someone to take care of me, sweep me off my feet, and take my breath away. And that night, I meet Aidan. He said hope came through that day, and he was totally right. It did. He is my destiny. We belong together. He makes me feel alive, which is the best feeling in the world. The pull we feel between each other. The magnet. The need for each other's bodies is indescribable. When we fuse, nothing else exists. We do fit together perfectly and move in perfect harmony. I don't have to be the strong one. He takes all of my stress away. I am so lucky. I smile as I recall the first time he said "disarray love" to me, and our love letters in the sand, our first walk on the beach, the first time he held me all night in my bed, holding my hand, the card that said he was falling for me, the kiss in the bar, when he carried me up the stairs and said to close my eyes, seeing my sexy man leaning on the car waiting for me. I love to remember the look on his face when I said yes I would be his. I giggle inside about splashing in the pool, the swings, the tickling, his hands fluttering over his heart, the funny pictures on the bed. He is my home. He said I set him free. He has done the same for me. The old me has melted away as our hearts beat together. I lean up and kiss his cheek. He kisses the top of my head.

I can't wait to get home and focus on just the two of us. We saved each other. Love does heal and wins in the end. He spoils me with all of his goodies. The wood box, the dress, his heart around my neck, the concert. The letter he sent saying I made him laugh again and that he lives for my smile and would die for my kiss. I tingle as I think of how he helps me escape. He really has extracted every ounce of my sexual pleasure. Aidan must feel it. He squeezes his arm tight around me. I am going to be safe in his arms forever. We wished for the same thing, as our thoughts mirror each other, and the hurt disappeared from his eyes. We are twin flames that made a promise until the end of time. We are complete. Our love is all that matters.

Aidan is behind me holding my hand. The magnet is hard to pull apart this morning. I have to go to work and I remember he will be joining me. I sneak into the shower and mentally prepare myself for the month ahead. The hot water is soothing. When I step out of the shower, I see my clothes hanging on the back of the bathroom door. I grin and shake my head. I get dressed and finish my hair and makeup. I look at myself long and hard in the mirror.

I smile and say, "Better me today."

When I come out of the bathroom Aidan is not in bed. I find him in the TV room. He is on a ladder positioning a big wooden G on the shelf next to his A. My heart skips a beat. *How did he? When did he?* He turns around and flashes a big smile. I flush. Somehow he manages to still surprise me every day.

"Are you ready to go baby?" he asks as he climbs down.

"Yes Aidan."

He extends his hand and I take it. He leads us outside and he opens my door. I admire him as he drives. *My Aidan. My dark knight. So in control, so confident.*

He drops me at the front door of my office building.

"I'm going to make a call and then I will be in the lobby."

"Yes Aidan."

He opens my door and takes my hand. He kisses the top of it and I walk in.

When I get off the elevator, I hear weird music playing from Beth's desk. I look around but don't see her. *Where is she? The singer is screaming. It's just horrid.* I squint my eyes.

My cell phone interrupts my thoughts. It's Aidan.

"Hello."

"Hi baby. I just heard. It's going to be a stormy week."

Zing!

www.ingramcontent.com/pod-product-compliance
Lightning Source LLC
Chambersburg PA
CBHW061553170626
46811CB00001B/188